D1391765

HUNTER KILLER

BRAD TAYLOR, Lieutenant Colonel (Ret.),
is a twenty-one-year veteran of the U.S. Army
Infantry and Special Forces, including eight
years with the 1st Special Forces Operational
Detachment—Delta, popularly known as Delta
Force. Taylor retired in 2010 after serving more
than two decades and participating in Operation
Enduring Freedom and Operation Iraqi Freedom,
as well as classified operations around the globe.
His final military post was as assistant professor
of military science at The Citadel.

BRAD TAYLOR

HUNTER
KILLER

An Aries Book

First published in the UK in 2020 by Head of Zeus Ltd
An Aries book

Copyright © Brad Taylor, 2020

9 7 5 3 1 2 4 6 8

A catalogue record for this book is available from
the British Library.

ISBN (HB): 9781838937713
ISBN (XTPB): 9781838937720
ISBN (E): 9781838937744

Typeset by Divaddict Publishing Solutions Ltd.

Printed and bound in Great Britain by
CPI Group (UK) Ltd, Croydon CR0 4YY

MIX
Paper from
responsible sources
FSC
www.fsc.org   FSC® C020471

Head of Zeus Ltd
First Floor East
5–8 Hardwick Street
London EC1R 4RG

WWW.HEADOFZEUS.COM

To my Deputy Commander of Everything, for keeping the ship sailing through the storm

There are hunters and there are victims. By your cunning, you will decide whether you're a hunter or a victim.

—*General (Ret.) James Mattis*

1

The road in front of me was empty. Just a narrow alley leading to the entryway I intended to penetrate. A fetid, cobblestone lane built centuries ago, it was dimly lit, with more shadows than light and piles of trash hiding what may lie within.

Anywhere else in the world I would have silently cheered at the luck, but here, in Salvador, it raised the hackles on my neck. Empty roads in Brazil were like hearing the wildlife in a jungle suddenly go quiet, all the birds and monkeys realizing there was a predator afoot.

I was in the historical section of the old capital city, with plenty of folks less than a hundred meters away at restaurants and bars, but nobody was walking down this alley. Meaning there was a reason for the lack of activity. It was counterintuitive to anything I'd felt before, where the bystanders were most often the threat. Crowds allowed camouflage for individual hostiles, like pickpockets, but more important to me, they prevented offensive actions by a team.

There were just too many cameras and cell phones in today's world, devices that recorded an event no matter how careful one was, so an empty alley was the perfect approach for me, and yet, I'd learned in my short time in Brazil that empty meant dangerous. For some reason, the humans here knew not to enter, an instinct that I should pay attention to.

Unfortunately, that was out of the question because a bad guy, my target, held my best friend's life in the balance.

I turned to Aaron, and said, "That damn alley is going to be trouble. I can feel it."

He knew what I meant. We didn't worry about the "trouble," per se; we worried about the mission, and whatever was waiting for us there could hinder that.

He said, "Hey, we only have twelve hours before the clock is up. That's a blink of an eye for hostage rescue. We need to go tonight, or we're not stopping what the police have in motion."

I said, "Shoshana seems to think this is bad juju because of the monks. Maybe she's right."

He chuckled and said, "My wife is a little off. Like you."

I nodded, but still hesitated, running through my options. He squinted his eyes and said, "You believe her. You think this is going to go bad because of what she felt."

I said, "Aaron, cut the crap. She's crazy all right, but sometimes she has a point. That's all."

He withdrew a Glock pistol, press-checked the chamber, and said, "One way or the other, we need to make a decision. And I think you're afraid of her saying 'I told you so' because of this alley."

I grunted a laugh and said, "Yeah, something like that. But you're right. Too late now."

I clicked my earpiece and said, "Koko, Koko, I'm about to penetrate. What's your status?"

Koko was the callsign of my partner in crime, Jennifer, so named because she could climb like a monkey. She said, "I'm good. On the roof over the balcony. The OP is in position, and I have a clear shot."

"Roger, all. Carrie, Carrie, you have lockdown of the front?"

Carrie was Shoshana's callsign. Because she was bat-shit crazy just like the Stephen King character.

Ironically, the man I was working to save had anointed both of them with their callsigns. Which is why they were both willing to risk their lives to free him. They loved him as much as I did.

She came back, "This is Carrie. Front is secure. But I still think this is a mistake. We should not be assaulting a church. It's bad. Bad all the way around."

I looked at Aaron and said, "Yeah, I agree, but I don't get to pick where terrorists stay. I just wipe out the nest, wherever that ends up."

She said, "It's not the church itself. It's something else."

I took that in, then looked down the alley. I said, "You want to help here? I think I have your bad feeling, too."

She said nothing on the net. Aaron whispered, "Good call. The front is facing the tourists. She's not needed out there. Get her in play."

Through a combination of means, we'd tracked our target to the back of an old convent tacked on to a UNESCO World Heritage Site. Called the São Francisco Church, it had existed since the sixteenth century, with an ornate Gothic façade that now was the anchor of a square housing outdoor cafes and art galleries.

The front of the church—and the square it faced—was a completely safe place for tourists in the old capital of Salvador, but just outside the light, down the cobblestone streets we were on, the predators prowled, waiting on a stray lamb to leave the lights and laughter.

I took a look down the dimly lit alley, seeing the narrow confines of the ancient street snaking down the left-hand wall of the church, reconsidering whom I was asking for help. I'd left Shoshana to pull security within the crowds of tourists for a reason.

Off the net, to Aaron, I said, "I'm not sure that's so smart. She's better protecting us defensively. Out front. Away from the action."

Aaron said, "Because you don't trust her offensively?"

"You're damn right. She's a walking disaster. Better for Jennifer to do it."

"Jennifer's on the roof. Shoshana's perfect for this and you know it. Jennifer would be better as bait, with her blond hair and innocence, but Shoshana's the next-best thing."

He turned away for a moment, then looked me in the eye, saying, "Shoshana's a killer, but she's pure. She won't do anything if it's not warranted. Honestly, I'm more concerned about you."

Aaron had seen what I was capable of, and he was hitting at the core of the mission. Could I maintain control? It was a good question, because in an earlier life, he'd almost killed me, and in so doing, he'd killed a friend of mine. The results hadn't been pretty. He'd seen what I was capable of when I was walking the edge, leaning way over, and now I was operating in that same zone. Something he knew about.

I said, "I'm good. Don't worry about me. Just worry about the threat."

He nodded, but I could see he wasn't convinced.

Shoshana came back on the net, whispering with an urgency neither Aaron nor I understood, "You feel something too, Nephilim?"

Aaron grinned, and I returned it, holding up a finger before he got on the net. I said, "Yeah, but it's not because of some damn ancient church. It's because I can't get to entry. I don't want a gunfight. I need quiet, which means I need you."

"So you want me to do what?"

"Walk down this alley from the back. Expose any threat that may prevent our entry."

She said nothing for a moment, then came back, "That's what you want? Me as bait?"

Aaron's eyes widened, and I saw him reaching to key his mike, him saying, "That's not how to get her to execute."

I held up my hand again and beat him to the punch, saying, "Carrie, this is the threat. *This* is what I feel. And this is what I need."

Aaron and I looked at each other, and I felt my cell phone vibrate in my pocket. Shoshana came back on and said, "This is Carrie. I'm moving to the south of the alley. I'll be coming south to north. I'll have the light on my phone going."

I pulled out my cell, saw it was Jennifer, and realized she didn't want to talk on the open net. I held it up, then whispered to Aaron, "Tell Shoshana that all we need is to flush out any threats. We'll handle it. I don't need any crazy shit here. She just walks toward us until someone triggers. Or until she reaches us without a trigger."

Aaron nodded and I answered the phone, saying, "What?"

Jennifer said, "You're going to let Shoshana loose in that alley, after you felt a threat? Let's back off. Attack a different way."

I saw a pinpoint of light at the back of the alley and said, "Too late. She's in."

Jennifer said, "That's a bad call. She'll kill anyone who threatens her."

I said, "If it's the guys that we're hunting, I don't give a shit."

She said, "Pike, don't go there—"

And I hung up, watching the light. Not wanting to think

about what I'd just said. Not after what had happened to my friend. She knew where I was headed, because she'd seen it once before. I knew it, too.

The difference was I wanted it.

The light bounced down the alley until it was abreast of our entry point, and Aaron and I began slinking down the lane, hiding from the streetlights behind us, stepping over the trash to avoid the noise. We closed the gap, both wound as tight as a tripwire, waiting. And it came.

Two men assaulted Shoshana from both sides of the alley, one from behind a dumpster and the other from a gap in the bricks.

They slammed into her in a synchronized assault, and we took off running, reaching them just as they gained the upper hand. I saw one man cinch his hand into Shoshana's hair, then bash her skull into the cobblestones. The second had his arms wrapped around her legs, pulling out a blade that glinted in the moonlight.

They were in total control, right up until we reached them. Aaron slammed his boot into the man holding her hair and I jumped on the man holding her legs. I caught a glimpse of their fight, and then was subsumed with my own.

He began attacking me, attempting to hammer my face with elbows and fists, and then hit me with the knife in my forearm. I blocked the initial blows, returned them with my own, then felt the blade slice through my jacket, nicking my flesh.

The wound he caused split open the blackness, the anger inside me boiling out. I gave him everything I'd bottled up over the last week. I abandoned my "team leader control" and let the beast run free, looking for vengeance.

I battered his face, trapped his wrist against his torso, the blade now useless, circled around his body, and wrapped him up in my arms, pressing his head forward into his chest. He began frothing at the mouth, flailing his one good fist, and then gave up, dropping the knife and raising his other hand in an effort to surrender. It did no good. I wanted a release, and I worked to achieve it. I pressed him further, going deeper, until I felt his neck snap.

The sound split through the pain, jerking me out of my darkness. I let him sink to the ground, looking at Shoshana and Aaron. Both were staring back at me, Shoshana holding the other attacker in a joint lock, facedown on the ground.

She said, "You were worried about me going crazy? What was that?"

I shook my head, clearing the beast, not sure what I'd done. I said, "Let's go. Put him out."

She nodded, then asked, "Permanently?"

Because that's just how she thinks.

Not liking what I'd just done, I said, "No. Not permanently."

She said, "He's Russian. He's not a common predator. He's here for *you*."

For the first time, I noticed that the man I'd fought wasn't from Brazil. I searched him, finding a passport from Saint Kitts. The same passport I'd found on the Russian I'd killed in Charleston. The one who had murdered my friend.

The blackness came rushing back.

This is all tied together. And it ends now.

She looked at me expectantly, and I closed my eyes, reliving the explosion and the charred body.

Shoshana said, "Pike?"

I locked eyes with Aaron, and he didn't flinch, just stared at me, letting me make the choice. Not judging in any way.

A part of me wanted to call Jennifer. Wanting someone

7

to stop the slide I was on. She was the only one who could prevent it. I didn't. Like a junkie feeling the heroin, I enjoyed what I was doing.

I stepped over the edge of the abyss.

"Kill him."

2

One Week Ago

Nung heard his boss swear out loud and shout, "Nung! Get your ass out here."

He stopped packing several laptops and rose from a pelican case. He tossed in some bubble wrap and strode to the front of the company's makeshift do-it-yourself office, more of a trailer than a structure. He opened the aluminum door, feeling the oppressive humidity of Myanmar hit and begin to soak his shirt, a relentless cycle that didn't faze him, unlike the men he worked for. Being from Thailand, he had long ago ceased caring about the sweat/air conditioner sequence, but the men who'd hired him despised the furnace of Myanmar. He poked his head out and saw his boss attempting to talk in sign language to a Burmese official. Meaning they were doing nothing but waving their arms.

His boss saw him and shouted, "Come on. Get over here."

He called himself Domingo, but Nung didn't believe that was his boss's name, because he knew the man was from Russia. Well, he didn't *know* Domingo was from Russia, but the fact that he spoke Russian was an indicator. The subterfuge wasn't particularly alarming to Nung, as he'd spent most of his life straddling the gray area between legal and illegal. In the end, Nung hadn't questioned the name because he, himself,

9

was operating under the same subterfuge—his name wasn't Nung, the Thai word for "one," just as his brother wasn't named Song, for the Thai word for "two." The similarities, though, ended at the use of an alias, because Nung took his job seriously, wanting to earn his pay.

Unlike Domingo.

Nung reached the scrum, seeing Domingo's false eye staring off into space, something that was always disconcerting to him. He never understood why the man didn't wear a patch—or at least make sure his eye was looking forward. He heard Domingo say to the other contractor, in Russian, "This idiot is as bad as the dumb-asses we were hired to help. Thank God this contract is over."

Nung showed no emotion. The men he worked with had no idea he understood Russian, and he wanted to keep it that way. He'd learned plenty about their operations over the past four months on the contract, and all of it could be lucrative for his father and family.

A lithe man of just under six feet, he was taller than most Thais because of his heritage. His father was American—a Caucasian who'd flown for Air America out of Thailand during the secret war in Laos and Cambodia, where he'd worked more than just an aircraft for the CIA. After the war had ended, his father had stayed in Thailand, using the contacts he'd developed during the war to create a black market empire in the seedy underbelly of Bangkok. He'd married a Thai, and had raised his sons in the family business. Because of it, Nung had grown up—not *immoral*, but certainly amoral.

His father had owned a brothel in the famed Patpong red-light district, which catered to foreign nationals. Unlike the other brothels that trafficked in underage boys and rough sex, he'd trafficked in exotic women. Russians, Swedes, Ukrainians. You name it, he had them.

Nung grew up in that world, so much that when his mother had died when he was at the age of four, he'd been raised by a Russian nanny. A woman his father had taken a liking to and had pulled out of the lineup for a softer life. She'd shown a greater intelligence than most his father had brought over, but the winning attribute was a true affection for his sons.

The woman had been his life for years while his father worked, never acting as if she was doing anything for money, showing what he had later learned was love. A strange concept he'd never understood as a child, given his father's transactional life.

She was killed in a car accident after Nung had gone to a university, but her lasting legacy had been a touchstone of caring that was the only bit of emotion he had. Well, that and the fact he could speak Russian. Something he kept hidden from his current employer.

He knew that Domingo had no idea, the thought fanciful. How could a Thai hired to work in Myanmar speak Russian?

But he did.

In English, the chosen language between them, Nung said, "What's the problem?"

Domingo said, "The problem is I can't tell what this idiot is asking. We were told to clear out of this camp now that it's operational but he wants to keep our sensors. That's not happening. He wants them, he can buy his own."

Nung worked for a group of Russians called Wagner, a private military contractor from the Russian Federation that had been hired by the government of Myanmar to help with the repatriation of the Rohingya, a persecuted group who had fled from a genocidal effort by the government to eradicate them from existence.

They were a Muslim subset of the population of Myanmar, with its own language and customs, and the government had tried to kill them off for years, but really ramped up efforts in 2017, in a concerted attempt to cause them to flee or die, a final solution.

After the rapes, murders, and burning of villages, the government got what they wanted; the Rohingya fled to Bangladesh, like they'd done for decades before, but this time it had a new twist; the world was more connected, and the atrocities were caught on the internet. It was, in fact, a genocide.

Embarrassed, the government of Myanmar had begun trotting out a hundred excuses for what had occurred, and offered to repatriate the ones who'd fled. And that was where Nung came in.

Now wanting to look like the good guys, the government had begun receiving the people back into the Rakhine State, albeit into refugee camps because their homes had been burned to the ground by government troops. Wagner had been contracted to build the camps. And they needed local help.

Nung, because he spoke the language, had been hired through his father's contacts to interact with the Burmese. It wasn't lost on him that even though they'd reached out to his father for help, they were not as respectable as the Red Cross.

He didn't mind, though. He could take the insults and the less-than-noble actions he witnessed Wagner conduct. It was all business.

Until it wasn't.

Nung saw Domingo push the man, then said, "What's

the problem? Let it go. Those sensors were paid for by the contract. You've already made the money on them."

"Bullshit. That's wrong. They paid for my services. If they want the sensors, then they need to buy their own. Tell him he's fucked."

Nung said some words to the official, and he began waving his arms again, incensed. Domingo slapped the Burmese official's hands out of the air, and Nung considered translating the wrong way and causing a fight. He'd seen how the Burmese treated the Rohingya, and it wasn't as pure as the state propaganda machine put out. The man in front of him was just as bad as the man behind him. They were both evil, and it would be nice to see them destroy each other.

He did not.

In short order, he had the situation resolved, the Burmese official walking away in a huff. He turned to the Russian and said, "Continue packing?"

Domingo said, "Yeah. I want to be out of this shithole in the next four hours. Let them deal with it now."

Two hours later, Nung finished sealing the rest of the office equipment while Domingo and the other man talked in the shallow office to his left. As usual, they were speaking in Russian, and as usual, Nung was listening. He didn't really care what they did with the Rohingya, because he was paid for a service, and he provided it. But in his heart he did. He hated the Russians because of what he'd seen. They hadn't done a damn thing to really help the refugees because the government hadn't cared. It was all a joke for the press.

The Rohingya members had been abused and castigated from the moment they'd created the first camp, and nobody seemed to give a damn, least of all the Russians of Wagner— which was the express purpose the Russians had hired him: helping to facilitate the resettlement of the refugees. It aggravated him. He could deal with the blood and violence, because he'd done it himself, but it was always against an enemy who understood the rules. Not a bunch of families that were being persecuted solely because of their heritage.

He'd called his father only once, and had been told to continue, because the Russian connection was a good one, and he'd been forced to choose. Family meant everything to him. There was no allegiance beyond that. Family was all. And so he'd continued. But he held a growing hatred, and while they treated him as the hired local help, they had no idea of his skills.

Luckily for them, they'd never see it, and he could finally go home, serving his father and expanding the family business.

Shoving more bubble wrap into another pelican case, Nung heard Domingo talking on a phone in the next room. He heard discussions about an operation in Brazil, and then Domingo became heated with the man on the phone, saying his men were already there and they couldn't afford another compromise like the one in France.

Nung perked up, no longer packing the case. Domingo glanced out the door and said, "No, nobody can hear me. I'm working with savages."

Then he said, "Are you sure? The same ones who killed Tagir? They're in Brazil?"

Nung worked around the box, pretending to pack but really moving closer to the door. He heard, "Yeah, I got the email. I'm looking at it right now. Are you asking what to do? I'll tell you what to do. Cut the head off of the snake. You know where he is. You got the information for Grolier Services, right?"

Nung heard the words and had to physically stop himself

from showing a reaction. Domingo continued, "I don't care who they saw in Brazil, you kill that fuck in Charleston, and it'll end. Get it done."

He heard the phone slam, then Domingo stormed out of the office, looking at Nung and saying, "What the hell is taking so long? Pack that shit up."

Nung said, "What's the rush? We've been here for four months."

Domingo said, "It looks like I'm going to Brazil, and I need to leave immediately. Get it done."

Nung nodded, watching him stomp out of the trailer. As soon as the door had closed, he went into the small office where Domingo had talked. The one with the desktop computer he was not allowed to access. He saw the window on the computer was open, the time-out for the password not yet engaged.

He went to email. He glanced behind him, seeing the outside door still closed. He pulled up the first email and saw nothing but Cyrillic lettering. He cursed under his breath.

While he'd learned to speak Russian, he couldn't read it. He highlighted all of it, then pasted it into Google Translate. The words that came out were a little schizophrenic, like an old telegram, but there was enough for him to make out:

The group highlight in Switzerland be highlight in Brazil. Two members seen in Salvador. Cannot stop say who else is involved. But military contract people not people might prevent success. Presidential campaign is reaching apex and that though Lulu oilfields are in doubt. Recommend another Operation Harvest. Target Grolier Recovery Services now, before they harvest operation.

Nung read the words, and inwardly curled. What he'd

heard earlier was correct. They were after Grolier Services. He had no idea why, but it made him bristle.

He heard the door slam open outside, and closed down the Google Translate page. He went outside the small office and saw Domingo glaring at him.

He said, "What?"

Domingo said, "What, what? What the fuck are you doing? Pack this shit up. I want to go."

"I was looking at preparing the desktop in your office."

"Don't touch that. I'll do that myself. I have to use the sat dish to get some plane tickets. Those fucks in Moscow want me to fly tonight. It never ends."

Nung said, "To Charleston, in the United States?"

"Fuck no, someone else is doing the easy work. I have to go to Moscow, then Brazil." And then something clicked in Domingo's brain. "How the fuck do you know about Charleston?"

Nung reverted to what Domingo knew; a dumb-ass savage. He ducked his head in supplication and said, "When you were on the phone, the only word I heard you say in English was Charleston. I'll get this packed up soon."

Domingo nodded, staring at him for a beat. Nung knew for all his bluster, he was not a dumb man. He'd seen it over five months. Nung bent down to the closest pelican case, packing up office equipment, and waited, feeling his eyes on him.

After five brutal seconds, Domingo left, shouting at his men. And Nung made his decision.

He knew the man who owned Grolier Recovery Services. He knew what that man had done for his younger brother. And he knew that only one thing counted in this world.

Family.

Something Domingo would learn the hard way.

3

Amena found me in the bathroom and said, "Why do you pick such fights? This is supposed to be a party."

Looking in the mirror, and honestly a little embarrassed at my actions, I said, "Because it's just some friends coming over. We don't need to turn this into a New Year's Eve gala."

She caught my eye in the reflection and said, "So you guys are fighting because you don't want to work? Is that it?"

I turned from the mirror, and she continued, "I'm not saying you're wrong. I'm just trying to learn what to expect here in America."

I knew she was toying with me, because she was smart as a whip and had picked up "being American" within a few weeks of arrival, now acting like any other thirteen-year-old teenager.

Amena was a refugee from Syria who had done some good deeds for America. Well, that's putting it lightly. She'd saved a ton of lives, all because she thought it was the right thing to do, risking her own life and almost giving it in the process. And because of it, I'd saved hers, bringing her to the United States.

Taller than an average thirteen-year-old, with tan skin, black hair, and black eyes, she was beautiful in an exotic sort of way. Her looks caused tourists to comment when we were out and about on the peninsula, asking where she was from, which initially aggravated the hell out of me. I was trying to protect her status, and some bloated lady from a cruise ship would act like she wanted to pet the strange animal. I took it as an insult, but Amena never did. She thought it was a compliment, and honestly, she *was* something exotic. In more ways than one.

Playacting like she was trying to determine how a man and woman behaved in America, she was really trying to cool the fight, because she was torn between loving me or loving Jennifer. She wanted us both.

I turned to her and said, "No, this isn't how it is in America. I'm just being an asshole."

She giggled and said, "Then why do you do it?"

"Because I'm stubborn."

She nodded and said, "I know. Now what?"

I sighed and said, "Now I have to eat crow."

And I'd finally said something American that made no sense to Amena. She scrunched her eyes and said, "Eat crow? Like a bird?"

I said, "It's just a saying that means I have to go admit I was wrong. How about you go out there and assist? With something too big for you to do? And then you come back here and ask me to help?"

She caught on immediately and raced out, wanting to end any disagreement between her hero, Jennifer, and me. Wanting to get back to the affection that gave her a blanket of security. Thirty seconds later, she was back, saying, "Can you help me with the tray of shrimp? It's too big for me to move."

I smiled, which brought out a grin of her own, and out we went.

I entered our living room, saw Jennifer scowling, and Amena said, "He's going to help me. Because I can't move it."

I looked at Jennifer and said, "I can't tell her no."

Jennifer's expression softened, and I knew she understood this was my way of giving in. She motioned me over, saying, "I could use some help as well."

I went to her, and she put her arms around my neck and kissed me on the lips. "It would be a lot easier if you just did the work, without the fighting."

I grinned and said, "I know."

Jennifer gave me a radiant smile back, melting any notion of contradicting whatever she wanted, and Amena practically broke the windows with her own beaming face, happy to have solved the dilemma.

Although deep inside, I *still* thought this was bullshit. All we should have been doing was packing.

Jennifer and I were slated for a mission in Brazil in a few days, hunting some Hezbollah financiers at the tri-border region, and normally such preparation would be old hat, but now we had Amena. We were working to find her a permanent home, but that took time.

Jennifer had come up with a stroke of brilliance, asking Kylie Hale, the niece of Kurt Hale, the commander of our unit, if she would house-sit while we were gone. Kylie had some history with Jennifer—meaning once upon a time, Jennifer had saved her life. She was currently wandering about trying to put her recent degree in English literature to use—meaning she was researching graduate schools—so she'd readily jumped at the chance to travel to Charleston for a salary that involved nothing more than watching Amena.

She'd arrived yesterday to become acquainted with our routine, and I thought we were set. Then she'd asked if her boyfriend could visit while we were gone. I didn't have a problem with that, because her boyfriend also happened to be on my team, and he was following Jennifer and me to Brazil shortly, so it wasn't like he could get in any trouble. I'd said fine, and she informed me he was coming today, suspiciously sounding like it had already been planned. Just to cap it off, later in the day, my commander, Colonel Kurt Hale, called and said he was passing through town and wanted to visit— which I knew was bullshit. Kurt was never just "passing through." There was an agenda in play, but with all three descending on our house, Jennifer had decided to throw a party, which made me grumpy.

Jennifer saw I was still less than enthusiastic and said, "Why don't you head to the store? I forgot a few things that I need for tonight. Amena and I can finish up here."

I jumped at the chance, snatching a grocery list out of her hand and racing toward the door.

"Take the Jeep," she said, "My car's blocked in." And I knew she was punishing me. It was only October, and Charleston should have still been a muggy swelter, but we'd had an early cold snap, making the air temperature about fifty degrees. She knew I hadn't replaced the top to the Jeep, and would therefore freeze while driving it.

I didn't care, because driving that beat-up CJ was better than her little Mini Cooper. It was my pride and joy—and a tax write-off, because it was our company vehicle, the rear quarter panel adorned with an emblem that said Grolier Recovery Services.

I climbed in, turned the old-fashioned key, and backed out our little drive, inching into the street while praying nobody slammed into me.

On the surface, Grolier Recovery Services helped facilitate archeological work around the world, and to that end, Jennifer and I made a pretty good living. We did about three jobs to one in the real world, working for various agencies that wanted the best at deciphering the mundane world of geopolitics and antiquities. The remaining job was what we really existed for—finding a bad guy and planting him in the ground, paid for courtesy of the United States government.

The cover work that facilitated our ability to conduct counterterrorism operations around the world had been pretty lucrative—enough to buy a small two-story row house on Wentworth Street just off East Bay on the Charleston Peninsula. It was a little fixer-upper with a narrow gravel drive on the side just big enough to fit three cars end to end. Jennifer and I were constantly rotating vehicles in and out, but the worst part was getting onto Wentworth Street from the blind alley.

I made it out okay and shot over to the Harris Teeter grocery store a couple of blocks away, getting out and reading the list. I immediately realized I should have checked it in Jennifer's presence, because it was full of inscrutable things that caused me to wander the store like a Buddhist monk searching for the secret to life, texting her questions about each item and sending pictures when necessary.

I knew she'd given up when I saw a FaceTime call from her. I answered and she said, "I'm not sure how you managed to make it through life not knowing how a supermarket works."

I said, "I know where the Doritos and beer are located. Sometimes the milk, but you're making me find a bunch of stuff with foreign-sounding names like Gruyère cheese. That stuff wasn't even in the cheese section."

She shook her head, saying, "Just come back with what you have. Kurt's already here. I'll go back out. You win."

I said, "I'm doing my best! I'm almost done."

She glanced away from the phone, and then leaned into the screen, whispering, "He wants to talk, so get your ass home."

I said, "About what?"

She glanced away again, making sure she was out of earshot and said, "I don't know, but I need you here for whatever it is, because I don't think it's good."

4

As soon as she said it, I knew Kurt was here about Amena. And Jennifer knew that she wouldn't be able to fight whatever he was going to say, but I sure as shit could. It was sort of my specialty.

I nodded and said, "I'm on the way."

Kurt Hale and I had a unique relationship. On the one hand, he was my direct superior—the commander of Project Prometheus and the one who gave me my operational orders. On the other, we were almost as close as brothers, with a deep friendship that had lasted for decades. We'd first met when I was assigned to his troop in a special mission unit, and we had both been promoted up the ranks, serving together multiple times. When he'd created Prometheus under a previous presidential administration, he'd recruited only the best of the best for the teams, and I was his original hire, the first person to go through Prometheus Assessment and Selection. Kurt trusted my judgment, going so far as to allow Jennifer to attempt A&S as a female civilian when everyone else said he was crazy, and I trusted him as a commander. But that didn't mean I wouldn't fight him on Amena.

Like I said before, that was sort of my specialty. While we were closer than blood on the friendship front, when he wore the commander hat, I was more than willing to tell him he was full of shit—and I was one of the few who could get away with it.

Two minutes later I was pulling in behind a late-model rental car, our little drive now three-deep in vehicles. I exited, looked up, and saw Kurt Hale on my second-floor balcony, leaning on the rail and holding a beer. He said, "Running errands for the partner. How domesticated."

I smiled, reached in to grab the two small bags I had, and said, "Yeah, well, it pretty much ended in failure. I'll be right up."

A minute later I'd given my bags to Jennifer. Kurt was still on the balcony with the door closed. She said, "He's going to take Amena. That's why he's here. He pulled all those strings with the Oversight Council, and now he has to make it good."

The Oversight Council was the board that oversaw all Project Prometheus activities, which included my team. Nobody ever mentioned the program name out loud, calling everyone associated with it an innocuous nickname: the Taskforce. While GRS was doing pretty well on the commercial front—enough to let us buy this house—it's primary purpose was as a cover to allow penetration of denied areas for one reason: to drive a stake into the heart of threats that could affect U.S. national interests.

I knew the Council was not happy with my decision to bring Amena to the United States because it had caused too many questions about how she jumped the line, potentially exposing the cover of GRS. How does a barely there company bring home a refugee and pass through customs and immigration without a hitch? The answer was because I had some people on my side, very important people who'd greased the skids. And that was making the Oversight Council nervous, since it would take only one thread to unwind the GRS cover, which would then unwind Project Prometheus and jeopardize the careers of anyone associated with it. Because Project Prometheus was decidedly illegal. An extrajudicial killing machine that was sanctioned at the highest level.

I passed Jennifer the bags and said, "I couldn't find the damn cheese you wanted."

Amena came up, pointed at the balcony, and said, "Why is he here? Is it me?"

She was like an animal that could smell a threat, having lived on the edge of survival for much of her short life. I looked at her and saw the pain of losing the first bit of sanctuary she'd ever experienced. And I realized I didn't want her to leave. For the first time in close to a decade—really since the loss of my family—I was content with my life, and I wanted that feeling to remain.

I brushed her cheek and said, "Don't worry about it. At least for this trip."

"Promise?"

I said, "Yes, doodlebug. I promise."

Jennifer heard me use the nickname that was once my daughter's and smiled. Amena relaxed. I turned to Jennifer, saying, "Just keep getting ready. I'll see what's up."

I grabbed a couple of beers and exited onto my upper balcony. I shook Kurt's hand, handed him another beer, and he said, "I hear Kylie is your new nanny."

I said, "I guess that depends. What's up with the sudden visit?"

He demurred, saying, "Looks like GRS is making more money than I remembered. This is a pretty nice house."

Which wasn't really true. It was an old row house that required enormous maintenance against plumbing leaks, pests, and electrical problems, but it *was* on the peninsula of Charleston, which was pretty cool.

I said, "So you want to cut my pay? Is that it? Because the Taskforce doesn't pay me nearly what I'm worth. I get a fortune helping some university do nothing more than excavate a dig. Shit, the last three jobs I did bought this house. I get peanuts from you dodging bullets."

He laughed and said, "I should have never let you two go find that temple in Guatemala. I've never heard the end of it."

"You never would have had GRS without it. We're the deepest cover organization you have."

He turned serious and said, "What's the status with Brazil?"

I said, "We've got the contract locked in with the university for the Jesuit UNESCO site, and it's a stone's throw from the triple frontier. Easy for us to work there and penetrate the area."

The triple frontier—or tri-border region—was the juncture of the borders of Argentina, Brazil, and Paraguay, a Wild West area heavy with Hezbollah activity. GRS always had to have a reason for operating, and we'd found one in the Rio Grande do Sul state in southern Brazil, an ancient Jesuit church called São Miguel das Missões that was slowly falling apart. A university, in coordination with the United Nations, wanted to stop the passage of time, and they'd hired us to help facilitate. Which was perfect, because we were going to use it to put some Hezbollah heads on a spike.

Kurt said, "Sounds like it's tracking."

"It is. Knuckles and Brett are already down there, prepping the battlefield. They head to Salvador in a couple of days, and Jennifer and I will link up with them there. But you know that. You're the one who fought to keep them on my team."

I was unique in the Taskforce in that I was a pure civilian now. Brett was a paramilitary member of the CIA and Knuckles was in the Navy. It had been a fight to allow me— now a civilian—to be the team leader of active-duty guys, but neither Brett nor Knuckles would have it any other way. We were a family that had bled together when *I* was on active duty, and while others in the government fought the decision on purely bureaucratic grounds, Kurt understood what teamwork meant.

In the end, the Taskforce was a strange beast, and it was just one more permutation from the norm. Kurt Hale had fought for me, and I'd regained my leadership position after I'd left active duty. After I'd crawled out of the abyss.

He just nodded, and I could tell he was thinking about something else.

I said, "Okay, sir, what's the point of this visit? It isn't our trip to Brazil, because you see those SITREPs. Just get it out."

He sighed, then looked at me, saying, "The Council has found a place for Amena. But you're not going to like it."

"What's that mean?"

"They want to repatriate her into the system. Put her into the refugee flow back in Syria."

He saw my face and said, "Wait, wait, she won't be put back into danger. She'll just be placed in a camp outside of Syria, either Jordan or Lebanon, and she'll get preferential treatment. She'll be back here in a year, maybe less."

I looked at him and said, "Are you fucking serious? Is that what *you* would do?"

He frowned and said, "Pike, there is more at risk here than

her. I'm trying to do the best thing for her, but you short-circuited that. Don't blame me. *You're* the one who brought her here on a covert aircraft after a covert mission. It's hard to explain."

I leaned back and said, "So she's not worth the destruction she will cause if anyone makes the connection."

He nodded and said, "That's about it. I'm here on behalf of the Oversight Council. They wanted to jerk her ass outright. I told them to hold off."

I said, "How much time do I have?"

"What? You have no time. This is it."

"Bullshit. I'm going to Brazil in the next few days. How much time can you get me?"

"What do you mean?"

"Let me get this mission done first. Give me some time to cushion the blow. Don't take her tomorrow. Sell it as 'Pike's gone on a Taskforce mission. Can't take her now.' How hard is that?"

He said, "I don't know if I can do that."

I said, "Sir, I'm asking. I have never asked before. Give me this. I've given you my blood. *She's* given you *her* blood. All I'm asking is for a trip. Fuck those assholes in the Oversight Council."

He nodded, not looking at me. He said, "Okay, Pike. I'm with you. I'll delay it, but it's going to happen. You need to get your head around that."

I said, "I'll get my head around it when I need to. She's not going back to Syria. That's the end of it. Fuck the Oversight Council."

He looked at me to see if I was serious, and Jennifer came out on the balcony, saying, "Pike, I have to go back to the store. You didn't get everything I needed."

She'd clearly heard what I'd said and was trying to defuse the situation. And it worked. Kurt and I stared at each other for a beat, then he said, "I'll go. You guys stay here."

I said, "Sir, you don't want to try to find what she's making. It's impossible."

He laughed and said, "Not everyone is a Neanderthal. Let me go. You guys need to talk."

He walked back into the house, and Jennifer looked at me. I shook my head. Amena peered at me behind the door, and I felt crushed. All I'd done was give her hope, and now that was going to be devastated.

Jennifer followed behind him, and I could see her giving him instructions on what to buy, the things that I'd missed. I watched him go down the stairs, and then saw him appear below me. He looked up and said, "I can't get out."

I said, "Take my Jeep."

I tossed the keys down, and he caught them, looked at the Jeep, and said, "This is probably the biggest risk I've taken since I was running shotgun with you in Iraq."

I laughed and said, "And I kept you alive then."

He crawled into my CJ-7, stuck in the key, turned the ignition, and an explosion erupted, shredding his life in a fireball that turned the Jeep into a shrapnel blast of flying parts.

I was thrown back, feeling the shock wave of the explosion and dully hearing the tinkling of auto parts spackling the roof.

I sat up, staring in shock at the inferno below me, the Jeep burning furiously. It made no sense. I couldn't get my mind around it. I saw the body in the driver's seat, slumped over with its hair on fire, an arm dangling outside the door by a piece of tendon still connected to the shoulder, and felt a helplessness. I placed my hands on the railing and began to squeeze, a white-hot rage coursing through my body.

Kurt Hale was my mentor, my protector, and the man I always wanted to emulate. The one man I had always wanted to be. He had been family, and now he was dead. Because of me.

Because I was the target.

5

Nikita Voronin—aka Domingo—passed by Red Square and slipped down an alley two blocks from the Kremlin, cinching his jacket tight against the coming winter. He found the entrance to a liquor store, nodded at the man working the register, and went to the back, stopping at a small metal door without any labels. He glanced behind, saw the store was empty, and knocked, looking up at a camera affixed to the wall.

He heard an electronic lock break free and entered, finding the interior distinctly different from the utilitarian shop on the other side of the door. Paneled in dark wood, with antique artwork on the walls and crystal chandeliers providing the dim lighting, it was as if he'd entered a museum.

A hulking figure put his hand to his chest, and he allowed himself to be searched. The brute finished and waved him forward. He entered an office, seeing an ornate wooden desk. Behind it sat his boss, Dmitri Pavlov.

Nikita said, "It's done."

An older man slowly going soft, Dmitri still had the steel in his eyes from his days in the Spetsnaz forces of the old Soviet Union, but the chaotic world that followed the fall of the Berlin Wall had allowed him to leave his past of death, focusing on a future of profit. The ensuing years had been good to him, so much so that his gut had swollen as he exploited the fruits of the post-Soviet world, even as he paid others to do the fighting.

Dmitri leaned back in his chair, lit a cigar, and said, "You're positive? I don't want this man messing up my operations a second time."

Nikita said, "You mentioned that before. What happened?"

Dmitri blew out some smoke, waved his hand, and said, "We had a simple mission—in Monaco of all places. What the hell could go wrong there? Recover a phone from a child who'd stolen it. I sent a man against her, and he was thwarted. I sent a *team* to help *him,* and they were thwarted. Only two of them lived."

Nikita said, "Luca and Simon. The two who saw the men in Brazil."

"Yes. They recognized the same man who prevented them from accomplishing their mission. A black man who is uncommonly good at fighting."

"If he's so uncommonly good at fighting, how did Luca and Simon escape?"

Dmitri grinned and said, "This, I do not know. Someone did kill Tagir and the rest of the team, but not Simon and Luca. Could have been they were interrupted. Could have been something else. But that action did lead me to investigate further, and I found the company I gave you. They're like ours, I'm sure; a hidden military effort cloaked in a legitimate corporation. I didn't bother to do anything about it earlier because there is no profit in revenge, only downside, but now the black man has been spotted in Brazil, and that is no coincidence. Which is why I chose to interdict first. And it seems it went smoothly."

Nikita said, "Yeah, we found the company, then located the target's house on the Charleston Peninsula, in the United

States. He had a Jeep that my men observed, with the company logo. We rigged it, then waited. It didn't take long. The target initiated the interdiction, and he was incinerated."

Dmitri sat up and said, "Wait, you used a car bomb?"

Miffed, Nikita said, "Yes. It was the easiest way for a standoff attack. I didn't want to engage with the target, with all the forensics, cameras, and other things around. You wanted an 'accident,' and interacting with the target is always messy. Too many ways to determine that a 'fall,' isn't really a fall."

"But a car bomb is messy. It'll beg all sorts of questions. Charleston isn't Beirut."

Nikita smiled and said, "You pay me for a reason. He drove an old CJ-7 Jeep, and we built a special device. When it's explored forensically, it'll look like the Jeep had a compromised fuel system. There is no evidence of foul play."

Dmitri nodded. Nikita said, "Isn't that what you wanted?"

"It is. As long as he's dead."

Nikita laughed and said, "He is, I promise. Unless he can walk out of fire."

"The men?"

"Still in Charleston. I'm going to let the scrutiny die down a little bit before they leave. I don't want to give anyone a reason to look for a connection, unlike what happened in Dubai or Turkey. I'll keep them in reserve there. Unless External Branch considers that too expensive."

Dmitri smiled and said, "External Branch won't care. If they've succeeded. But Global Engagement might have an issue, since they're still on that account."

Nikita scoffed and said, "Then get them off of the Global Engagement pay line. That entire contract in Myanmar was a waste of time anyway. We made a pittance and I had to suffer every day because of it. I work for External. I give a shit about Global."

Dmitri laughed and said, "So you don't enjoy the 'hearts and minds' of our global strategy?"

"No, I don't. I enjoy the sharp edge of the spear."

Dmitri leaned forward and said, "Good. That's exactly what I wanted to hear, because the target set has expanded. It's no longer three members of Petrobras."

Nikita perked up and said, "That could be a problem. You can't add a target at this late date. It takes months to build up a pattern of life, and we need to eliminate them within a week. We already have the data on the others."

"Calm down. In this case his pattern of life is advertised."

Dmitri passed across a picture and Nikita recognized it.

"No way. A politician? That's insane."

Dmitri tapped the picture and said, "Unfortunately, the other three deaths matter little now, unless we remove this man."

"Why? You're talking about killing a potential head of state. Corporate attacks are one thing, but this is political. We don't do that."

"We do when it serves our interests."

Nikita put his hands on Dmitri's desk, leaned forward, and said, "You have to help me out here. I get I have no need to know, and I was good with that for the Petrobras executives, but this is another order of magnitude. I could expect some help if I were caught doing the executives, but if this one goes bad, I know I'm getting gutted."

Dmitri started to retort at the insolence and the lack of trust, and then held back. He knew Nikita would see it for what it was: a lie. And he needed Nikita to execute.

He said, "Okay. This doesn't leave the room. You know Operation Harvest as the killing of the Petrobras men in order to gain some oil concessions, but it's much larger. In a nutshell, it's the control of the entire Lulu oil fields off the coast of Rio de Janeiro, and with it, the de facto control of the country. For Mother Russia."

Nikita took that in, then said, "How?"

"Brazil has found the largest deposits of crude and natural gas in the twenty-first century, but they can't get it out of the ground. There are plenty of people competing to help, and our national company, Rosneft, has been shut out. They don't want to work with a Russian institution because of Rosneft's deep ties to Venezuela. That's where we come in. We have some people in Petrobras who are not, shall we say, squeamish about Rosneft's less than stellar reputation. But they are thwarted by others."

Nikita nodded and said, "Okay, okay, I get that. It explains the other targets. But why the politician?"

Dmitri took a deep drag on his cigar and said, "Have you heard of the Carwash scandal in Brazil?"

Nikita studied the wall for a moment, searching his memory, and said, "Yeah, I think so. The one that caught a few Brazilian politicians flatfooted?"

Dmitri laughed and said, "Yes. But it was much more than a 'few' Brazilian politicians. It was pretty much the entire political class. *Everyone* in the party in power was involved in the bribes. Everyone had their hand in the till, taking bribes from all manner of oil companies funneled through Petrobras, which means we're a little late to the show."

"Why?"

"Because the man our bosses have been working with was the ex-president. He was running for another term, and leading handily, meaning all we had to do was get rid of a few Petrobras sticks, replacing them with someone of a more *Carwash* bent. But he was just informed he can't run for president anymore, even though we're within sight of the election."

"Why?"

Dmitri laughed and said, "Because he was sent to jail for corruption. You can't make that up. He was winning the election from jail, but the high court said he is ineligible while serving his sentence. So the party put up someone else, and he's miles behind this man."

Dmitri stabbed a finger into the picture on the table and said, "A firebrand that came out of nowhere, whose entire platform is getting rid of corruption. So, naturally, we can't have that. We need the stand-in to win. Which means we need to get rid of any competition. Can you do it?"

Nikita ran his hands through his hair, thinking of the implications. And the rewards. He said, "Yes, I can. But it'll be costly."

Dmitri laughed and said, "Of course. But costly for whom? Surely you don't expect my hands on this, do you? I gave you the clean passports, and I pay your salary."

Nikita drew back and said, "That's not what I meant. I mean it'll be costly to get it done in the timeline you envision. The election is in two weeks. Not a lot of time to plan, but money can overcome some of that."

Dmitri pulled out a bottle of vodka and two glasses, saying, "You will have the money. And I was joking earlier. You will have the protection as well. This comes from the highest place. It's not about oil fields. It's about influence. NATO takes over one country after another in our near abroad, and now it's time to return the favor for the United States. The idiots in Brazil helping us have no idea, just as the Crimean Peninsula didn't."

"So this is about more than money?"

"It's always about more than money. We're altering the election of a sovereign state not for the profit of cash, but the profit of influence."

"But the United States is aware of our actions in the past. Even the Europeans are aware of election meddling. Something this overt will be challenged, and quite possibly backfire."

"The Europeans don't care, and as for the Americans, we have a company that's helping shape Brazilian opinion. One that's well placed in the political establishment. It's one more bit of Kompromat to use. If this goes bad, the company will want to distance itself from their efforts, and they'll use their own levers of power to do so with the United States. It's a win-win."

Incredulous, Nikita said, "You have a United States company working on Operation Harvest? How on earth can you not be sure they aren't penetrated?"

"They work for profit. Not ideology. And they work in the world of social media manipulation for the election. They've done it all over the world, and all they know is that they've been hired to support a candidate from Brazil. They don't know the hand behind the payment."

"That's not good enough. Have you screened them? I mean individual members."

"Yes, of course. If it'll make you more at ease, the owner emigrated from the Soviet Union, much like the president of Google. While I'd love to have Google in my pocket, this company will do. They have their hand in the politics of the United States, and are also the ones who established the investment fund that got you the Saint Kitts passports. They make a profit with that as well—and not just to us, although we certainly leverage it."

Nikita took that in, and realized he wasn't going to win a fight about trust, even if it was his ass on the line. He either took the mission or he didn't, but there remained an outstanding threat.

"What about the men still in Brazil? The ones from Grolier Recovery Services that Luca and Simon identified? They're still running about."

"They're not a threat. They should be flying home as soon as they hear their boss is dead."

"If it's like you say, I'd rather not rely on hope that they do so."

Dmitri poured two shots of vodka, hoisted his glass, and said, "I guess that'll mean upping the target deck to six. But I wouldn't worry too much about it. They can't fight without a leader."

6

I squeezed the handset, wanting to throw the phone against the wall. I could tell I wasn't winning the argument. George Wolffe, the deputy commander of the Taskforce, did not want to hear what I had to say.

"Sir, all I'm asking for is some computer work on the video I have. I'm not asking to start hacking into U.S. systems."

"Pike, you yourself said that the fire marshal called the explosion a natural event, and the damn ATF backed up their assessment."

Which was true, but there was no way what had happened to Kurt was a coincidence. The ATF didn't look hard enough, which is why I wanted the video analyzed. After all, if the ATF knew what we really did for a living, they'd be digging deep into about forty different terrorist groups. They didn't, and so that left me.

I had just driven the Jeep to the store before tossing the keys to Kurt, and everything had been working fine. If the fuel line were leaking like they said, collecting in a puddle, wouldn't it have registered somehow? Wouldn't I have seen a stain on the stone, or felt something out of whack? Or did it just happen that day? I realized that the cause the ATF and fire marshal blamed had to start sometime—and today was just as good as any other—but in the back of my mind, there was no way I could make sense of the fact that my personal vehicle had killed my commander—and my friend. It *had* to be something else.

I said, "Sir, they did say that, but they also said their finding was just a guess due to the damage. They can't determine conclusively, and they aren't looking based on our answers about enemies and threats against us. We told them the cover story and backed off. Someone needs to investigate that isn't a threat to our cover. That's what I'm trying to do."

"They determined conclusively that there was no malicious interference. The *rest* is just speculation. Look, I get where you're coming from, but we have enough on our plate right now just covering who Kurt really was and why he was there. Let's deal with that right now."

Kurt held two jobs: one as the CEO of Blaisdell Consulting, aka the commander of Project Prometheus, and another his "real job" working on the Joint Staff as a colonel in the United States Army. His death on my lawn was causing a headache, because now the national command authority had to publicly state why a staff officer from the Pentagon was killed at a house in Charleston, South Carolina. And they had to do so without involving Grolier Recovery Services, because the thread was there to pull by any conspiracy buff who wanted to find it.

I said, "His niece was my nanny. He was visiting, period. That should hold up and it's no reason to deny my request."

I could hear the exasperation coming through the phone, George wanting to placate me, but not wanting to go where I wanted. "Pike, it's not going to happen. The entire Taskforce is on stand-down. We're in uncharted territory here, and we need to prevent any exposure. That's the mission."

"Sir, that's my point! If this was a targeted hit, then we *are* exposed. Someone knew enough to find out where

I live and to target me. They didn't do it because I dig up pottery shards with Jennifer. They did it because I work for the Taskforce."

I heard him take a breath, then, "Pike, I know this hurts. It hurts everyone, trust me, but you of all people know that sometimes bad things just happen. It doesn't make it a conspiracy. Two people pedaling by your house thirty minutes before Kurt died does *not* make this a targeted hit. More importantly to the discussion, how did your interactions with the police go?"

The video I wanted the Taskforce computer geeks to analyze was from my home's surveillance cameras. After the explosion—after I'd raced out of the house in a futile attempt to save Kurt's life, and after the nightmare of police vehicles and fire trucks—I'd reviewed the DVR footage and seen nothing except two males biking down the street. Something that was completely ordinary in Charleston. But I didn't want it to be.

I said, "I didn't talk to the police. I'm camped out at our office. Jennifer's handling the police conversations, and we're good. She gave them the story about Kylie and it's set in stone. No reason to go looking anywhere else. She told them I'm out of town."

"Why? Why did you flee the damn scene? That's going to look like you're hiding something."

"Because someone tried to kill me, and I want them to think I'm dead."

"Damn it, Pike, you're going to cause the very thing we're trying to prevent!"

I heard nothing but breathing for a moment, then, "Okay, look, find a way to get back home. If you have to act like you heard about the death, then came racing back from some business trip, do so, but in no way do I want the police to scratch their heads over why the owner of the Jeep started sleeping at his office the night his Jeep blew up. Do you understand?"

I said, "Yes, sir."

"Pike, that's an order. No more conspiracy theories. No more hiding out looking for the bad man. Understood?"

"Yes, sir, I got it."

"Give me an update tomorrow."

"Will do."

But I had no intention of standing down.

He said, "Pike, I'm sorry. We all are."

I said, "Thank you, sir." And hung up, thinking about my options.

George was probably right, and I just didn't want to face the fact that Kurt had died by a random event. The same thing had happened with my wife and daughter years ago, and it had ripped me apart, the senselessness of the loss driving me into a world of self-destruction.

A few years ago I had been the defender of freedom, a man at the pinnacle of the Special Operations community. One that was called upon when the worst had happened. Or so I'd thought. I'd answered that calling even when my wife had begged me to quit, after years of combat. I'd agreed to stop, but I'd done one more deployment because the mission was a siren call. A thing that defined me more than my family.

Until I'd learned that it didn't.

While I was gone, both my wife and daughter had been murdered, and it had shredded me, like pulling a tree out of the ground, the roots ripping in pain. *I* was the one that was supposed to be in danger. I was the one protecting *them*. And

I had learned a hard truth: everything I'd done to protect my nation had done nothing to protect what I held dear.

The loss had caused what I call my dark time. Something that was joked about on my team, but never in my presence, because it was very real. All too real. I had dropped into an abyss that no one should ever enter. A place where I came close to attacking anyone I met in the hope that they would kill me and relieve the pain. I was too big of a coward to do it myself, and was willing to force someone else to do the honors, even if it meant me defending myself and killing them instead. Because I couldn't let someone kill me.

It was a bad, bad time, and I wondered if maybe I was subconsciously trying to prevent the beast from returning, looking for a meaning to Kurt's loss.

I'd done that with my family, and in the end, their deaths were just as nonsensical as this one. That fact had almost crushed me once, and I was working mightily to prevent the beast from coming back.

This morning, I woke up in my sleeping bag disoriented, unsure of where I was, and the explosion had come back—the one that had ripped Kurt's life away. Last night, as I prepared to go to sleep, I'd recognized where I was headed—recognized the symptoms of the scar tissue ripping, the beast wanting to roam—and I'd wanted Jennifer with me, the one person who could stop the slide I was on. The one person who had seen me when I'd slipped over the edge before. But I'd abandoned her to deal with the fallout of Kurt's death, while I hid trying to make sense of the disaster.

I stared vacantly at the television across the room, an old movie playing with the sound muted. I picked up my phone to check in with Jennifer, and it dinged with an iMessage, the number blocked.

I read, You in Charleston?

I figured it was from someone in my past who wanted to get together, but now was not the time. Before I could reply, my phone dinged again, Sorry. This is Nung.

What the hell? Nung was a crazy half-breed Thai mercenary I'd worked with a couple of times, and I'd helped his younger brother get into a high-class boarding school as payment. Another time, he'd helped me and ended up with the ill-gotten gains of a group of Irish terrorists for the effort. He was spot-on deadly in a crisis, but had the moral compass of a computer. I had no idea why he'd be contacting me. I hadn't seen him in years.

I typed, Long time no see. Yes, I'm in Charleston, you here?

Will be tomorrow. In air now, on Wifi. Need to talk.

This just got stranger and stranger, but given this was coming from Nung, it was par for the course, because I was pretty sure his middle name was "strange."

I typed, About what?

In person. Don't want this over wifi.

I narrowed my eyes, watching the bubbles form another message. When they appeared, all of my previous doubts evaporated like a dream fragmenting in the light of dawn.

You and Jennifer are in danger. Watch your back until I arrive.

I felt the beast stir, the first tendrils of anger slithering out, escaping the scar tissue of pain I kept bottled up.

Someone is *hunting me.*

And now it was my turn.

I dialed the personal number of a guy who worked in the Taskforce Network Operations Center—colloquially known as the "hacking cell"—hoping that because of the death of Colonel Hale, he would be home and able to answer his phone. He did.

"Hey, Pike. We're all devastated up here. It's terrible news."

"Thanks, Creed, but that's not why I'm calling. I need some video work done. I need the best you can do to give me facial ID of two men. They're pretty grainy right now."

Bartholomew Creedwater was my go-to computer geek at the Taskforce, not only because he was very good at his job, but because he was willing to bend the rules if I asked. Even given that, I could hear the suspicion leaking out of the phone.

"Pike, we're all on stand-down until they can sort out what to do about Colonel Hale. They've even given stand-down orders to anyone operational who's not in the midst of a critical mission."

I said, "I know that. I just got off the phone with George. I'm not asking for covert penetration of a computer network. I'm asking you to enhance a video from the surveillance cameras on *my* house. As a friend. But you can't tell anyone at the Taskforce you're doing it."

I heard nothing for a moment, then, "You want me to keep it secret? Why?"

"Because I'm going to kill them."

7

One more person did a double take at Luca's appearance and Simon chuckled, saying, "You look about as out of place here as those two dykes we saw on the canoes yesterday."

Luca grunted and said, "They might think we're a couple, but I promise, if they do, they know who's the man and who's the bitch."

Simon frowned, but he couldn't debate the sentiment, given Luca's size. He was a mountain of flesh, a man who clearly spent more time in the gym than he did at anything else, his ropes of muscle rippling with any movement. With a ponytail of brown hair and a brow that looked straight out of a documentary on cavemen, he stood out at the Amazon jungle resort. But then again, he'd stand out anywhere except on the set of a Conan movie.

His teammate, Simon, was lean and wiry, with a tribal art tattoo crawling out of his shirt and up his neck, giving him a seedy appearance of having just left prison. Both of them made little effort to blend in, but that wasn't a threat, as the lodge catered to foreigners of all stripes. They weren't the strangest couple at the lodge, but they *were* the only one who didn't care about the extravagant expanse of jungle surrounding the grounds.

Every other patron traveled to this location to see the Amazon up close. To experience one of the few remaining rain forests on earth. Luca and Simon couldn't care less. They were here for one reason only: the elimination of the ethics lawyer for the Petrobras oil company.

Just a year before, that position inside Petrobras had been a joke. A whitewash of any and all ethical violations perpetrated by the giant conglomerate, giving the company a veneer of respectability while the executive in the position had to swallow that his mission was to ignore his mission. Now, as the Carwash bribery scandal continued to reach into the corporation, snagging executives left and right, the position had grown teeth, aided by a career prosecutor who was looking for the truly corrupt ones to prove that Petrobras was a good, noble institution that only had a few bad eggs.

As such, the executive needed to go. The bad eggs wanted some breathing room.

Simon said, "Hurry up. That damn family is headed in, and you know they're going to sit on the couch and suck up the bandwidth. Tell me we can execute, because I'm sick of this jungle shit. Let Kolva come clean up the mess. It's his target."

The executive was a new target for them. There were three teams in Brazil, and each had a mission to execute, without any coordination. Luca and Simon's original target had been the ombudsman from Petrobras—someone who was determined to prove she was above reproach, and someone who held significant sway on the assignment of concessions in the lucrative Lulu oil fields off the coast. They'd followed her to Salvador, developed a pattern of life, and were prepared to eliminate her when Simon had recognized a threat. An American he'd encountered before, on another continent. One who was skilled enough to almost kill him.

His appearance could not be ruled a simple coincidence.

Luca typed on the computer and said, "Don't fucking

blame me. It's not my fault we're here. I told you we could handle both of them. You're the one who contacted higher. And got us into this god-forsaken jungle mess."

Their boss at Wagner had switched teams, under the simple theory that if the Russians could recognize the Americans, the same was also true. Thus Luca and Simon had been given the ethics lawyer, the target package passed off in a seedy hotel.

The target had been headed to a vacation in the Amazon when the package had been passed, along with his wife and eight-year-old son, and so Luca and Simon had followed, ending up at a jungle lodge that had no connectivity at all, save the thatched-roof bar and reception area that maintained a Wi-Fi connection that was decidedly slow.

Luca watched the other family enter up the steps, the mother and father nodding and smiling like everyone else did at this backwater location, proud to be "roughing it" at a five-star lodge that had every amenity on earth, and making Luca want to show them what it *really* meant to live in the jungle. Where one was not only struggling against the elements for survival, but was actively fighting other humans on the hunt. Not one living in a sheltered luxury lodge with air-conditioned rooms, expansive buffets, and tours that gave a taste of the wilds without actually entering the wilds.

They took a seat across from him on the couch, the two kids scampering down the steps to a billiard table. Luca made sure his computer screen was hidden and kept working. The wife asked, "Are you two going on the Cayman search expedition?"

Simon gave a lukewarm smile and said, "I think so. Well, at least I am."

They'd been at the lodge following their target for four days, each split by two tour events. Luca and Simon had traveled with the lawyer on canoe trips, excursions to native villages, Amazon jungle hikes, and boat explorations deep into the Negro River basin for wildlife sightings. All had offered several opportunities to eliminate their target, but they had been on hold since the sighting of the Americans, which had been decidedly frustrating. Simon felt they should be allowed to continue here, since the threat was in Salvador, but he'd been overruled, his command stating that a single sighting didn't mean a single threat, and there was a plan in place to stop all of them, seen and unseen.

Given that, tonight was the last chance at this venue. Tomorrow the executive and his family were taking a seaplane back to Manaus, forcing a complete reset on the attack. This compelled them to begin anew, and Simon didn't like it. The Amazon lodge was the perfect location. All he needed was the execute authority.

The small sitting area became crowded with people and the nighttime wildlife beginning their catcalls while Luca still worked the VPN to his headquarters. A guide entered the reception area wearing rubber boots and holding a large battery-powered spotlight. He said, "Let's go find some wildlife."

Luca ignored him. He looked up from the screen to Simon and whispered, "We're a go. The guys in Salvador have been neutralized."

Simon said, "How?"

"I don't know. The boss said they took out the command and they're no threat. Either way, we're finally a go."

The group around the table stood to leave and Simon looked around, saying, "He's not here."

Luca cursed under his breath and said, "He's leaving tomorrow. This is it."

The guide passed out life vests in the light of the reception area, and the group stood to leave, following the native down the narrow path to the dock at the Negro River. Simon sat with his life vest in his hand, hesitating, and they both heard a man shout, "Hang on! Wait for us."

They saw the target arrive with his wife and child. The guide smiled, tossed them a few life vests, and Simon stood, saying, "I'll keep them in sight. You have two hours."

Luca smiled and said, "I won't need that long."

Luca waited until they'd been gone for twenty minutes, drinking a vodka and cranberry juice from the bar. The bartender asked why he hadn't gone on the boat trip, and he'd simply said, "I have some packing to do."

He left the reception area, walking in the darkness to his bungalow on the narrow path. He entered his room and went straight to his suitcase, pulling out a barometric explosive device. He checked that the settings were correct, then wrapped it in a box, complete with paper he'd stolen from the small gift shop on the outskirts of the compound. Satisfied at the camouflage, he left the room, slinking back down the dark path.

Before he reached the reception lodge, he took a right, walking up a set of wooden stairs and continuing into the darkness until he was at a bungalow all by itself, one with a view of the jungle, much larger than the room he had. It was the best the resort had to offer, which worked out for him, because it was separated from the lowly huts of the other patrons.

He approached the door, his head on a swivel in the darkness, the bungalow illuminated faintly by trail lights set into the earth. He saw no one. In thirty seconds, he had the cheap lock of the bungalow picked and was in the room. He went straight to the suitcases on the floor, all three mostly packed, with a scattering of clothes about the room. He found the gift that the target had purchased earlier—a handmade sculpture of wood now bound in a box just like the one he held in his hand.

He removed the gift, replaced it with his own, and then heard, "What are you doing here?"

He snapped upright, seeing a maid holding a trash bag. He cursed inwardly, not believing his luck. He'd forgotten about the trash removal.

The plumbing at the lodge was not strong enough to take toilet paper, forcing the guests to place their wiped waste into the trash can next to the toilet. Because of it, maids came multiple times a day to empty the trash, when the residents were known to be on a tour. It was an amateur mistake, but one that had to be dealt with.

Luca said, "Hey, sorry. These guys are friends of mine and I'm just leaving them a gift."

"How did you get in?"

"They left me a key."

"They can't leave you a key. There is only one."

Luca walked toward her, seeing no fear. Yet.

"They left me *their* key."

She nodded, and he slapped a hand over her mouth, bringing her to the floor. She tried to scream, but the only sound that escaped was a muffled gasp. She began fighting, and he wrapped her up in his arms, his enormous muscles shrouding her in the death he was bringing. Her eyes went wide, and she began bucking. He snatched a towel off the floor, the moisture from a shower still prevalent. He looped it around her throat and began torqueing it tighter and tighter. Her skull snaked back, her arms slapping him in the face, and he lowered his head, all the while holding a hand on her mouth.

Her body went into a frenzy of spastic flailing, but he kept the pressure, his head tucked into his shoulder against her thrashing arms. Eventually the thumping grew less frantic, until it was just a twitch. Luca stared into her eyes, knowing that was the key. Her lungs fought for air, pumping desperately for life, and then her eyes went from wide-eyed fear to half-lidded, like she had passed out drunk. He cinched the towel tighter, held it for another twenty seconds, then let her go, her head smacking the floor and lolling to the side.

He sat up, assessing the situation. The primary mission was to cause the death of the target without suspicion. And he'd now caused suspicion just because the maid was dead.

But the family was due to leave tomorrow morning. Their death would happen at ten thousand feet. All he needed to do was separate the maid from the bungalow. Give himself some space.

Luca was not an in-depth thinker. He was a killer. A guided missile that didn't think about what he was doing or how. He was the man one pointed at a target, and he would execute. He could do the mission assigned, but he didn't spend a lot of time anticipating second- and third-order effects. For the first time in his life, that lack of attention would work.

He went back to the suitcase, made sure that the package he'd created was the same as the one he'd taken, then hoisted the maid on his shoulder. He opened the sliding door to the bungalow, walked out on the balcony, and unceremoniously dropped her over, hearing the body crash into the jungle below.

He left the room, circled around the lower ledge of the bungalow, and found the body. He hoisted it onto his shoulder again, the weight no more to him than a bag of dog food, and walked into the jungle until he was about a hundred meters away, the lights from the lodge like fireflies in the darkness. He dropped the body into a draw, seeing it sag into the hole, one hand appearing to cloy the ground to prevent the tragedy. He kicked it away, then slunk back up the hill, going to his room.

Two hours later Simon returned to their bungalow, and Luca was now in bed. Simon asked if there had been any trouble. He said no, and rolled back over to sleep.

At nine in the morning, they both went to the breakfast buffet at the open-air restaurant. While eating, they heard the seaplane land, the patrons in the restaurant all talking about how neat it would be to take a plane instead of the three-hour van trip back to Manaus.

Simon looked at Luca and said, "You sure that thing will work?"

Luca said, "I didn't design it. I'm sure it's packed."

They heard the plane take off, with most of the patrons rushing to the edge to see it go. And they got much more than they wanted.

The plane rose into the air, lazily circling the jungle, then a small explosion puffed out of the starboard side. The plane fought to regain control, trailing smoke, but it was a futile endeavor. The entire breakfast entourage watched the aircraft dive into the jungle, exploding on impact.

The patrons began screaming, everyone running amok, and Simon said, "Well, that's one target down."

Luca said, "That's not the target I want. I want those fucks from Switzerland."

8

Knuckles ended the call on his cell phone and stood for a moment, letting the masses of people swirl around him, lost in thought, still having trouble assimilating what he'd heard. A man walked in front of him holding out a cup, and he shook his head. The man wandered away, and Knuckles entered the Mercado Modelo once again, winding his way through the myriad of stalls and ignoring the vendors thrusting all manner of things in his face. He took a left onto a set of stairs to the upper level, then threaded his way through the tourists and locals, heading toward the balcony restaurant. He nodded at the hostess, then returned to his table, seeing Brett looking at him expectantly.

He took a seat and said, "This is going to end badly."

Brett laughed and said, "Because we have to go home before you find some female companionship?"

"No. Because that call was from Pike."

Knuckles saw the next laugh die. Brett asked, "What did he say?"

"He said we stay."

Brett took that in and said, "We can't stay. We're flying home tonight. We got the order from Kurt. This is done."

"Pike says the order didn't come from Kurt. He wants us to stay. The entire Taskforce is on stand-down, and he wants us to hold in place."

"Huh? He can't countermand Kurt. We got the order."

Knuckles looked at him and said, "It didn't come from Kurt. Kurt is . . . Kurt's dead. Pike just told me. He's gone."

Brett's eyes went wide, and he said, "What the fuck are you talking about? Are you serious?"

Kurt had been the only commander of Project Prometheus since its creation, and both men valued and respected him. The blow was as hard as could be imagined, not the least because of the way Knuckles had learned. A simple phone call. No warning. No preparation. As harsh as it was, both of them had experienced combat loss in the past multiple times, learning to compartmentalize the pain. A friend next to the shoulder in one instance, then the life gone, the body slammed to the ground by the unforgiving gods of war. There would be no histrionics, but the psychological learning curve didn't make the news any easier.

Knuckles said, "Yeah. I'm serious. Apparently there was some kind of car accident. I don't know any more than that, except Pike doesn't think it was an accident. He thinks the men who did it are tied into some assholes here, in Brazil. We didn't get an order from Kurt. We got an order from the Taskforce."

Brett took that in, then said, "That makes no sense. How did it happen?"

"I told you. He had some sort of accident in Charleston. At least the police are saying it's an accident. Pike doesn't think so."

The waitress arrived and they fell quiet. She cleared their plates, leaving the bill. Brett waited until she was walking away, then said, "If what you say is true, we should definitely go home. We're out here on a limb, without a mission. The

Taskforce has control, and they've told us to go home. Hezbollah will have to wait."

"What if Pike is correct? What if it's not an accident, and we're sitting near the men responsible?"

"How on earth would Pike know that?"

Knuckles redirected the conversation. "Didn't you say you thought you recognized a guy at the airport when we flew into Salvador? That guy with the mountain of muscles?"

"I was just spitballing. Making a joke. He *looked* like a member of the team we took out in Switzerland, but come on. The odds of that are astronomical."

"I don't believe in coincidence."

"We haven't seen them since. If they're here doing something that's tied into Kurt's death, wouldn't we see signs? We've done nothing but have a vacation."

Knuckles paid the bill and stood up, saying, "One more day won't hurt. If Pike doesn't turn up anything, we can always fly home tomorrow."

He turned to leave and Brett said, "What are we going to do?"

"What we were going to do before the Taskforce called. Head over to Vera Cruz on the ferry. Check out that old fort. Spend some time on the beach. Whatever we want to do."

Brett followed him into the swirling masses of the Mercado, saying, "I think your first instinct was right. This is going to end badly."

Knuckles smiled, and they broke out into the sunshine, the ferry terminal a hundred meters away. In front of them were two groups of protesters shouting at each other and waving signs, police in between them trying to keep the peace.

Knuckles said, "Shit. I thought things in the U.S. were bad.

This presidential election is getting out of control. I don't want to be here when the vote comes down."

Giving the protesters a wide berth, Brett said, "Well, when your front-runner is told he can't run because he's in prison, what do you expect? And you're just changing the subject. What are we doing here now? What's the mission? We're no longer on the Taskforce dime. They ordered us to go home. And Kurt's dead."

Knuckles abruptly stopped walking and pointed a finger at Brett, the anger leaking out. "Yeah, he's dead," he said. "You don't give a shit about that, that's on you. You came late to this game, but I worked with him from day one, and if Pike wants a day, he gets a day. What about you? You want to go home?"

Brett took a step back, recognizing the attack wasn't against him, but instead was a by-product of the news about Kurt. He said, "Hey, easy."

Knuckles relaxed, shook his head, and said, "Sorry. Look, just give Pike some time. He's working something in Charleston. We owe Kurt at least that."

Brett said, "You know I'm with you. If it's real, I'm the first through the door, but you have to admit, this is a little strange, and it has the potential to compromise us. We've lost the backing of the Taskforce."

Knuckles forced a smile, no humor coming through, and said, "You haven't seen what I have. If Pike says it's real, it probably is, and I'm willing to give him the benefit of the doubt."

Brett slowly nodded. He said, "I've seen it as well. But I've also seen that guy go off in a rage. I'm on your side, but let's make sure that being on the side of Pike is the right thing. That's all I'm saying. We have the national command authority telling us to come home, and we have Pike saying we stay. After Kurt's death."

Knuckles said, "I hear you, but staying one more day isn't the end of the world."

They circled around the protesters and Brett said, "One day. Okay. But this isn't going to end well. You know it and I know it."

Knuckles didn't respond. They reached the ferry terminal just before an SUV pulled up, a prim woman of about thirty-five exiting, wearing designer clothes and holding the hand of a child. She entered the building followed by a hulking bodyguard dressed in a black suit. They followed behind her, entering the line behind tourists and day workers. Right in front of them was a group of four locals, all wearing worn clothing and cheap backpacks, rubbing elbows with the woman and her charge.

Absorbed in the phone call he'd just received, trying to make sense of his new world, Knuckles ignored the line until the security guard bumped him. The man apologized, bringing him out of his funk. Knuckles smiled and accepted the apology, then saw the crowd in front of him—day workers scraping by for a living and a woman with a bodyguard. He enjoyed the contrast, not the least because it was a reflection of his own team.

Knuckles was broad-shouldered and tall, with ropy muscles and a shaggy head of black hair that made him look like a beach bum. His partner Brett was an African American, and a short fireplug of muscle that just crested Knuckles's shoulder when he stood fully erect, with a close-cropped Afro and a T-shirt celebrating a famous Salvadorian drum troupe. They couldn't be more different on the outside, but that difference helped them blend in.

The original capital of Brazil, Salvador had the dubious distinction of being the entry port for the slave trade in Brazil's past. Because of it, the town was a mix of African descendants and Brazilian natives, which meant that Brett looked like he belonged. *He* was the one who provided the camouflage for the team, as anyone seeing him would assume he was local—and by extension, so was Knuckles.

They paid for their tickets and dutifully followed the line down the worn dock to a large ferry, the captain's berth on top, the bottom adorned with rows of plastic chairs bolted to the floor, the sides of the boat open to the air.

Knuckles took a seat on a bench that ran the length of the side, leaning over to see the water. Wanting to break away from the weight of the earlier conversation, Brett said, "You can take the SEAL out of the water, but the water always calls him back, huh?"

Knuckles smiled and said, "Same for you, Jarhead. Same for you."

In short order, the ferry was under way with only about half of the seats taken, the boat plowing out of the harbor toward Itaparica Island, the shore visible in the distance.

The boat entered the strait between Salvador and the island, and Knuckles stretched out on the bench, closing his eyes and saying, "Supposed to take forty minutes."

Brett leaned back, then punched Knuckles in the thigh, saying, "Check out the guys that were in front of us."

Knuckles cracked his eyes and saw the four ragged locals all bent over, digging into their packs with a purpose. When they rose up, they were holding an assortment of weapons. One fired into the air and started screaming in Portuguese. Another began racing to the ladder leading to the captain's deck. The others began herding the ferry passengers to the center of the boat, away from the sides.

Knuckles said, "You have got to be shitting me."

The security man protecting the woman drew a pistol, fired once, and then was cut down in a hail of bullets. The woman fell on top of her child, covering the body. Two men ripped her off the child, throwing her into the center. The other man began rounding up the rest of the passengers. He reached Knuckles and Brett and began waving a weapon, screaming and pointing.

Brett raised his hands over his head and said, "I fucking told you this was going to go bad."

9

I watched two more ex–frat boys enter the rooftop deck of the hotel—a couple of thirty-somethings dripping Rolexes and designer labels and looking for a new conquest. They did a double take when they saw Jennifer, then looked at me with what I took as amazement. It used to annoy me, but now it just made me secretly smug. I glared at them, because that's what the alpha male does, and they moved on. Jennifer, of course, was completely oblivious.

Honestly, we *did* look a little like beauty and the beast. She is blond and lithe, with a body like a surfer and a face from the same type of calendar. I'm not making anyone's calendar, unless it was for pirates. With close-cropped brown hair and a scar tracking through the stubble on my cheek, I look a little craggy. But, hey, I have a great personality.

She took a sip of her Coke and said, "How long do you want to pursue this?"

"Until it's done. We either confirm or deny these assholes. And so far, it's falling in the confirmation column."

She toyed with the circle of water on the table from her soft drink, then said, "You don't know that. All you know is what Nung told you last night. He might be wrong, and this whole thing could be a mistake."

I knew what she was afraid of. Me going into berserker mode in a misguided attempt at retribution for Kurt's death. And she was right, up to a point. I *would* kill those fucks when I found them, but I would be positive of their culpability before I did. Something she wasn't sure I was capable of. But I'd learned a thing or two since I'd known her, and I knew she had learned as well. We'd grown on each other, leaving my view of the world more aligned with hers, and hers more aligned with mine. Right now, she wasn't sure what to think.

She'd had a hard couple of days dealing with Kurt's death, and it was showing. Her smile, once a brilliant thing that would light up a room all on its own, was broken, like a cracked mirror reflecting her soul. It was the same thing I'd seen when Decoy had been killed right next to her, the first combat trauma she'd experienced, and *that* had been hard. She didn't want this to be the same. She wanted to believe that it was an accident, making the death just the fate of God instead of the work of men trying to kill her and me, but instead murdering her friend. It was something she couldn't tolerate if it were true, and not the least for Kylie's sake.

Kylie had come to our house as our guest, as a favor to watch Amena, and now Kurt was dead. An uncle she cherished more than her own father. Jennifer didn't want to be even tangentially responsible for that. The initial night had been a kaleidoscope of emotions—a blur in my memory— Jennifer and Kylie trying to absorb what had happened while I tried to find out why. Kylie had become distraught, and Jennifer had taken over, calling in Kylie's boyfriend, Veep, to help out while I'd fled to plan my next moves. It made me a coldhearted bastard in Kylie's mind, but there was a purpose behind it. Because I knew it wasn't an accident, and no matter what Jennifer thought about my propensity for violence, one thing was true: it was coming.

I said, "Hey, if these guys don't pan out, I'm done. But you have to admit, it's pretty strange they're here on Saint Kitts passports. Just like the Russians Nung worked with. And *he's* the one who said they were hunting us. That wasn't my imagination."

The video I'd sent to Creed was paying huge dividends. In his effort to locate the cyclists, we'd learned that they had passports from the island of Saint Kitts, which would have been a strange thing in and of itself, but we'd also found out that Saint Kitts had what's known as an "investment passport," which basically meant if you dumped enough money into the country, you earned a passport. An American company called Monte Cristo Analytics had started a booming business of investment opportunities in Saint Kitts solely for the facilitation of passports, and now everyone from Iranian Quds Force members to drug cartels used it to circumvent immigration controls and sanctions around the world.

She raised an eyebrow and said, "Yeah, well, Nung's not the most trustworthy guy when it comes to this. Just because these guys have a passport doesn't make them evil. His motto is just kill 'em all to be safe."

I smiled and said, "He'll be up here in thirty minutes, and we'll know. Don't worry, I won't kill anyone until then."

Nung had landed in Charleston late last night, and when I'd picked him up, he had a story to tell. He'd found evidence that a Russian private military company called Wagner was gunning for my company, and somehow they'd made the connection that we weren't what we said we were. Just like them when they operated around the world.

He'd said they'd recognized someone in Brazil from Grolier Recovery Services—which meant Knuckles and Brett—and that his boss had issued orders to kill me to defeat whatever we had planned. In effect, cut the head off the company to short-circuit our mission. I had no idea what that meant, how they'd recognized Knuckles and Brett, or why they cared. We weren't even looking at Wagner or anything remotely Russian. We were targeting Hezbollah in the triple frontier of Brazil, and we had no indications of any Russian play, but it was enough to keep digging. And I had a handle that would allow just that.

Creed had analyzed the video I'd sent him, and had given me a pretty good photo of one of the men, with the other still being a little sketchy. It was a physical identification I could use if I ever bumped into the man on the street, which wasn't much of a help, but Creed had found something else: working through the video, he'd found that the two dumb-asses were riding bikes from a rental company called Holy Spokes.

Dotting the entire peninsula, it was a version of Uber for bicycles. Tourists used an app to unlock a bike, then took one, pedaling around the Holy City. When they were done, they put them back into one of the racks pre-positioned around the peninsula. It was the perfect way to see our fair city if one didn't care about being tracked, but it was abysmally stupid if one did, because every bike had a GPS tracker in it to prevent theft, and in order to rent it, one had to use a credit card.

Creed had worked his magic and found the traces of every bike on the Charleston Peninsula. He'd narrowed down the bikes that went by our house using time stamps, and then had located the credit card used from the app. From there he'd figured out where else the credit card had been swiped, and had found the Restoration Hotel on Wentworth Street, along with a complete profile of the men. And yes, they were from Russia, using a passport from Saint Kitts.

A swank place with limited rooms, it had a rooftop bar that Jennifer and I were currently in. Ordinarily, going to the hotel of a target that could recognize us would be a nonstarter, but we knew that our targets were on a ferry headed out to Fort Sumter, a tour that took at least a couple of hours. They were actually enjoying their time in the Holy City after committing murder, which steamed me.

I'd done a deep dive on the hotel itself, trying to figure out how to penetrate the target's rooms for confirmation of my suspicions, and Creed had come up with another brilliant plan: Each room had an Amazon Alexa—a voice-activated device that would turn on the lights or the TV or tell you the weather. The Alexa was a pretty sweet little gadget, but had one flaw: It was always listening, waiting to wake up. Amazon would tell you that it would only turn on its microphones if it heard an initiation phrase, but Creed said we could turn it into a damn recording device if we could access the Wi-Fi it was on. The Wi-Fi in question being a hotel network, that was easy enough. I made Nung rent a room.

He went in, and using Creed's instructions, had modified the Alexa in his room. Because the device was designed to find all others on the same network for home use, linking them together for whatever advertising uses Amazon could find, it was an easy fix to locate the one in our target's rooms. With a few hardwired soldering efforts from Creed and a small circuit card loaded with malware, Nung had our Alexa talking to the two target rooms, and we'd let it sit for a day, exporting everything it heard. Now we were waiting for the recordings—or more precisely, waiting on Nung to provide a translation of what he'd heard, because these guys spent all their time speaking Russian.

At first, I had been exasperated at the wall placed in front of me, because there was no way I was going to get a Taskforce interpreter to translate anything they said. Then I was surprised, because it turned out Nung—of all people—spoke Russian.

10

Jennifer toyed with her drink, not looking me in the eye. She said, "What if this is bad? What are you going to do?"

I saw the angst on her face, put my hand on hers, and said, "I'm going to do what I do."

She pulled her hand away and said, "We don't have a team. We don't even have a mission. You can't just kill someone here in Charleston."

I said, "They did."

"That's not the same."

I let her words settle, saw her turn her eyes away, and said, "It isn't?"

She leaned back and said, "No, because we aren't *them*. You don't want to go back there."

That hurt. *Back there* was a cesspool I was living in when we first met.

I said, "So just let this go? Let them get away with killing Kurt—when they are trying to kill us?"

She reached across the table and took my hand again, saying, "No, that's not what I mean. I . . . well . . ."

No other words came out, and I said, "Look, if this is real . . . if they murdered Kurt . . . they pay the price."

"And what is that? Are you going to turn them over to the police? What is justice in your mind?"

Now it was my turn to let go of her hand. I leaned back and said, "No. You know where this is going."

She said, "Pike, I'm not sure I can do that here. We live in America, not Russia. Just because—"

I cut her off, saying, "Just because what? Just because it happened in our own hometown? Instead of Russia?"

She snapped back at my comment and said, "No, because it's wrong. And when I did it before, it almost destroyed the both of us."

I realized she was more concerned about what my actions would do to *me* than she was about the lives of the men. She was afraid of me crossing the line, because once upon a time, she'd crossed it, too.

After Jennifer and I had collided, and I'd gotten her into the Taskforce, we'd conducted an operation in Dubai, and she'd been captured by the man who'd murdered my family. She'd barely managed to escape with her life, but in so doing, she'd found proof of his culpability in my family's destruction. She hadn't said a word about the assault, but had given me the proof of my family, and then had directed me at the man like a guided missile, seeking her own private vengeance. In an unspeakable rage, I'd targeted the wrong man and had come within a half pound on a trigger of killing him.

The chase had torn us both apart, ripping at the very fabric of our beings, until each of us was almost destroyed. In the end, I'd killed the murderer of my family, and I don't think she'd ever forgiven herself for that, even as she wanted him dead. She'd seen the beast in the mirror and hadn't liked it.

She was trying to protect me, and in so doing, protect herself. Something she felt she'd failed to do in Dubai.

She took a breath, saying, "Okay. Okay. I get it. *If* this is real. But you really don't want to go there. You need to back off and think. You need to be Pike. Not the man I met years ago."

I locked eyes with her and said, "This is going to get bloody. You need to trust me. I have never asked that of you before, but I'm doing it now."

She waffled, averting her eyes and seeking a way out of the path I was on. She said, "But we *still* have no team. Pike, we have nothing to execute anything even if we wanted to."

Not letting any emotions play across my face at her acquiescence, I said, "We have Brett and Knuckles in Brazil, and we have Nung here in Charleston. And we have a couple others who owe us a favor."

"Who?"

Before I could answer, Nung walked onto the deck. A six-foot guy with a hint of Asian in him, he glided like a cat, and acted like one as well. He didn't seem to give a damn about anything. Except family, and somehow, we'd earned that right.

He sat down, handed me a sheaf of papers, and said, "I was right. They are bad. There are three of them, and they're hunting your men in Brazil."

I took the stack and said, "Three? There are three targets? Not just the two we've identified?"

"Yes. They have one man who never leaves the suite. Guarding it, as it were."

Which was something we did when we had classified or other secret stuff we didn't want the maids to find by accident. The "Do Not Disturb" sign only worked so well.

One more indicator.

I focused on the readout—basically everything said in the room over the last twenty-four hours—and it was damning. Conversations between the targets, and one-way conversations on a cell phone to someone in Brazil, it detailed everything they had executed since they'd been here, including laughing about my death, not realizing they had missed.

I felt the rage grow, begging for a release, and suppressed it. I passed the sheets to Jennifer and said, "It's real."

She took it, read a few lines, then looked at me with trepidation. I said, "Don't worry. I'm not going to run down there and kill them right now."

Nung said, "There is only one there. They won't be back for a couple of hours."

I smiled and said, "So we have some time for planning. Before we go to Brazil."

Jennifer didn't like the sound of that, but she said nothing. Nung said, "Pike, I can help here. I owe you that, but I cannot go to Brazil. You will be on your own there."

Jennifer leaned forward. "That's what I was saying earlier. Let's take this to the Taskforce instead of going off half-cocked without a team."

I pulled out my cell phone and dialed a number, saying "I'm not talking to the Taskforce. They don't believe what's happened, and they're chickenshits even if they do."

She said, "Pike, come on. We aren't the Russians. We can't go on a tear killing people for what they did."

I put the phone to my ear and said, "Yes, we can. It's the one thing we *can* do. Kurt is dead because of these fucks, and for whatever reason they tried to kill me. It's in Brazil. I'm going to stop it."

Exasperated, she said, "How? We have no support. No team."

I held up a finger, saying into the phone, "Hello, Pumpkin King. It's Pike Logan. And it's time to repay the favor you owe me."

11

Alek Sokolov watched the man behind the counter slice off the top of a coconut and put a straw into it. He passed it across, then tended to another patron as Alek stepped away from the bar, moving to a rickety table on the side of the thatched hut. He glanced around, seeing nothing but locals walking down to a small spit of beach, going toward a group of kids playing a game that looked like volleyball, but where they used their feet instead of hands. And they were surprisingly good at it.

Alek broke away from the game, checking his watch, and saw he was within the window. *He* wasn't late. Nikita was, but Alek sure wouldn't make any waves about that. Not with the news he had to give, and knowing Nikita's hair trigger to anger.

Alek glanced back at the fort behind him, known as Forte de Monte Serrat, the last bastion of protection for the old Brazilian capital during the colonial days. It was an icon of Salvador but was now fading into disrepair. He watched groups of street urchins playing on the grounds, hanging on an anachronistic artillery piece from World War II, the area sprinkled with cups and other trash.

He knew the urchins had more interest in fleecing him from his valuables than they did in the history. They had no sense of understanding of the land they were on, and it aggravated him. Something he intended to change. If they didn't appreciate their history, they wouldn't care about their future. And he was going to alter their future.

The guy behind the bar, a black man with Rastafarian dreadlocks, hollered at him, saying, "You want another coconut? Or you going to sit here all day at my table not paying?"

Alek said, "I'm waiting on a friend. When he gets here, we'll get another one."

The Rastafarian nodded and went back to his work. Alek glanced back toward the fort again and saw the kids had scattered. Then he saw why.

Nikita was coming down the flagstone path, and as always, he projected an air of anger. Of a volcanic temperament that was begging to be released, and the children seemed to pick up the vibe like rabbits sensing an earthquake. Or maybe it was his false eye bobbling about, always looking away from where Nikita was focused, giving the man a demented persona that kept anyone around him off balance. Alek hated it, but knew Nikita treated it as a badge of honor, having lost his eye fighting for Mother Russia in Ukraine.

Because of his past ruthlessness and clinical skill, Nikita had been placed in charge of Operation Harvest—the entire Brazilian effort—and Alek knew he was feeling the pressure. Which didn't make the news he had to give any easier.

Nikita took a seat and said, "Target two is gone. Poor bastard crashed in a plane in the Amazon." He smiled, and Alek smiled back, mightily ignoring Nikita's left eye staring off into space.

Nikita said, "What about the target here?"

Alek glanced away, then said, "Hang on. I promised this guy I'd order something when you got here."

He stood up before Nikita could say anything and ordered

a couple of coconuts, waiting for the Rastafarian man to hack off the top and jam in a straw. Alek paid him and returned to the table.

He put one in front of Nikita and took the other to his side of the table.

Nikita said, "What the hell is this?"

"Coconut milk. It's good. Take a sip."

Nikita ignored the straw and said, "How fucking long have you been down here? You're going local on me? Who gives a shit about a coconut drink? What's going on with the next target? I owe a report."

Alek set his coconut on the table and said, "We've had a problem."

Alek watched Nikita's left eye wander, but the cold blue steel of his one good eye remained steady.

Nikita said, "Problem?" as if the word were foreign to him.

"Yes."

"What?"

"Our target was on a ferry to Itaparica Island this morning. Just a day trip with her security, same guy we've seen all week long. Nothing special, except also on that boat were the two men that you were worried about. The Americans. Their appearance definitely spiked our interest."

He paused and Nikita said, "And?"

Alek took a breath and said, "Believe it or not, the ferry was hijacked on its way to the island. It's currently about a hundred meters offshore, anchored against a lighting buoy with four armed men aboard, including explosives."

Nikita blinked and said, "You're kidding me."

"I wish I were. It's some criminal group called Primeiro Comando da Capital. The PCC. They're a bunch of thugs that hold sway in most of the favelas around Brazil. They're screaming about prisoner releases and a bunch of other shit. Threatening to kill everyone on the boat if their demands aren't met."

Alek waited on Nikita's famed temper to appear, watching him closely for signs of an eruption. Nikita glanced down the street with his one good eye, then said, "You think the Americans have something to do with this? That it's a fake attack to disrupt our plans?"

Alek said, "No, I don't. If anything, it's being done by the Cardosa campaign to help his election. That's what my contacts are saying. He engineered it because he's the 'law and order' candidate."

"What? So that asshole made a deal with thugs to take over a boat so he could crow about how that shit won't happen if he's elected?"

"That's what I'm hearing. And that guy is our final target."

Nikita scoffed and said, "He's just as corrupt as any of them. Hell, maybe we should co-opt him instead of working the line we're on."

Alek relaxed, realizing he wouldn't be to blame. He watched the eyeball for a moment, waiting on Nikita to tell him what to do. Wanting to please him.

Nikita stared into the sky for a moment, and a smile began to form. He focused on Alek and said, "This may be just what we need. Our primary target may have just made our mission work."

"How?"

"We need the death to be blamed on something else. We need plausible deniability for anything we do. We used an aircraft in the Amazon, but that guy didn't have any security. This target does, and it's hampered our ability to get close enough to kill her. Now we can use the PCC. All we need to do is botch any rescue, forcing them to kill our target. Even better, they can kill the Americans while they're at it. What's the police response?"

"A special unit called the BOPE arrived today from up north in Bahia. They're the crisis response for things like this, sort of like our Alpha group. Special weapons and special tactics. They're usually used for high-risk warrants and working in the favelas, but they do hostage rescue as well. They don't take a lot of shit."

"Can we get to the commander?"

"Yeah, I'm sure we could work that. We have the contacts, but why?"

"We need to convince him to force this thing to end badly."

"I don't think he'll be susceptible to a bribe. The BOPE are the elite of the police down here. They don't get in if they're corruptible."

Nikita ignored him, asking, "How many men on your team?"

"Four. But I told you—"

Nikita cut him off, saying, "Call the team in the Amazon. They're headed to Rio for the primary target, but he can wait. We have his schedule. Get them up here. We need more manpower."

Alek said, "Okay. That's easy enough." And waited, not wanting to risk Nikita's wrath.

Nikita said, "Can you get a safe house without any connection to us? No credit cards, passports, or anything else?"

"Yeah, I have some local talent that works in a church here. It used to be a working convent, but now it's just a church that tourists come to take pictures of. The convent portion is still there, though. It has dorm rooms and plumbing, and is off-limits to the tourists. I already prepped it in case we needed to disappear quickly. Why, though? I told you the BOPE captain wouldn't take cash."

"Every man has a price. Maybe it's not cash, but it's something. First order is to find out if the captain's married. Second is to locate his wife."

12

I heard my earpiece break squelch, then heard, "Two on the move. Third in place."

Finally.

It had been a day and a half since I'd confirmed the Russians' culpability in the death of Kurt Hale, and I'd had no luck at all building a pattern of life to interdict them. Which was to be understood, given the circumstances. It wasn't like they were driving the same way to work at the same time each day, and it was frustrating.

I had three primary problems. One, I felt the press of time. I had no idea why the Russians were staying in Charleston after the hit, but I assumed it was to ensure a gap in coverage before they left. If the authorities somehow linked them to the death, it would give them plausible deniability. What foreigner would stay at the scene of a crime if they could flee to their home country? Given that, sooner or later, they'd feel comfortable leaving, and if it were sooner, I'd miss my chance.

Two, killing them outright would be the easiest thing, but with the sparse information Nung had discovered, I needed to interrogate one of them. Preferably the one who kept using the phone to call his higher headquarters. Killing them as an act of revenge—while satisfying—wasn't going to solve the problem. I needed a crack to break it all open, which brought up my final problem: I needed to separate the men to get one alone.

I knew what two of the men looked like, but the third—the one who stayed in the room guarding it—I had no idea. He would be the easiest, but the fact that he stayed hidden all day told me he was some support flunky. I'd get him in my own sweet time, which left the other two, and they were hard men who never separated.

But I had an ace in the hole to force it. All I needed was a setting where they felt secure, and after a day of waiting, I had one.

They'd made reservations at a steak house called Michael's on the Alley, which was about as perfect for interdiction as we were going to get.

I acknowledged Nung's call and said, "Koko, Koko, five minutes. Nung, need to beat them here."

I was already in the parking garage next to Michael's, knowing they'd show up here. They might park on the street, but with the mess of parking in Charleston, I doubted it. Jennifer—aka Koko—was stationed outside, giving me early warning when they arrived.

Nung called, "I'm moving. They're in the same rental. Black four-door Hyundai."

Jennifer said, "Got it. Eyes on the garage entrance."

I said, "Nung, go ahead and get set."

My phone buzzed, and it was Jennifer, not wanting to talk on the net. Exasperated, I said, "Yeah?"

"Pike, what are we doing? You keep talking about building a pattern of life, and now we have it. What's the end state?"

Honestly, I'd been avoiding this conversation. We'd spent the last twenty-four hours on the tactical side of things. She was now asking the strategic question.

I said, "The end state is figuring out why these guys killed Kurt and why they're fixated on Knuckles and Brett. That's the mission."

She said nothing, but I could hear her breathing, sitting inside the lobby of a hotel adjacent to the entrance of the garage. I said, "Jennifer, you there?"

She said, yet again, "Pike, I don't think this is right."

I said, "I agree, but I didn't choose this fight. And neither did you. Get your head in the game."

The phone disconnected, and I wondered if she'd have the strength for the endgame. She said she did, but the moment of truth was the last time you wanted to find out your teammate couldn't commit. Couldn't execute what was asked. It was a weak link, and one I'd never had with her. But she was crucial to the outcome, because she was the bait.

To make matters worse, my callout to Israel had my other teammates arriving right in the middle of this operation. Shoshana and Aaron were landing in twelve minutes, and all I could do was get them an Uber to my office on Shem Creek. They wouldn't know it until they turned on their phones and received the text messages. I could only imagine the pain I was going to feel for that.

Nung called and said, "In position."

I replied, "Koko, Koko, status?"

"Still clean."

We'd had a full day to build up an attack plan, and Michael's on the Alley was the best choice for an ambush. It was a steak house built into an old Charleston structure, situated on—of course—an old alley. It was actually three establishments: an Italian restaurant on the left, Michael's on the right, and a cocktail venue called Victor's Social Club in the center. All were connected, sharing the bathrooms located in Victor's.

We'd explored it today, under the auspices of using the venue for an event, and had learned that the entire second floor spread across all of the restaurants, had one elevator entrance, and was unused tonight. Well, unused by someone having an event.

I fully intended to use it.

Jennifer called, "Target entering garage. I say again, target entering garage."

I said, "Roger," and ducked down, watching the right-side mirror. Two minutes later, their vehicle passed me, climbing higher.

I said, "Target acquired. Nung, you set?"

"Yes."

"Okay, let them settle in for dinner. You trigger and then we play the shell game."

13

I waited an interminable amount of time, still tucked down low in the seat of my car. Eventually I began to think we'd missed them. Finally, Nung came on, and said, "In the restaurant. I'll signal when they're set at the table."

Whew.

I said, "Roger that. Jennifer, meet me outside Victor's."

I got a reluctant "Roger all" and opened my car door, slinking through the parking garage until I could see the alley. I surveyed, and saw nothing out of the ordinary. I went to a corner in shadow and waited. Jennifer found me thirty seconds later.

She immediately confronted me. "What the hell are we doing here? What's the end state?"

The fact that she cursed at me was an eye-opener. Because she never did that, which meant she wasn't on board. Sitting alone with only her thoughts to keep her company had caused her to retreat from her earlier acquiescence. I glanced out to make sure we were still clear and said, "What I'm doing is finding out who killed Kurt."

I looked her in the eye and said, "*That's* what I'm doing. You on board, or not?"

She shook her head and said, "Don't give me that crap. I'm all about finding who killed Kurt. Don't put that on me. That's not my question. What are we doing *here*?"

"Exactly that."

She looked down, shuffling her feet, then let out, "You want to murder the people here. I'm not sure I can do that. This is it. A cut line. I'm not going to murder someone in Charleston because you ask."

She caught my eye. She wasn't fighting me. She was begging. I said, "All I want to do is learn what they know. That's it. Knuckles and Brett are in danger in Brazil because of these fucks, and we need to find out why."

She nodded and said, "So, you won't kill them? If you find that out?"

I heard the words and said nothing, because I couldn't lie to her. I could kill without remorse, but I couldn't lie to her. It was a strange world I'd entered when we met. A thing that just was. Lying to her was worse than the death I was about to bring.

She said, "Pike?"

I said, "Look, if you were in Vietnam on patrol and a VC element came in front of you, you'd open up. They don't know you're there, but they're the enemy, and it's completely within the international law of land warfare. This is not any different. They are the enemy. Because we're in an American city means nothing. Because they aren't wearing a uniform means nothing. Can't you see that? This is an ambush. It is *not* murder. And they deserve every bit of the pain that's coming to them."

She looked at me, seeing the blackness. She nodded. And then she said, "I understand. I want *you* to understand. This is more than them, this is about *you*. Would you kill someone who survived the ambush? After he was your prisoner?"

And that was the crux. She was right. An ambush was justified, but slaughtering soldiers who surrendered after the smoke cleared was, in fact, murder. So I could kill the men inside before I had them in my custody, but doing so after the fact made me a murderer. But killing them beforehand would deprive me of the very reason I was here: intelligence on their operations.

Something I didn't want to think about. I said, "Get in the building."

Her face grim, she said, "Pike, I'll kill anyone who did this to Kurt, but only in a fight. And I won't harm anyone who didn't. You understand that, right?"

I heard the words and realized she thought I was out of control. And maybe I was. I said, "Yes, of course. Just get staged outside the restaurant. You know me. This is good."

She glanced up the alley, then back at me. She said, "I'm the bait. I get that. Don't use that to force me into your problem."

Meaning don't use her to kill, even by secondary actions.

There was only one way I believed I could separate the two assholes eating dinner, and it was to have Jennifer walk in front of them. I knew that they would recognize her on sight, and would be shocked at her appearance. The coincidence would be too much for their suspicious minds to absorb; they'd want to follow her to see what she was doing, but wouldn't be alarmed enough for a full-on play. I was sure the leader would send his underling to check her out. Once Nung had the subordinate under control, I'd confront the boss, taking him up to our little interrogation room.

At least that was my plan, if Jennifer would execute.

Jennifer started to back away and I took her hand, saying, "This is the real world. They killed Kurt. I didn't bring this fight to us, but I'm going to finish it."

She nodded, not liking the words, and we heard, "They're

at the table, drinks ordered. Button cam is in place, and I'm moving to the second level."

The transmission ended, and I looked at Jennifer. Waiting. She said, "Okay, Pike, I'll get this guy in the nest. But that's it."

I said, "That's all I want."

She gave me a wan smile, leaned in, and kissed my lips. She said, "I love you for who you are. Don't do anything that would change that."

I wouldn't have been more shocked if she'd pulled out her Glock and started firing it in the air while hopping up and down and yelling like she was in a Yemeni wedding. We'd danced around our relationship since we'd met, and I'd eventually resigned myself to a more "friends with benefits" than actual commitment. Most of that was my fault, because I was petrified of rejection, but she'd never committed, either.

She started to walk away, leaving me slack-jawed. I said, "Wait, what?"

She grinned and said, "Have I not said that before?"

Completely outside the mission, now at a loss for what was happening, I said, "Uh . . . no. You've never said that before."

She walked to the door saying, "Don't make me regret it."

14

Felipe Costa pulled off Avanida Sete de Septembro, swinging his police motorcycle up to the guard shack that controlled an imposing iron gate. Behind it, he could see a modern building towering forty stories in the air. It was where the rich and famous lived, and a far cry from the favela where he had grown up.

In a country split decidedly between the "haves" and the "have nots," the people beyond the gate lived in a rarefied air that fully 99.9 percent would never come close to experiencing, important enough in Salvador—the original capital city of Brazil, where old money ruled—that even as the commander of the Special Police Operations Battalion, Felipe couldn't enter unless he was invited.

Not that he wanted to visit. He had his hands full with a hostage crisis on a Salvadoran ferry that was spinning out of control, the hostage takers growing more and more unstable, and a presidential election that had thrown the whole event into the stratosphere, with one presidential candidate leveraging the event for his own ends and upping the pressure exponentially to resolve it one way or the other.

And he was beginning to believe the candidate wanted a messy resolution to help his campaign.

He gave his name and identification to the guard in the shack, and in minutes a man came out from the expansive lobby of the complex, showing him where to park his motorcycle.

Felipe complied, then on the walk inside asked, "Who am I meeting?"

The man said, "I don't know. I'm just the visitor guide. I'll take you to the room, but I have no idea who's behind the door."

Felipe nodded, feeling a kinship with the worker, because he had no idea, either. All he knew was that someone high up in the hierarchy had ordered him to come, saying that a group might have a way to a peaceful resolution of the crisis. Maybe it was a person with enough clout to cause the crazies on the boat to give in, which was worth the trip.

They rose to the thirty-fourth floor, traveled down a hallway big enough to ride a horse through, and stopped at a suite with bright red brazilwood double doors—the tree from which Brazil derived its name, and one that was forbidden from being harvested in the modern age. A status symbol that showed the power of the people behind it.

The worker rang the doorbell and then vanished down the hallway, leaving Felipe alone.

The door swung open and Felipe saw a large Caucasian man with a ponytail, his biceps threatening to split his T-shirt. Inside were two other men, one with some sort of tattoo crawling up his neck and the other with a thin mouth and an eye staring off into space, making him look crazy. He felt confusion. They were not dressed with an air of wealth, and none looked remotely like a native. The man who opened the door said, "Felipe Costa?"

Felipe heard a distinctive accent, but he couldn't place it. He nodded and the man continued in English, saying, "Please come in. We wish to help you with your current dilemma."

Felipe hesitantly entered the room, and the one-eyed man stood, saying, "I apologize for the secrecy, but it is necessary. My name is Nikita." He held out his hand and Felipe took it, the eyeball staring off to his left disconcertingly. Nikita pointed at the tattooed man and said, "This is Simon," then turned to the muscled giant and said, "This is Luca."

Felipe shook their hands and Nikita pointed at a chair, saying, "Sit."

Felipe did, and Nikita continued, saying, "We're from a powerful organization outside of Brazil, but with significant investments here. I know this is odd, but my group wishes to help."

Now more confused than ever, Felipe said, "How?"

Nikita said, "Before we get to that, where do we stand with the ferry?"

Felipe hesitated again, off balance, and Nikita put a hand on his arm, saying, "You were given instructions to come here, correct?"

Felipe nodded, unsure of which eye to look at, and Nikita smiled in an attempt to calm him, but it had the opposite effect. Felipe thought he looked like one of the feral dogs from his favela.

Nikita said, "So he trusts us to help. That's why he sent you. There are no secrets to be kept if you want our advice."

Felipe thought it over, then said, "The ferry is anchored on a buoy about a hundred meters from the dock at Vera Cruz."

"And the threat?"

"From what we can tell, there are four to six armed men inside, holding about eighteen or twenty hostages."

"You're sure of this?"

"Fairly sure. We have a command post set up at the ferry terminal that overlooks the harbor, but it's hard to see inside.

The ferry has clear plastic sheeting that can be rolled down in inclement weather, and they've used it to obstruct our view. We can see somewhat, but not distinctly. We do believe that they have placed explosives on the four corners of the bow and stern."

"How do you know this?"

"We can see backpacks, and they've told us this is what they contain. We're in contact with terrorists through the boat's radio in the captain's hold. We don't know it for a fact, but we have to assume."

"And the BOPE is prepared to assault the ferry?"

"We were, but this has generated so much national attention that the government might turn it over to the GRUMEC. Maritime attack is not a BOPE specialty."

Nikita said, "GRUMEC? What's that?"

"It's the Naval Special Forces Combat Divers' Group. I don't think they should be used. They have some counterterrorism experience, but nothing like my men. Their expertise is sabotage and demolitions, not hostage rescue. They train on it, but my men have executed this mission multiple times in the real world."

"If they take over, will you still be in command?"

"No. It will shift to a military operation, not a police one. We'll just provide assistance to them."

Nikita glanced at the other men, then said, "We need you to be sure that doesn't happen. We need *you* in control."

Felipe narrowed his eyes and said, "Why is that?"

Nikita nodded at Luca, and the mountain of a man circled behind Felipe's chair. He felt an inexplicable tendril of dread.

Nikita laid a manila folder on the table and said, "This is going to be shocking, but please do not shout or attempt to escape."

He opened the folder, and in it Felipe saw a picture of his wife and daughter, both tied to a chair, a gag in their mouths, their eyes wide open in fear. Felipe jerked upright, then felt Luca's hands on his shoulders, pinning him to the chair.

Nikita said, "I know this is confusing, but we have a special request. If you follow through, they will be released. Can you do that?"

Felipe nodded dumbly, his ricocheting thoughts competing for attention in his mind.

Nikita patted him on the knee and said, "Good. Good. You do right by us, and they'll be released unharmed."

Felipe found his voice. "What do you want?"

"We want you to botch that rescue. We want all on the ferry to die."

15

I waited a beat for Jennifer to get settled near the entrance to Michael's, still reflecting on her last words. Wondering if she was using them as a weapon to control the outcome of this mission. As leverage forcing me to choose—her, or vengeance.

I knew that wasn't like her. She'd shown in the past that she didn't have that sort of subterfuge in her—which was precisely why I didn't ever lie to her. Out of respect for her moral compass.

The last time she'd thought I was going off the rails, she'd simply left me, disgusted at my perceived moral failings and not wanting to associate herself with actions she felt were beyond the pale. She'd overcome that, and had grown to understand the less than black and white of our world since then, so maybe she'd grown in other ways, too. Maybe more of me was rubbing off on her than she or I cared to admit.

My radio came alive with Nung saying, "You guys getting the feed? The appetizer's arrived. Need to execute before the meal. You wait until they have a steak, and they may not take the bait and decide they'd rather eat."

I snapped out of my thoughts, pulled out my phone, and started an app called "sticky-cam." Essentially nothing more than a high-speed version of those "Ring" doorbells, and named after a video game by some egghead Taskforce member's attempt at humor, it was tied to a camera that Nung had slapped under a table with a view of our targets. About the size of a large button, with a battery life of only thirty minutes, it wasn't high-definition by any means, and only gave video, with no audio, but it was good enough for this work.

I saw the targets eating what appeared to be calamari, one tall and lanky with a head of black hair cut like the Beatles, the other's skull shaved bald, with a full beard, as if he were trying to prove he could still grow hair on his head.

I said, "Koko, you ready?"

She said, "Roger."

"Let me get set at the bar and I'll trigger."

I walked into Victor's, seeing a scattering of leather couches and some high-backed chairs around tall cocktail tables. To my front was a long marble bar with a mural behind it reaching the twenty-foot ceiling. There was a smattering of patrons, not overly crowded, but enough to hide me.

I took an empty bar stool on the left side—the Italian restaurant side—and away from the steak house holding my targets. Both restaurants had access to the cocktail bar via a hallway behind the bar and mural, and that was where both the restrooms and the elevator to the second floor were located.

I glanced at my phone, appearing to surf social media and looking like thirty other patrons sprinkled around the bar. I saw the targets in place and said, "Nung, you getting the feed?"

"Yes. I see them."

"Roger. Get ready to execute. If they don't break free in five minutes, we'll go to plan B."

Plan B was for Nung to stage outside to pick up surveillance, and for me to walk by the table. I wasn't supposed to know what they looked like, but they sure as shit knew what I looked like, and most assuredly would react, either following me or leaving the restaurant. If they came to me, I'd handle it. If they fled, Nung would take control. But I didn't think that would be necessary. Jennifer would be enough.

I heard, "Good to go," and said, "Break, break. Koko, you're cleared to execute."

Thirty seconds later I saw her enter the restaurant, talking to the hostess. The bearded one facing the door stopped with his fork halfway to his mouth, staring. He dropped his food, leaned over, and hissed something. The other target with the bowl-cut whipped his head to the door, then turned around, whispering. I really wished I could hear what they were saying.

Jennifer walked up to them, circled around their table, smiled and nodded, and then was lost from view. Bowl-cut leaned over and said something, pointing in the direction Jennifer had gone. Mr. Clean put his napkin on the table and stood, nodding his head. Beatlemania remained seated, taking a sip of beer.

Bingo.

I said, "Koko, Nung, Baldy is on the move. Bowl-cut is remaining in place. Call when you have control."

I got acknowledgment and waited, which was the worst part of this. Jennifer was literally fifty feet away from me, behind the wall at the back of the bar, standing next to a smug Russian who might just kill her. I hoped he thought he'd see what party she was going to, then report back, but you never knew what curves Murphy will throw your way. The enemy always gets a vote, no matter how smart you think you are.

I glanced at my phone, seeing Bowl-cut still seated, and heard, "Pike, this is Koko. First target down. I say again, we have control of the first target."

I smiled, wanting to see the face of the asshole at the table when I marched up to him. And then the enemy voted.

Bowl-cut stood up, walking out of view of the camera. I said, "Second target unsighted. Out of view."

"Where's he going? Is he coming here?"

"I don't know. Stand by. I need to find him on foot."

"Don't get compromised."

I bit back saying, "Oh, yeah, I hadn't thought of that." Instead I said, "Stand by. He may have just gone to the bathroom."

The problem here was that *I* was their target, so I'd be known on sight, which would cause a significant issue. I was supposed to appear after the first target was acquired, scaring the shit out of the second when he saw a ghost with a pistol under the table.

I slinked behind the bar and peeked down the hallway to the bathrooms. I saw Bowl-cut standing in front of the elevator, waiting.

I whipped back around and said, "He's coming up. I say again, he's coming up."

Jennifer said, "Did he see you? What happened?"

"I have no idea, but this is about perfect. I'll let him get in and be right behind him."

In the original plan, I was supposed to force him to the upper level with a little threat and my pirate stare. Now I wouldn't have to do that. He was walking right into my trap. Sometimes you eat the bear, sometimes the bear eats you.

I heard the elevator ding, waited a beat, turned the corner, and saw the door close. I let it ride for a second, then hit the button to go up, getting ready for the interrogation. Psyching myself up for what was to come.

A man came down the hallway and I glanced at him, expecting him to enter the men's restroom. He did not. He came to the elevator and stood next to me, waiting as well, acting like he knew where he was going. He nodded at me, and I nodded back, frantically afraid that he was a manager going to retrieve something on the floor above.

But then, why wouldn't he be asking me what the hell *I* was doing. There was nothing going on on the second floor. It was used as a private venue for wedding receptions and other events, and I knew it was empty tonight. Because I'd discussed renting it.

Is this the third guy? The one who "never" left?

The elevator door opened and we both entered. The door closed, and we began to rise. The man had backed into the corner, studiously staring at the elevator door. He didn't look like some sort of killer, but he most certainly didn't look like a restaurant manager. Dressed in jeans and a fashionably untucked shirt, he *could* be with the restaurant. Maybe.

We had picked the corner above the Italian restaurant to conduct the interrogation, so I had some time when the door opened. If he went that way, he'd have to go down, immediately. If he went the other way, I'd follow, just to keep him in sight. The upper deck spanned all three venues, so we might be able to let him do whatever he was riding the elevator for and continue the mission.

I heard an unmistakable snick, something that would be unknown to just about one hundred percent of the population, but I knew what it was. An automatic knife.

I glanced at the man and saw a bead of sweat rolling down his brow. And that was enough.

I rotated around, slamming my forearm into his cheek while trapping the arm hidden behind him. He kneed me in the groin, then punched me in the neck with his free hand. I bashed his head into the steel of the car, the door opened, and I flung him as hard as I could out of the elevator.

He slammed into the wall just outside, bounced back, and I threw two jabs in his face, then swept his legs out from under him. He hit the ground hard, then raised his knife, swatting at the air.

Behind him, I could see Nung doing battle with Bowl-cut, and Jennifer farther in, holding a pistol on Baldy, his hands flex-tied to his front, on his knees, with Jennifer alternating between looking at the fight going on with Nung and her target.

My explosion out of the elevator caused all of them to reassess what the hell was happening. Nung used the surprise to gain the upper hand on Bowl-cut, and I saw him wrap the man in a death grip. Jennifer turned to me and I saw Baldy leap up, diving on her for control of the pistol.

The man on the floor used the distraction to leap to his feet, stabbing forward with his blade. I dodged it, half of my mind on Jennifer, trapping his arm and whirling him over my hip. I slammed him to the ground, saw Jennifer on her back, then her kicking out, launching the guy into the air. He hit a pillar and bounced off; she took a knee and lined up her sights.

I gained control of my target and shouted, "Shoot him!"

Baldy stood up and raised his arms in surrender, shaking his head, begging for mercy. She hesitated, and he ran to a window, leaping through it.

Losing the concentration required for a death fight, focused on Jennifer's survival, my man rotated out of my hold, swung his blade, and barely missed my chest. I dodged back, seeing the blade whip through the air.

I snarled, slamming him in the head with a closed fist, bouncing his skull against the hardwood floor, stunning him. I snatched the wrist holding the blade and used both of my hands to jam it backward, shattering the bones. He screamed, and the knife fell free. I rotated around his body, scraped up the blade from the floor, jerked his head back, and slit his throat, both carotid arteries spewing out a fount of blood. I kicked him away, letting him flop on the floor as his life force leaked out, and looked to Nung.

His target was down, permanently.

I stood up, sweaty and bleeding. Jennifer glanced at me, ashamed. She said, "Pike, I couldn't. He was standing with his hands up. I just . . ."

I went by her, running to the window. I looked out, and saw the ending of the movie *Halloween*. All that was missing was the creepy music, because the concrete below was empty.

I went back to her, and she said, "I just couldn't . . ."

I took her pistol, saying, "I know. You did the right thing. It's okay."

She glanced down, not believing my words, and I could tell I was putting her in a bad place. One she didn't belong in. I raised her chin with a finger, bringing her eyes up to mine, and said, "You did the *right* thing." I smiled and said, "Something I wouldn't regret. Lucky for you."

And my words resonated. She gave a tentative smile, relieved. Nung said, "We must leave, now."

He was as calm as ever, as if he'd just broken a dish and not killed a man in cold blood. Or more correctly, like my stray cat licking its paws after it brought me something dead as a present.

I said, "Check the bodies for electronics and passports. That entire action was because they were talking. And find the car keys."

Jennifer said, "I already have the stuff from the guy who jumped."

I smiled, saying, "Well, then, there you go."

Nung said, "I have two sets of keys. And the electronics. We're complete."

Meaning we had both cars. I said, "Perfect. Let's beat that asshole back to the hotel. He's got no phone to call an Uber or cab, and he's going to look a little stupid asking for a cell with his hands flex-tied."

Nung said, "What about this mess? There's no way to cover it up."

The room looked like a slaughterhouse. Nung had managed to kill his man without any blood, but I'd slit my target's throat, and the floor was coated in it, with some on me.

I went through the implications in a nanosecond and said, "Nung, swap shirts with me."

"Why?"

"Because you're right. We need to close this out, and I can't have blood on my shirt. You guys are going to walk out of here like nothing happened."

Nung said, "I'm pretty sure walking out of here like nothing's happened isn't going to close this out."

I smiled and said, "Jennifer, take a picture of their passports, to include any previous travel, then leave the passports on the bodies. Finding them completely stripped of identification will cause major questions in all directions. Leave the cops a thread. Saint Kitts is going to drive this city crazy, but it won't lead to us."

Jennifer said, "What are you going to do?"

Putting on Nung's shirt, I said, "Go back down and get a rum and coke. Then close out my tab. You guys never entered as far as they know. Nung, get the button camera on the way out. Jennifer, just get out of the building. The only one here that's stamped is me."

I finished replacing Nung's shirt, which was a little tight, and said, "We good?"

Nung looked at the sag in his new shirt and said, "No. This thing doesn't fit."

Incredulous, I said, "Are you bitching about my shirt? Really?"

Nung smiled at me and said, "This will work to get out of here."

I said, "Then let's go, and pray that the police aren't good enough to figure this out."

We started jogging to the elevator and I said, "Nung, please tell me you disabled the camera in the elevator."

From our reconnaissance, we knew there were no cameras on the upper floor, and none in the hallway to the bathroom, but there *was* one inside the elevator.

He looked at me like I was insane. He said, "Of course I did."

The elevator doors opened, and my phone rang. I checked the number, seeing "unknown." I answered, and heard, "Uber? Really? You can't even pick us up? Is that what my skill is worth?"

The doors closed and I said, "Sorry, Pumpkin King, but something came up. Meet Jennifer at a place called the Restoration Hotel. Right now."

I heard nothing for a second, then, "Why?"

"Because I might need your skills."

16

Nikita padded around the opulent penthouse, staring at his watch every ten seconds. He had to report the progress of Operation Harvest to Dmitri, and they were behind schedule. There was only one target down, and he'd withdrawn most of the teams to Salvador to deal with the second—a woman, no less. And so he paced, rehearsing what he was going to say. He knew he was correct in his decision, and that Dmitri would understand—if he could frame it correctly.

When his digital watch struck 2 P.M., he dialed the phone. It rang twice, and then a man with a flat voice answered saying, "Black Sea Holdings." Nikita said, "Group chat number for Harvest."

The robotic man said, "Two twelve."

Nikita disconnected from the cellular network and brought up a VPN app, checked to ensure he was on Wi-Fi, then double-tapped it. A screen cleared, asking for a group number. He typed in 212, and waited.

The application was a voice-over-internet-protocol that was encrypted end to end and completely off the cellular network, chosen because it was unbreakable and untraceable. While Nikita couldn't use it point-to-point with other cell phones, Dmitri insisted it be used when communicating with Russia.

Because he's always looking out for himself.

He heard Dmitri pick up. "Sir, did you get the situation report on the lawyer?" Nikita asked.

"Yes. Good job. I'm still waiting on news about the Mines and Energy minister and the Petrobras ombudsman. What is the status of them?"

"We're tracking both, but I've had to consolidate the teams for the ombudsman. It's under control."

"You were given such a large team precisely to execute concurrently, not sequentially. We have a two-week window. That's it. And we have the primary target to deal with."

"Well, sir, to meet the timeline, I'm going to need more men. We ran into a problem that's also an opportunity, and it's caused a consolidation of my manpower. We have the ombudsman in our sights, but it's complicated."

He explained the current situation with the ferry in Salvador, then waited on the response. When it came, it wasn't what he expected.

"I can't give you more men immediately. We've run into a problem in Charleston, and Global Engagement Branch is skittish. Your team missed the man we were targeting from Grolier Recovery Services."

"Missed him? What are you talking about? My team saw him incinerated."

"Your *team* saw someone *else* incinerated. If I remember right, when I asked you if you were sure, you said, 'unless he can walk out of fire.' Well, it looks like he did."

Nikita could feel the sarcasm coming from the phone, and understood he was standing on a trapdoor. He said, "How do you know? The next day the press said it was him. Was there a sighting?"

Nikita heard laughter, then, "The man you killed is named

Kurt Hale. Something your men would have learned had they bothered to wait a few days for the press to sort out their own bad reporting. And yes, there was a *sighting*. Your target set a trap and killed two men from the team. A third barely escaped."

"Killed them? In Charleston?"

"Yes. In Charleston. I knew they should have flown home immediately. Sergey is the only one who made it out alive—and even he barely did so. He's holed up at a cheap motel near the airport, waiting on a flight out. Luckily, the deaths are being blamed on some drug competition from the Caribbean. Nobody has connected us to the action, unless you fuck something else up."

Nikita tried to process the information. One second he was fighting for more men on a sanctioned mission, and the next he was being berated for screwing up a hit he didn't even have control over. The last time he'd talked to Sergey, they were headed out to some fort in the middle of the harbor, enjoying life. And now, according to Dmitri, most of the team was dead.

He focused on the mission. "Did Sergey make it back to the hotel? Sterilize the room?"

"He tried to, but he was beaten to the room by the GRS men. He saw the target enter the lobby and just kept walking."

Jesus Christ. "So they have everything in the room?"

"I haven't personally debriefed him yet. He's flying out tomorrow. Due to your incompetence, I'm closing that out."

"Sir, he can't fly out. We need to recover the equipment. At a minimum, recover the laptop that was in the suite."

Nikita heard Dmitri's voice take on a sharpened edge. "Why? What was on the laptop?"

Nikita hesitated, then said, "Information about that

specific target. Intelligence that could prove damning, like the Brits found after we targeted Skripal in England."

"Is that it?"

"There might . . . maybe, be some information about our operations here. There shouldn't be, but I haven't seen the computer."

Nikita waited, then heard the anger come through the phone. "You fucking idiot. You cross-pollinated operations?"

"Wait, sir, there aren't two different operations going now. I'm executing Operation Harvest, and you put this target on my list. I had to coordinate with the team before I began operations down here. The laptop should be clean, but I can't be sure. Don't let Sergey leave."

"What would you have me do, you fuckup? We're about to cause an international incident, like those idiots did in England. We've muddied the waters enough in Charleston. We have two dead men there, and a car bomb *you* initiated. It won't take much to connect the two. You mentioned Skripal, and that's exactly what I'm worried about. When Russia's hand was exposed, it was a worldwide mess of pressure. We don't need that here."

"Sir, Harvest has only begun, and it was *you* who said this man was a threat to successful execution. You put him on the target deck. His men are still here, and I can eliminate them, but the head is still alive, and we don't know how many more he controls."

Nikita could almost sense Dmitri's brain turning over the implications. He pressed forward: "If you want to end Harvest because you think we're already compromised, then so be it. But if you want me to continue, that target in Charleston needs to be eliminated. If what you say is true, it means stopping him now more than ever. Before, he was just a possible threat, but now he *knows* we're hunting him. It's a setback, but it'll be worse if we don't go on the offense."

Nikita waited, hearing nothing. Then, "What do you suggest?"

"Let me continue with the mission. Reinforce both Sergey and myself. Give him what he needs to eliminate the head of GRS in Charleston and give me what I need to execute down here."

"I'm not sure taking that man head-on is smart. He's a hard target, and as you said, he knows he's being hunted now."

"Hard target or not, he needs to be dealt with. His men are down here for a reason, and I promise it's because the United States wants the influence we're trying to get here. They are no different. GRS is probably working for Exxon. We need to be bold."

Dmitri said, "Maybe, but being bold and being stupid are the flip sides of the same coin, with only a twist of fate determining the difference. I'm not sure which one you are."

"Sir, I have his men down here, just as I described. Give me more men for the other targets and let me execute this mission. Give Sergey what he needs and let him work the Charleston target set. We'll eliminate not only the ombudsman, but the GRS problem."

"Okay, but I don't need another mistake. GRS is proving resilient, and I have to answer to powerful men."

"You won't get one. GRS may be resilient, but they aren't superhuman. Give me command of the men in Charleston, and I'll solve that problem. As for here, I own the police response, and those two GRS men on the ferry are trapped."

17

Knuckles waited until the sun was well past the horizon, a full moon providing feeble illumination on the water. He checked the sleeping guard curled on the bench bolted to the gunwale, leaned over, and poked Brett in the thigh, saying, "It's time."

Tonight marked the second cycle of darkness since they'd been taken hostage, and Knuckles knew the longer the crisis continued, the more unstable it would become. The hostage takers were at first arrogant and cocksure. Some type of criminal element with a sliver of grassroots insurgency, throughout the second day they had grown surly with the pressure—as always happened when a group took other human beings as pawns.

The hostage takers were tolerable now, but Knuckles knew it was only a matter of time before the terrorists began to crack. It caused him to worry. They needed to resolve this before the terrorists began fraying, losing the ability for rational thought.

On the plus side, the terrorists had shown they'd thought through the problem, and hadn't simply stopped their planning at the moment of capture. They'd dictated to the police how the ferry would be fed, down to the type of boat that would bring supplies, and had planned for a sustained control of the situation. That told Knuckles that the fraying would take longer than an ordinary hostage situation, such as a bank robber who had no intention of taking captives but now was stuck with them.

All of that was a good thing in Knuckles's mind, as it gave him space.

The captives had been given water and a basket of fruit, brought to the ferry on a wooden skiff from the town of Vera Cruz. A single man had been allowed to pilot the skiff, and he remained in the back, working the throttle while the gunmen all glowered, looking for some team of commandos to spring forth from the boat. When that hadn't occurred, the skiff had returned twice more, delivering jackfruit, papaya, and bananas.

The terrorists had shown planning in other areas as well. While the passengers were all corralled in the center of the ferry for control, and not allowed to roam about, they were given the use of one bathroom at the stern of the boat, going in pairs under the watchful eye of a guard. It was the only movement permitted, and it was synchronized, with each individual guard knowing what was required. That was both good and bad.

Good because it showed detail orientation to the problem they'd caused. They'd not only studied the floor plan of the boat prior to assaulting, but had also determined the control of the hostages throughout the crisis, meaning they wouldn't spaz out at the first hitch in their plan. Bad because it also meant they'd probably synchronized a response to any assault, either from the hostages or from the police.

Knuckles had studied the cycle of the terrorists, and had noticed that only one was allowed to sleep at any one time. And so he waited after nightfall until the one chosen for rest had been down long enough to be asleep.

He wasn't thinking of attacking the remaining two down

below. Like the care and feeding of the hostages, the terrorists had put some thought in their plan for control, and never congregated together. The three awake were always separated, providing no way to eliminate the threat before one could begin to defend himself, especially since one always remained upstairs in the captain's chair. And it would take only one, as all of the terrorists had made clear they each held a daisy-chained initiation device that would cause the four satchels of explosives to detonate. Because of that, Knuckles's goal wasn't to eliminate the threat, but to engender someone else to do so. Someone with the skill to succeed. All he needed was a way to alert them that he was in trouble.

In the initial attack only the woman's bodyguard was killed. Every hostage was searched, especially for cell phones and all identifying articles such as wallets and passports. The cell phones had been turned off and placed in one knapsack, the wallets and passports annotated for communication with the police and placed in another. Both were stored at the back of the boat, near the toilet everyone was forced to use.

Brett sat up, looked around in the darkness, then whispered, "You sure about this? We get caught and it might be the end."

Knuckles said, "Yeah, well, I'm pretty sure unless we get some help, it's the end anyway. You got a better idea than just sitting here waiting on some Neanderthals from Brazil to try a rescue, or these guys to decide they want to show they're serious? You know the first they'll kill is anyone who they think is a threat. That woman will live. You and I will not."

Brett chuckled softly and said, "Nope. But if we get in a fight, I'm going down swinging, which means this whole boat is liable to blow. I'm not dying on my knees with a barrel to my forehead."

Knuckles looked at the woman with the child. She was

curled up around him like a lioness, protecting him from whatever the men with guns wanted to extract, her expensive clothes now being used as a makeshift blanket to give them warmth. It reminded him of the stakes.

He patted Brett's thigh and said, "Same here, brother, same here. But if you give me cover, it won't come to that. We missed our contact window, and the Taskforce has got to be wondering why, but they won't pull the trigger on a Prairie Fire without some additional reason."

Prairie Fire was a code word alert for a Taskforce element in mortal jeopardy. Once initiated, everything stopped, with all assets within the area of operations dedicated to helping the team in trouble. It was rarely used, and Knuckles knew the Taskforce wouldn't initiate the protocol just because of a missed SITREP. So he needed to push a little bit, which is where his phone came in.

A special iPhone, designed from the ground up with features that were hidden from the casual user, it had a beacon inside that would signal not only their location, but the fact that they were in trouble.

If he could get to it.

He didn't want to steal the phone and keep it, thereby jeopardizing the rest of the passengers, because he had no idea if they'd take an inventory of the backpack in the future or would search him at a later date. Finding it on his person would mean his instant death—and possibly someone innocent, just to prove a point.

All he wanted to do was take it into the bathroom with him.

Knuckles said, "Remember the play?"

"Yeah, you go first, get to the door, then I shit my pants, pushing you out of the way."

Knuckles smiled and said, "But you don't really need to shit your pants. Just act like it."

Brett chuckled and said, "I've been saving in this gas for hours. Someone's going to get it. You sure you can get that beacon up and running in the time we have? It's not going to be more than a few seconds."

"Nope. I'm sure I can shove that phone in my pants before they see, though. You'll just have to do the dance twice."

Brett stood up and said, "Let's get it on."

He waved his hands to the guard at the bow of the boat, and pointed at his groin. The man nodded, then held up two fingers. Brett knew the drill. The guards wanted to prevent going to the bathroom over and over, so they demanded two at a time, forcing the passengers to hold their bladder until another was ready. Brett tapped Knuckles, who stood as well.

The woman with the child heard the commotion and raised herself to her elbow. He glanced at her, and she locked eyes with him, as if she wanted something. He furrowed his brow, and she nodded. Meaning . . . meaning, what?

She lay back down, keeping her eyes on him. The guard approached, showing no fear. The routine had been performed seven times this day alone with the passengers, and he held a Czech Scorpion pistol. Enough to cause the timid hostages to back down.

He prodded them to the stern of the boat, where the backpacks were laid out on a bench, the toilet to the left, adjacent to the gunwale. They both stopped, looking suitably timid. The guard nodded, and Knuckles advanced to the door. He put his hand on it, then Brett leaned over and grabbed his stomach, groaning. The guard showed concern and Brett let loose a bout of flatulence that caused the guard to reel back, holding a hand over his face and cursing.

Brett flung Knuckles to the side in an apparent desperate effort to access the toilet. Knuckles fell toward the bench, snatching the cell phone knapsack as he dropped between the row of seats. He heard the toilet door slam shut and began digging in the darkness, not even bothering to look behind him. If he were discovered, it was the endgame. Knowing the guard had seen him snatch the bag mattered little at this point. He had either succeeded or he'd lost. He rapidly dug through the phones, waiting on a shout. None came. He located his, slid it in his pants, and replaced the bag.

Brett staggered out of the toilet, holding his hands to his stomach. The guard stayed back, waving his hands in front of his face. Knuckles rose, looked at him, and saw no suspicion. He waited for approval and the guard, standing away from Brett, nodded.

Knuckles entered the head, locked the door, then ripped the phone out, powering it up. Waiting for it to boot, he tapped his foot, aggravated at the time, glancing at the door, sure the guard would break it down for no reason whatsoever.

Finally, the screen cleared, and he brought up the music app. He went to a particular song, hit play, waited a beat, then shut the phone down again. The beacon would transmit now whether the phone was on or off.

He relieved himself, exited the head, looked at Brett, and gave an imperceptible nod. The guard waved his machine pistol at them, and Brett bent over like he was going to launch another volley of gas, holding his stomach and groaning. He pointed at the toilet and the guard turned his face away, nodding his head. Knuckles sidled to the right, until his back was over the bag on the bench. He reached behind him, raised the flap, and dropped in the phone.

A few minutes later, Brett exited, wiping sweat off of his

forehead. He said, "I'm sorry. That fruit you gave us is not good."

The guard shoved them both forward, back to the center of the hold. They sank into a bench and he left. Brett looked at Knuckles and said, "So?"

Knuckles smiled and said, "So, Prometheus Five is now transmitting."

The woman on the floor woke up, staring at them. Knuckles smiled at her, and she locked eyes with him, saying nothing. Studying him. He winked and saw her eyes grow wide. He put a finger to his lips, and she nodded, then sagged back into her makeshift blanket of clothes, snuggling with her son.

Brett caught the movement. He waited until she was down again, then leaned in and said, "I think she's a fighter. Nobody else on this boat is."

"I agree. Something to consider."

Both were thinking about the endgame. It was coming, one way or the other. They both knew that situations like this never ended peacefully. After a moment of silence, Brett said, "You think anyone is going to get that call?"

"Yes. I don't know how long it'll take, with the shit storm going on in D.C. right now, but I'm pretty sure that it'll get to Pike eventually. Even if the Taskforce is on stand-down, Pike will come."

Brett lay down on the seats, curling his arms under his head, and chuckled, saying, "Oh, goody. We get the wrecking crew. Can't wait to see how that works out."

18

I listened to Shoshana's report, then said, "So you think it's worthless to stay any longer?"

It was getting close to 11 A.M., the check-out time at the hotel, and our target had yet to return.

She said, "Yes. He's not coming back."

Aggravated, I snapped, "Okay, go ahead and crack the room. Get what you can, but don't take anything. Extract any digital stuff in place. If you need additional kit, call me back. We'll get it to you."

I heard, "Hey, I'm not making up bad news just to aggravate you. No reason to get cranky."

I rubbed my forehead and said, "I know, I know. Sorry. Just enter the room and get what you can. I'll see you back here."

Last night I'd sent Jennifer racing back to the Restoration Hotel, meeting our new teammates Aaron and Shoshana. I'd waited in the bar drinking a rum and Coke—because I'd damn well earned it—and somebody had finally found the bodies. There was an enormous police response, which wasn't surprising. For Charleston this was like a Mexican drug cartel rolling heads into a disco in Cancun. It had exploded on the news, and this morning I'd learned that the police were on that very track. They believed that bad elements from the Caribbean were attempting to smuggle drugs through the port of Charleston, and some sort of feud had caused the deaths. Which suited me fine.

The Israelis and Jennifer hadn't had any time for pleasantries, and since they were the only ones not currently burned for surveillance work, she'd given them Nung's keys to his room, the access code for the Alexa hack, the description of our target, and told them to burrow in, waiting. If Mr. Clean showed up again, they were to take him down, calling us for backup and exfiltration. Alexa was the trigger. Any noise that occurred in that room would be heard by them.

Aaron had balked, not wanting to start an operation on such a shoestring bit of information—not even knowing why—but Jennifer had told him we didn't have the time because the target could return any second. Surprisingly, Shoshana had agreed, and Aaron had reluctantly assumed the mission. She'd left them, then met me at the Grolier Recovery Services office, where I'd begun planning for our trip to Brazil while waiting on a jackpot call that never came.

Jennifer stuck her head into my office and said, "What happened?"

"No joy. Aaron and Shoshana are headed back here."

"And the room?"

"Don't know yet. They're going through it now."

She nodded, then hung in the doorway. I said, "What?"

"Nothing. Just wondering how you're doing."

I smiled. She was always more worried about others than herself. If she offered you iced tea, and then your house started burning down, she'd ask you if it was too sweet. Right before she put out the fire.

I said, "I'm fine. Really. But we've got a lot of work to do before we fly."

She said, "Maybe leaving here right now isn't such a good idea."

I sagged back into my desk chair and said, "Come on, Jennifer. We've been over this. Kurt's death leads to Brazil, and we already have our visas ready from the original mission."

"Aaron and Shoshana don't have visas."

"They don't need them. They're from Israel." I tapped my temple and said, "Always thinking."

She grinned at me and said, "Pike, we have no thread, and we have a lunatic Russian on the loose. Do you really think it's smart to leave Amena and Kylie here alone?"

I paused, then said, "Are you telling me you want to hunt *him*?"

She looked embarrassed, then said, "Well, yeah. Bird in the hand and all that. We need to eliminate the threat here, then go forward."

That was a little bit of a revelation.

Before I could say anything, she said, "We can get his digital trail from the room. There's bound to be something inside it for a thread. We find that, then we hunt his ass. Eliminate that threat before going to Brazil. What do you say?"

I put my hands behind my head, leaned back, and said, "I say that's a damn good idea, little Jedi. How do we stand with the safe house?"

Before she could answer, we heard, "Hello? Anyone home?"

Jennifer stuck her head outside my office and said, "Back here." She turned around and said, "It's Kylie and Amena. Take care with what you say."

I started to reply, and Amena pushed through Jennifer, running to me and giving me a hug. I hugged her back, and saw fear in her face.

I said, "What's up, doodlebug? Why the long face?"

She said, "Why are you making me move out?"

Thinking of Kurt's final words, I misunderstood what she was asking. I said, "Wait, what? You aren't moving out."

She said, "Then why are you making me pack clothes? Pack a suitcase?"

It dawned on me she was talking about the safe house.

I laughed and said, "Nobody's making you 'move out.' You're just relocating here in Charleston for a few days. That's all."

Her arms still around my neck, she looked into my eyes, trying to sense a lie. She said, "Why would we do that?"

I glanced at Jennifer, and she was giving me the stink-eye, not wanting me to tell the truth, but I'd learned that Amena could smell subterfuge a mile away. And she'd understand why, based on her past life.

I put my arms around her and gave her a hug, saying, "There are some bad men looking for me, and I don't want them to find you."

Jennifer said, "Jesus, Pike! Is that necessary?"

Amena glanced from me to her, then back to me. She sighed, the relief evident on her face. She sagged into me and said, "That's the best news I've heard all day."

I chuckled and said, "Don't worry. You aren't getting rid of me that easily. I just want to make sure you're safe."

She sat up and said, "Why are bad men always finding you? What did you do?"

I sat up and said, "Me? Seems like the last time it was you."

She frowned and I laughed to defuse the situation, saying, "Just kidding. Someday I'll tell you, doodlebug. But not today. Just pack a bag and enjoy the beach house."

She grew concerned and said, "What if you don't come

back? How bad are the people looking for you? Is it like Switzerland?"

I glanced away, not wanting to think that my life was now more important to others than it was to me. She said, "What?"

I said, "Don't worry about me. I'm going to hunt them first."

She said, "Was the man in the car working for you? Is that why he's dead?"

And I felt the blackness again. A deep pool of tar dragging me down. Jennifer stepped in, taking her hand and saying, "Come on, honey, we have a lot of work to do, and you need to pack."

Amena realized she'd touched a scab and didn't resist Jennifer's pull. She stood up, and Kylie entered the room. I hadn't seen her since Kurt's death.

She looked at me with loathing, and I rose, walking to her. She said, "Don't . . . Don't."

But I did. I wrapped her in my arms and said, "Kylie, I'm so sorry. I'll find them. I promise I will."

She started crying, saying, "Why'd you leave? Why did you run?"

Unspoken was the blame that I'd killed her uncle. The man she revered more than any other. I rubbed her back and said, "I had to. The same reason you're taking Amena to a different house. It'll be okay. I promise, it'll be okay."

Veep entered the room, saw the display, and stood, awkwardly shifting from one foot to the other. I broke my embrace with Kylie, brushed her hair aside, and said, "Veep will take care of you two until we get this resolved."

Nicholas Seacrest—aka Veep—was supposed to be traveling to Brazil with me, but that was no longer in the cards because of the Taskforce stand-down, which worked in my favor. A member of Air Force special operations, he was the youngest on my team and looked like a Boy Scout, but looks could be deceiving. His callsign VEEP came from the fact that when he'd joined my team, his father had been the vice president. The national command authority had tried to force him into a safer military occupational specialty because of his family, and he'd refused, instead coming to me. I routinely kidded him about his millennial creds, but underneath the Boy Scout façade lurked a killer. Now his father was the president, and I was going to use him to protect what I held dear.

I kissed Kylie's forehead and said, "It'll be okay. I can't bring Kurt back, but I can find out why he was killed."

She nodded, brushed her hair out of her eyes, looked at me one more time, but said nothing. And then she left the room. Veep waited until she was gone, then said, "So take them to the new place?"

I said, "Yeah. It's probably for nothing, but it's better this way. Take them back to my house, get whatever you need, and get out. Don't return there until you hear from me."

He nodded and turned to leave. Amena left Jennifer, ran to me, and wrapped her arms around my waist, saying, "Don't go. Come with us."

Veep left, embarrassed at the display.

19

Answering emails in his office in Crystal City, Virginia, Clyde Marion saw a notification from the WhatsApp manager on his computer desktop. Surprised, he closed out of his email manager, clicked into WhatsApp, and saw an instant message from a man who was never supposed to contact him in the United States.

He hesitated to answer. The man on the other end of the line was firewalled from every other contract he conducted, relegated to a partition of the company known as "Deep Purple" because of his associations.

Monte Cristo Analytics had grown from a little backwater social media advertising influencer for housewives trying to sell skin care products to a full-blown player in the world of manipulating public thought. Named after the famed gold mine in the San Gabriel Mountains of California, it was both a tribute and a middle finger directed at the squalor of the trailer park where he'd grown up, a decrepit shadow of the promises the mine once held. The name now assumed a double meaning because of the data mining the company conducted, cloaking what Clyde truly represented, just like Alexandre Dumas's Count of Monte Cristo—and not unlike Clyde himself.

Born Gregori Utkin in the Soviet republic of Kazakhstan, he had fled with his family to America after the collapse of the USSR, living hand to mouth in a trailer park. Clyde had despised his given name, having been bullied relentlessly because of it in that dusty, broken Californian town. As soon as he was old enough, he'd fled the trailer park and legally changed it to Clyde Marion—a name that worked much better in Silicon Valley than his foreign-made one.

Clyde checked to make sure the door to his office was closed, then clicked on the WhatsApp icon, seeing a chat request. He hesitated, checked the door again, then initiated a conversation.

-Why are you contacting me here? You know I'm in DC.
-*I need some help. Something only you can do.*
-I'm doing everything I can in Brazil. We've flooded WhatsApp with messages, and have a positive response rate on all of our Facebook work. The campaign is working. There's nothing else I can do, and you said my hands should remain unseen.
-*It's not the campaign. It's your contacts. Do you still have the contract with the Pentagon?*

That gave Clyde pause. He did, in fact, have a contract with the Pentagon to study the effects of disinformation on the future capabilities of warfare, both offensive and defensive, but he didn't advertise that he was using the very thing he was studying for an election in Brazil.

He typed,

-I might. Why?
-*Don't worry. I don't want to infect our relationship with a Russian disease. I just need some information.*

-What?
-*There is a colonel named Kurt Hale. Have you heard of him?*
-No. Should I?
-*He works in the division that has your contract. J3.*

Clyde frowned. Surely he wasn't expected to know every single man on the joint operations staff at the Pentagon. There were literally thousands.

He typed,

-No. Never heard of him. Why?
-*He's dead. Made the news.*
-So?
-*I want to know what he did. Where he worked. Can you check that?*

Clyde hesitated. Working for various foreign governments and independent actors was one thing, but this could constitute actual spying. The man on the other end sensed the hesitation.

-*I'm not asking you to hack his computer. Just look him up in the Pentagon directory. It's open source information.*

Clyde paused, then typed,

-It'll cost you.
-*It always does. Put it on the bill for Brazil.*
-Stand by.

Clyde minimized the chat room and whirled his chair to another computer, one hooked into the Pentagon's secure database. He spent five minutes typing, then furrowed his brow. He dug deeper, but came up empty.

Strange.

He turned his chair back to the other desktop and pulled up the chat window.

-You still there?
-*Yes. What did you find?*
-He works in J3 SOD. The Special Operations Division. But he doesn't have an office listed. In fact, he's got nothing listed. He's just a name in a phone book. I can't find a single thing in the database that he's had a hand in. Nothing. What is he?

Clyde waited for two minutes, getting nothing back. He typed,

-You still there?
-*Yes. Can you dig deeper? Find out what he's doing?*
-I thought you said he was dead.
-*Okay, WAS doing.*
-No. I don't work with SOD. I have no contacts.
-*It would be lucrative. Very lucrative.*
-I just told you I have no contacts, and my contracts with the Pentagon are already lucrative. What is this about?
-*I think he was part of something secret, and it's affecting our operations in Brazil. I need whatever group he was involved in to back off.*

Clyde released the keyboard like it was molten. He leaned back, wanting to delete the entire thread. He saw,

-You still there?

Clyde hesitatingly put his hands back on the keyboard.

-Yes.
-Is there some way to highlight him? Just shine a light on his death? It'll turn into a press story, I promise. He was a player in something deep.
-How? I don't have that capability, and I'm not going to risk my entire company on your request because of Brazil. I've done what I said I would.

Even as he typed it, he was thinking about a friend of his. Someone who was a firebrand about "American imperialism" and "unjust covert action." Someone who had grown up with the luxury of protesting in the United States even as his parents paid for his education. Clyde, having fled the Soviet Union as a child, and then scraped his way to the pinnacle he was now in, had no illusions about the world. Everyone was fair game—either getting played or acting as the player—and he wasn't averse to leveraging the relationship.

-Think about what I'm saying. I'm not asking for YOU to do anything. I'm asking if you have any contacts. You work with everyone. You have political clout. You have no one?

Clyde hesitated yet again, then typed,

-How much are we talking about?
-As much as the entire contract for Brazil. That's how much.

Clyde's eyes widened. Whoever Kurt Hale had been, he was clearly an important man. And a threat. He typed,

-I have a friend who is a staffer for a senator on the Intelligence Committee. My old college roommate. I could pass it to him and have him start an inquiry. Would that work?

-*Perfect. Let me know when it's complete.*

-Before I do, why? Why am I doing this?

-*Spare me the theatrics. Because you want to make some money. Like you did in Ukraine, Brexit, and Myanmar. Like you're doing in Brazil.*

Clyde leaned back, a little ashamed.
Because the man was right.

20

Amena repeated, "Come with me. We can stay together. All of us. Me, you, and Jennifer. You don't have to go do this."

I started to reply then heard, "Nephilim! I thought we were brought here for our skill. Not just sitting in a hotel room."

Shit. Bad timing.

Shoshana entered my office, all smiles, trying to look like a woman on vacation, even as she dragged in a bit of danger behind her like a rotting bridal train. A lithe woman without any voluptuous curves at all, she was more like a lanky teenage boy than the predator she really was.

Once an assassin for the vaunted Mossad, she'd been trained to kill at an early age, and because of it, she'd never learned what it meant to be normal. The operations she'd been forced to conduct had once twisted her into something beyond human, but she was mightily trying to rectify that now. Much to my chagrin, because she was always trying to emulate Jennifer—and she just couldn't pull that off. She was one of the best killers I'd ever seen, but had trouble operating like a normal human in civil society. She kept trying, though. I'll give her that.

We'd met under bad circumstances, and like Nung, I'd somehow become someone she trusted. A couple of years ago, I'd leveraged the entire United States arsenal to rescue her husband, Aaron, in Africa, and *that* was the favor she owed me. I'd be lying if I said I'd done it for that purpose alone, though. I'd done it because I loved her, in a family sort of way. She *and* Aaron. And maybe that was why she returned the favor.

She took one look around the room, seeing Jennifer, Amena, and me. She said, "So there's more going on than just the hotel room."

Shoshana had some weird skill at reading people. I would say it was borderline psychic, like you see on street corners with palm readers, but I don't believe in that shit. Even as a part of me did. She could just *tell* what someone was about. See into their soul. And she was reading us now.

Amena looked at her and drew into me. She said, "She's a killer just like the others."

Which brought me up short. Maybe Amena had the same skill.

Shoshana snapped her head to the child, sucking up her essence like she was breathing incense. She went from Amena to me and said, "She's with you?"

I smiled and said, "Yup. She's with me."

Shoshana nodded her head, now intrigued. She said, "She's a fighter. Where is she from?"

Amena looked at her fiercely and said, "I'm from America."

Which brought a smile. Shoshana clearly knew that wasn't the case. She walked over to her, putting a hand on her cheek, then looked at me, saying, "She is not wanted here. Is that it?"

I pulled her hand away and said, "Cut that out, Shoshana. We don't need it now."

Shoshana squinted at me, reading me. *Aggravating* me.

Amena stared at Shoshana, seeing something inside her, and because of it, she believed what she'd just heard. She said, "Is what she said true? I'm not wanted here?"

I started to protest, pushing Amena behind my back like I was protecting her, when Shoshana squatted down to her level, took her hands and said, "No. That's *not* what I meant. I meant I see your pain. I have not been wanted as well. But I'm wanted *here*."

Shoshana looked at me, and I swear I thought I saw her eyes well up a little. Which would have meant hell had frozen over. She locked eyes with Amena and said, "It's the ones who really want us that matter, not the ones who want us discarded."

Amena heard the words and understood them at a level only Shoshana could reach. She nodded and said, "I get it. I'm like you."

Shoshana grinned, seeing something nobody else could, and said, "Yes, you do understand. But you're not yet like me. And hopefully you never will be."

She stood and said, "So, you have a Syrian refugee you're hiding. What else are you not telling me about this mission?"

Amena's eyes grew wide, and mine about slammed shut. I pushed Amena to the door and said, "Why don't you go wait outside for Veep."

I waited until she was out the door, then snapped, "Stop that shit in her presence. She is on thin ice, and she doesn't need to know it. As far as she knows she's good to go. Don't get her worrying about what *might* happen."

Jennifer stepped between us, saying, "Hey, let it go. Pike, she's just being Shoshana."

Taken aback, Shoshana raised a hand and said, "Wait. I didn't mean anything."

I glowered at her. She continued, "I'm sorry. I just saw the connection. And the conflict. I meant no harm, Nephilim."

Jennifer broke the tension, saying, "Shoshana, we've had a significant event. And we could use your help."

No sooner had the words left her mouth than Aaron entered the room, sensed the tension, and smiled, saying, "I see nothing's changed."

I sank into my desk chair and rubbed my eyes. Aaron caught the reaction, and his smile faded.

Jennifer said, "It's a little different this time. What did you find out from the target room?"

"It was a suite, but not a lot there. Some luggage, nondescript clothing, no documents or other pocket litter. They were thorough. There was a laptop, but no other electronics. We bypassed the screen lock, drained it, went back to our room to make sure it transferred, then came here."

"So you found something?"

"Yeah, but it's all in Russian."

"No issue." I shouted, "Nung!"

He appeared, took one look at Shoshana and Aaron, and said, "So you *do* have another team."

Shoshana glanced at him, then said, "You called another before us?"

"No, Nung was the one who came to me with the threat."

"How long have you worked with him?" Meaning, *Should I trust him?*

She talked like he wasn't standing right next to her. He took it like he wasn't standing right next to her, saying nothing. Because that guy just didn't give a shit.

I said, "Since before I met you. Don't worry, he's just as deadly as you are, but he has a skill you don't. He speaks Russian."

I turned to Aaron and said, "Bring it up. What did you find?"

Aaron placed a laptop on my desk, booted it, and said, "We found a trove of emails off a Proton server that were stored on the computer hard drive. But it's all in Russian."

"Nung, can you translate it?"

He approached the screen, saw nothing but Cyrillic lettering, and said, "I can't read that."

Confused, I said, "But you speak Russian."

He said, "I speak it. But I can't read it. I can use Google Translate, if you want."

"Are you kidding me?" I scrolled through the find and saw it was large. I said, "There are like a hundred emails. Google Translate isn't going to work for that. I need more precision than that."

He shrugged and said, "I cannot help here. I'm sorry."

I exhaled, then said, "Yeah, well, it was worth a shot."

Aaron said, "I might have some connections who speak Russian. Someone discreet, but I'll have to send it to them."

I knew he was talking about Russian Jews who were now employed by the Mossad. It was tempting, but also risky. Anytime you involved Israeli intelligence, it was asking for interference. They would help, but they'd also stick their fingers in and swirl around to see if they could get something out of it—and that was something I didn't need.

While I was mulling it over, Nung said, "My flight leaves in three hours. I need to get packed."

That took me by surprise. "You're leaving? Just like that?"

"I told you I couldn't stay. Father wants me home before I'm compromised with your mission."

"You mean before you're smeared by my actions with some Russians that your father might want to work with again? Because it could affect future business?"

He smiled and said, "Now you think like me."

I shook his hand, saying, "I didn't mean that. Thank you for coming, even if it was too little too late. You didn't have to, and I would have no thread without it. I owe you one."

He waved that away, saying, "That last payment will work for a decade." And I knew he was talking about twenty-five million dollars in Bitcoin I'd inadvertently given him the last time we'd worked together. Jennifer stood on tiptoe, giving him a peck on the cheek. She said, "Thanks for the help in the restaurant."

He simply nodded, and walked out without another word.

Shoshana watched him go, then said, "I like your friend. He should stay."

I looked at Jennifer, wondering how our friend group had shrunk to a robotic half-breed Asian and a psychotic Israeli assassin. At least we had Aaron. Someone who was somewhat normal.

I said, "If you like him, you'll *love* the mission."

21

Shoshana took a seat in another chair, put her feet on the wall, and pushed, sliding it across the floor on its casters like a child. She said, "Which is what, exactly? You've flown us here like the world was on fire, then had us sit in a hotel room doing nothing."

Without preamble, Jennifer said, "Kurt Hale was murdered. Killed with a car bomb at our house. The Taskforce is no help. They're all on stand-down."

I saw Shoshana's eyes widen and said, "It's true. He's dead, and the man that killed him was trying to kill me. I got most of them last night, but one escaped. He was staying in the hotel I had you watch last night. He poses a threat to us, and we want to find him."

I saw a little of the darkness I fight inside her, too. She said, "You should have called us earlier, instead of Nung. We would have come."

I said, "I had no idea. This whole thing just split open in the last forty-eight hours, and Nung brought the first thread. I didn't know what I had. Shit, even the Taskforce doesn't believe me. Nobody does. Outside of this room, that is."

"So what are we doing?"

"We're going to find that bald guy—if he's still here and not back in Russia—and wring him out."

Aaron said, "I'm sorry about your loss."

I said, "I appreciate the sentiment, but I could really use your skills. That guy is still running around, and I have a lot of vulnerable points. The girl you saw is one. We're another. I want to tie this off into a bow quickly."

Shoshana said, "So it's here only? Find that man and be done?"

I looked at Jennifer and said, "We need to find him first, but that's not the end."

"What does that mean?"

Jennifer raised her eyebrow, and I thought about how much I was going to say. Considering how far I would go in the description of the mission. There was a mystery in Brazil that I wanted to uncover, but in so doing, I wanted to kill every single one of those fucks. It was a dilemma. Deceive them about my true goals, or just spill it all?

And then my Taskforce phone rang with its unique tone, telling me an encrypted call was coming in.

I looked at the phone like it was possessed by a demon. Jennifer showed the same expression.

I held up a hand and said, "One moment." I went to the table, picked it up, and said, "Hello?"

Without preamble, George Wolffe said, "What do you have Knuckles doing in Brazil?"

So they figured out my delay.

He wasn't Kurt, but George Wolffe was an old hand from the CIA's paramilitary division. He'd conducted more dubious operations than the rest of the Taskforce combined, and his loyalty had always been to the men, not the machine. Kurt had run a few missions with him before the Taskforce, and they'd become friends, then coconspirators determined to fix the inherent conflicts between the intelligence community and the military machine. Together they'd built Project

Prometheus from the ground up with nothing but guts and sheer will. I knew he'd taken the loss of Kurt as hard as I had, and I hoped he'd listen to me.

I feigned ignorance. "Sir, Knuckles and Brett were down there for the Hezbollah mission. That's all they've been working on. But before you recall them, I have information from here in Charleston that might be pertinent to their mission."

"They missed their SITREP last night. And the night before that. Today Creed was doing maintenance in the commo room and Knuckles's phone was giving a Prairie Fire alert."

That was the last thing I expected. "Sir? Are you sure?"

Aggravated, Wolffe said, "*Yes,* I'm sure. We've tried to make contact with each of them. Both phones go straight to voice mail like they're turned off. They won't ring through, and they haven't been back to the hotel. We checked. Now I want to know what the fuck you're up to."

I knew instantly what had happened. It was the Russians, and I needed to convince Wolffe of that. I only hoped that Knuckles's Prairie Fire wasn't too little, too late.

I said, "Sir, listen to me. I was right, and the Taskforce is under attack."

I told him what I'd found in Charleston, explaining what I'd done, to include the Taskforce help I'd leveraged. He was incredulous, not even knowing where to begin.

He stuttered, "You . . . you killed Russians in Charleston? With a guy from Thailand? Using Taskforce assets? Jesus, Pike, this is a disaster. What the hell are you doing?"

"Sir, they were hunting me, but killed Kurt instead. No matter what those weenies in the Oversight Council think, we're exposed here, and we need to tie it off."

He took a moment to reflect on the meat of what I'd said, beyond the actions, then said, "You're sure of this? I mean, positive?"

I had never realized in the past how much trust I'd enjoyed with Kurt. If I'd said it to him, it was written in stone, and the floodgates of Taskforce support opened on my word.

I said, "Sir, I'll give you a complete roll-up later, but right now I need Taskforce help. Knuckles is in trouble, and I need to get there as soon as possible. I also need three cell phones drained and a translation of a bunch of Russian emails."

"Pike, there *is* no Taskforce. The president himself has put us on standby until Kurt's death is safely resolved. There is *no* movement."

I wanted to squeeze the life out of the phone. I said, "Fucking go tell him the situation."

"If the Oversight Council hears what you did, it will not encourage them to help. It'll shut us down for good. Hell, they're liable to put us both in jail just to save their asses. It's an old rule of D.C. The first to leak is the whistle-blower. The rest get rolled up."

I said, "Then do it without telling them. You have the talent in the building. You just told me Creed was there today. Shutting us down doesn't mean we can't operate. It just means we're doing it without sanction."

I heard nothing from the other end, but remained quiet.

Finally, he said, "What do you need?"

"What I told you before—strictly support. I need forensic exploitation of those phones, a translation of documents. And the Rock Star bird with a package. I'll do the rest."

He said, "And men? How many operators? You can't do this by yourself."

I glanced around the room, seeing Jennifer, Shoshana, and Aaron waiting.

I said, "I don't need any operators. I have my own team now. And they're a wrecking crew."

22

Nikita walked to the expansive plate glass window to get a better signal, then said, "Has the team arrived?"

"Not yet. They get in this afternoon. But I've got no angle on the target. Both he and the blond girl have disappeared."

That little nugget was the last thing Nikita wanted to hear. It could mean the man was flying here to link up with his team. He still had no idea why Grolier Recovery Services was involved in his mission, but they needed to be stopped. Wherever that guy had gone, it was necessary he be found.

"You've been on the house?"

"Yes. I installed some surveillance kit. The only people who've returned are the little girl and her nanny. They came for about five minutes and left with suitcases."

Nikita squeezed his eyes shut, experiencing the weird feeling of one orb working naturally with his body while the other felt like a marble in his head, his eyelid still registering the sensation of sliding over it. It was something he never grew used to, and it aggravated the hell out of him.

He said, "Tell me you know where they went."

"Yes, of course. They have a house nearby at a place called Sullivan's Island. But they aren't the threat."

Nikita said, "That's true, but they can *contact* the threat. Get the men and get those two under control. We won't need to find the target. He'll find us."

He hung up, sat in the chair looking at the phone, and heard a knock on the door.

What now?

He said, "Come in."

Maksim, the team leader of the men targeting the ombudsman, entered the room, looking hesitant. Which wasn't a good sign.

Nikita said, "What's the problem?"

Maksim's team was the one Nikita had switched out with Simon and Luca. Originally dedicated to the lawyer in the Amazon, he was now leading the primary team against the ombudsman. And he was failing in his duties. Nikita had little patience for whatever was going to come out of his mouth.

Maksim said, "Latest surveillance report. I think we have an issue."

Nikita read the report, the silence growing pronounced, then said, "So you think the commander will not obey?"

"Sir, he's making the daily contacts as instructed, but he's surly on the phone. He's now outside our influence and on the edge. I'm not saying he won't obey, but I believe he needs an extra incentive."

Nikita glared at him. In truth, he didn't like Maksim. Thought him weak. He'd taken on the ombudsman mission, and had so far done nothing but provide excuses, even sending his second in command, Alek, to report failure. It was cowardly. Simon and Luca had taken out Maksim's target in the Amazon, and this man was doing nothing more than giving him another reason for failure against the original target.

One screwup after another.

Nikita laid the report on the table and said, "So you think he'll hold his duty to his badge above his own family?"

"I believe so. Without further encouragement, he very well may."

Nikita leaned back in his chair, rubbed his face, then said, "So we go Ukraine here. I don't get the issue. Show him the pain he'll get."

Maksim shuffled his feet, seeing the stray eye stare at the ceiling and wanting to be anywhere but here. He knew the extreme pressure Nikita was under, along with his propensity for violence. He said, "Okay. If you think that's best."

Nikita sprang up, snatched the man by the throat, and said, "If I *think* it's best? Is that what you said? Because *I'm* the one who fucked this up? Seriously?"

Maksim remained compliant, not even raising his arms at the attack, having seen what Nikita was capable of.

Nikita began to squeeze and said, "I'm sick of this incompetence. Luca and Simon had no trouble with your original target, and you have nothing but mistakes against a *woman*."

Maksim coughed, and Nikita threw him against the wall, saying, "You fucking sicken me. Give him an incentive. Do I need to tell you that?"

Maksim ignored the pain his shoulder took against the wall, straightening up and simply nodding. It took every bit of human effort not to rub his throat, and thereby show weakness. He stood, mute. He saw Nikita's wayward eye stare off into space, then the good one fixate on him with a fury Maksim didn't want to confront.

Nikita said, "Play hardball. Just like Ukraine. You know what that means?"

Maksim nodded. He hadn't been with Nikita in Ukraine, but everyone on the Global Engagement payroll had heard the stories. He knew exactly what Nikita meant.

Nikita turned to the expansive window overlooking the bay, gazing in the distance as if he could actually see the hijacked ferry. He nodded, then turned back around, saying, "Yes. Give him a reason to continue. But no nipples this time. Just a finger. Deliver it to his operations center. We'll save the nipples for later."

Felipe stood in front of the sink in his small bathroom, staring into the mirror. Wanting the man staring back to give him an answer.

They'd set up a command center in the Second Naval District Headquarters building a mere stone's throw from the ferry launch point on Salvador, a decision Felipe was now regretting. The headquarters itself was perfectly situated for the mission—a stately two-story building, with an ornate garden out front, old anchors and other artifacts across the grounds, and an open access to the sea at the back tied into the Salvador harbor. On the plus side, it had the communications infrastructure, planning space, and the ability to launch an assault if they so chose, but it also had a problem: it was a naval headquarters, and the commander of the Combat Divers' Group was using that fact to great effect. He'd stormed into the headquarters and immediately began circumventing any and all attempts by Felipe to control the situation.

Which meant controlling the outcome.

Felipe could see the commander had glory in his head and didn't really care about the outcome. They'd had an initial discussion about overall command, and immediately the navy man had started talking about amphibious assaults involving submarines and over-the-horizon naval infiltrations. It was incredible. It was like the man was trying to justify his budget, and wanted to use every single crazy idea they'd ever rehearsed.

A submarine? Really? Felipe knew through experience that the crux of any assault wasn't the infiltration, but the last five feet to the door. How would a submarine help with that? They'd still have to exit, get in a rubber dingy, and advance. Something they could do very easily from the base he was in right now. But the navy men were adamant about pulling off a Hollywood movie.

The plan was insane. Felipe had been involved in no less than seven hostage-barricade situations—some with the very group they now confronted—and the navy men seemed to think that the theatrics would enhance the mission. He knew they were wrong.

Even as he argued, he thought about his mission. His *new* mission. At one point, with the insanity at peak level, he thought about just acquiescing, because the assault was guaranteed to fail. But he didn't, because he *needed* to control the outcome. A failed assault didn't mean the men on board would kill the hostages.

He looked in the mirror, searching for an answer in the reflection. Wanting a solution to what he'd been given. His choice was impossible. Kill more than twenty innocents to save his family, or kill his family. He knew what the right thing was, but he couldn't bring himself to do it. He would have gladly given his life on an assault to save innocents, and now he was being asked to give his family's life.

He ran the water in the sink and splashed his face. He made his decision. He would control the assault, and he would save everyone on that boat. Every. Single. One.

He heard a knock at his door, and turned from the

bathroom, hesitatingly walking into the small atrium of the apartment.

He opened the door, seeing nobody on the outside balcony. But there was a package on the floor. He picked it up, seeing it was leaking something.

He opened it, and then sank to his knees.

23

The plane lifted off from Charleston, circling around the air force base before putting in the power, throttling out over the Charleston Harbor. I watched my city fall away and wondered if it would be the last time I saw it, because I might be fighting an extradition treaty after what I was about to do.

Once we were out over the ocean at altitude, Shoshana approached my seat, Aaron right behind her. She said, "I must say, you Taskforce guys always fly first class. Are we going to blow this one up, too?"

We were on a Gulfstream 650, an aircraft ostensibly leased to Grolier Recovery Services, but in reality owned lock, stock, and barrel by the Taskforce. Hidden inside its walls was every manner of death and surveillance capability I could envision, giving me a very healthy capability for violence. The last time Shoshana had been on such an aircraft, we'd destroyed it over the ocean, with her very narrowly avoiding death in a parachute.

That had been in Brazil. And now we were going back.

I laughed at her joke and said, "I sure hope not. I damage this one and I'm pretty sure we'll be using a Greyhound bus for future transportation."

The bird itself looked like something Bill Gates or a rock star would use—which is the reason everyone in the Taskforce jealously called it the "Rock Star" bird—with large leather seats facing each other two-by-two and a table in between. Shoshana took the window seat across from Jennifer and Aaron sat down across from me. Jennifer smiled at them but kept banging away on her laptop, doing her usual research for where we were going.

Shoshana took a sip of water from a bottle, then said, "What's up with the little girl?"

I grimaced and said, "Not your concern. She's just a distraction at this point. Probably a bad decision."

Shoshana waited a beat, and when I didn't say anything else, she said, "You know that's a lie. I could see it before you even opened your mouth. You hide your emotion behind some body of armor because you're afraid."

Jennifer tried to pretend she was engrossed in whatever bit of history she was studying, but briefly glanced up from her computer at the exchange, and Shoshana caught it, saying, "Even Koko knows. We all know."

I wanted to tell her to just shut the fuck up, but I knew it would do no good. Ever since she'd married Aaron, she was convinced she'd reached a level of emotional maturity that I just did not have. Because of it, she was always lecturing me like she was a trained psychotherapist, instead of just plain psycho.

I leaned back and said, "Amena knows what she means to me. I don't need to prove it to you. I proved it to her."

I paused a beat, then said, "Just like I proved it to you two, once upon a time. If you remember."

Shoshana snapped back at my words. She'd felt she had the upper hand and wanted to delve into Amena because of it, but *I* was the one who'd saved Aaron solely because she'd asked. No questions, no waffling, I'd done it because I thought it was right, and I hadn't staged a bullshit touchy-feely interrogation after.

Jennifer saw the fight coming and was well versed in it, because it always happened between Shoshana and me. To anyone looking from the outside it would appear as if we wanted to slit each other's throats, but it wasn't like that. It was more like two siblings fighting over a worn-out toy in the toy box. Neither of us wanted it, but by God, we were going to bitch if the other one got it.

Jennifer raised her hand and said, "Pike, stop it. Aaron and I have better things to do than listen to you drive Shoshana into a rage."

I said, "Hey, wait a minute. She started it!" And that broke the tension, with Aaron and Jennifer laughing. Shoshana, having never had a childhood, didn't get the joke, but she smiled anyway, wanting to understand.

Aaron took Shoshana's hand and said, "You spoke the truth about Africa, and I'm here because of it. But I need to know just what it is you're asking of us."

I exhaled and said, "It's helping Knuckles right now. I can't ignore his beacon."

Aaron took that in, then said, "The beacon hasn't moved. It's been on that island since it started broadcasting." He left unspoken why that mattered: if the beacon hadn't shifted location at all, the odds that Knuckles still had it were not good. Or if he did, it was because it was on his dead body.

I said, "Yeah, I understand. We'll see what's happened with the beacon, but I'm more focused now on the clues you guys brought back from the laptop in the hotel room. We have at least two Russian phones we can track, and I have no doubt that his missed contacts and that beacon are because of whoever owns those phones."

"The emails also detailed some other targets the Russians are interested in. Are you looking to interrupt the execution of those missions as well?"

"Maybe. It depends on what we find. First on the deck is Knuckles."

Aaron nodded, toyed with his water bottle, then said, "And second on the deck is vengeance for Kurt?"

I felt my expression harden against my will. I said, "Let's deal with Knuckles."

Shoshana leaned forward, penetrating me with her gaze. She said, "Is Kurt going to affect you on this?"

"No."

She squinted her eyes and said, "Liar. I can see it. You're boiling, just like I was in Africa. You're on a suicide run, wanting to destroy them."

I bristled and said, "It's not like that at all. Knuckles is the priority right now, and Kurt's death won't do anything to alter that mission."

Jennifer raised her eyes from her computer, and Shoshana caught the look. She said, "You see it, too."

Aaron said, "Pike, I owe you my life. It's why I'm here, and I'll do whatever you ask. But I need to know what you're asking."

I said, "Because it might upset your business like Nung was worried about? Because your ex-Mossad contacts in the corporate world are hip deep with Russia, giving them cyber capabilities to hack our infrastructure?"

I saw the disgust form on his face, and immediately regretted the words. Shoshana said, "I misjudged you in Africa. Misjudged your motivations and your loyalty. Don't do the same with us."

Before I could answer, Aaron said, "Pike, I'll give you my

life if it's required. I just want to know what the mission is, and right now, I don't think even you do."

He was right. I could operate on an even keel, I knew, but just below the surface was a need for vengeance. A darkness in my soul that I constantly fought to keep under control, and the loss of Kurt was making that very, very hard. Left unsaid was what would happen if I learned the Russians had killed Knuckles.

Even I had no idea what I was capable of if that came to pass.

Jennifer said, "Pike, I think I found out why that beacon is seventy meters off the coast of the island."

From the time the beacon had been initiated, it had sat just offshore of Itaparica Island, never moving. Since I knew Knuckles was heading there the day he disappeared, we all surmised that the grid was just off a bit. The beacon operated on the cell network, using a GPS chip that was reporting a grid close to the location, but with a greater circle of probable error. Happened all the time.

I said, "What's that?"

"There has been a hijacking of a ferry from Salvador. It's been taken over by a criminal gang, and they're threatening to kill everyone on board. It's making national news in Brazil and becoming a flashpoint for the presidential election. Everyone's talking about it."

"And? What's that got to do with Knuckles?"

"The ferry is offshore of Itaparica. I think Knuckles is on it."

24

Knuckles leaned over and grabbed yet another banana, smelling the fetid sweat coming out from under his shirt when he did so. An animal odor that he'd usually experienced while in a hide-site for a week, not when he was supposed to be enjoying a paid vacation. He leaned back, peeled the banana, and glanced at the guards.

They were still diligent, rotating on time and, outside of a few arguments, not showing the deterioration he had feared.

Brett said, "Same ol' same ol'. You think that beacon did anything?"

"I don't know. I'm sure there's some turmoil going on in D.C. because of Kurt, so maybe not. But we need to be ready. Even if it's some Brazilian JV team that assaults, an assault is coming."

He looked around at the passengers slouching in seats, and caught the eye of one man. One who had looked at him with interest in the past, but not like he was trying to signal anything. More like he was reading the captors for a possible threat, like he was looking for something or someone. He was definitely suspicious.

Knuckles leaned back in his seat and whispered, "I don't think there are four terrorists on this boat. I think there's another one planted in the passengers."

"The guy with the shaved head?"

"Yep. You've seen him, too?"

"Yeah. He keeps looking at us, and not like he's concerned about his welfare. Like he's concerned about what we might do."

Knuckles said, "I know," and continued glancing around. He caught the eye of the woman with the child, now leaning against a bench. She was rubbing her hand on her son's back, and appeared to be waiting on his eyes to reach her. When they did, she squinted, then slightly nodded at him.

Knuckles said, "Interesting."

"What?"

"Nothing. Keep your eye on the starboard guard. I'm going to talk to that woman."

"You move, and you'll get slapped again."

Earlier, Knuckles had made the mistake of walking to the stern, where the water bottles were located. He'd done so without a buddy, as was required. One of the guards had freaked, running at him and yelling. He'd stopped, raised his hands, and received a butt-stroke to his gut, bringing him to his knees.

Knuckles said, "Just moving one row over. I'm going to squat down, below the chairs. Tap me when the guard's looking away."

Brett said, "What about the hyena?" Meaning, the guy they'd both identified as a possible false flag. Knuckles glanced at him and saw his eyes closed.

Knuckles said, "Now better than later. Just keep an eye on him and see if he wakes up."

Brett nodded, and Knuckles sank below the guard's view. He glanced over at the woman and found her staring at him. He winked, and she nodded.

Brett tapped him on the shoulder, and he scuttled down the

row, going over the other passengers on his hands and knees. He reached her and took a seat next to the boy. She sat up, then leaned over, whispering closely. "Are you American?"

He nodded, surprised at her words. Not because of what she said, but because her accent clearly indicated she was American as well.

An attractive brown-haired woman of about thirty-five or so, she dressed and looked like a Brazilian, but then again, that may have just been his prejudice. Throw her into Manhattan and she would have blended in just like everyone else.

He said, "Yes. Like you? Why are you down here with a security man?"

She gave him a quick smile and said, "Yes. I'm American, and I have a security man because I'm in danger here. I need help."

He chuckled and said, "Lady, we all need help on this boat."

She said, "No, you misunderstand. I'm in a powerful position at Petrobras. I'm responsible for complaints of corruption, and I think I've shaken a few too many branches on that tree."

Knuckles looked at her in a new light, saying, "You don't think this is random? You think this ferry was taken specifically because of *you*?"

She nodded, then said, "Have you heard of Carwash? It was a big scandal down here involving Petrobras. Most of the politicians in the national government were implicated on bribes and extortion, and Petrobras was excoriated."

"Yeah, I read about it, from a year ago, but what does that have to do with you?"

"I was hired to clean up the mess. 'A new start' I was told. I came from the United States, outside the politics of

Brazil. I worked as an arbitration lawyer in the oil industry before, and was told they wanted my expertise. I think my expertise was more than they bargained for. The prosecutor who was pursuing the original Carwash case died in a plane crash six months ago. An 'accident.' This is no different."

Knuckles nodded. "I can see how you'd believe that, but these guys have no indication of working with the state. They're the real deal. If it were about you, they'd find a reason to smoke you in the first twenty-four hours. The fact that you're still alive means they're not after you."

She stared at him for a moment, then said, "How do you know?"

"Because I do this for a living."

She nodded, then said, "I thought so. I could tell. My name is Willow Radcliffe. My brother is in the navy. He looks like you."

"Like how?"

She glanced around, then whispered, "He's a SEAL. You know what they are?"

Knuckles almost laughed at the theatrics, but he didn't. He also didn't let on what he did, but the statement was a revelation. There was such a thing as a brotherhood, and it extended to family.

Instead, he said, "I've heard of them. He's allowed to have hair like this and wear Puka beads? I've never been in the military, but maybe I should look into it."

She faltered, realizing she'd made a mistake. She sagged down, cradling her son and said, "Okay. Don't tell anyone what I just said. Especially about my brother. They'll kill me for sure."

The earnestness of her fear made Knuckles's decision easy.

He sagged down next to her until they were shoulder to shoulder. He said, "So why did you bring me over?"

She said, "Nothing. I made a mistake. You looked like my brother. You and your friend. I don't mean your hair or your clothes. I meant your eyes."

She hugged her son and started crying, curling into a ball.

Knuckles put his hand on hers. She stiffened, but didn't move. He said, "You are right, partly."

She whispered, "How? You're like my brother?"

He caught her eyes and said, "No. I'm no longer like your brother. I was him at one point, but now I'm much worse. And so is my partner."

He saw her eyes widen and said, "Why did you bring me over? It wasn't to give me a sob story about your boy."

She looked at her son, then back at Knuckles and said, "Are you serious? Are you as good as you say you are?"

He grinned and said, "Well, if your brother is a SEAL, you already know that answer. Of course I am."

She glanced left and right, then said, "My son has a knife in his sock. My brother gave it to him, and he's never without it. It has caused issues on more than one occasion, but he always has it. And they didn't search him."

Knuckles said, "Like a pocketknife or something?"

"Yeah, but it's huge, and it auto-opens when you flick it. Elliot gave it to him for Christmas. Told him they were no longer making them and that it was a collector's item. The damn thing is dangerous. I've tried to get him to get rid of it, but he won't. He shoved it into his sock the minute this happened."

Knuckles said, "Can you get it to me?"

She nodded, then woke up her son. He rolled over, and she whispered to him. He snaked a hand toward his ankle, rolling up a leg of his jeans. He pulled out something with black slab grips and looked at him. Knuckles held out his hand.

The boy said, "You know how to use this?"

"I do. If the time is right."

He passed it over, and Knuckles recognized the knife—a Zero Tolerance 300. A hefty folding blade much larger than anyone would carry on a daily basis, but built rock solid with a large belly on the blade. It was coveted by men like him, and it was something he'd give, if he had someone to give it to.

The boy said, "Will this help?"

Knuckles looked at Willow and said, "Yeah. It'll definitely help. Have you kept it sharp?"

The boy squinted and said, "Sharp enough to shave." Like he was being tested.

Knuckles grinned and said, "You guys just stay low. Something's going to happen before the sun comes up tomorrow. I don't know what it is, but if it's what I think, you'll be okay."

Willow said, "And if it's not?"

Knuckles looked at the boy and said, "If it's not, then we make our own luck."

25

George Wolffe walked into the West Wing unsure of what to expect. He was now the default commander of the Taskforce, but the Taskforce, as far as he knew, no longer existed.

He'd spent the last four days doing nothing but shutting down operations and burying cover organizations, and then he'd been told to report at the request of the Principals Committee of the Oversight Council—the core group who adjudicated Taskforce activity, but there was no reason for him to be called to brief, because there was nothing to report.

Unless someone had heard about his release of the Rock Star bird and Pike's flight to Brazil.

He went through the security procedures, then waited outside the Oval Office. The door opened, and he entered, seeing President Hannister behind the Resolute Desk and a group of people, all staring expectantly at him.

He marched in between the two couches, faced the president, and said, "Sir, you asked for me?"

President Hannister said, "Yes. Thanks for coming. You know everyone here, I assume?"

Wolffe glanced around the room, seeing the secretary of defense, the secretary of state, the director of the CIA, and the national security advisor. Nobody else.

So, this *was* the principals of the Oversight Council. Which wasn't good. It wasn't about some CIA thing he'd done in his past or some congressional oversight prep work he'd done. He was about to get slammed for releasing Pike, but he had no idea how they'd learned about it.

He said, "Yes, sir. I think we all know each other. I spent most of my time in the back of the room while Kurt briefed."

Hannister nodded and said, "I don't have a lot of time off the calendar, so I'll make this short. We have an issue. Where are we with Taskforce operations?"

Was that a trick question? Wolffe said, "Sir, all operations are on stand-down. We have two teams to redeploy, but nothing of any interest is happening. They're just waiting on flights home. Why?"

Alexander Palmer, the national security advisor, said, "We're getting an inquiry into Kurt Hale's death. We need to put it to rest."

Wolffe turned to him and said, "Who? If it's a press report, give them the standard blurb. What's the issue?"

The secretary of defense said, "It's not a press report. It's some shithead on the congressional select committee on intelligence. He's asking who Kurt Hale is—or was—and wants some answers as to why he was in Charleston. What he was doing."

Wolffe was shocked. Completely blindsided by the statement. He said, "Are you saying someone on the intelligence committee is asking questions about an accidental noncombatant death? In the United States?"

"Yes. That's what's happening. And he's not doing it because he's mildly curious. He's saying he thinks the committee has been kept in the dark, which, of course, they have been. We have no idea why, but we're hoping you do."

Wolffe shook his head and said, "No, sir. I don't. But we own the chairman of the house committee on intelligence.

Easton Beau Clute. He's an Oversight Council member, and he owes us."

He saw everyone glance everywhere but to him, and he said, "What? Use your political leverage. What am I missing?"

Palmer said, "It's not from the House. It's on the Senate side, and it's not a senator. It's some staffer that's digging, and we can't leverage Easton because in so doing we may cause the senator himself to start asking questions."

"Seriously?"

"Unfortunately, yes. We don't even know if the senator is aware of what the staffer is asking. We have no idea why he's doing it, but we're sure if we bring in the House side, it'll just convince him he's right. He's a true believer type. A guy who's been bitching for years about covert action and renditions. He's the one who pushed a vote on the AUMF."

The AUMF—otherwise known as the Authorization for Use of Military Force—was the bedrock of legal authority for the invasion of Afghanistan after 9/11. Since then, it had been used for the invasion of Iraq, Libya, Syria, and the reintroduction of forces into Iraq against ISIS. Pushing a vote for its legality wasn't something Wolffe was against, because in his mind it was way outdated, and now being used far outside of its mandate, but none of the operations conducted by the Taskforce fell even close to legal authority. The only ones who sanctioned his missions were in this room, and he could see why the questions would cause angst. Forget about the AUMF; if this asshole had a thread to the Taskforce, he'd burn it all down.

He said, "True believer or not, he's got nothing to go on. Why's he asking?"

Amanda Croft, the secretary of state, said, "We don't know. That's why you're here. He's discovered you somehow.

Apparently, you're tied into Kurt through the Pentagon phone book. He's now asking the CIA for answers because he found your name."

Incredulous, he said, "How is that? I'm still officially listed as working in the Counter Terrorism Center."

He looked at Kerry Bostwick, the director of the CIA. Kerry said, "George, we don't know. There are so many different conduits. You've been at every Oversight Council meeting—"

Wolffe cut him off, "Which are off the record and not recorded."

Kerry raised a hand and said, "I get that, but every activity you've done—plane tickets, conferences, corporate holdings—has been next to Kurt. This guy has made the connection, and we don't know how. All we know is that he's pushing, and he's asked for the CTC directorate to bring you out. For questioning."

"Are you shitting me?"

"No. Someone's feeding him information, and we don't know who it is, but whoever it is knows something. They knew to point him this way. Which creates a problem."

"Which is what?"

"One, we want to ensure that all Taskforce activities are shut down. We can't have anything go wrong. Two, we don't know who gave him the information to look in the first place. Kurt was a noncombat death. There's no reason to investigate it."

Wolffe said, "And three? That's not enough to get me here. You've all seen the updates. We aren't operating anymore. Do you want me to investigate? Figure out who the leaker is?"

Palmer said, "No. Three is we need you to vacate Washington. He wants to interview you, and we can't let that happen. Kerry has deflected so far, but we need you gone."

Wolffe nodded, then said, "Where? Where am I going as a 'CIA' officer?"

President Hannister said, "We'd like you to go to Charleston. Get out of D.C., and give Kerry here a reason to stall, but also figure out what the police are doing in Charleston. There has to have been something for him to become suspicious, and if it didn't come from here, in D.C., it had to have come from there. Talk to the police down there and see what you can find. There's a reason why this guy is looking at us, and we think it's from Charleston."

Hannister paused, then looked at him with a little bit of harshness and said, "Unless you know of another reason."

Wolffe wondered yet again if someone had found out his actions with Pike. He said, "No, sir, I don't. Sounds good to me. Charleston is the promised land, according to Pike. I'm sure I could stay with him, and I could maybe find something out. Is that it?"

Palmer said, "Yes, that's it. Thank you for the agreement on that. Pike losing Kurt is something we don't want to get out of control, given his past. There is too much in play right now that he won't understand. Get out of town and stay there. And make sure Pike isn't planning something that would be . . . something we'll regret."

Wolffe nodded, realizing the true meaning of this meeting, and hoping his face wasn't betraying him. He said, "Sounds good. Anything else?"

They shook their heads, with Wolffe seeing them starting to close folders and rise. He turned to go and bumped into Amanda Croft on the way out the door. She said, "You have a minute?"

He nodded, and they exited the Oval Office with the rest

of the principals flooding out to attack their regular day jobs of running the most powerful country on earth.

He said, "Ma'am?"

She waited until the hallway was clear of anyone hearing her, then said, "What are you doing about the Prairie Fire alert from Knuckles? I understand that Taskforce activities are shut down, but surely you're doing something? Off the books?"

Amanda Croft was an enigma to him. A firebrand who had achieved the position of SECSTATE through sheer force of will, she'd been against most Taskforce activities because—in her world—diplomacy was better than the violent means Wolffe controlled. But he knew she was also intimate with Knuckles—something nobody else on the Council was aware of.

In the recent past Kurt had brought Knuckles to testify at an Oversight Council update for an operation in Africa, and she'd taken a shine to him. The next thing Kurt and Wolffe knew, Knuckles and Amanda had become an "item." Knuckles was a manwhore of the first order, and it had been a shock at first, but Kurt and Wolffe had kept the secret. It was all close hold in the Taskforce world, and they'd maintained her confidence even as Kurt had confronted her on the relationship. But it was real. "Dating" would be a stretch, but she most definitely cared about his life.

Which begged the question of what she was asking. She was a principal of the Oversight Council, sworn to uphold their activities. Was she fishing for information and using her connections with Knuckles to sniff out subterfuge? Or was she really asking because she cared? Wolffe had worked in the wilderness of mirrors long enough to know he wasn't going to show his cards just because she asked.

He said, "Ma'am, I know about you and Knuckles, but you heard the Council. I can't do anything about him."

She took the comment in stride, knowing he was already aware of the relationship. "Can't? Or won't? I don't believe you'd let a man die because of us politicians. Am I wrong about the Taskforce? Was what Knuckles told me wrong? It's really about the politics and not the man?"

He shuffled his feet and said, "I can't do anything about Knuckles. My hands are tied. I have to go to Charleston and put out some fires."

She looked at him with a touch of disgust and said, "So you're not something different. You're just like us."

She turned and began walking away, and he made a decision. He touched her arm, saying, "*I* can't do anything. But there are others who can."

"Who? Someone I can get in motion through State?"

He saw how earnest she was, and committed. He said, "Not anyone *you* can get in motion."

She relaxed, understanding his words. She said, "Someone I've seen brief before?"

He looked into her eyes for a beat, the silence heavy, and then said, "I can't comment. Officially, there's nothing I can do. Just like you."

She considered for a moment, then said, "*Not* like me. I can help, if I was told how to do it."

He smiled and said, "Well, if you'll stay by your phone, maybe there's something you could do. Behind the scenes."

She nodded slowly, understanding what was being asked. She said, "Do I know him?"

"I can't comment on that."

She nodded again, then pressed forward: "I understand. Are you going to meet someone in Charleston to prevent something, or are you going to Charleston because we asked, and he's already gone?"

With a straight face, he said, "Rest assured, I'd never send someone on a mission outside of the charter. I have no idea what I'll find in Charleston, but I'll be doing my best to execute the mandate of Project Prometheus."

Amanda smiled and passed him a card, saying, "Nice choice of words. That's my direct number. Just in case someone wants to disobey the Oversight Council and you need some advice."

26

Nikita ignored the chopsticks and dipped a piece of nigiri into a tray of soy sauce with his hands, then slurped it down, saying, "Pretty good sushi from this backwater place."

Maksim nodded, staring at the mess he'd ordered. It looked like some toilet roll that had been decorated with fluorescent frosting from the leftovers of a rainbow birthday cake. Alek caught the look, hoisted a piece of sushi with his chopsticks, and said, "Told you. Never go for the chef's special."

Nikita laughed and said, "No, no. That thing is perfect for Maksim. All pretty on the outside, but pure trash when it comes time to execute."

Maksim bristled and Nikita waved his hand, saying, "Calm down. I'm just wondering how much you paid for this room. Since I've given you authority to spend money."

They were sitting in a side alcove of a restaurant called SOHO, on the shore of Salvador and just a stone's throw from the navy base housing the police response for the ferry. From the window, they had a wide-open view of the bay, with nothing but a beaded curtain separating them from the other tables on the deck.

The restaurant was sparsely occupied, and, due to the chill, most of the other patrons were eating inside, but one couple had braved the ocean wind to eat outside, next to the water.

Maksim said, "It was free. I just had to ask. Don't worry, I'm not driving up our expenses."

Nikita said, "Good, because they're getting high enough already." He made no mention of the costs for the help of his cyber friend in the United States, keeping the operation compartmented, just as he did with the teams in Brazil, but this operation in Salvador had forced him to consolidate.

He said, "Where do we stand with the ferry? When can we move on to the other targets? Time is growing short, and I have people to answer to."

"It's tonight. The police captain took your incentive to heart. He's regained operational control, and they plan on assaulting prior to daylight, when the terrorists are at their most vulnerable."

Nikita chuckled and said, "Can we not convince him to attack when they aren't at their most vulnerable?"

Maksim said, "Sir, there's only so much people will believe. A failed raid is one thing, but stupid planning in advance will open up the operation to questions. He'll get what we want. He's going to trigger the explosives on the boat during the assault. It will be enough."

"Are you sure he's on our side?"

Maksim grimaced and said, "No, he's most certainly not on our side. But he'll obey. That finger we sent was persuasive."

Nikita nodded, his weird eye looking over Maksim's shoulder, and Alek finally spoke. "There is another issue, however."

Nikita focused his good eye on him and hissed, "What now?"

"The captain said they're making headway with the terrorists. The government is negotiating, and the terrorists are capitulating. They may just give up."

Nikita dropped his piece of nigiri in disgust. "Is this from the captain? Is he trying to manipulate us?"

"It is from the captain, but I think it's true. There has been enormous pressure placed on the government to get this resolved. There are two Americans—not counting our target—and four from France. It's an international incident, and the government would rather negotiate out of this than assault. The only thing in our favor is that the terrorists are stubborn. The police captain thinks they're about to capitulate, but the government doesn't want to wait this out. Every day causes the situation to deteriorate, and our captain has been given the green light for an assault tonight. It's reached a head, but the terrorists don't know that."

Alek leaned back and said, "They might quit between now and tonight."

Nikita said, "Those two Americans are also our targets. They all need to die. We need a contingency."

Alek said, "Sir, I've already thought of that. We have an observation post in the bell tower of a church overlooking the harbor. We've been using it just to monitor the situation, but it'll duplicate as a sniper hide."

"How does that help?"

"If the terrorists give in, they'll simply drive the ferry into the dock. Once it's there, as the people exit, we can shoot one of the explosive bags. Even if it doesn't cause a chain reaction with the others, it'll kill our target. The police will storm the boat, but they won't waste time with EOD defusing the bags. They'll rush everyone off before they do that, and it leaves them vulnerable."

Nikita smiled, saying, "This is the thought process I'm looking for. Can you make this happen?"

"Yes. It's easy. Just give me the order."

"You have it. Now, what about the next target? Mr. Gabino Alves, the Mines and Energy minister? We're running out of time, and his stranglehold on the oil concessions needs to be broken."

Alek looked at Maksim, liking the compliments and not wanting to bring up bad news. He would leave that to Maksim.

Maksim said, "Sir, since we've consolidated here, we've lost contact with him. He was last seen in Rio, at the Petrobras headquarters. We know he's scheduled to escort a group of Chinese investors starting tomorrow, but we don't know if that means he'll stay in Rio, or go somewhere else."

Nikita scowled and said, "I thought we had enough manpower to track him? Not enough to execute, but enough to keep control of his movements."

"We did. I have a man still on him, but he can only do so much. Gabino has been unsighted at the headquarters for two days. It might just be a question of waiting."

Nikita considered, then said, "We can't afford to wait. If he's left Rio, we need to know. This thing will be done by dawn tomorrow, and we need to be able to react immediately to the next target. I have men on the way, but they won't be here in time. Reinforce the singleton. Talk to the people in the Petrobras headquarters. Find out what he's going to do. We need a pattern of life right *now*."

Maksim hesitated, then said, "Sir, that's going to leave us short here. I have to maintain security on Felipe's wife in the church, then man the sniper hide. Each of those requires at least four. More for the long term. They need to sleep sometime."

"Well, you don't have that. How much could a sniper's hide need? A guy with a gun and a guy pulling security. As for the safe house, one guy inside with a gun is enough. She's a woman."

Maksim said, "Sir, it's not the woman, it's the threat—"

Aggravated, Nikita cut him off, saying, "You fucks have never worked on the edge, where you were supposed to succeed with only what you have. The team only needs to stay awake for one night. Pull one of them."

"We need security outside the site. A man inside can control her, but he needs protection."

Nikita slammed his hand onto the table and said, "Figure it the fuck out."

Both Alek and Maksim jumped at his outburst, then glanced outside, seeing the couple at the table staring at them.

Nikita pointed a finger at Alek and said, "You get to Rio." He turned to Maksim. "You stay here. And I want no more fuckups."

Maksim said, "I'll do everything you ask, but I was wondering about Sergey. He's sitting on a team in Charleston, in America, doing nothing. Can't we get him here to help? He won't arrive until tomorrow, but we could use him."

The words seemed to make Nikita even angrier. Maksim saw his wild eye staring into space and his face grow red.

Nikita said, "Sergey is committed. He's dealing with another problem."

27

Sergey Ivanov watched the small child enter the house, followed by the nanny. He stared at the nanny's rear, carrying groceries with her hips swinging, and thought about what he could do before he killed her.

They entered the side door of the old wooden house, and he studied the street. Getting a feel for the battlefield and his new mission. Yesterday, he'd been on the way to the airport to fly home when he'd been given a redirection. Far from leaving, he was to receive a new team and continue the attack against Grolier Recovery Services, making him glad he'd taken the initiative to follow the nanny from the original target to this one.

The house on Sullivan's Island was located on a side avenue, the second-to-last one on a dead-end street that butted up against a park called Fort Moultrie—some asinine triumph for the United States of America. Sergey hadn't bothered to check out the grounds, because in truth, history bored him.

He'd taken a ferry to Fort Sumter with his now-dead partner, and that had been nothing but a slog through a history of a civil war he cared nothing about. He'd lived through civil wars, having seen the death and inhumanity. Having *provided* the death and inhumanity. He really didn't give a shit about an American one. All he cared about was the mission.

And that nanny's ass.

He keyed his radio. "Target is in. We wait for nightfall, and we go."

28

I got the call from Aaron saying the meeting was breaking up, and he had no good audio. Which was a bummer. We were running out of time, and it was forcing me into an endgame I didn't want to execute.

I said, "Did you get *anything*?"

"Yes. A little. They were in a separate room, but it had a beaded curtain, so the lip-synch game was up. We switched to microphone and picked up a little. But not enough, I'm sure. The translations are broken, but there's enough to prove you were right."

Through the help of George Wolffe and Creed, we'd located the phone that was tied to the Russian in Charleston, and then had traced it to a high-end condo complex in the city of Salvador, Brazil. From there, after about a seven-hour surveillance effort, we'd identified the man who owned it—some freaky-looking guy with an eyeball that was always staring off into space.

Surveillance efforts always took time, sifting out the wheat from the chaff, and I didn't have that luxury. I'd have liked to watch this guy for three days to develop a pattern of life, but one was all I was going to get, because I knew the ferry hostage crisis was reaching an endgame.

He'd left the complex, and we followed, stopping at a sushi restaurant called SOHO. The place had a little bit of a mall around it, complete with a parking garage, so it was no effort to get in undetected. I'd thrown Aaron and Shoshana against the target using a button camera with a little twist from the Mossad: facial recognition software designed to read lip movements.

They'd introduced it to me on another operation, and it was the bomb for outside surveillance. You didn't need to get close enough to hear, you only needed to get close enough to see. Then, the damn beaded curtain had cut that short, but Aaron also had a directional microphone that could be slaved to the same software for translation.

He'd heard something, or he wouldn't have said it, but I knew it wasn't going to be the golden egg. That would only come with wringing one of these guys out, which was where I stood now. I'd already determined that taking out goggle-eye in his gated condo complex was a nonstarter due to the security, but the two at the table presented an additional opportunity. Because they were meeting here, they obviously weren't staying in the same complex.

I said, "Call when they've left the table. We'll pick a target and follow, you catch up."

"Two are leaving. Pirate eye is staying behind."

"Roger that, but his callsign is Hannibal. I'm the pirate. He's the psycho. Calling him a pirate is an insult."

Shoshana came on and said, "Hannibal? Who is that?"

"Someone you might take a shine to. A psychopath."

Jennifer gave me a glare, and off the radio I said, "Come on. You know it's true."

She said, "You ever look in a mirror? She's here because you asked her to come. Just like you came when she asked in Israel. You two are the flip side of the same coin."

I glanced at her and, just to poke a bit, I said, "So that makes you like Aaron?"

She sank back in the seat and said, "No. Aaron is like her. He just hides it."

Surprised, I said, "You think that?"

Because I sure did. I'd seen those two together, and it was a little weird. Jennifer was my backstop in life. Her moral compass had led me out of a forest of evil, and because of it, I trusted her explicitly. Aaron was different. While he had the ability to keep Shoshana in check, he seemed to do so out of tactical considerations instead of any moral constraints. But I was surprised that Jennifer felt the same way.

She said, "Yeah. He's like her. He hides it, but if it came down to murder or the mission, he'd murder."

I said, "So if it came down to the mission here or me, you wouldn't kill?"

She looked at me, and I saw the pain. She said, "No, no. That's not what I meant. Don't put me there, Pike. Don't make me choose between your life or murder."

I held up my hands, shocked at her words. I said, "Murder? Hey, that's not what I meant at all. You said something before getting in that elevator in Charleston. Was that a play? Or did you mean it?"

She glanced out the window of our car, saying nothing. I now feared the response. She might, in fact, have been playing me, and I wasn't sure I could handle such a revelation.

I said, "Hello?"

She turned to me and said, "You said something in the back of an armored car in England. Did you mean *that*?"

A couple of years ago we'd managed to stop a terrorist attack on the London Eye due to some serious heroics on her part, and had been unceremoniously arrested for the help. While sitting in the back of a British paddy wagon I'd blurted out my feelings for her, but before she could even register what I'd said, we were hip-deep in rescuing Kylie—my new nanny—from a bunch of Irish terrorists.

In the end, we'd both pretended as if my words had never been uttered. I now realized she was just as afraid of rejection as I was, and it brought a sense of calm.

I took a step off the ledge.

"Yes. I meant it."

I saw a hint of a smile escape her, and the iPad between us dinged, then our radio came alive.

"Two are moving, I say again, two are moving. Hannibal stayed behind."

I picked up the iPad and saw a picture of two men, one of average height, with a shock of red hair and a mustache, the other thicker, with a receding hairline and crooked teeth. On the net I said, "Roger all. We'll take the follow. Break off of Hannibal when you can. Leave before he does but make it casual. I'll vector you in to our location."

Off the net, Jennifer began prepping for a surveillance effort, pulling out beacons and other useful things. She said, "If I didn't know any better, I'd say you planned that."

I chuckled, relieved at the interruption. I started our vehicle, saying, "I'm good, but I'm not *that* good. Let's get in view of the taxi stand."

The two men who'd met with Hannibal had arrived by two separate cabs, so it was a fair bet they'd leave the same way. Now all I had to do was pick one of them.

We drove around the deck, reaching the exit, the entrance to the SOHO restaurant on our right, and the road out from the little mall area on our left. Right in front of us were three cabs lined up.

We waited, and, looking at the surveillance photos on the iPad, Jennifer said, "Which one do you want to take?"

I said, "I think the guy with crooked teeth. He looks a little older and overweight. The other one looks like he keeps in shape. That means he's a cog in the wheel, used for the hammer, and the other guy is more like management."

"What about Hannibal?"

"Yeah, he'd be the best one, but that bastard is living in a fortress, and so far he hasn't shown anything of a pattern." I slapped the dash in frustration and said, "We need more *time*."

She ignored my outburst, as always, and started packing a small knapsack, saying, "Time is the one thing we don't have. From the news reports, this is being treated like the search for the Boston Marathon bomber, with all the presidential candidates using it as a club. It's going to come to a head sooner rather than later."

I glanced out the windshield, saying, "I know, I know," then the targets appeared.

I said, "There they are."

The two men walked right in front of the garage, and I stared at them hard, wondering if they had been involved in the death of Kurt Hale. Wanting to confront them right on the street. I felt my pulse increase at the thought, and Jennifer caught the change, rubbing my arm like she was calming a growling dog.

I tracked them to the taxi stand, but instead of getting in separate cabs, they both entered a single one.

"Shit."

I needed them separated, just like I did in Charleston. Taking on two guys was asking for trouble.

Jennifer said, "Wait on Hannibal?"

The taxi started moving and I put our car in gear, saying, "No. Let's see how this plays out."

29

We swung out on Avenue Lafayete Countinho, the main coastal road, heading toward the lower old town. We passed the harbor, then the naval headquarters, the front full of police cars and other government vehicles, officials coming and going, all managing the chaos of the hostage crisis. Which was a good sign.

With that much activity, they probably hadn't settled on an assault plan yet. Or maybe they had and now everyone was getting briefed.

We reached the Mercado market and the cab pulled over, dropping the passengers off. I swung in behind it, finding no place to park. The cab pulled away and I knew I was going to lose them.

I said, "On you. Keep in contact with them. Get out."

Jennifer bailed without another word. Singleton follows were the absolute worst, and not something I would have done if I had a choice, but she knew the constraints we were under and took on the mission without complaint.

I circled around the Mercado, now headed back the way I'd come, not finding anywhere to ditch the car. Aaron came on the radio: "We're out. Where do we need to stage?"

I said, "Come to the Mercado. As soon as you find a place to park, do so. Meet me at the elevator."

The city of Salvador was built on an escarpment, where

the lower part, near the water, held the oceangoing economic engine, and the upper part the residential neighborhoods. Since the founding of the city, the citizens have struggled to find a way to overcome the vertical distance between the two, with the Jesuits in the seventeenth century starting the march of progress using a rope and pulley system.

Eventually, in the nineteenth century, they built the world's first public elevator. Called the Lacerda Elevator, after the man who had initially envisioned its creation, it had undergone many renovations, and now it housed four cars that could take more than a hundred people at a time to the top of the escarpment twenty-four hours a day. Standing out as a landmark seen throughout the lower city, it was a tourist attraction as well as a fixture of life for those living in Salvador.

Because of the layout of the city, I was betting that the Russians were headed to the upper level, to their bed-down site at a hotel or house, and the elevator was the quickest way to interdict them.

I whipped a U-turn and pulled into a parking lot in front of a decrepit, crumbling building. I had no idea about the rules for parking, but didn't really care.

I leapt out, calling Jennifer, "Koko, Koko, what's your status?"

"Still on them. They're walking deeper, doing a lot of talking."

"Intentions?"

"Not sure. They aren't headed to the elevator, though."

Damn it.

"Okay. Keep on them. Aaron and Shoshana are inbound."

I locked the car and jogged across the street to the entrance of the elevator, waiting on the rest of the team. We'd either chase after Jennifer, or we'd meet her here later. There was no way they were staying on the lower level, as all the hotels were on top, so sooner or later, they were headed up.

I saw Aaron stalking through the crowds, a half a head taller than everyone else. In Brazil, where everyone on the street was predator or prey, nobody bothered him at all, because he was most definitely a predator.

Behind him was Shoshana, assessing her surroundings while she walked, constantly in a state of red. She would determine a threat four minutes before the threat even decided to rear its head. Together they were a deadly combination, and I was glad I had them.

He reached me and said, "Maybe we should have stayed with Hannibal."

"Yeah, maybe. Let's see."

Shoshana saw my angst and poked my shoulder playfully, saying, "It'll work. Koko will find a way."

No sooner had she said it than Jennifer called. "They're at the train. They're going up."

Shoshana smiled and said, "There you go."

Besides the elevator or walking a five-mile circuitous route to get to the upper city, there was a funicular railroad called the Plano Inclinado Goncalves. Built in the 1800s, it had gone up and down for more than a century before being closed from neglect and lack of funding. It had reopened in 2014 to great fanfare, and was just as popular as the elevator.

I poked Shoshana back, rolled my eyes at Aaron, and keyed my radio, saying, "Koko, roger all. We'll meet you at the top. Let 'em come out first and we'll pick them up."

We turned and entered the elevator entrance, which, far from being like an elevator in a hotel, looked more like a bus station, with lines leading to a lady taking money.

We paid the pittance required, then crammed into a car that was about three times the size of a hotel elevator, riding over two hundred feet to the top. The opposite door opened, and everyone piled out onto a concourse that looked like a concrete boarding gate to an airplane, the view toward the harbor spilling out below us.

We speed-walked past the crowds and exited into a courtyard lined with buildings from the seventeenth century, the exception being a squat one-story mess that was apparently someone's attempt at art deco in 1970.

We jogged past it, and I saw a police presence milling about, then a sign proclaiming it as some sort of city hall, which meant we weren't doing any shenanigans near it.

We kept going until we hit a large cathedral and Shoshana said, "Left. It's to the left."

We reached the back of the cathedral and saw the entrance to the funicular, hemmed in on all sides by buildings. It would be the easiest surveillance box I'd ever set up.

There was a flow of people exiting the station, but I wasn't worried about missing our targets, because unlike the elevator, with four cars that worked 24/7, the funicular had only two cars, and, being pulled up and down the escarpment by a cable, was much slower. I was sure we'd made it to the top while Jennifer was still waiting.

I called, "Koko, Koko, we're set. Status?"

I got back two clicks and nothing else. Meaning she was on the train with the targets and couldn't talk.

I positioned Shoshana and Aaron on the road that led by the entrance to the cathedral, while I took an alley that threaded behind the back, leaving the east-west road we'd used to get here open. It was a risk, but if they were going in that direction, they would have taken the elevator. Why walk a longer distance to the train only to walk back in the other direction where the elevator was located?

Inside the station I could see two empty bays for the trains—really more like a trolley car than a train—meaning one was coming up and one was going down. After about a minute, I saw a car slide into the docking slot, then the people begin to exit. In the line I recognized the targets, but still didn't see Jennifer. I faded into an alcove, waiting.

The riders filed by me, some taking the southern road to the entrance of the cathedral and others heading toward city hall. None came down my alley. Eventually, I saw the redhead, then crooked teeth, and held my breath. Waiting on their choice.

They passed by me, then the road to the elevator, and I called, "Trigger, Trigger. Carrie, they're coming to you."

Shoshana said, "We have them."

"Roger. Koko, what's your status?"

"Coming out now."

I saw her exit the station and showed myself. She jogged up and said, "No issues. The car was so packed I was right next to them. I got a Copperhead on the redhead."

I said, "You're kidding. Where?"

She smiled and said, "Underneath the seam of his jacket. Don't worry, he won't find it like the North Korean's did."

A small disk about the size of a quarter, the Copperhead was a beacon that felt like a cloth bubble with liquid inside. A burst device that projected a signal to satellites, it had an adhesive backing that would let it be affixed to just about anything and a battery life of nine hours of continuous transmission, with a chemical compound that literally ate itself as it expended power.

Once the bubble was broken by Jennifer—which was

how it was initiated—it would blast a signal out every thirty minutes, giving it a life span of a week, which was the good news. The bad news was the signal it gave was so weak that tall buildings had the potential to block it, much like listening to satellite radio in a car in the city, but it would still give its burst faithfully for our satellites to pick up, then transmit to our Taskforce phones. It wasn't optimal, as there were major time gaps in coverage between transmissions, but it was certainly better than nothing.

I smiled at her and said, "Never cease to amaze me."

She slapped my stomach and said, "I'm waiting on the same."

I grabbed her hand to prevent more damage and keyed my radio, saying, "Carrie, what's the status?"

"We're still headed south on Largo de Jesus. They've crossed over into a pedestrian-only area full of restaurants and shops. We're hanging back a bit in case they stop."

I looked at the map on my phone, found the only road with Jesus in the name, and saw they were about a hundred meters away. The pedestrian square ended at a church, with a single avenue running in front perpendicular to the square. I said, "We're going to parallel you on the north side, one road over."

Jennifer and I jogged down an alley on the north side of the square, continuing until it dead-ended into a road called Inacio Acciole. I held up, and Jennifer pointed south, saying, "That's the church at the base of the square."

I could see an ornate façade of carved granite rising into the air, a small courtyard in front, and an alley leading down the side. I said, "Aaron, Carrie, we're set at the end of the square."

Aaron came on, saying, "Pike, they kept going all the way to the church. They just entered."

I turned to Jennifer and said, "What is it? Why would they go there?"

I knew she had already studied the entire city and would have an answer that made sense. I was wrong. She said, "I have no idea. It's the Church of Saint Francis, and it's just a tourist attraction now. The chapel is decorated completely in gold leaf, one of the most ornate in the world. It used to be a convent as well, but now it's just a church. There's nothing inside to see besides the chapel."

What the hell.

I said, "Pull up the Copperhead and see if it's sending."

She did, saying, "Nothing. We're either in between transmissions, or it's getting blocked by the building."

I got on the radio and said, "Carrie, Aaron, stage at one of those outdoor cafes on the square. We'll take the north. Just give us a trigger."

The street we were on was narrow, with cobblestone from centuries past and the buildings butting right up to the edge, leaving little in the way for hiding. There were some shops selling local goods, but unlike the pedestrian square, there weren't any outdoor cafes to allow us to sit and blend in.

I speed-walked down it searching desperately for something to allow us to hang around for a few minutes, and found an open door, sunlight spilling through. It wasn't someone's house. I peeked through it, seeing a dark corridor stretching out to an open area. I entered, finding myself in a hallway that opened up into a courtyard. I kept going, finding some sort of amphitheater, the place overrun with litter and feral cats.

I stepped out onto the stage and they scattered, running like they knew I was a threat. Which I was.

Jennifer, following behind, said, "Didn't expect this."

I said, "We'll stage right here. Wait them out."

Jennifer's phone vibrated and she glanced at it, then did a double take, saying, "I have a beacon lock. It's at the southeast corner of the compound. Outside the chapel, where the old convent was."

Before I could process that, I heard, "Pike, Carrie. Snaggletooth just exited as a singleton. He's headed your way."

Why would only one of them stay inside? And why in the old convent?

I looked around at the deserted amphitheater and had an idea. I said, "Roger all. Close down the back door."

Jennifer looked at me with a question, and I heard Shoshana say, "Why is that?"

I locked eyes with Jennifer, and, into the radio, I said, "We're taking him down right here."

30

Riding up in the funicular rail car, approaching the station for the upper city, Maksim said, "You'd think they'd limit the number of people they allowed inside this thing."

They docked and the old sliding door opened, the people in front of him spilling out. Alek said, "It wouldn't be so bad if everyone took a bath once in a while."

Speaking Russian, neither worried about anyone exiting the car understanding them and taking offense. They broke out into a courtyard, a fountain to their right and an alley to their left. Maksim began walking at a rapid pace, not saying another word until they were past the ancient Saint Basilica Cathedral. Even as he knew nobody could understand him, he took no chances with the words he was about to utter.

When they were finally walking two abreast, with nobody near, he said, "So it looks like you're heading to Rio. Leaving this mess behind."

"Yeah. I'm sorry about that. I don't want to leave you in the lurch."

Maksim chuckled and said, "I'd go, too, if I could. Nikita is losing it, and I don't think it's going to end well. He'll need someone to blame, and anybody here will be on the deck."

"If I go, you're sure you'll still have enough to take care of the woman and the kid, and also execute the sniper contingency?"

"You heard Nikita. We have no choice now. Anyway, it shouldn't be an issue. Let me talk to Kolva when we get in. He's trained. I'll brief him and get him over to the island with a weapon."

They entered the pedestrian square and Alek looked at his watch, saying, "It's getting late, and that sushi restaurant didn't do a whole lot for me." He pointed and said, "That place has a pretty good seafood stew called moqueca or mopeca or something. You want to get some food? We both have a long night ahead."

"No time. If those idiots on the ferry give up and I haven't set the sniper, it's mission fail."

Alek understood the unstated peril for failure and, in truth, was relieved to be leaving, although by being given responsibility for the next target, he would be in the same situation as Maksim very soon, and Nikita would probably be in a worse mental state, if that was possible.

They walked the rest of the way in silence, passing outdoor cafes and art galleries, eventually reaching the entrance to São Francisco Church and Convent. They entered the building, going right by the man selling tickets for admission. He simply nodded, letting them pass.

They walked into an open courtyard in the back, the second floor ringed with a balcony. Maksim said, "Any trouble with the staff?"

"None. The money was enough to keep them quiet. But that might change if they know we're hosting a kidnapping."

They reached a staircase and rose to the second floor, passing rooms no longer used, the wooden door frames crumbling from the ravages of time.

Maksim said, "They haven't even come to see what you're doing? Not curious at all?"

They reached a corner room, the door bigger than the others. Alek said, "No. I told them such curiosity would result in pain. They've seen enough crime down here that they don't want to rock the boat. All they want is the money."

He opened the door and Maksim entered a large suite, the plaster crumbling from the walls, water stains from leaks in the roof framing a window looking onto an outside balcony where a man was seated, surveying the street below. Snaking from a hole in the ceiling was a single bulb hanging from a wire. To the left was a hallway leading to two bedrooms.

Maksim said, "Not too bad."

Alek grimaced and said, "Try shitting in a bucket for a week. It gets old."

"Security?"

"During the day, it's just that observation point on the balcony. At night, I'll post some security in the alley, but it's been quiet for the most part. Biggest threat has been gangs of kids that roam around here."

Alek threw a bit of plaster at the window, waiting until it bounced. When the man turned his head, he waved his arm and said, "Kolva!"

The man rose and entered the room, looking uncertain, glancing between them both. Maksim gave him his new mission, telling him that time was of the essence.

When he finished, Kolva looked confused. He asked, "So I'm not to help on the assault?"

"No. You only engage if that ferry makes it to the harbor intact. If they peacefully resolve this, you wait until you identify the target, then set off the explosives."

"And if they don't go off? I have no idea if a bullet strike will do it."

Maksim didn't even want to think of that eventuality. He

said, "Let them go. We'll have to reengage. Killing her with a sniper shot to the head won't look accidental."

Kolva left to pack his belongings, and Alek said, "With both of us leaving, it's going to set back security on this place. Only four left, and they have to sleep sometime."

Maksim walked down the hall to the room on the right. Inside was a girl of about eight, hunched over in the corner, her arms around her legs. Next to her was an older woman, her black hair askew, her wrists flex-tied to her front, a bandage on her left hand with an empty space where the pinky finger would have been. She'd heard them approach, and grew fearful when they appeared at the door, drawing back as if she were trying to magically disappear into the wall.

Maksim gave not a thought to her fear or the pain he'd caused. He said, "This'll be over tonight. The men can go without sleep for one night. Just make sure whoever you leave in charge knows what to do with the woman. I want this place vacated tomorrow, the bodies gone, no trace we were here."

He went back into the barren living room and Alek followed, saying, "If Nikita wasn't so hell-bent on that guy in the United States, we'd have the men we need without worrying about shuffling back and forth."

Maksim said, "It is what it is. We don't know everything. If killing him helps out, then let's kill him."

Alek scoffed and said, "That guy can't affect us down here. He's in the United States. If he could, he'd be here, which means those men in Charleston are wasting their time."

Maksim said, "I'd rather be in Charleston hunting a single man than down here with this mess. Pay's the same either way."

Alek laughed and Maksim said, "I have to go. Good luck in Rio."

He left, taking the stairs two at a time, walking through the courtyard and back out onto the street. He took a left, thinking about what Alek had said. The men in Charleston could most certainly be used better down here, but he wasn't going to question Nikita.

If the American target was bad enough to scare Nikita, then it was probably worth the diversion of men. His only comfort was that the American couldn't make his current ferry mess any worse. Not unless he could get here from the United States in the next twelve hours on some magic carpet.

Now outside, Maksim saw a blond woman window shopping, looking at a string of leather purses hanging from a wall next to an open door. He recognized her as the same woman who'd ridden up in the funicular railroad car with him and Alek.

She glanced at him, and he smiled.

Holding his eyes, she said, "Execute."

The word confused him. Before he could respond, he was jerked violently off his feet into the open doorway.

31

Jennifer was looking at me like I had a horn growing out of my head. On the net I said, "How far has he gone? How much time do I have?"

"He's still in front of the convent, but he's not window shopping. He's walking with a purpose. We're behind him now."

Off the net, to Jennifer, I said, "I can't see when to get him. Get outside and trigger."

She said, "Pike, think about this. We have no planning in place. No exfil, no security, no nothing. You're standing in an abandoned amphitheater we found six minutes ago."

I said, "No time. This may be our best bet. Get out and let me know when to execute. I won't be able to see him until he's abreast of the door, and by then it'll be too late."

"Pike—"

I cut her off with a snarl, "Just do it!"

She slitted her eyes and didn't move. Feeling the press of time, I wanted to snap at her again, but I knew that wouldn't work. I settled for logic, saying, "Jennifer, this is our best chance. Don't think about Kurt. Think about Knuckles."

She shook her head and started walking back to the street. She didn't even turn around when she reached the door, letting me know she'd accomplish the mission, but not liking where I was headed.

I'd be lying if I said it didn't have an effect. I had been fully planning on killing this guy once I wrung him out, but now I wasn't so sure. I had the same problem I had in Charleston— namely, killing him in a fight was one thing, but putting a bullet in his head after I had him under control was another. It was a cut line with Jennifer, and I understood it.

Even though I *knew* he deserved to die.

Jennifer came on the net, saying, "I have him in sight. About forty seconds. Carrie, you close?"

Shoshana said, "Right behind him. Keeping to the side. You'll see me when he breaks past the alley from the convent."

Aaron said, "Two pedestrians coming up the alley. They might break the plane of the street in view of the kill zone."

I said, "Interdict them. Ask them questions. Act like a tourist."

"Roger. Moving."

Shoshana said, "Two more coming out of a shop. Directly to my front."

Shit. I thought about just letting him go. And then thought about Knuckles, stuck on a ferry with a beacon he trusted. Knowing I was going to move heaven and earth to get him free.

I said, "Koko, distance?"

"Twenty seconds. I have Carrie's targets. They're moving the other way. Backs to us now."

And I felt a surge of energy. If Jennifer had wanted to stop this assault, she wouldn't have made that call. She was intentionally letting me know it was clear. Because she trusted me.

I heard "Ten seconds," and sidled to the doorway, keeping just inside the gloom.

"Five seconds."

I started to pant, feeling the adrenaline rise.

"Execute."

I stepped out of the door and saw Snaggletooth engaging Jennifer across the small street, his back to me. I reached out, grabbed the top of his jacket with my right hand, his belt with my left, and ripped him backward through the door, flinging him into the concrete wall.

He bounced off it hard, landing on his back, but to his credit, he didn't act like an ordinary civilian would, collapsing in total shock. He raised his legs up and rotated his back on the ground like a turtle, seeking the threat.

He found it.

I leapt on him while he was still dazed from the wall, batting his legs aside and locking up his arm, rotating around and jerking forward until he was on his knees, his hand upturned in front of him, the palm facing his nose.

I pressed forward and he screamed. I let up and said, "Stand the fuck up. Slowly."

He did so, finally looking at me. I saw no recognition.

So these assholes down here don't have the target package from Charleston. Or I'm making a big mistake.

I said, "You speak English?"

He shook his head no.

I said, "Portuguese?"

He just looked at me. Jennifer entered the hallway, then Shoshana. I said, "Where's Aaron?"

Shoshana took in what was happening, then glanced my way. She said, "He's on the way, Nephilim."

She used my given name as a spear to let me know she thought like Jennifer, and I'd lost my mind. *As if anything I did could compare to her crazy ass.*

I said, "Lock down the door," then turned to Snaggletooth saying, "He and I need to talk."

Jennifer looked at Shoshana, and they seemed to agree on something. They went to the door, protecting me.

I turned to my target and said, "Look, I know you speak English. I know you're Russian. I know you work for Wagner, and I know you tried to have me killed, but you killed my friend instead."

At that, I finally saw recognition dawn. It brought a spasm of rage, me wanting to break his fucking neck right then. He was complicit, and he would pay the price.

He saw the change in me, and I recognized the fear. Which was good.

Aaron entered the little hallway, speaking Hebrew. Shoshana answered him, and I had no idea what they'd said, but I couldn't let my target know that. Showing confusion to him was showing him a way out.

I glared at Aaron, and he went to English, saying, "We can't stay here forever. I suggest letting Shoshana do the interrogation."

I thought about it, then nodded. Shoshana had a weird ability with people. Not only was she just plain scary, but she was also a trained interrogator. A skill that was more useful than my bashing about, because within three questions, I was liable to just slaughter him out of pure malice. I needed information, and I wasn't sure I had the ability to listen to the answers to get it. The beast inside of me was breaking through the bars.

I said, "Check that door behind you."

He did, and it was a small closet, about eight feet deep. I turned to Snaggletooth and said, "Look, you have one chance here, unlike my friend you murdered. You can tell us what you know about that ferry in the harbor, or you can die."

He locked eyes with me and said, "You and I are in the same profession. There is no reason to lie to me. I am dead. You know it, and I know it."

I said, "Your death will be up to you." I waved my hand and said, "He's all yours, Shoshana. No reason to be easy on him, since he's sure he's going to die anyway."

I saw her turn to him, the dark angel coming out, giving him the full force of her unearthly wrath, and he shrank back. She took his wrist from me, rotated him around, and kicked him into the closet. Aaron followed behind, his gun drawn, saying, "We'll be but a minute."

Jennifer hissed from the doorway. I went to her and she said, "We don't have a lot of time here. The longer we stay, the more the chance of compromise."

I said, "I know. It'll be okay. Just keep eyes out on the street."

Shoshana came out of the little room, floating her weird gaze over me. She said, "How much pressure do you want me to use?"

I said, "I don't give a shit. Faster is better than slower, put it that way. I need to know what they've got on that ferry. What their plan is. How long do we have."

She looked at Jennifer, then back at me. She said, "And when I'm done? I'll get the information, but then what?"

I said, "Just get the information. We'll worry about exfil afterward."

Shoshana left the hallway, and I felt Jennifer's eyes on me. An awkward silence followed. Finally, Jennifer broke it, saying, "You can't kill this guy in cold blood. Let me get him out of here."

Exasperated, I said, "Where, Jenn? Where are we going to take him? Our hotel room? We have no Taskforce assets, and we sure as shit can't let him go free."

I saw her eyes grow cold. She said, "So you *are* going to kill him. And I set him up for that."

I said, "This is about Knuckles and Brett, not about him."

She said, "It's about *you*. You alone."

Shoshana came out, interrupting us, Aaron dragging our target out behind her. He had a little blood running from his ear onto his shirt but otherwise didn't look the worse for wear.

She read the situation, but ignored it, saying, "I have the information. They haven't engendered the ferry heist. It's truly a hostage situation, but they have controlled the outcome. They have a policeman in their pocket who's going to make sure the 'rescue' goes bad, killing everyone on board."

I took that in, saying, "Okay, who's the policeman? How do we get to him?"

"He's the man in charge of the entire assault. Apparently, it's going down tonight."

"What do they have? Are they paying him? What's the control?"

"They have his wife and daughter."

Which caused the beast to slither inside of me. I cocked my head and closed my eyes, not wanting it to take over. Jennifer saw the reaction and said, "Pike . . . Pike . . . this isn't about your family."

I snapped my head up and snarled, "You fucking think that makes it right?"

She recoiled, and Shoshana approached me, getting in my face.

She said, "No, she *doesn't* think that makes it right. But

you could make it wrong. I will do what you ask, but you'd better make sure in your heart."

A shadow blotted out the light from the door, and five youths entered, all of them between eighteen and twenty, laughing and joking. They saw us and stopped. One look at them and I knew they weren't in a Boy Scout troop.

32

The lead man took in our situation, seeing a guy on the ground, his face a little battered, a string of blood running onto his shirt, his hands flex-tied to his front, and said something in Portuguese.

Shit. This just went bad.

I glanced at Jennifer, telling her in one look to get ready. She gave me a long blink, telling me she understood. I stepped in his path and said, "Sorry, no habla."

He smiled and turned around to his friends, saying something else in Portuguese. They laughed, and then advanced. He looked at me and, in broken English, said, "You doing something wrong here?"

I said, "No. You misunderstand."

He pointed at Snaggletooth and said, "What do I misunderstand?"

He turned to our target and said, "Would you like some help?"

Snaggletooth said, "Yes, yes, please. They've kidnapped me."

Aaron shoved him to the ground, and I said, "Look, we don't want any trouble. We have a disagreement with this man. That's all. I'm sure you have the same problems all the time."

The leader turned to me and said, "Well, maybe we all have a disagreement. *You* understand?"

He held out his hand, rubbing his fingers together, asking for a bribe. Shoshana approached, and I looked at Jennifer, then the ceiling, knowing what was coming.

She said, "Get out of here. Now."

He said, "Get out? This is my area. You—"

And that was all he was able to say before she ripped his legs out from under him, slamming him to the ground. Aaron jumped forward, pinning the man to the left against the wall, Jennifer closed on the man to the right, and I thought, *Jesus Christ. Can't anything be easy?*

Two of the men fled at that point, leaving the rest under our control. Shoshana leaned over the leader, getting in his face and saying, "You will leave here right now, if you want to live."

In our focus on the threat, the one thing we'd forgotten was our target. I stalked to the guy who looked like the second in command, the one Aaron had pinned, and caught a flash of movement. I whirled, and Snaggletooth sprinted by me, right out the open door.

In an instant, I realized our mission was about to be compromised. If that guy got free, Knuckles was dead. I turned to Jennifer and said, "On me," then whirled back to Aaron, saying, "You got this."

Shoshana squinted her eyes at me and I said, "They're all yours," then raced out the door, chasing down a guy who could eliminate any chance of saving Knuckles.

I entered the street, heard Jennifer fall in behind me, and looked left and right. I saw our target running flat out away from the church. I took off after him, the sparse pedestrians glancing at us and jumping back. He wove down the cobblestone streets, dodging pedestrians, and I slowly gained.

I heard Jennifer's feet behind me, keeping pace. She was just as fast as I was, but I was wishing it were Brett behind me. That man was a freak on foot, and we'd have this guy in a bag within a block. But that wasn't going to happen, because he was currently captured on a ferry, about to die, and the man I was chasing was going to cause it.

He glanced back, saw us getting closer, and dodged into a new alley, sprinting flat out. We followed, closing the gap to fifty feet. He kept going and burst out into a square, the expanse of space covered with some type of drum troop, all of them banging away and dancing. On the far side of the square was a cardboard cutout of Michael Jackson plastered to a balcony, an open door beneath with a string of T-shirts for sale with his image.

He dodged through the drummers, the men jumping left and right trying to avoid him, and we followed, closing to twenty feet. He glanced our way, saw us gaining, and a drummer stuck his foot out, tripping him. He hammered the cobblestone, skidding forward in front of the open door with the Michael Jackson memorabilia.

I snatched him off the ground and piled into the door, finding myself inside some sort of exhibit. I saw a black man on a stool, looking at me in shock, a stairway behind him. I said, "I'm with the American FBI. This man is a criminal."

Snaggletooth started to fight me, and I punched him in the nose, then dragged him behind the man and up the steps to an open room, flopping him on the ground.

Jennifer reached me and said, "What the hell do we do now?"

The black man ran up the steps, saw us, and said, "You didn't pay."

It was surreal. I had a guy at my feet with his hands cuffed and blood on his collar, and this guy was asking for money? I said, "Pay for what?"

"Pay for the picture."

I looked at Jennifer and she said, "This was the location for a Michael Jackson video. This man's house was used. He makes money now by tourists taking pictures."

I shook my head and said, "You have to be shitting me. Switzerland with Queen and now this? Is there any country we go to that doesn't have a rock star?"

She grinned and said, "Not yet," then turned to the man and said, "Yes. Sorry. We're going to need quite a few pictures." She held out a wad of cash—more than he would make in a month—and said, "Will this work? Can you keep anyone else out while we take them?"

He saw the money, grinned, and said, "Yes, yes. That will work. I'll keep people away."

He disappeared, and Jennifer looked at me. "Now what?"

I honestly didn't know. The target looked at me as well, waiting. I could kill him now, which is what I wanted to do. Maybe. I wasn't sure. I hated him, no doubt, but it no longer rose to the level of murder. And I thought I had a way out. Something to solve the problem of keeping him off the street while not killing him. But it would take a bit of work.

I called Shoshana, "Carrie, Carrie, you there?"

I got back "Yes."

"Status?"

"We're good here. Location?"

I gave it to her, then said, "Don't come here right away. Go get your vehicle. I want to transport this guy somewhere else."

Jennifer watched me, but said nothing.

Shoshana said, "Roger all. Do we need a place outside the city?"

Meaning, *do we need a place to dump a body*. Jennifer heard it and slowly shook her head.

I looked at her and said into the radio, "No. You said they had control over this guy through the police, right?"

"Yes."

"Well, I'd like to turn him over to the police. All I need is a vehicle."

I saw Jennifer's eyes open wide, taking in my words. She had been sure I was going to kill him. And I really wanted to. But she was right.

I thumped Snaggletooth on the head, bouncing it into the floor, saying, "This fuck doesn't control me. Only you can do that."

I saw the relief wash across her face like a wave, and she said, "What did you mean with Shoshana? About the police?"

I said, "It's the longest of long shots. But it's worth pulling the trigger, and might just be the key to saving this shit show."

She said, "What're we doing?"

I smiled. "Turning him over to the police."

She looked at me like I was crazy, and I probably was.

I dialed my phone, calling George Wolffe.

33

In no particular hurry, George Wolffe let the other passengers flow around him, all anxious to get out of the Charleston International Airport. Having a carry-on, he went straight to the car rental counter.

He got his keys, then walked out the door to the rental lot, checking his watch to make sure he wasn't going to be late. He unlocked a late-model Hyundai Sonata, threw his suitcase in the trunk, then felt his phone vibrate.

Seacrest.

He pulled out his Taskforce phone and saw a blocked number. He answered, saying, "Hey, bud. Being the president's son doesn't mean I'm at your beck and call. You still work for me."

He heard, "What?"

"Who is this?"

"It's Pike, and I need some help."

Wolffe was momentarily confused. He said, "Pike?"

"Yeah. Why would you think I'm Veep?"

Wolffe laughed and said, "I just landed in Charleston. I'm meeting him for dinner."

Wolffe heard the same confusion through the phone that he'd felt. "Why on earth are you in Charleston? What's going on?"

Wolffe told him of the Oversight Council meeting, ending

with, ". . . it seems getting me out of the district was the best course of action. You know how it is. Hide until it blows over."

Pike said, "This isn't going to blow over. That asshole is getting a feed from the Russians. This isn't random."

Wolffe took a seat behind the wheel of his car and said, "Whoa. Come on. Let's not go all conspiracy theory here."

"Sir, I'm telling you this is planned. Someone down *here* is feeding that narrative. It's not in Charleston. They're trying to get us to quit."

Wolffe started the car and exited the airport, saying, "Pike, I think that's a bit much." He heard Pike start to protest and cut him off, saying, "What do you have? What's the point of this call?"

Pike told him, and Wolffe couldn't believe how quickly he'd become operational. But he should have known when he'd allowed him to go. Turning Pike loose was guaranteed to get results. All that remained was whether the results were something anyone wanted.

Wolffe heard the words coming out of the phone and almost rear-ended a car trying to get onto Interstate 26. He slammed on the brakes and said, "Wait, wait, stop. You have a Russian contractor under your control?"

"Yes. He's in the trunk of my car."

"Jesus Christ, Pike, what are you doing?"

"I'm saving Knuckles and Brett, *that's* what I'm fucking doing. And I need your help to do it."

Wolffe said nothing, entering the flow of traffic toward Charleston. He heard, "Hello? You still there?"

Finally, he said, "What do you need? You said no operators. I can't give you manpower."

"I don't need manpower. I need the U.S. State Department.

There are U.S. citizens who are hostages on that ferry, and I'm betting the State Department is involved. Have we offered the Brazilian authorities military assistance? Given them advice on how to solve the problem?"

"Pike, I have no idea. That's not what we do."

"Well, it's what we do now. I need to get in to the head man. The guy running the show, and I need to do it in the next four hours."

Wolffe looked at his watch and said, "Pike, it's after five here. After six your time. There's no way that's happening. Everyone's gone home."

Even as he said it, he remembered Amanda Croft's words. Pike said, "I don't give a shit what time it is. Jesus Christ, this isn't a nine-to-five problem. There's a crisis down here, and I can solve it. I promise the crisis response cell here in Salvador didn't break down at five P.M."

Wolffe smiled in spite of himself. Before he'd been buried for years in the political world of D.C., trying to get men like Pike the operational authority to work, he'd been operational himself. In truth—like Kurt Hale—he was more Pike Logan than a Senator Covermyass.

Pike started in on another tirade and Wolffe cut him off, saying, "You might be in luck. Let me make some calls. The SECSTATE is on our side."

He heard Pike exhale, then "Seriously?"

Wolffe laughed and said, "Yeah. Apparently, Amanda Croft has a thing for Knuckles. Which I'm about to use. Stay by your phone."

Pike said, "Thank you, sir. I can't keep this guy in my trunk forever, and Jennifer won't let me kill him."

Wolffe hung up, wondering what sort of shit storm Pike had started. He thought about the breach of intelligence.

In his heart, he knew it wasn't true, because it was just too crazy. There was no way some staffer on the Senate Select Committee on Intelligence was compromised by a Russian influence effort. That was just wild internet ramblings.

But Pike had a supernatural ability to ferret out things like this. Wolffe had seen it in the past, and he'd always been proven correct. If he said he believed it was coming from Brazil, it just might be true.

He crossed the Ravenel bridge, saw joggers and walkers enjoying the view. He envied them. Their biggest worry was the weather. They didn't have the heavy weight of death on their minds.

He'd hoped this diversion to Charleston would allow him the same experience as the joggers, giving him the chance to relax for a moment. And maybe get a touchstone for Kurt's death. He'd helped form the Taskforce with Kurt from the ground up, and, while he would never show it, felt Kurt's death like a brand burning into his skin.

All he wanted was closure. He wanted to believe it was a bad gas line in an old Jeep. Not that someone had hunted Pike and ended up killing Kurt. But if that's where it led, he wouldn't shy away. He'd get the vengeance Kurt deserved, regardless of what the Oversight Council said.

And he had a wrecking machine to do it.

34

Sergey watched the man leave the house, walking without a care in the world, not looking for the danger he represented. The inside of his car was starting to stink, Gatorade bottles full of piss on the floor and cigarette butts scattered about. Sergey had been in place for over eight hours, and now he finally had what he wanted. It wasn't fully dark yet, but it was close enough.

He watched the man reach the end of the driveway and thought he wasn't that much of a threat. He was fit, no doubt, but he didn't survey his surroundings like a predator. He might be a challenge in a ring, when he knew the attack was coming, but he was too stupid to react to a threat that appeared out of nowhere. Sergey decided his plan was correct.

The man entered a car and drove away.

Sergey clicked his radio and said, "It's time. Get here."

He heard, "You said wait for darkness. The sun hasn't even set. Let's wait."

Sergey said, "We don't know how long that fuck's going to be gone. Get your ass here. It's now."

He heard, "Roger. On the way."

Ten minutes later a car pulled up with three men inside. Sergey exited his own vehicle and said, "Park it right here. For easy access."

The men started withdrawing weapons, checking chambers,

turning on lasers, and loading magazines. Sergey gave them the time to work, then said, "You ready?"

The lead man nodded, and they walked up to the front door as bold as if they were delivering a UPS package.

Sergey knocked, and the nanny answered. Before she could say a word, he put a barrel into her face. She melted, and they flowed in.

Sergey said, "Where's the girl?"

The nanny stammered, saying, "She's not here. She went to play."

Sergey slapped the barrel into her forehead and said, "Don't lie to me."

The younger girl sprang up from behind a couch and tried to run through the open door. He caught her in his arms, whirled her around, and slammed her into a wall.

The men behind him laughed at the display. One closed the door, effectively cutting off any escape.

The girl sat up, holding her head. Sergey walked to her and said, "Lay on your belly."

She said, "No."

He raised his pistol, but instead of putting it on her, he aimed at the nanny. She cringed. The girl lay down, the other men pinning her to the floor.

Sergey said, "We don't want to hurt you."

The girl fought the men for a moment, then stopped. She said, "You have no idea of the pain you're asking for."

In complete control, Sergey leaned down, getting into her face. He was humored by the response. He said, "Really? I don't?"

She looked at him with unadulterated hatred and said, "Yes. You should leave here now."

"And why is that?"

She said, "Because I'm family."

Confused at the answer, and wanting to show he was in control, he slapped her face and stood up, saying, "What's that got to do with it?"

The girl actually smiled at him, a twisted expression full of rage.

She said, "Everything."

35

I pulled into a small parking lot across the avenue from the naval headquarters, right in front of a decrepit building constructed sometime in the nineteenth century, but now abandoned and rotting from the inside out. It was the closest place I could find without trying to penetrate the police barricade—which, given that they searched every vehicle, made driving right up to the headquarters a nonstarter. I most certainly couldn't let them find what I had in the trunk. At least not yet. I wasn't so sure about the safety of the lot, though. There was plenty of space, but no other cars, which had to be for some reason.

I looked at Jennifer and said, "Keep on your toes. Anyone gives you shit, show them your badge and tell them we're with the U.S. State Department. If it escalates, give me a call."

She grinned and said, "I think we can handle not getting towed."

I smiled. "That's not what I'm worried about. More like another goon squad showing up wanting the car stereo. It's getting dark, which may be why nobody else is parking here, but you can always sic Carrie on them. They screw with you, turn her loose. It'll be like Stephen King for real."

I glanced at Shoshana, waiting on the inevitable give-and-take we always enjoyed. I didn't get it. She said, "Nephilim, just get us the chance to help the ferry."

She floated her gaze over me, and all my attempt at humor left. I said, "I will. I promise. Get to work on an assault plan for the convent. Figure out the room from that beacon lock and the best way in. Leverage the asshole in the trunk to confirm."

Jennifer was already working the issue using satellite imagery, Google Maps, and a reach-back to Creed at our secret Taskforce cell for any blueprints of the church. I said, "Aaron, you ready?"

He said, "Not really. I think maybe you should go in alone."

I said, "We've been over this. Two is better than one. Two experts on counterterrorism, here to give some advice. I go in by myself and I might be shuffled to the back. Two counterterrorism commandos? We'll look like an official delegation."

"I'm not American. We start talking tactics, and everyone will know."

I laughed and said, "Get out of the damn car. Nobody in that room will know the difference between Israeli or American tactics. And I want to team up on the police chief. Trust me."

He nodded and I said, "At the end of the day, what you know is what I know. There is no difference."

We exited the car and he said, "You do the talking."

I said, "Fine by me. Just make sure that badge is visible."

It had been a whirlwind since I'd tackled the guy in the Michael Jackson house, with me coordinating the exfil of the target, then coordinating for my entrance into the vortex of the hostage rescue of the ferry. I'd originally thought my call to Wolffe would be wasted breath, forcing me to make a choice about killing the asshole we'd captured, but it hadn't. Amanda Croft had come through.

I hadn't spoken to her personally, but I would, because her intervention had given us the ability to potentially solve this damn thing. We'd been given U.S. State Department badges, and access to the crisis site, ostensibly as experts in hostage rescue because U.S. citizens were on the ferry.

We'd arrived at the U.S. consulate in Salvador and everyone had looked at us like we were superhuman, breaking open the heavens for help. Amanda's call had put them all on edge, and we were treated like royalty. I'd taken the badges, turned to leave, and one young girl had stopped me, saying, "You're here to stop that ferry thing, aren't you?"

I'd said, "Ferry? What are you talking about? I'm just here for a conference."

She turned away, embarrassed, and I broke protocol, because if this went bad, at least someone would remember I'd tried.

I touched her arm, she turned around, and I winked, saying, "Yippee ki-yay, motherfucker."

She looked at me like I'd lost my mind, and I said, "Never mind."

She scurried away, and Jennifer slapped my arm, hissing in my ear, "You are *not* allowed to talk to Department of State people. *Ever* again."

I laughed, exiting the consulate, saying, "We got the badges."

Now, we were about to use them, but I still didn't like leaving the car. The final rays of the setting sun were leaving our parking lot in a gloom that wouldn't matter in the United States, but was asking for trouble in Brazil.

I tapped the driver's-side window and Jennifer rolled it down. I kissed her on the lips, saying, "See you soon."

Shoshana flicked her eyes to Aaron, then squinted. He sighed, muttering, "Thanks for that."

He went forward to the passenger side and did the same. Jennifer looked at me, and I could see the laughter wanting to break out from her eyes. I winked at her, and Shoshana got her kiss.

We walked away and Aaron said, "I'm getting sick of competing with you two."

I jogged across the avenue and said, "I thought I was the loser in this shit."

He laughed and said, "You have no idea how much she's obsessed with you."

I glanced at him and he said, "In a good way. Trust me."

We reached the first ring of police and I grinned, saying, "As long as it's in a good way, I don't mind."

A uniformed officer stopped our advance, saying something in Portuguese. I held up my badge and said, "Get me the U.S. State Department liaison."

He looked at the badge, then at me. He said something into his radio. Thirty seconds later a short, balding man pushed his way through the crowd. He reached us and said, "You the terrorism experts?"

I held up my new badge and said, "Yes."

He stuck his hand out, saying, "Thank God. Alonzo Walsh, State. I'm in over my head here, barely treading water."

I shook his hand and said, "I'm Pike Logan. This is Aaron Bergman. We need to see what they have planned."

He turned and said, "Follow me."

As we walked up to the front door with him he asked, "Who are you with?"

"Another government agency."

He glanced at me, but didn't push it figuring we were CIA.

He opened the door and I saw a whirlwind of activity, men rushing in and out, and a large table in the center of the room strewn with papers and photographs. On the wall behind the table was a map of the harbor, three men pointing at it and talking options.

I said, "Where's the commander? The guy in charge? I need to meet him."

Alonzo nodded and said, "Felipe Costa. He's the commander of the BOPE unit here. Sort of like our SWAT teams. He's usually in an office down the hall."

He started walking toward the left, down a narrow corridor adorned with pictures of naval battles and portraits of old dead guys. I asked, "Does he speak English?"

Alonzo stopped at the third door and knocked, saying, "Yes. Pretty well."

Someone behind the door shouted in Portuguese, and Alonzo opened the door. Seated behind a desk was a man of about forty-five, with a shock of black hair and a pencil mustache. Alonzo introduced us, and I could tell Felipe was annoyed.

He came around the desk and shook our hands, but said, "This is a Brazilian problem. Understand that up front. This is not, nor will not become a United States operation, no matter how many citizens you have on that ferry."

I turned to Alonzo and said, "We need to speak to Felipe alone, if you don't mind."

Alonzo went from me to Felipe, then back to me. He couldn't decide if he should be insulted or happy. He chose happy, saying, "Fine by me. I want out of this whole mess."

He left the office, closing the door behind him. Felipe crossed his arms over his chest and said, "I have significant problems here and do not have time to entertain two American FBI agents."

I don't know who told him we were FBI, but if he wanted to believe that it was fine by me. I said, "Felipe, we know you have significant problems. Bigger than just some crackpot hijackers. Russian problems."

His mouth fell open and I said, "I have a Russian in the trunk of my car right now. I want to turn him over to you. Not just to the police, but to someone you trust. Someone who can keep their mouths shut. I know these assholes have leveraged your family for your compliance. I'll get your family back. In return, you'll let me and Aaron in on the assault of the ferry. Sound good?"

He was speechless.

I said, "Felipe?"

He found his voice and said, "Who are you?"

"Just somebody who hates those Russians as much as you do. Do we have a deal?"

"No. Give me the information. I'll get my family back my way."

"Felipe, if this is to work, it has to remain secret. You can't leave here. How are you going to do that? You're the commander of the biggest crisis in the country. If the Russians think you're working against them, they're liable to cause some other disaster on the ferry. Trust me on this. It's what I do. I'll get your family back. You get the Russian in my trunk."

He considered me for a moment, then somebody stuck his head in the door, rattling off a sentence in Portuguese. Felipe answered him, then, after he'd left, he said, "I have to go. They're ready to brief me. The assault is happening tonight. There's no way I can stop it now."

I repeated, "Do we have a deal?"

He nodded his head. I couldn't imagine the pressure he was under, but he seemed to be handling it well. He said, "Okay. Wait here. The next men that enter the office will be the ones to take custody of the man in your trunk."

He opened the door, then turned, asking, "I had already resigned myself to their deaths, and now you've shown up. Are you as good as you seem to think you are?"

"Better. I promise."

36

Kylie took Amena's hand and gave it a squeeze. Amena looked at her and saw fear, but also a little quiet strength. Amena squeezed back, but in truth, she held no fear. This wasn't like Switzerland. This was the United States. She'd been through the fire, and had absolute belief in her new family. If anything, these jerks had made a significant mistake.

Kylie said, "Be strong. We're going to be all right."

Amena furrowed her brow and said, "Of course we are. Why would you say that?"

Amena's blind faith caused Kylie to smile for the first time. She said, "Yeah, honey, you're right."

But Kylie didn't believe it. She knew what these men were capable of, having been on the brunt end of a group just like them. Her only hope was Nicholas Seacrest, and he wouldn't return for hours. Even when he did, he'd walk into a killing field. These men would ensure it. And the leader kept leering at her, causing a different unease. He may not do anything to Amena, but Kylie was fair game.

They'd been inside for close to two hours, sitting on chairs in the kitchen without being given any reason for the intrusion, and she could tell the leader was getting antsy.

He entered the kitchen, nodded at the two men watching them, and Kylie shrank back. He said, "What the hell is taking your boyfriend so long?"

"I told you, he went to dinner with a friend. He's not going to be home until late."

The bald man leered at her, then put his hand on her thigh and said, "Lying to me won't make me go away. But maybe if you offered something else, I might think about it."

She slammed her legs shut, knocking his hand away. She said, "Don't."

He laughed and said, "Or what?"

"You're making a mistake. If you leave here now, I promise I won't tell them."

He laughed again and rubbed her thigh, causing her to cringe. He said, "You miss why I'm here. I *want* them to know about this. It's the whole point."

He passed her a cell phone and said, "I'm sick of waiting on your boyfriend. Time to get this in motion."

Confused, she said, "Who do you want me to call?"

"Pike Logan."

Amena heard the name and it caused the first spike of fear in her. The fact that he knew Pike's name and wanted Kylie to call him meant that this was bigger than a simple home invasion. They were here because of him. Just like had happened in Switzerland. She was going to be punished because of something he had done.

And then she remembered her own phone. A Taskforce one with a special application that had saved her in Switzerland. A way to tell Pike they were in trouble. She surreptitiously glanced at the bald-headed man, seeing him engaged with Kylie.

She slid off the chair and the bald-headed man saw her immediately, saying, "What the fuck do you think you're doing?"

She recoiled, saying, "Nothing. Nothing."

"Get back in the chair."

She did, seeing Kylie tremble. Kylie said, "What do you want me to say to Pike?"

"Just tell him what's happened. I'll do the rest."

"Why?"

"Because you want to live. That's why."

Amena only half-listened to the conversation, looking at her backpack, and the salvation inside of it.

For all of her youth, Amena was more mature than most her age. She knew that Veep would be coming home, and walking into an ambush. She also knew that the minute these men called Pike, he would unleash a vengeance they could not comprehend. She'd seen it, up close. And yet she understood that Pike's actions would only be retaliation, not salvation. He was too far away to stop what they had set in motion. Unless she could short-circuit their plan.

Which required her to get her phone. There were four men in this house, and she needed to give Veep a fighting chance. She needed to split them.

She looked at Kylie and said, "Call Pike. Do as they say."

Kylie shook her head and said, "No. No way."

The bald man grabbed her by the hair and said, "This could be a pleasant diversion for you. Or for me. Make the call."

Kylie started to weep and Amena said, "Do it. Before he hurts you."

Kylie took the phone, looked at the leader, and said, "You have no idea what you're about to do."

He grinned, showing tobacco-stained teeth. He said, "Let me worry about that. Dial."

She did, punching in the numbers and waiting for the call to go through. Amena saw the leader and the other men fixated on Kylie. She paused a beat, then leapt off her chair, racing to the sliding glass door at the sunroom in the back of the kitchen, snatching up her backpack as she passed it.

She had a split-second gap of surprise before the two security men sprang up. She frantically worked the lock on the door, the men leaping over chairs to get to her. One came within arm's length when she ripped it open. She went through it, and the two men collided together trying to stop her, spilling onto the ground. She sprinted out of the back of the house, leaping over a small picket fence and running straight into a park. She heard the leader shout at the men to follow and dug into her pack on the run.

Struggling to maintain her pace while searching the bag, she rifled through it until her hand settled on metal. She pulled out her phone. The one given to her by Pike Logan. She threw the pack behind her, hoping to slow the men, and tapped on the music app, still running as fast as she could.

She tried to scroll to a specific song, but had trouble running and reading at the same time, the darkness hindering her. She glanced behind her and saw the men coming, but far enough away. For a split second she slowed to a fast walk, ignoring the men and concentrating on the phone. She found the song.

U2's "I Still Haven't Found What I'm Looking For."

She clicked on it, shoved the phone in her back pocket, and began sprinting toward the ancient brick walls of Fort Moultrie.

She heard the slap of footsteps behind her and ran as fast as she could, knowing her phone could bring devastation on these men.

She just wasn't sure anyone was listening to it.

37

George Wolffe took a bite of his hamburger and said, "I swear, my phone hasn't stopped ringing since I came down here. I should have gone to a cabin in the woods."

Nicholas Seacrest laughed, but without any humor. Wolffe could tell he was nervous. Wondering why the acting commander of the Taskforce was in Charleston instead of Washington, D.C.

He put him at ease, saying, "Hey, kid, I'm here because they want to hide me. I'm not checking up on you."

Seacrest nodded, picked at his plate, and said, "Well, it's sort of strange to see you show up unannounced. Does my dad know you're here?"

Wolffe laughed and said, "It was your dad who told me to come."

"Did he tell you to send Pike?"

His beer halfway to his lips, Wolffe paused, wondering what to say. How far to go. Wondering if the president's son would value the Taskforce mission over loyalty to his father.

Seacrest saw the reticence and said, "It was a good call. Just in case you're wondering. Don't worry, it's not like I talk to my dad every day giving him an update."

Wolffe smiled and said, "Then no. The president of the United States has no idea what I've done. But others do."

"Who?"

Wolffe's phone rang. He looked at the caller ID and said, "Speak of the devil. This never ends."

"Who is it?"

"SECSTATE. Hang on."

Wolffe walked out of the bar onto the deck surrounding the restaurant, Seacrest seeing him talking and waving his hands in the air. When he returned, he said, "I'm going to throw this damn thing in the ocean."

"What's up?"

"Nothing. Croft helped Pike in Brazil, and because she did, she thinks she deserves constant updates."

"Why does she care?"

"No reason. Other than political."

Seacrest laughed and said, "Other than sleeping with Knuckles, you mean."

Shocked, Wolffe said, "You know about that?"

"Shit, sir, he's on my team. Of course I know."

Wolffe took that in, then changed the subject, saying, "Why's this place called Poe's? What's up with the 'Raven Burger' on the menu and the Edgar Allan Poe memorabilia?"

"A little historical legacy. Edgar Allan Poe was stationed at Fort Moultrie down the street when it was still an active-duty post, and apparently he got a lot of inspiration for his books here."

"No shit?"

Before Seacrest could answer, Wolffe's phone vibrated again. He cursed, saying, "That's it. Into the ocean."

He answered, and Seacrest heard, "Which phone?"

Then, "Why?"

Finally, "No way. Check the transmission. Pike's in Brazil. That's a mistake."

Wolffe hung up, looked at Seacrest, rubbed his face, and

said, "Creed's telling me that Prometheus Three is transmitting a Prairie Fire emergency, here in Charleston, but Pike's in Brazil."

Seacrest snapped up, saying, "Prometheus Three? That's Amena's phone."

"Amena? The refugee? She has a Taskforce phone?"

Seacrest leapt out of his chair saying, "Yes, she does. Those fuckers are here, right now."

Wolffe saw the fear on his face and said, "Whoa, wait. Let's not go crazy. It could be anything."

Seacrest grabbed his jacket off the back of the chair, threw a wad of cash on the table, and said, "You do what you want. Amena is with Kylie. And both are in a safe house picked by Pike. I'm out of here."

He jogged to the door and Wolffe followed, saying, "What are you going to do?"

Seacrest didn't answer, running to his car in the parking lot. Wolffe reached him and put a hand on his arm, saying, "Take a breath here. We need to explore a bit before we charge in like a bull."

Seacrest said, "Can you work a weapon? Do you know how to use one?"

Wolffe chuckled at his eagerness, saying, "Son, I was shooting people in a country you couldn't find on a map while you were in grade school. Take a breath here."

Seacrest opened the trunk of his car, exposing an arsenal of weapons. Wolffe saw it and said, "Jesus Christ. What the fuck is this?"

"Pike said the men who killed Kurt might be coming back. I'm the one dedicated to protecting them. And I've wasted my time talking to you instead of protecting them. That alert is real. Amena or Kylie set it off."

Wolffe could have waffled. Should have waffled. As the commander of the Taskforce, he should have taken some time to figure out the state of play. Should have ordered Seacrest to stand down. But he'd seen men killed in the past precisely because of such actions.

He said, "You got something for me?"

Seacrest handed him a piston-driven H&K assault rifle and said, "Can you work that?"

Wolffe took it and said, "Yeah, I can work it." He pointed at the trunk and said, "What were you going to do if you were pulled over by the police?"

Seacrest slammed the trunk closed and said, "Tell them I'm a Navy SEAL. Instead of getting arrested, I'd become a hero on the news."

Wolffe smiled and said, "Where are we going?"

"The safe house. And we're hitting it hard. You good with that?"

Wolffe snapped the charging handle back, chambering a round, saying, "Oh, yeah. It's about time I could do something besides talk on the phone."

38

Shoshana took a seat at the outdoor table, aggravated at her assignment, even after she voiced her concerns about the target itself. Assaulting a church was bad. She could feel it in her core, but even given that, she knew, no matter what Pike said about her worth, he feared her skills. Feared what she would do if she were on the assault team.

Sitting within view of the church, at an outside cafe, Pike waited until the waiter had taken their drink orders before bringing out a tablet and starting his brief.

He said, "We don't have a lot of time for this mission. The BOPE guy told me the ferry assault is going down tonight, which means we need to do this quickly if we're going to have any influence on those actions."

He set the tablet on the table, showing Jennifer's research efforts, saying, "I think this is enough information to execute the assault. Anyone disagree?"

Shoshana said, "We have enough information, but the target should give us pause. I don't like attacking a church."

Pike said, "I don't like it, either, but it is what it is." He waited on her to continue, and when she did not, he said, "Okay, from what you guys found, it's the corner room, in the old guest suite for people visiting the convent. We know they keep an observation post on the balcony, and have to assume they have at least three inside. The balcony OP is the first target."

He turned and said, "That's you, Jennifer. You're sure you can get up?"

"Yes. There's scaffolding on the south side alley. They're doing renovations. It'll be easy."

Aggravated at her tasking, Shoshana cut in, saying, "If it's easy, I should go. We don't need her climbing skills here. We need what I bring."

Pike paused and said, "What's that?"

"You know. You beyond anyone else knows."

Pike looked at Jennifer, letting her give the response, and Shoshana saw he wondered about her as well.

Jennifer leaned back and crossed her arms, insulted. She said, "I can do the mission. Why are you asking about this? Because I questioned your willingness to murder a guy in cold blood? Because of that you now don't trust me?"

Shoshana said, "You're going to kill that observation post, and he won't see it coming. You're not going to ask him to surrender."

Jennifer said, "Yeah? So?"

Pike said, "So she's just making sure you can do it. It's a legitimate question."

"Because I didn't *murder* that guy in Charleston? The one with his hands in the air saying, 'Don't kill me'? Is that why? Pike, you know better than that. There is right and there is wrong. That's all. This is right."

Pike looked embarrassed, but Shoshana could tell Jennifer's actions in Charleston were *exactly* why he was asking. He pressed ahead, saying, "Okay, but Shoshana's got a point. When I call, you need to drop him, no questions asked. I don't give a shit if he's reciting the rosary or praying for his mother with cancer. He dies. Can you do that?"

Jennifer squinted, and, while nobody else at the table could feel it, Shoshana saw the heat coming out of her. Jennifer said, "Hold up your hand."

Confused, Pike did so. She said, "Your other one."

Intrigued, Shoshana sat up. He switched, spreading out four fingers, the fifth, the pinky finger, nothing but a stump. Jennifer said, "You remember when you lost that?"

Shoshana saw he knew where this was going, but she didn't.

In a cold rage, speaking in a monotone, Jennifer said, "*I'm* the one who killed the men in that room. I'm the one. The woman in this church lost the same finger, for the same damn reasons. Evil people with an agenda. That man on the balcony is complicit in torturing a mother and child, and I'll bring him the vengeance he deserves—*while* we assault. Don't *ever* question my commitment. But if we secure the target and a bad guy is still alive, wounded or otherwise, we're not murdering him in cold blood."

Pike slowly nodded, and Shoshana saw a hidden strength inside Jennifer she hadn't recognized before. Something Shoshana yearned to own.

Shoshana was an unrivaled killing machine, but deep inside she hated the talent she'd been given. In the past, Shoshana had executed targets just because she'd been ordered to, and those actions had caused her unimaginable pain because she'd known she was killing innocents, all on the order of a man who was evil. Unlike Jennifer, she hadn't been strong enough to say no.

It was a quality Shoshana revered. A thing that, in Shoshana's mind, made Jennifer something better.

She said, "I shouldn't have doubted you. I meant no insult. Truthfully, I just don't want to sit out front doing nothing but pulling security."

Jennifer relaxed, nodding at Shoshana. Aaron spoke for the first time, saying, "This is not our mission. We support, and we have to lock down the front door. Prevent interference. That's your job. Enough discussion."

Coming from anyone else, Shoshana would have snarled an answer. Coming from Aaron, she simply nodded, saying, "I understand."

Exasperated, Pike said, "Are we done?"

Shoshana gritted her teeth and Pike said, "Okay then. You stay right here. You're squirter control for anybody who runs out of that church and early warning for anybody trying to get in."

He didn't wait for acknowledgment, turning to Jennifer. "You got the OP. When I'm outside the door, I'll call. You drop him, and Aaron and I are breaching. You meet us inside."

Once again, he didn't wait for any questions. He turned to Aaron and said, "We've got the assault down the alley. Final door, up the staircase, and in. Anyone inside that's not a forty-year-old female or a child is dead."

He looked around the table, his eyes daring the assembled group to respond to his next question. "Anybody have anything to add?"

Shoshana thought about asking for a better mission, but Aaron caught her eye. She remained silent.

Pike said, "Okay, then. Jennifer, you go first. Call when you're on the roof, and we'll work our way to the alley. Shoshana, you stay right here. We'll be back within ten minutes."

Jennifer stood, put on a small backpack, and began walking

away without another word. No witty banter, no kisses, no nothing. Shoshana realized Jennifer had been deeply insulted by her words.

Shoshana stood, and Aaron touched her arm, saying, "Let her go. It'll be okay. Let her focus."

Shoshana nodded, unsure, and Pike's cell phone rang. He took a look at the number and said, "Jesus Christ. What now?"

He answered, and Shoshana saw his face blanch. She read him in only the way she could, and saw his aura go black.

He said, "Don't worry. Don't worry. I'll get help," then a pause, followed by "No, *you* listen to *me*, you fuck. Let them go."

He said nothing for a moment, then clenched his fist, turning in a circle, looking like he was going to lash out at the first person who approached. His aura went to red. In a voice from the grave, he said, "You let them go and I'll let you live. You don't and I will carve you up."

Then he looked at the sky and said, "Okay, Okay. Don't hurt them. Promise me that."

He heard a few more words, then put the phone down. Whoever had called had hung up.

She said, "What was that?"

Still thinking about the call, Pike glanced at her with a ferocity she'd never seen before. An animal hatred that rivaled her own. He said not a word, dialing his phone. It rang out, with nobody answering. He tried another number, and got the same result.

He tilted his head back and screamed into the air, causing the patrons in the restaurant around them to whisper and stare.

Aaron stood up and said, "Pike, what is it?"

Panting, Pike said, "They have Kylie and Amena. The Russians do. They told me to stand down or they'll be killed."

Pike was close to hyperventilating, his breath coming in short gasps, his hands unconsciously squeezing like they held a man's throat.

Aaron turned to Shoshana and said, "Pay the bill," then took Pike's arm and led him into the middle of the square, away from everyone else. Shoshana threw much more than was required on the table and followed.

She saw the red remained. Pike was on the verge of exploding.

Aaron said, "What happened?"

"I fucking told you. They have my daughter and her nanny. Kurt's niece. I can't get anybody to answer their phone. Veep's cell rings out. Wolffe's cell rings out. They've killed them, I'm sure. And they want me to stop."

Shoshana said, "Your daughter?"

Pike shook his head and said, "I meant Amena." He squeezed his fists again and muttered, "I'm going to kill every single one of those fucks."

Shoshana saw the unadulterated pain, like alcohol on an open wound, and said, "We can stop here. Let what they have planned go. I'll come with you to Charleston."

He looked at her in anguish, saying, "And then the woman and child in the church die. Along with Knuckles."

She saw his pain and said, "I'm sorry." She touched his cheek, saying, "We must do what is right."

Jennifer came on the radio, saying, "This is Koko. I'm set."

She saw Pike take a breath, getting control. Returning to normal. His voice as cold as a stone in a river, he said, "Time to execute."

He turned and walked away. Shoshana looked at Aaron and said, "He's not ready for this."

Aaron nodded and said, "Just stand by. There's still a woman inside who needs saving."

He turned to go, and Shoshana pulled his arm, bringing them close. She said, "Don't get killed because he's out of control."

He smiled and said, "Stand by the radio. If anyone can shut him off, it's you."

39

Seacrest took a right on the adjacent road from the safe house, driving with only his parking lights. He wanted to get close, but not close enough to trigger a response. He said, "We need to approach the house from the rear, but it backs up into the Fort Moultrie park, so we can't get there in a car."

Wolffe said, "What are you thinking?"

"Stop one road over, walk into the park, and hit the place, hard."

"We get in a gunfight here, it's going to be messy. We have no cover here in Charleston. No embassy to run to."

Seacrest looked at him and said, "Messy is better than the alternative."

Wolffe pulled back the charging handle on his H&K and said, "I'm with you."

Seacrest pulled the car over next to a squat brick house on a narrow blacktop road, trees surrounding the residences built in the seventies. He said, "This is it. The target is one road up. We'll swing around the Intracoastal Waterway. There's a dock at the end of the park. The target house has two breaches: the front door and a sliding glass door off of the kitchen, facing the park. We'll circle around it, I'll breach the glass door with a rock or brick or whatever I find, and we assault. You good with that?"

Wolffe said, "Good running around Charleston with an assault rifle looking for a gunfight? Yeah. Beats talking to the Oversight Council, even when we get arrested."

Seacrest laughed in spite of himself, saying, "Pike picked this house because of the location. They're all rentals around it, and all of them are vacant. We could probably set the damn thing on fire and nobody would notice for hours."

Wolffe nodded and said, "Let's get it on."

They exited the car in a rush, the street black, no lighting at all. They circled around a one-story ranch, reaching a backyard that butted up against the Intracoastal Waterway behind Sullivan's Island. Seacrest began jogging, dodging yard ornaments and jumping over fencing. They reached a large concrete dock, a wide open expanse of grass to their left.

Seacrest veered into the green, seeing light spill out from a lone house at the end of a street. He took a knee, saying, "That's it. The door is on the east end."

Wolffe squatted down next to him, saying, "We only have a two-man assault. Need to dominate quickly. If we give them time to mass, we'll lose. We need to kill them one at a time."

Seacrest nodded, and they advanced more slowly, eyes bouncing left and right, barrels forward, looking for a threat. They reached the yard surrounding the house, a small four-foot picket fence marking the territory.

The sliding glass door was open, a sheer curtain flapping in the breeze from the wind. Just inside the door was Kylie, sitting in a chair sideways to them. To her left was a man with a weapon, leaning against a wall.

Seacrest whispered, "We're outside the ring of light. You get close, right up against the wall. I'll pop that guy from here, and you enter. I'll be right behind you when he drops."

Wolffe nodded, then realized they had no radios to coordinate. He said, "What's the trigger?"

"That guy hitting the floor."

Seacrest's phone vibrated in his pocket, and he silenced it. A second later, Wolffe's went off. Wolffe silenced his as well, grinning and saying, "Looks like someone is trying to stop this thing."

Seacrest said, "Too fucking late for that. Go."

Wolffe went forward, avoiding the light spilling out from the house, snaking over the small fence and sliding down the wall until he was next to the open door. He could see nothing but blackness in the park, but knew that Seacrest could see him from the spilling of light. He went to a knee, his weapon ready, and waited, looking through the door.

He saw the man fiddling with his rifle, and Kylie twitching in the chair. The fear on her face clawed at him, and he glanced back into the darkness, wondering about the pause, feeling the adrenaline coursing through his veins. Begging for the assault to begin.

He heard a muted spit, whipped back around, and saw the rifle man's head explode. He fell forward, Kylie screamed, and Wolffe entered the house, his weapon seated into his shoulder. He scanned the room the girl was in, saw no threat, and turned to the next room.

He entered it just as a man came running into the kitchen, so close Wolffe didn't even get the chance to fire. The man collided with him and Wolffe reacted instantly, dropping his weapon on its sling, cinching the man's neck, and throwing him over his hip, slamming him into the floor.

By the time he landed, Seacrest had entered, gun and eyeballs looking for a threat. Kylie jumped toward him and Seacrest said, "How many? How many in here?"

She said, "That's it. Just two."

Wolffe punched the man on the ground in the face, hammering him until he went unconscious, then stood up, regaining control of his weapon and holding the barrel a foot away from the man's head.

Seacrest hissed, "You're sure? No more in here?"

Agitated, Kylie said, "Yes. The other two are chasing Amena."

Seacrest stiffened at the words and said, "What?"

"Amena. She ran out the back. She's being chased by the other two."

"Does she have the phone Pike gave her?"

"I don't know. I think so. She ran out of here with her bag. Nick, they're going to kill her."

The elation of their perceived success vanished. His face grim, he turned to Wolffe and said, "Get me the feed from that Prometheus alert. Send me a grid from her phone to mine."

To Kylie, he asked, "Where did she go?"

Kylie pointed and said, "Right out that door."

Seacrest glanced at Wolffe and said, "This site is all you. I'm outta here," and raced out the door.

Wolffe started working his phone and the man at his feet woke up. Wolffe pointed the barrel at the man's head, talking to Creed and getting the Prometheus alert sent to Seacrest.

The man rolled over, sat upright, rubbed a glob of blood from his nose, and chuckled. Wolffe hung up the phone and said, "Glad one of us can laugh about this. Even if it's someone who failed a Mr. Clean casting call."

He turned to Kylie and said, "Find something to tie him up with."

The man said, "You have no idea of the pain you've just

brought yourself. We would have only killed the girl. Now we'll kill you and anyone connected to you."

Wolffe ignored his words but kept the barrel on him, watching Kylie stand up unsteadily. He asked, "You okay?"

She nodded, saying, "What about Amena?"

He said, "Veep's on it. Shouldn't be too long now. Find something for this guy."

The man continued, saying, "This doesn't have to be ugly. We get what we want. When I talked to Pike, he was agreeable. You should be, too. Trust me."

Wolffe heard the words and, incredulous, he leaned down until they were face-to-face. He said, "You called Pike? And told him you had these people as hostages?"

"Yes. Just like my men will have whatever you hold dear hostage. Let me go."

Wolffe shook his head, unable to assimilate the stupidity. He reiterated, "Does Pike know you tried to kidnap Amena and Kylie?"

Confused, the man repeated his threat, now sounding weak, "Yes. Like is going to happen to you."

Wolffe dialed his phone, wanting to short-circuit the wrath that was coming. The phone rang out to voice mail. He cursed.

Kylie said, "What's wrong? We're safe."

Wolffe looked at the man on the ground and said, "You have no idea what you've done."

The man spat out, "*You* have no idea."

Wolffe squatted down and raised the man's chin with the barrel of his weapon, saying, "In this world there is a measure of skill waiting to be exposed, whether it's playing football or playing a piano. Very few reach a master class of talent. It takes something to trigger. Something unique to get an ordinary human to do extraordinary things. Usually, it's pain in life."

The man looked at him in confusion, wondering where the conversation was headed.

Wolffe tapped his head with the barrel of his weapon and said, "Pike Logan's talent is death, and he learned it through the loss of his family. You were dumb enough to threaten his new family, and because of it, you just elevated him into the master class."

Wolffe dropped his chin and leaned back. He said, "Pike doesn't care about your mission. He doesn't care about your money. He doesn't care about your threats. He cares about his family. He's the fourth horseman, and you opened the seal. Far from *you* stopping him, I might not now be able to."

40

Shoshana sat at her table like a guard dog on a porch waiting on its owner, perking its ears at every twitch of noise. The waiter came back to her, confused, saying, "I thought you had left. You paid the bill. Did you want change?"

She said, "No. You can keep it. I'm just waiting on someone. Can I get a glass of water?"

He nodded and left the outdoor area, retreating to the interior of the restaurant. Shoshana returned to watching the street, restless.

She saw a group of youths advance through the pedestrian area, laughing and horseplaying with each other, but with a violent edge. She tracked them with her eyes, seeing that others avoided them. They were a threat, and she wondered if she should alert Pike and Aaron. She decided against it, then heard her radio come to life.

"Koko, Koko, this is Pike. I'm about to penetrate the alley. What's your status?"

Jennifer said, "I'm good. On the roof over the balcony. The OP is in position, and I have a clear shot."

"Roger all. Carrie, Carrie, you have lockdown of the front?"

She keyed the mic and said, "This is Carrie. Front is secure. But I still think this is a mistake. We should not be assaulting a church. It's bad. Bad all the way around."

She heard, "Yeah, I agree, but I don't get to pick where terrorists stay. I just wipe out the nest, wherever that ends up."

Looking at the square around her, trying to pinpoint her unease, she said, "It's not the church itself. It's something else."

She waited, then heard, "You want to help here? I think I have your bad feeling right now, where I'm at."

It was a confirmation of her fears. Something bad was out there, and only she and Pike could sense it. She said, "You feel something, too, Nephilim?"

She heard, "Yeah, but it's not because of some damn ancient church. It's because I can't get to entry. I don't want a gunfight. I need quiet, which means I need you."

"So you want me to do what?"

"Walk down this alley from the back. Expose any threat that prevents our entry."

She said nothing for a moment, disgusted. She snarled, "That's what you want? Me as bait?"

Pike came back with the same ferocity, saying, "Carrie, this is the threat. *This* is what I feel. And this is what I need."

She understood that Pike was finally asking for her skill. Wanting what she offered even as he'd sat her on the sidelines for the same reasons. It was time to get in the fight.

She stood up and said, "This is Carrie. I'm moving to the south of the alley. I'll be coming south to north. I'll have the light on my phone going."

The waiter came out with her glass of water and she said, "Sorry. I have to go."

She jogged to the end of the pedestrian square, seeing the group of youths right in front of the church, laughing and drinking out of something in a bag. They glanced at her but made no move to interfere.

They were not the threat.

She used a road on the south side to circle around the back of the church, walking rapidly in the darkness. She reached the rear of the building, a two-lane thoroughfare running behind it. She saw a group of men standing outside an auto repair shop, the light from an overhead lamp making them look sinister.

She began gliding down the back of the church and they had no idea she was even there. She saw the balcony of the target room, then the man in the observation post, sitting in a chair watching her. She tried to locate Jennifer on the roof and failed due to the light. But she knew she was there, and that the man had minutes to live.

She reached the alley Pike was on, pressed against the wall, and glanced down it, seeing nothing but trash on the cobblestone lane. She pulled out her cell phone, turned on the flashlight, and began walking like she belonged.

She was hyperaware, all of her senses assessing her surroundings. She felt the very air around her, sensed even the hairs on her arms, everything coalescing in a kaleidoscope of protection only she could generate. She walked forward, waiting on the inevitable.

And then it happened.

A man came out from the side of the alley and attacked. She blocked his strikes, kneed his groin, grabbed his head by the hair, and another man slammed into her, bringing her to the ground. She began fighting, unleashing a ferocious response. The first man bounced her skull into the stone, stunning her, then the other wrapped up her legs, preventing her from moving. They gained the upper hand, she saw a blade, and then they were hammered by a cyclone of violence, one man ripped off her like he'd been sucked into the vortex of a tornado, and the other releasing her to fend off the new assault.

She locked up his arm, twisted hard, and he fell to the ground, screaming in pain. She saw Aaron above her, a suppressed Glock 23 in his hand, but he did nothing. Letting her work.

The man shouted in Russian and she realized this was about the target. They weren't random criminals looking for an easy score. They were here for Pike.

She turned to the other fight in time to see Pike Logan lose control. Pike had wrapped up the man from the rear and the target surrendered, dropping his knife and holding up his one free hand, begging for his life. Pike ignored the gesture, his face a mask of rage, snapping the man's neck like he was making kindling for a fire. She was shocked at the action.

She'd killed on command for the majority of her life, and, while she knew most were justified, others who had died at her hand hadn't deserved it. She'd never had the strength to say no, and she wanted to believe that Pike was different. Seeing Pike kill the man when he was no longer a threat—when he was actively giving up—left her bare. She wanted to believe he was pure.

He was not.

She looked at him standing over the body and said, "You were worried about me going crazy? What was that?"

She read confusion and doubt, his aura changing. He pointed at the man she held and said, "Let's go. Put him out."

She nodded, then asked, "Permanently?"

She saw him look at the dead body at his feet, then he said, "No. Not permanently."

She knew Pike didn't understand what the man underneath

her represented. She said, "He's Russian. He's not a common predator. He's here for *you*."

She waited on the order, not wanting to hear what she knew was coming. The man at her feet stared up at her, completely under her control. The command didn't come. She saw Pike grappling with himself, the rage bubbling out again.

Shoshana said, "Pike?"

Pike looked at Aaron, then back at her; she saw his aura turn a vibrant red.

He hissed, "Kill him."

She forced the man onto his stomach, him begging for life. Her left hand still controlling his arm, she held out her right for Aaron's pistol, and Aaron hesitated. She looked into his eyes and he slowly shook his head, but he handed her the pistol. She put the suppressor against the man's skull, and he whimpered.

She held it there for a heartbeat, then whispered, "No."

She looked at Pike and for the first time in her professional life drew a line. She said, "No, we don't kill this man. It's not right."

Aaron gave a slight nod and she torqued the Russian's wrist back hard, causing the man to keen like a wounded rabbit. She snapped the bone, and he passed out.

She looked at Pike and said, "I will not push you into the abyss."

41

Amena sprinted through the darkness, reaching the parking lot of the Fort Moultrie visitors' center, the men behind her still coming strong through the grass of the park. She reached the road that separated the modern center from the ancient fort itself, and a light rain began to fall. She heard the slapping of feet on the asphalt of the parking lot and darted across the road.

She reached the walled exterior of the old fort and went left, following the brick and stone until she came up against a chain link fence that was anchored to the edge of the wall.

She scaled it, flopping on the far side, now into the fort itself. She sprinted up a berm until she was adjacent to a radar tower built during World War II. She squatted down, listening.

She heard the men searching, trying to find where she had gone. She peeked over the side of the berm and saw them frantically probing the fence line, then one pointed down it, into the old bastions leading to Charleston Harbor and away from her.

That wouldn't do.

Her goal was to keep them out of the house, and she knew that if they didn't find her—if they ran down the fence line without discovering her—they would return to the house for further instructions, possibly taking Kylie somewhere else. She couldn't afford for them to give up.

She stood, a part of her brain wondering about her sanity. A year ago, she would have fled the area completely, leaving behind the threat and leaving Kylie to her fate. Now she was embracing it.

Because of family.

Pike Logan had broken open heaven and earth to save her once, and he would do so again. She just needed to play her part, which meant keeping these jerks in the game.

As they walked away, she frantically searched the ground around her, her eyes settling on a cinder block laying in the grass. She kicked it over, letting it roll off the berm and crash into the pavement below. The men turned around at the noise, and she gave them a half second of her shadow in the harsh glow of a vapor lamp, then sprinted away.

She heard them coming, heard the chain link rattle from their climb, and she darted into a tunnel, waiting in the dampness, an emergency exit bulb faintly illuminating the stone, but she didn't need the light. She knew exactly where she was.

Constructed during the Revolutionary War, Fort Moultrie had the distinction of being the site of the first major patriot victory over England. Since then, the fort had been built and rebuilt as a coastal defense for the United States, finally falling into disuse after World War II. The repeated renovations had left the old fort riven with a mishmash of bunkers, batteries, and armories all interconnected by tunnels, and had become Amena's playground. Since they'd moved to the safe house, it was the only place that Veep let her go alone. With the presence of the national park police and heavy tourist traffic, he'd allowed her to leave their safe house and scamper across the grounds. Because of it, she knew every square inch.

Unlike the men chasing her.

She heard the men rattling around like drunks near the old radar post, then begin rushing down the hill, reaching the entrance to her tunnel. They were so close she could hear them breathe. One said something in Russian, and she heard the footsteps separate.

She crept away from the entrance, wanting to always maintain an escape route. Always leave herself a way out. She knew this tunnel went all the way through the fort, with bunkers left and right. She slid down the stone wall until she reached an ammunition hold built for the Civil War, knowing it had a ladder that led to the surface in the rear. She entered it, crouching down and scurrying across the concrete. She knelt in the darkness, breathing with an open mouth and listening.

She heard footsteps in the tunnel, then a shouted command, the two men trying to coordinate a systematic search, one outside and one inside. The footsteps grew louder and she saw a flash of light.

A gun light.

The flash startled her, and she felt a moment of panic. Like an idiot, she'd expected the men to be operating on her playing field. If she had to run in the dark, so would they. Or so she'd planned.

She knew the bunker was barren concrete, with nowhere to hide. She realized she was caught. She'd expected them to run right by, and then she'd come out, make a noise, and cause them to run in a different direction. But that wasn't going to happen.

She heard the footsteps slapping concrete, the light flashing closer and closer, and reached for the ladder. She began climbing, getting into the shaft above the bunker, pulling her feet up out of sight, and then heard the other one above her, shouting directions. She froze, not wanting to make a sound.

She saw the light reach the entrance to her bunker, then heard the man say something in a language she didn't understand. The man above her shouted back and moved on. She clung to the ladder like a spider in a rainstorm, afraid to move.

She saw the light enter the bunker and felt her phone vibrate, demanding attention. She ignored it, waiting on the man to leave.

He did so, the space falling blessedly dark.

She pulled the phone out of her pocket and hit redial for the missed call. It connected and she heard Nicholas Seacrest, breathless, "Amena?"

She whispered, "Yes. Yes."

He wasted no time determining her status, saying, "I have a grid, but it's showing you inside the fort. I'm coming, but I need to know where you are. The grid is off."

And she relaxed.

There were very few people Amena trusted on this earth, but Seacrest was one of them. He'd saved her life in Switzerland, and since then, since the death of Kurt, he'd proven that he cared. He was family.

He wasn't Pike Logan, but he *was* a wrecking machine.

She said, "The grid is correct. I'm in the fort. There are two men after me, and I'm going to set them up for you."

He said, "Set them up? Wait, I'm at the fort. Where do I go?"

She gave him directions to the fence, then for where she was, saying, "You'll see the end of the tunnel when you reach the berm. I'm coming straight out of it. The man in here will be chasing me."

She heard nothing for a moment, then, "I'm over the fence. I see the tunnel. Stand by, I'm coming in. Don't put yourself in jeopardy. I'm here."

She watched the light fade from her bunker and said, "I'm coming now."

She heard, "Amena! No!"

And she took off running. She heard the man with the gun light whirl at her noise, and then give chase. She sprinted as fast as she could, hearing him shouting in Russian to his partner. She broke out into an open field, felt the breath of the man right behind her, and then heard him grunt like he'd been hammered with a sledge.

Still running flat out, she looked behind her, and saw the man on his back, Veep above him. She slowed, turned around, and the man sprang up, bringing his weapon to bear. She saw two flashes of light from Veep's muzzle, the sound from the bullets muted by his suppressor, but the damage violent. The man staggered like he'd been hit with a baseball bat, then folded over, collapsing on the ground.

She ran back to him and he said, "Are you fucking nuts?"

She said, "There's one more. One more bad guy."

He looked like he was going to explode, hissing, "I don't give a shit about him. We got Kylie, and we need to move. Get clear from here."

She said, "We won't be clear with this man running around. We weren't clear before, when Kurt died. It's why we're here now."

Veep bent down, took the pistol from the dead man's hand, and shoved it into his waistband, saying, "Are you sure you're thirteen?"

Hearing the Russian above them, searching the berm, she said, "These guys won't stop. I've seen it before. *You've* seen it before. They'll just keep coming, unless we end this."

Veep started to respond and she held up a finger, listening. She said, "He's on top of the hill, by the radar tower."

Veep raised his rifle and said, "I'll meet him there."

She said, "No, no. We need to trap him. Ambush him. Up top is open ground. A killing field. He'll shoot you before you can find him. Go through the tunnel. On the far side is an empty room. I'll bring him."

Veep said, "Amena, that is insane," and turned to climb the berm. She grabbed his arm and said, "Don't go up there. You don't know this place like I do, and the way to win is inside, not up top."

He paused and she begged him, "Please. You go up top and he'll kill you, and then he'll kill me."

She glanced at the radar tower, hearing the man stomp around. She pleaded, "*Please*. Get in the tunnel."

Veep paused for a second, then said, "I can't. If you get hurt . . ."

She pushed his back toward the dark entrance, saying, "I know, I *know*. You won't be able to live with yourself. Trust me. Just do it."

He jogged into the tunnel. She waited a beat, then made a noise with her foot. The target didn't bite. She tried again, and heard him shout something in Russian, trying to find his friend, then began to shuffle away from her.

Not good. She searched the ground around her and found an aluminum soda can. She kicked it into the brick, the noise rattling into the night.

That did it.

She heard the footsteps running, saw the man drop from

the top of the berm, take one look at the body on the ground, and then draw a bead on her head with a pistol.

She took off running, straight into the tunnel.

He followed, and she heard a crack, then the whine of a ricochet, and realized he was shooting at her. Something she hadn't considered.

She unconsciously ducked and kept going, hearing two more shots, the bullets snapping right next to her head. She panicked, now no longer thinking about setting him up, but only getting away. She sprinted down the tunnel blindly, the fear giving her a burst of adrenaline, desperately trying to reach the Civil War bunker.

She felt the kiss of the fourth round snap by her earlobe before the sound of the gunshot reached her, and she knew she was dead.

She dodged to the right and passed by the opening to the bunker without even realizing it, then heard another shot explode in the tunnel, but with a different pitch. The man behind her screamed. She whipped her head to the rear and saw Veep standing above her tormentor, his rifle shouldered like an extension of his body. He squeezed twice more, the light on the rail illuminating the damage he inflicted.

She slowed, then ran back to him. He was breathing heavily, the death he'd delivered pressing home.

He saw her and shook his head, saying, "I have no idea why I agreed to watch your ass. You are a piece of work."

The adrenaline coursing through her, she felt a grin leak out and said, "I'm family. That's why."

42

I couldn't believe that Shoshana had refused to kill her target. I thought about putting my own barrel against his head and she read it in me before I could even draw the pistol, saying, "No, Pike. Jennifer is right. This isn't about him. It's about you."

Aggravated, I said, "What the hell are we going to do with him? Let him just run off? We have a hit coming."

She pulled out a pair of flex-ties from her jacket, bent down to him, and began binding his legs and arms. She said, "I'll babysit him. You had me out front wasting time anyway. I can do both. I'll post on the corner. You do the hit and then we'll exfil."

I said, "We don't have time for that shit."

"Yes, we do. I'm the one bringing the exfil vehicle, and you have to get out both the woman and the child anyway. I'll pull the car right up to your breach point. It can stop here for five seconds. We'll turn him over to the police as well."

I shook my head, looked at Aaron, and said, "You ready?"

He nodded, and we jogged down the alley to an ancient side door. I knelt down, saying, "Light."

He put a beam on the lock face and I started working my tools, saying, "She's really pushing the limits of my endurance."

He chuckled and said, "She thinks she's protecting you.

She has seen the beast inside herself, and she doesn't wish that on you. Killing that man would be crossing a line. She is done with that."

I turned around and said, "Are you kidding? She's crazy as a loon."

He said, "No more so than you. Trust her."

I went back at the lock and felt the dead bolt come free. I glanced at him and whispered, "Breach."

He raised his weapon, and I swung open the door, letting him flow inside. I followed behind him, my own Glock 23 drawn, and we found ourselves in an old sacristy, velour chairs and dark oak all around. Just like the floor plan Creed had sent us. At least something was working out.

We threaded our way through the darkness, entering a hallway and taking a knee. I whispered, "Staircase should be right at the end."

Aaron nodded, and we slunk forward, each step a deliberate one, heel, toe, heel, toe, making sure we were silent as a shadow.

We reached the end and I saw the faint edge of the stairwell, a light at the top giving us faint illumination. I tapped Aaron, pointed up, and he nodded. I got on the radio and said, "Koko, Koko, we are at LCC," meaning we were at the last covered and concealed position before we assaulted. "Are you ready?"

She came back immediately, saying, "Roger. What took so long?"

I said, "Later. Carrie, this is Pike. Are we clear?"

Shoshana said, "Yes. Target is secure. No issues."

I went up the stairs, hearing nothing but the rustle of clothing from Aaron behind me. We reached the top, I peeked around the corner, and saw our door, a single bulb above it illuminating the hallway.

I clicked the radio and said, "Koko, Koko, breach in sight. Stand by."

"Roger."

I knew she was now worming forward on the roof and lining up her sights.

I broke out of the stairwell and slunk down the hallway, checking the knob on the door. It was locked.

I drew a hand across my throat and Aaron rotated the pack on his shoulder, pulling out a small explosive charge. I took it, placed it just above the doorknob, where the lock was set, then unspooled the wire from it.

We staged on the left side of the door, away from the blast, and I handed Aaron the initiation device. He nodded, and I called, "Koko, Koko. At breach. I say again at breach."

She whispered, "Standing by." Meaning she had the man in her crosshairs. In a mantra I said, "Five . . . four . . . three . . . two . . . one, execute, execute, execute."

On the first execute, Aaron cracked our charge, the explosion shattering the night, the door splintering inward. I raced forward, my barrel leading the way. I met a man in the foyer, a pistol in his hands and a look of shock on his face. I put a double tap into his forehead and kept going, waiting on the rush of men.

There was none.

Aaron split to the left. I went right, and then saw Jennifer drop onto the balcony, entering the room with her own weapon out.

The rest of the apartment was empty. We cleared it rapidly, until I reached a final door down a hallway. I kicked it in, seeing a woman cowering with a bandage on her hand. She looked up at me, her clothing soiled, her makeup streaked, and said, "Por favor, por favor, no."

I dropped my weapon, and Jennifer flowed in behind me, wrapping the woman in a blanket from the floor. She looked confused, like maybe it was a trick, her daughter behind her showing hope, but with an edge of disbelief.

I said, "Do you speak English?"

She nodded, and I said, "We don't have a lot of time. You're safe now. Just listen to Jennifer here."

Jennifer leaned into her ear and whispered something, and the woman nodded her head, going faster and faster at every utterance like she was about to break her own neck. She grabbed her daughter and wrapped her tightly.

I left the room, finding Aaron at the door to the balcony. Outside, on the slab of concrete, I saw the body of the man Jennifer had killed, a single bullet hole right between his eyes.

Aaron said, "Shouldn't have doubted her."

I patted his shoulder and said, "Yeah, you and me both. Time to exfil."

I called Shoshana, saying, "We have jackpot. I say again, jackpot."

She said, "Moving."

Jennifer came out of the room with the woman and child. She glanced at the body on the balcony, then her eyes settled on me. I thought I'd see doubt, but I didn't.

She gave me a ferocious smile and said, "This one was good. Very good."

She helped them to the door, one arm around the woman, another holding the child.

43

Wolffe heard a noise at the back of the house and ceased his interrogation of the Russian. He pointed to Kylie to get behind him. She did so, and he raised his rifle, aiming at the sliding door but keeping his knee on top of his prisoner's neck.

The curtain fluttered in the breeze, and then Amena appeared. Wolffe exhaled and Kylie rushed to her, crushing her, wrapping her up in her arms. Nicholas Seacrest entered, and Kylie rose, the emotion finally spilling out.

He embraced her, whispering in her ear, but looking at Wolffe.

Wolffe stood, keeping control of the Russian below him, and said, "Where do we stand?"

Seacrest said, "Two dead at the fort. We need to go."

Although he expected it, Wolffe muttered, "Shit. Not what I wanted to hear."

Seacrest described what had happened, including Amena's actions, and Wolffe shook his head, saying, "So she's as crazy as Pike?"

Seacrest set his weapon against a wall and said, "Probably more so."

Amena was unsure how to take that. Was it a compliment? An insult? She settled for just sitting in a chair, swinging her legs back and forth to burn off the adrenaline.

Seacrest took Kylie's hand, returned to Wolffe, and said, "We have no idea of the scope of element against us. We need to pack up and get out. What did that guy say?"

Wolffe leaned on the man, driving his knee into his neck and causing him to groan. He said, "Not much. He claims his team was the only one here, but I agree, he could be full of shit."

Seacrest said, "Any word from Pike?"

"No. He won't answer his cell."

The second the words left his mouth, his phone went off, vibrating on the table next to him. Wolffe said, "Watch this guy," and picked up the handset.

Seacrest raised his barrel toward the Russian's head and Wolffe looked at the screen, saying, "Speak of the devil."

He clicked the green button and said, "Why the fuck won't you answer your phone?"

He heard nothing, then, "Is this George Wolffe?"

"Yeah, who else would have my cell?"

He heard a sigh, then, "Shit, sir, I thought you were dead because you didn't answer *your* phone. Look, are you still in Charleston? I got a call, and Kylie and Amena are in trouble. I need you to find Veep and—"

Wolffe cut him off, saying, "A little late for that. What's happening in Brazil?"

Pike replied, the trepidation dripping out, "What do you mean? A little late?"

"I mean your little refugee initiated a Prairie Fire alert on a phone you gave her—without authorization, I might add—and Veep and I interdicted the problem."

Pike said, "Interdicted? Interdicted what? What happened?"

Wolffe told him, relaying the assault and Amena's efforts at the fort. He heard Pike turn away from the phone, saying something to someone else, then, "So Kylie and Amena are secure?"

He laughed and said, "Yeah, why? Is that a surprise? Me working a weapon is like fantasy shit or something?"

"No, no, sir. I mean, I've just been worried sick. These fucks called me and ordered me off of our mission. They put Kylie on the phone, and if I could have reached through it, I would have, slaughtering every one of them. Just like you did."

Wolffe ignored the accolades, focusing on the one word that mattered. He said, "What do you mean, 'mission'? We have no mission. What have you been doing?"

"Nothing that we haven't talked about. Working on freeing Knuckles and Brett."

Wolffe felt the hairs on his neck rise. "That was supposed to be you as a liaison with the Brazilian assault element. Is that what you mean?"

"Uh . . . yeah. That's what I mean. Is Amena there?"

"Yeah. She's fine."

Wolffe walked into the den, out of earshot of the others, saying, "But we need to talk about her situation. I know this isn't the time, but we don't get to pick the time. With Kurt dead, she's a weak link. If someone finds her, and then finds GRS, we're in trouble. There is no explanation for it all. They'll crack open the Taskforce, and we know now that someone's looking."

All he heard was, "Bullshit. Give her the phone."

Wolffe said, "Pike, we have a serious problem here. This

shit I just did in Charleston is another brick in the wall. We need to solve this problem. Find a solution for her. A permanent solution."

Pike said, "Permanent solution? What the fuck? You sound like a Nazi."

Wolffe couldn't believe how Pike had twisted his words. He exploded, saying, "Have you lost your mind? Don't put that on me. I just told you I'm with you. We aren't going to throw her to the wolves."

Pike said, "Wolves? She'd probably survive that. Kurt told me you assholes were going to send her back to Syria. Let me talk to her."

Wolffe said, "Now's not the time."

Pike came back, and Wolffe recognized the heat in his voice. "Put her on the phone."

Wolffe relented. He walked back into the kitchen and caught Amena's eye, saying, "It's Pike. He wants to talk to you."

Surprised, she said, "Me?"

He said, "Yes."

She glanced first at Kylie, then at Veep. She rose, trying to hide the pleasure of Pike wanting to speak to her, and her alone. She took the handset and glanced at the others in the room, attempting to cloak the triumph of her being chosen among all of them. And failing.

The act brought a smile from Wolffe, and he began to understand Pike's attachment.

She took the phone, her face serious, saying, "Hello?"

She listened and nodded, saying, "Yes, we're fine. I had to run, but Veep came through. He really—" and Pike cut her off. She paused for a moment, Wolffe hearing the chastising, and she finally said, "I know what you told me, but I had to make a choice."

Pike continued berating her. She squinted her eyes, then said, "You're *not* the boss of me."

Wolffe could hear the laughter from the other end even as she talked. Pike said something else, then Amena smiled, saying, "I'm okay with 'Doodlebug.' If you don't yell at me anymore."

She passed the phone back to Wolffe, saying, "He wants to talk to you."

He took the phone, looking at her and saying, "What was that all about?"

She smiled and said, "Nothing. Just family stuff." Clearly enjoying the disciplining she'd received.

He grinned and said, "I know the feeling. I think I'm about to experience it."

He took the handset and came right to the point, saying, "Pike, what's going on in Brazil? You were supposed to just advise and assist. What 'mission' are you talking about? You mean the Russian you took out, right?"

"No, sir. That Russian gave us intelligence, and I used it on a flex target. A different target."

"What different target?"

Pike said, "Uhh . . . I made a deal with the assault captain. I help him, and he helps me. And now it's time for him to pay the bill."

"Wait, wait. Stop. What deal?"

And Pike told him what he'd done, holding nothing back. Wolffe was incredulous. He waved at Veep, letting him know he was leaving the room. He walked out onto the deck and said, "You assaulted a church? One that's a UNESCO landmark? Jesus Christ, Pike, you could have caused an international incident."

"Could have, but didn't. Let it go. I have the police captain's family, and he owes me a favor. I'm going on the assault. I need you to alert Knuckles's phone. Can you do that? Even if it's turned off?"

"Wait, wait. I might need Oversight Council approval before you execute a Taskforce action."

Pike chuckled and said, "There *is* no Oversight Council. There is no Taskforce. There's only Knuckles and Brett, and I'm going to free them. Can you alert his phone?"

Wolffe ran his hand through his hair, not wanting to step out on the limb. But he did. "Yeah. I can get Creed to do that. Knuckles's phone doesn't exit the cell system even if it's turned off. The only way it won't work is if they've taken out the battery, but why?"

"I want him to know we're coming. You alert that phone, get it to ring or buzz or whatever that thing's capable of, and he won't even need to answer. He'll know."

Wolffe took in the words, then said, "Okay, Pike. I'll do it. But after that? Then you come home?"

He heard nothing from the phone. He said, "Pike? You come home?"

Pike said, "No, sir. I'm not. Rescuing Knuckles won't solve our problem. The Oversight Council thinks that just giving up will prevent our discovery, but that's not going to happen. Someone down here knows that Grolier Recovery Services is not what it appears, and they're going to keep working to expose us. I'm going to stop it."

Wolffe knew he had to get a handle on Pike before he caused an incident nobody could explain. He needed to get him to understand what he was doing.

He went into commander mode, saying, "Pike, that's not going to happen. You're coming home."

He thought he heard Pike chuckle, and bulled ahead, saying, "You get Knuckles, and get out. You've done enough. You keep going and you might just prove what they're trying to expose. We can find them through others. Through the established intelligence community."

Pike snapped, "You sound like those cowards on the Oversight Council. The only one with any balls is a woman who hung her neck out to get me the chance. We choose your course of action and the way this ends is with the Taskforce shut down permanently out of fear because these guys are still running around. They'll win."

Wolffe said, "Pike, it's more complicated than that. Listen to yourself. We have a Senate inquiry into Kurt Hale's death. He died at your house, for God's sake. If that guy makes a single connection to Grolier Recovery Services, it's a short leap to Amena, and an even shorter leap to your actions in Brazil. You've done good work, but don't take it further."

Pike said, "Because you're afraid?"

The insult caused Wolffe to explode, "Because it's fucking illegal! And if you want the Taskforce to continue, it needs to remain in the shadows. Think of Amena here."

And with those words, Wolffe thought he'd finally penetrated. Pike said nothing. Wolffe said, "Okay, so we agree."

Pike said, "We agree on one thing. Those fucks attacked my family. Tried to kill them."

He said, "What's that mean?"

Pike said, "It means they made a mistake. The man pulling the strings is still down here, doing evil shit. He killed Kurt, which is bad enough, but he made a mistake attacking my family. I can't let that stand."

Wolffe tried one last time, "Pike, think about this. What am I supposed to tell the president?"

There was a pause, then Pike said, "Tell him I'm going to burn it all to the ground."

44

Alek exited the Rio airport baggage claim and faced a throng of people, half holding signs with someone's name, the other half unregistered cabbies trying to catch a customer.

Tired beyond measure with the travel from Salvador, the clock climbing past midnight, he prayed that Nikita's man was here. The last thing he wanted to do now was spend time trying to find a place to stay for the night. He needed a good night's sleep before he began tracking his designated target because from what Nikita had told him, he was going to be starting from scratch, with the man having vanished. And failure was not an option.

He waded through the crowd, growing concerned, then finally saw a man in the back, holding a sign with his name on it. Short and wiry, with a broad Slavic face, he had the dead eyes of a killer, standing next to a pillar and ignoring the flow of passengers exiting.

He approached and, in Russian, said, "I'm Alek."

The man smiled, showing broken teeth that apparently hadn't seen a dentist in years. He stuck out his hand and said, "You can call me Pushka. Nikita said you were coming to help, but I think I've solved our problem."

Alek said nothing in the crowded entryway. While he didn't believe anyone spoke Russian near them, he'd wait until they were in the car.

Pushka noticed the pause and understood. He pointed at the small roll-aboard suitcase and said, "Is that your only bag?"

Meaning, had he brought something for the mission. Something given to him by Nikita. Alek said, "This is it. Nikita said you had what we needed."

Pushka nodded and said, "Car's right out front. Let's go."

They exited through the swarm of people and loaded up into a dented Ford Fiesta, Pushka taking the wheel. He pulled away and threw a manila envelope in Alek's lap, saying, "That's the target."

Alek opened it, first seeing a photograph of a man in a crisp suit. He looked to be in his midsixties, with distinguished features and a severe cut of salt-and-pepper hair. In truth, he looked exactly like the men who paid Alek's salary. A man of power.

He pulled out the target's description, wading through pages of analysis to get to the synopsis. He read:

1. Gabino Alves, Mines and Energy minister of Brazil.
2. Responsible for the oversight of all natural resources in the country. Currently engaged with Petrobras for the release of parcels of the Lulu oil field and predisposed to ignore Rosneft advances. Vehemently opposed to Russian expansion.
3. Leverage points: Implicated in Petrobras bribes in the Carwash scandal, but no hard evidence. May succumb if operatives can glean proof.

Alek knew he was reading original operational parameters, because he wouldn't be in the country holding this packet if the third measure had been met. He flipped the page, and saw he was correct.

A short statement read, *All efforts beyond lethal approaches have failed. Gabino rebuffed overtures, and our information campaign against him failed to be effective. Recommend future efforts be dedicated to grooming a replacement. Recommend termination.*

Pushka left the urban jungle of the city and began traveling along the coastal road. Alek said, "Where are we going?"

"A sweet hotel at Copacabana. Right on the beach. We're almost there."

He pulled into a circle drive and Alek closed the packet, saying, "What the fuck are we doing here?"

Pushka said, "We originally tracked the target to here. His house is in São Palo, but when he travels to Rio, it's always to this hotel."

Alek looked at the ostentatious hotel and didn't like it. He said, "This is asking to be remembered."

Pushka shrugged and said, "Hey, all I do is follow. I didn't choose this hotel. The target did."

They exited, Pushka giving the keys to a valet. They went inside, Alek dragging his suitcase. A bellboy came out, asking if he could help. Alek said no and kept going. The bellboy looked incensed, and Alek glared at him, causing him to shrink back.

Pushka whispered, "Don't make a scene. *That* is what will get you remembered. The people here don't worry about a couple of bills."

Alek relinquished the suitcase, disgusted, but let the man roll it behind them.

They rode up to the fourth floor, remaining quiet. The

group reached the room and Alek tipped the boy, then closed the door. He said, "That was absolute bullshit."

Pushka said, "We're not in a safe house. You need to blend."

Alek took a look at the minibar and said, "Looks like you've been blending just fine."

Pushka smiled and said, "When in Rome . . ."

Alek tossed the target packet onto the bed and said, "What did you mean in the airport that you might have solved the problem? I thought this guy was in the wind."

"He was, but I've been staking out the downtown Petrobras headquarters. There's this weird church right across the street that's perfect for surveillance. Looks like a gigantic pyramid and has a continuous flow of tourists."

Alek rolled his hand, telling him to get to the point instead of bragging about his skills.

Pushka said, "Okay, anyway, I knew sooner or later he'd return, and yesterday he did. After he left, I called my contact that runs security for the front desk and learned he's in town for a few days."

"You have his schedule? Or do we need to track him?"

"I don't know his schedule tomorrow, but I do the following day. He's taking some Chinese investors on a little trip. Playing tour guide."

"Where are they going?"

"I don't have an hourly schedule. I only have what the guard could relay, but I know one point of inflection. One place we can interdict him."

"Where?"

"The Christ Redeemer statue. They're headed up to it the day after tomorrow."

45

We pulled back into the same spot we'd been in before, the car now packed with enough people that I felt like I was about to drive into a circus. I said to Jennifer, "Okay, only Aaron and I are going in. Just like before. Hold fast here."

From the backseat, the mother said, "What are you doing? Are you selling us?"

I laughed and said, "Selling you? Shit no."

I pointed across the street to the naval base and said, "Your husband is planning an assault against a ship that holds my friends. I saved you so you could save them."

She didn't look convinced, her arms wrapped around her daughter. I said, "I know you have no reason to believe me, but please don't try to run away. You are safe. I promise."

She nodded, and Shoshana said, "Pike? Outside the door."

I looked out the window and saw a group of thugs, much like the ones who had interrupted our interrogation earlier.

The mother moaned, then said, "I knew it. You're going to sell us. I have money. Let me buy my freedom. Please. Don't give my daughter to them."

I muttered, "What. The. Fuck. Is this place a walking criminal enterprise?"

I turned back around to her and said, "No, I'm *not* selling you."

Jennifer said, "Pike, maybe we should park somewhere else."

I clenched my fists, then muttered, "I don't have *time* for this shit."

Aaron said, "Maybe Jennifer's right," but I ignored him, swinging the door open just as the first man reached me. I didn't even give him a chance to say anything, rising up and slamming a hard right cross straight to the temple, snapping my hips and putting my entire body weight behind it. He fell to the ground, unconscious.

I looked at the other men in the group, raised my pistol, and said, "Get the fuck out of here."

They took off running, breaking apart like a pack of roaches caught in the light, all searching for a place to hide.

I turned back to the car and said, "Aaron, can we go?"

Aaron chuckled and climbed out, saying, "By all means."

In the back of the car, the woman's eyes about popped out of her head, the realization of what I'd done sinking home. She said, "You . . . mean what you say?"

Jennifer said, "Pike always means what he says. You're safe."

She climbed out of the car, purposely bumped her hip into mine, for the first time letting me know that she was over my earlier questioning of her commitment, and thought that punch was pretty sweet. Which made me feel better, because I was about to put her in the wringer again.

She said, "I suppose this is our mess now?"

I said, "Yeah, if you don't mind."

She leaned over the body I'd eliminated and said, "Shoshana, you want to give me a hand?"

Shoshana said, "Gladly."

I looked at the woman, her mouth agape at the turn of

events, and said, "Just stay here. These two will protect you. You'll see your husband soon."

She nodded dumbly, but the daughter gave me a thumbs-up.

Aaron and I jogged across the street and met the phalanx of police. I said, "Get me the U.S. liaison."

We repeated the dance of radio calls, and Alonzo Walsh came out, saying, "Where the hell have you been? You said you were going to dinner. That was four hours ago. I thought I was through with this shit show."

I said, "Sorry about that. Something came up. Get us in."

He shook his head and said, "I did some checking. Nobody's ever heard of you guys. The embassy doesn't know who you are."

Aggravated at one more blockade to Knuckles, I snatched him by the throat, causing the police around us to spring back, but afraid to interfere in a U.S.-only affair.

I bent him over backward, my anger starting to get the better of me. I said, "Why is *everyone* against me? I don't have *time* for this shit. Get me in."

He nodded his head rapidly, and I released him. He stood up, rubbed his throat, looked at me like I was a lunatic, then started walking to the door. The policemen relaxed, and we followed.

Aaron whispered, "I'm not sure you're diplomat material."

I said, "Should've known that the minute you met me."

We entered the lobby and saw a whirlwind of men, all scurrying about. I took in the room and knew they'd reached a tripwire. They weren't doing analysis for developing plans. They'd made the plan and were now trying to make sure it worked.

Not good.

We went down the same hallway and Alonzo said, "He's

under significant pressure. I mean *significant* pressure. We have U.S. citizens on that ferry. Please, think about that before you speak."

And I understood that Alonzo Walsh, a State Department flunky, actually cared. I smiled and said, "I won't jeopardize them, I promise."

He nodded, then knocked on the door.

We entered, Alonzo leading, and I saw Felipe with a phone to his ear. He said something and hung up. I turned to Alonzo and said, "Time for you to go."

His face flushed and he said, "I can't do that. I have my orders, too."

Aaron saw where I was going, stepped around me, and said, "Just leave the room. Now."

He turned on that weird Israeli vibe that Shoshana had, and I thought Alonzo was going to soil his pants. He scurried out of the room.

Felipe said, "We go soon. The assault is on." Like he didn't want to know about his family, but I could tell he was begging for the information.

I said, "Your wife and child are in a car about two hundred meters from here. They're safe."

He blinked at me, stammered something, then collapsed into his chair, cradling his head in his hands, his breath hitching.

I said, "You okay?"

He looked up and said, "Are you lying to me?"

I leaned over his desk and said, "No. Family means everything to me. The men who took yours also tried to kill mine. And I'm going to bring it to a close."

He sagged back in his chair, took a breath, wiped his eyes, then said, "Let me talk to my wife."

I said, "We don't have the time for that. Take me at my word. You'll speak to her face-to-face soon. What's happening with the assault? You said it was tonight."

In a monotone, he said, "The mission is in three hours. A GRUMEC unit is going to assault from a fast boat, with BOPE police as the main element."

I said, "How are they going to assault a boat full of terrorists looking for an approach? They're in the middle of the ocean. They can see everything."

He rubbed his head and, without conviction, said, "We'll be on them before they know we're there. We'll eliminate the threat."

What he told me was a recipe for disaster. I said, "Call it off. Tell the command you have new intelligence. Tell them you've found something else. Postpone the mission."

He looked up at me and said, "I can't do that. It's taken on a life of its own."

Not even meaning to, I turned into the men I was hunting, saying, "If you want to see your wife and child again, you'll figure out a way."

He snapped up out of his chair, his visage contorted in hatred. He said, "You utter one more word, and I'll kill you right here. I have enough enemies. One more won't matter."

And I was embarrassed at my words.

Aaron stepped forward, his hands in the air. He said, "My friend isn't that good at the diplomacy thing, but he's very, very good at hostage rescue. Please. Listen to him."

Felipe went from me to Aaron, then said, "Where is my family?"

I relented, giving up the one card I had. "They're in the parking lot across the avenue. I didn't mean what I said. I'm sorry. I would never hold them hostage, but that ferry has two very good friends of mine on it. *My* family. It's why I'm here."

He took that in, then said, "So I can just go across the street and get them?"

I dialed my phone, heard it answered, and said, "Put on the child."

I passed it to him.

Suspicious, he took it, and then I saw his face melt. He began talking in rapid Portuguese, then hung up.

He stood, regaining his composure. He said, "Thank you. I'm not sure how to express my gratitude. What do you want, for real?"

"I want you to stop this assault. Give me another day."

"What will that do? What's another day?"

"You guys give me a day, and before it's passed, I'll free that ferry."

46

Knuckles rubbed his face, feeling the grime from three days of living in the same clothes. He glanced at Brett and said, "I'm pretty sure that beacon didn't work."

Brett nodded, saying, "I was thinking the same thing. If they could have done something, the Taskforce would have been here by now."

They sat in silence, wallowing in the loss of hope for a moment. Brett broke the silence, saying, "So what do you want to do? We have about a one-in-five chance of getting out of here alive if we try anything. Every one of these guys has a detonator. We'd need to kill all four of them at the same time."

Brett glanced at the man sitting in the middle of the hostages, the one who had acted strangely, and said, "And that's not counting the other threats."

Knuckles looked at Willow Radcliffe and her child, saying, "Yeah, yeah. I hear you, but it's looking more and more like it's going to be on us. We need to prepare for the fight. These guys are breaking down. They can't take the stress much longer."

At the rear of the boat, near the toilet, a ringing began. Brett glanced at Knuckles, and he was just as mystified. It grew louder and louder, until the guards heard it.

One ran to the rear of the boat, searched around, then

cocked his head. He snatched up the backpack full of cell phones, then began digging inside. He pulled out one phone, the noise growing louder now that it was outside. He tried to shut it off, but couldn't get it to stop.

Willow jerked upright at the commotion, and the guard saw her, shouting, "Is this your phone? Is this yours?"

Confused, trying to get the cobwebs of sleep out of her head, she said nothing. The man advanced on her and said, "Why is this ringing? It's turned off. What have you done?"

She said, "I don't know. I have no idea. That's not my phone."

He advanced forward, and Knuckles saw the cell. Saw what it was. Saw why it was ringing. The other hostages began waking up, scurrying away from his wrath.

The terrorist reached Willow and screamed again, convinced there was a conspiracy. She tried to refute him, and he slapped her face, driving her into the deck.

Knuckles leapt up, saying, "That's my phone. It's not hers. Stop it."

The terrorist glared at him and said, "Why's it ringing? It's turned off."

Knuckles shrugged his shoulders and said, "I have no idea. You guys have had it the whole time."

The terrorist stormed over to him and punched him in the gut, causing Knuckles to double over. Brett leapt up and the terrorist put the barrel of his pistol in his face.

They stood silent for a moment, Knuckles getting his air back and Brett doing all he could not to break the terrorist's neck.

Satisfied at his control, the terrorist slammed the phone into the ground, splitting it open. He stomped on the remains, and the sound stopped.

He looked at Knuckles, now upright again, and said, "You try anything else, and I'll kill you."

He walked away, and Knuckles smiled, sitting back down on the bench. Willow crawled to him, keeping low, not wanting to cause another outburst.

She said, "Are you okay?"

Still thinking about the phone, he said, "Oh yeah, I'm more than okay."

Brett slid in next to him and said, "Only one reason that damn thing went off. It looks like your beacon worked."

Knuckles felt an infusion of confidence, for the first time feeling he was in control, like he was about to make breach with an unstoppable team behind him.

He said, "Yeah. The beacon worked, and Pike Logan is about to slam this place."

He caressed the blade the child had given him and said, "When it comes, we need to be ready."

47

The boat rocketed out of the harbor, going fast enough to leave a small rooster tail behind it. The men driving it were dressed like ninjas, wearing black fatigue pants and tops, complete with yellow letters spelling out BOPE on their backs and black balaclavas over their heads. They looked scary, but when I saw their eyes, I recognized fear. Not that I blamed them, because my plan was not something that would inspire great confidence.

Unless you were me, that is.

Jennifer and Shoshana were still wearing civilian clothes, but Aaron and I were outfitted just like the BOPE police, using uniforms borrowed from Felipe but without the vests and gunbelts. In its place we each had a single Glock 23 with an RMR holosight. Felipe, dressed in tactical gear like his men, but without the balaclava, showed more wonderment than fear. He said, "You sure about this?"

I said, "Yes. You can't assault that ferry from above the water. Especially with the explosives. If they don't set them off on our advance, they'll prepare and set it off on the assault. Best case, you only lose the hostages. Worst case, you lose everyone."

He caught my eye and said, "I wouldn't have followed their orders. I want you to know that. I wasn't trying to get anyone killed."

I said, "I know."

His eyes watered, and he said, "When I got her finger, I almost succumbed. But I couldn't do it. The most I could do was just go along with GRUMEC's plan. I knew it was crazy, but it was blessed by the government. They were all convinced doing anything was better than letting it go on." He shook his head and said, "It was easy. Giving up, I mean."

I patted him on the shoulder and said, "You didn't give up. If you had, I wouldn't be on this boat."

Somehow, through sheer force of will, Felipe had gotten them to delay until the following evening, which gave me this one cycle of darkness. He'd made up some bullshit story about checking on possible booby traps on the infiltration route or something like that, and then said he was going to conduct a reconnaissance. The GRUMEC had given him a boat and then had tried to come with him. He'd shut that down as the commander, saying he had explosive ordnance disposal capabilities the GRUMEC couldn't duplicate.

He'd retained control of the operation, and because of it, he did what he wanted—at least with the crisis site. He was under enormous pressure, because by the time we returned, he'd have to answer to a multitude of people—up to and including the president of Brazil—demanding to know why he'd postponed the assault, but by then, he'd be a hero.

I hoped.

Felipe changed the subject, saying, "You sure she can shoot?"

He was looking at Jennifer, and I said, "Yeah. She can shoot. All you need to do is keep the boat steady."

He'd offered a BOPE sniper, and while I would bet they were competent, I wasn't putting my life in the hands of anyone I hadn't seen operate. Jennifer had once hit a head shot from four hundred meters out—and not on a paper target.

The memory made me regret my earlier questioning of her commitment. Before we'd embarked on the boat—while we waited to transfer our latest Russian from our trunk to Felipe's men, using the same parking lot from before—Jennifer had pulled me aside, wondering if I'd lost faith in her. But I hadn't. I'd lost a little faith in myself. When *Shoshana*'s telling you you've got a screw loose, you probably do.

I'd said, "No. You were right then, but you're not *always* right. There is no black and white, but you want to make it that way. The world is a mess of gray, and we operate in it. Sometimes people just need to be dead."

Looking at me intently, she said, "I know the gray. It's not about the lives you end. It's about *why* you do so. You can't take it back. Ever."

I thought about the man I'd killed who had tried to surrender. I hadn't told Jennifer how he'd died, and I knew I'd dream about it for a long time. Not because he didn't deserve to die. I'm sure he'd done some pretty heinous things, and he would have killed Shoshana without remorse, but that was what separated me from him.

The fact remains that you can't be the good guy and do inherently bad things. The justification for the action only goes so far. Pretty soon, left to its own devices, the god of war has you justifying gas chambers because it's in the interest of the nation you've sworn to defend. There was a cut line, and I'd crossed it, and Jennifer had seen what crossing that line could do to me.

She looked at me intently, touched my cheek, and said, "Shoshana told me what she did. She was right, but I'd be lying if I didn't say I was surprised."

I chuckled and said, "I'm pretty sure you're rubbing off on her."

"Well, that's not a bad thing, is it? It's seemed to work pretty well with you, and look at us now. A couple of super commandos out saving the world while wearing a white hat. Or at least a gray one."

I nodded, not fighting her. She saw the shift, smiled, and said, "We'll get vengeance, but on our terms, not theirs. Okay?"

I chuckled and said, "Okay, but be careful what you ask for."

She said, "What's that mean?"

"We're going on the assault tonight. Aaron and me. You're going to be in overwatch, and I need the same trigger control I had in Guatemala. You'll be behind the gun; Shoshana will be spotting."

She said, "What?"

I saw the concern on her face and said, "You can make the shot. I'm not worried about it. It'll be three hundred meters or less, and the water's calm in the cove by the harbor. There's that terrorist who's always in the captain's cabin on the upper deck, and he's the only one we won't be able to immediately neutralize."

She nodded vacantly, thinking about my words, and I saw the reticence. I said, "What's the matter?"

She returned to the present, focused on me, and said, "I don't know about this. It's a night shot. What if I can't see the target?"

"He's in the captain's cabin. It's always illuminated. Don't worry about that."

She nodded again, but there was still doubt. I thought it was about killing. I was wrong.

I said, "What is it? You don't want to take a life?"

"Pike, no. That's not it. The shot is a single point of failure. If I miss, he'll blow up the boat. Kill everyone."

I said, "Then I guess you'd better not miss."

48

The boat reached the midpoint between the island, the twinkling lights from the houses and restaurants appearing like stars on the ocean, the landmass itself still hidden in the darkness.

Felipe said, "About ten minutes out."

I said, "Once we leave the boat, get in the protected cove and anchor. Jennifer will set up, Shoshana will spot, and all you do is sit. It'll be over soon."

He flicked his head to the stern and said, "You know that equipment is just for rescue purposes. It's not designed for what you're about to do."

Since we couldn't attack from the surface of the water on another boat, that left two options: one, parachute onto the deck of the ferry from above, then start slinging lead as we came down, or two, go under the surface. Since option one would only work in a Jason Bourne movie, that left option two.

At the rear of the boat were two sets of HEEDs–Helicopter Emergency Egress Devices—which were basically mini-scuba tanks designed to allow a helicopter crew to escape a crash in the water, where most of the deaths weren't from impact, but from drowning. I'd asked Felipe if his helicopter crews had them, since they flew over water, and he'd told me yes.

I said, "The HEED is designed to provide air underwater,

and that's how I'm going to use it. We've only got about a three-hundred-meter swim, and it'll work for that."

Aaron smiled, saying, "Don't worry, Felipe. We won't die on the infiltration. It's the final five feet that's going to be dangerous."

My assault plan was pretty simple and tailored for the threat. Instead of a fireworks show of a ninja assault force, only Aaron and I were going forward.

We knew there were four terrorists, and that they rotated sleeping duties, meaning only three would be awake at any given time. One was always in the captain's cabin, which was Jennifer's target. The other one or two were down below, which would be our targets.

Using the HEED, we'd swim to the concrete lighting buoy the boat was anchored against. From there we'd work our way to the boat, Aaron to the stern, where one target was located, and me to the bow, the location of the other one.

We'd studied videos of the ferry in action on various tourist websites and had seen children climbing up the old tires the ferry used as bumpers and diving off while the boat was under way, showing off for the tourists. I figured if a damn ten-year-old could climb up the side while the boat was steaming full ahead, two commandos should be able to do it quickly enough to neutralize the threat.

Felipe said, "How will I know when to come forward?"

"I'll call Jennifer. Or you'll see a giant fireball."

The biggest problem we had was communication while we infiltrated, since I couldn't talk while underwater, meaning they'd just have to wonder if we were getting shot at while we advanced. Once I was in position, I'd be able to get an earpiece in, but that was about it. Any problems beforehand and there would be no support. No help.

Felipe flashed his eyes at me at the fireball comment and I said, "I'm just kidding. I'll call, I promise. But when I do, you'll owe me another favor."

He looked at me with suspicion and said, "What?"

"That original Russian I gave you? I want some time with him. He's involved in more than just this. He's involved in the death of a friend of mine, and I want to know why."

He stuttered for a moment, then said, "That's impossible. He's in the custody of Brazil now. We'll deal with him."

Taken aback, I said, "What? That's not an unreasonable request, given what we've done here."

"It's not going to happen. I appreciate what you've done, but I have to respect Brazilian laws."

His words caused a spike of anger, forcing me to fight to keep the beast at bay. Jennifer saw what was happening and tapped Shoshana. They both came forward.

I said, "Listen to me closely, because I mean what I say. I *wanted* to save your family because it was the right thing to do, but if you don't let me talk to that Russian, you and I are going to have an issue. And you don't want an issue with me."

For the first time, his face reflected the fear of the men he'd recruited to drive the boat.

He said, "Pike, I cannot allow that to occur."

I snapped, "Why not?"

Shoshana stared at Felipe, reading him in her weird way. She said, "Because he can't."

I said, "What the fuck does that mean?"

She turned to me, and, as if Felipe weren't even there, said, "I don't know. But he can't. I can see it."

Felipe shrank into himself upon hearing her words. I saw shame flash through him, then he looked at Shoshana as if she were the devil incarnate.

I regained an even keel, glad it wasn't that he didn't *want* to, but couldn't. I said, "What did you do? Give him back to Russia? Send him to the embassy on the words of someone higher? After what he did to your family?"

He closed his eyes, shutting them so hard I could see the squint, an internal debate raging. He finally opened them and said, "No. He's dead."

My team sat in silence for a moment, the words he uttered incomprehensible. I said, "Dead? Are you serious?"

He looked embarrassed, and I understood exactly what had happened.

He said, "He tried to escape." But there was no conviction in his words. While I had been reining in my own fire for vengeance since I'd entered Brazil, I truly didn't fault his. I glanced at Jennifer, wondering if she was going to sour this whole mission, and she surprised the hell out of me.

She went to him, patted him on the shoulder, and said, "He shouldn't have tried to escape."

What the hell?

He relaxed at her words and said, "I'm sorry. Sometimes these things happen."

I let him know he was full of shit, saying, "Yeah, but not that often when the guy is tied up and handed to you. I needed him."

He started to protest, and I nodded at him, telling him it was water under the bridge, then said, "I don't want that other Russian to attempt the same thing. Understand?"

He nodded back, glad to be away from the conversation. I looked at Jennifer and said, "Let's make sure you and Shoshana know what you're doing with that weapon."

I dragged her to a pelican case about the size of a carry-on at the front of the boat. I knelt down and flipped the latches, revealing an Accuracy International AX-MC precision rifle, broken down into components. A bolt-action chambered for the Taskforce in 6.5 Creedmoor, it was a precision shooter's dream, and one that Jennifer had fired many, many times. Because of it, she knew I hadn't brought her over here to give her a class on the weapon's assembly.

As soon as the case was open, I said, "What the fuck was that all about? You know that Russian didn't try to escape, right? Felipe murdered a man you made me save and you pat him on the back?"

She gave me a little indignation back, saying, "Pike, it was done, and Felipe is our support for this. There was no reason to make him second-guess whether we might be a threat when you're about to get in the water, leaving Shoshana and me alone on the boat with a bunch of BOPE officers he commands. I don't need to be watching him while I'm trying to use the scope."

I shook my head and said, "You confuse the shit out of me. You think strategically when it matters, and tactically when I want to do the same damn thing."

Shoshana was standing above us, looking on intently. Jennifer glanced at her, then said, "I knew you were about to call him out on it, because you have no filter. I only care about *my* family. He can deal with his own demons for what he did. Something you won't have to do, because *you* did the right thing."

I grinned. "Always the smart one."

And she relaxed, smiling.

Shoshana said, "Good."

I turned to her and said, "What'd you say? What do you mean, 'good'?"

Looking like she was the sensei master, she said, "Good. This was good."

I laughed and said, "Get the weapon assembled and positioned. What will be 'good' is if you can get Jennifer on target as the spotter."

Jennifer started working the rifle in a practiced manner, snapping in the barrel, putting together the bolt, and attaching the bipod. Shoshana said, "Don't worry about the spotting. You just worry about Aaron."

Standing behind her, I saw him roll his eyes. I said, "I'm pretty sure he can take care of himself."

I felt the motor cut out on the boat, the hull now gliding silently on the water. Felipe came forward and said, "This is as close as we can get. Any closer and they may feel we're a threat."

I looked at Aaron and said, "Time to go."

49

Knuckles felt his eyes close, the sleep monster trying hard to take over his conscious mind. He snapped them open, glanced at Brett, and saw the same struggle. He leaned over and whispered, "Pike is taking his damn time. Dawn is about an hour away."

Brett let out a tired chuckle and said, "Maybe it'll be another cycle of darkness."

The suspect passenger heard their conversation and cracked an eye, his right hand in his jacket pocket, like it had been since they'd noticed him.

Knuckles caught the movement, put his hand on the knife, and said, "No. It's this cycle. My phone wouldn't ring tonight. He's out there."

I swam blindly through the darkness, staring at my Taskforce phone, the last known location of Knuckles's beacon plugged in and giving me a bearing. It was waterproof, but most definitely not made for underwater operations, and I hoped it hadn't locked up or lost signal underneath the surface, leading me astray on some vector that was no longer valid.

When I'd first broached the plan, I'd assured Aaron that it would work, but I truthfully didn't know, and we didn't have enough air in the HEEDs to recover from a mistake. If it was wrong, we'd be forced to surface.

To make matters worse, the cheap-ass diving mask and fins we'd purchased at a beach store were not really giving me the cutting-edge capability I needed. The mask made it hard to see the phone, and the fins made me feel more like an eight-year-old playing in a pool than a commando. The only good thing was the water wasn't freezing cold. We'd thought about using wet suits, but I wanted the camouflage of the BOPE uniforms at the end, so I'd opted just to swim in the fatigues. It turned out to be a good call, because, while it wasn't pleasant, the temperature was bearable.

I kept plowing ahead, following the compass bearing, Aaron behind me tied to my left hand by a length of twine, blindly trusting me. The bearing never changed, which was giving me growing concern. I couldn't be that good a swimmer to be directly on the line of march to the grid location without some shifting. Not with ocean currents and the darkness.

Five minutes into the swim I checked again, and I was headed straight toward the boat, the beacon showing it about seventy meters away—*if* the bearing was real, but I was now having my doubts. We only had between eight and ten minutes of air, which meant I had to make a decision: continue on, or break off and swim back. Or surface only to find us right next to the boat, alerting them to the assault and causing a catastrophe.

I slowed my swim, felt the line on my hand go slack, and turned, heading at a ninety-degree angle. The arrow shifted, aiming away from me, still on the same bearing.

So it is working.

If I could have, I would have smiled and high-fived Aaron. Instead I just congratulated myself on being a damn good swimmer, reminding myself to brag to Knuckles when I saw him.

I oriented back on the bearing, kept going, and reached the endpoint. I looked up and could barely make out the shape of the ferry against the faint light coming through the water. We'd made it. Now all we had to do was find the pylon.

We'd studied the ferry's location, and, while the terrorists had been smart to place it offshore to prevent an assault, they'd been limited in what they could do to keep it there, and had tied it to an old chunk of concrete that rose thirty feet out of the water, a large base at the bottom, but a thin concrete pillar that held a light to guide in the ships to the harbor. It was the only thing around that would allow us to prepare for the assault out of view of the men on the ferry.

I oriented on the bow of the shadow above me, then began swimming diagonally to the east, splitting off it. I went twenty feet and just about slammed into the cement pylon sinking to the ocean floor below me. I gingerly stuck out my hand, caressed the barnacles over the concrete, then swam around, getting behind it. When I was out of view of the boat, I rose, breaking the surface of the water.

I grabbed on to a set of concrete stairs at the base, holding off from the small current trying to push me into it, and Aaron broke the surface next to me.

He spit out the regulator of the HEEDS, dropping the bottle to a lanyard around his neck. "I thought for sure you were bullshitting me about that beacon trace. Especially when you stopped."

I grinned and said, "And you still followed me?"

He chuckled and said, "No. Hell no. Shoshana said it would work because she has some unreasonable faith in you. I followed *her*."

I withdrew my Glock, saying, "Maybe I should start listening to her."

I drained the water out of the barrel, dropped the magazine, and conducted a function's check. It worked fine. I reseated the magazine and saw Aaron doing the same. He said, "Maybe you should."

I said, "You and I both know that ain't going to happen. She's crazy."

He stifled a laugh and I pulled a balaclava out of my thigh pocket, wrung it out, and pulled it over my head. I said, "Okay, here we go. You have the stern; I'm swimming around the bow to the starboard side. Remember, once we've eliminated the threat, get all the hostages facedown, hands out."

His face went to stone, getting into mission mode. He nodded, put in his earpiece, pulled on his own balaclava, and said on the net, "Check, check."

I heard him and said, "Roger. Got you. Koko, Carrie, we're at LCC. Moving now."

50

Jennifer responded to Pike's call, her voice flat, "Roger all. Target acquired. Standing by."

What she didn't relay was the absolute fear rocking through her body. The AX-MC was a precision shooter's dream, leaving any mistakes not a function of the weapon, but a function of the shooter. And the platform she was shooting on was less than ideal.

She *did* have the target in her sights. She hadn't lied. With the optic at twenty-power, she could clearly see the terrorist through the window of the captain's cabin, the light above him giving her hyperclarity of his features, down to the acne on his cheeks, but the "calm cove" still had a swell, causing the reticle of her scope to bob up and down. She couldn't keep it still.

She said, "Shoshana, what's the wind now?"

Lying prone next to her, Shoshana said, "Jennifer, at this distance, it doesn't matter."

"Wind."

Shoshana held up a Kestral wind meter and said, "Still three miles an hour, still head on and zero value."

She dropped it and said, "What's the problem? I know it's not the distance or the wind."

"This boat isn't stable. It's rising and falling, and under the scope's power, it's like trying to settle a crosshair on the back of a bucking horse."

Shoshana said, "Is it steady? Or random?"

"It's steady."

"Ride it. Dry-fire now. Time it and squeeze."

Behind the scope, Jennifer exhaled and said, "I don't know if I can do this. Everybody on that boat is relying on me. If I miss, or even if I just wound him, he'll think an assault is imminent and kill everyone on board. All he has to do is press a button."

Shoshana rolled over and put her hand on Jennifer's shoulder. Jennifer looked at her, and Shoshana brushed a strand of hair out of her face, an odd, out-of-place gesture.

She said, "Jennifer, I would take this shot for you if I could. I can do it, but I'm not as good as you with that weapon. I know it and Pike knows it. Banish the thought of failure. Focus on the reticle. Focus on the bullet. Make it go where you want it to go."

There was such an intensity coming out of Shoshana that Jennifer was unsure of what to say. She nodded, and Shoshana rubbed her back and rolled over again, the gesture more intimate than the situation demanded.

At one time, Jennifer and Pike had thought Shoshana was a lesbian, and then had learned that she didn't understand such a distinction. Shoshana's concept of love had nothing to do with gender. If she cared about you, she did it with all of her being. If she didn't, she'd kill you without a second thought.

Shoshana commanded, "Dry-fire. Get the timing."

The conflicting nature of her commands and the intimacy caused Jennifer to shake her head, but the conviction from Shoshana gave her strength. Jennifer had learned early on that Shoshana had an unearthly skill at killing, and if she believed in Jennifer, the least Jennifer could do was believe in herself.

She settled down behind the stock, obtained a cheek weld, closed her eyes for a moment, then opened them. She watched the Christmas tree of the reticle rise and fall, rise and fall. She got the rhythm, took a breath at the bottom, exhaled at the top, then broke the trigger.

She repeated the maneuver, gaining confidence.

She did it one more time, and then the radio broke, "Koko, Koko, this is Pike. We are set. Need a read on the targets."

Jennifer felt the adrenaline start to rise and quelled it, not wanting to alter her rhythm with a racing heartbeat. She didn't dare shift the scope to find Pike at the bottom of the boat, instead relying on her spotter.

Shoshana said, "I see Pike. He's just below the ledge of the gunwale, holding on to one of those tires the kids use to climb up. He's secure, his target is above him at Alpha One, unaware."

She paused, and Jennifer knew she was scanning the back of the boat. After a few seconds, she said, "Target two is at the templated location on the stern at Charlie Five, just to the left of the latrines. He's sitting down on the gunwale. Aaron is unsighted."

To prevent the boat team from having to try to describe where the terrorists were by using landmarks on the ferry—like "He's near the third row of seats on the port side" or "He's by the anchor"—Pike had broken the boat down into sectors, with the length being numbered from one to five and the width from A to C, thereby eliminating any possibility of confusion.

Jennifer got on the net, her conscious mind not wanting to initiate, but she set the mission in motion anyway. "This is Koko. We have you. Your target is just above you, Alpha One.

You're in perfect position. Second target is at the projected location Charlie Five. Aaron is unsighted. I have my target with high confidence."

She didn't want to say the next words, but she did. "Ready to execute."

"Any sign of the sleeper?"

He was asking about the final terrorist. Jennifer knew that once Pike and Aaron eliminated the terrorists currently on guard duty, they'd need to get to the one asleep before he woke up and realized what was happening. Before he could simply press a trigger on a detonator. Before he could immolate everything she held dear.

Horrific thoughts racing through her head, she said, "Stand by."

Off the net, deferring to her as the command of their element, Shoshana said, "I can't see inside the boat. He could be anywhere."

Jennifer clicked back on and said, "Pike, this is Koko, fourth terrorist is unsighted. I say again, unsighted."

She waited, wondering if he would abort.

Pike came back, his voice as calm and cold as a mountain lake, "Roger. Understand. All elements, all elements, I have control. Stand by."

The words were as final as a guillotine beginning its slide. She was committed now, and Pike was counting on her. Trusting her. She banished everything from her mind but the reticle in her scope. She settled it on the man in the cabin, seeing the acne, seeing the eyes. Seeing the life. She didn't think about that. All she thought about was the rise and fall of the crosshairs. And the count from Pike. She heard nothing for a brief moment, then it began.

"Five . . . four . . . three . . . two . . . one . . ."

51

Jennifer's call about the final terrorist gave me pause. Hiding underneath the swell of the bow, clinging to a ratty tire dangling down with one hand while holding my pistol with the other, I debated about aborting. I was sure that I could eliminate the target above me, but we had four, and each one was a single point of failure. The ones who were awake didn't concern me, though. I had confidence in the team to eliminate those targets. It was the fourth one that gave me pause. If he was asleep, we stood a better than even chance of winning. If he was not, we would be in trouble.

But if I *did* abort, the next group of commandos would be an idiotic fast-boat assault with a group of wannabe ninjas, causing the ferry to explode when they were still out in the channel, killing my friends.

Knuckles didn't deserve that. He deserved my best, win or lose. If it went south, we'd both die, just like he would do for me.

I kicked off my tourist fins, dropped the HEED to the bottom of the ocean, and said, "Roger. Understand. All elements, all elements, I have control. Stand by." I gave a momentary pause, then began the countdown, "Five . . . four . . . three . . . two . . . one . . . execute, execute, execute."

On the first "execute" I began to hoist myself up the tire, putting my feet inside the well. Remaining in a crouch, I raised my pistol, still having not heard the rifle bullet break the sound barrier. We couldn't attack without the removal of the terrorist in the captain's cabin on the second deck, and the longer I crouched here, now in possible view of the terrorist, the greater the chance this thing would end up a debacle. I started to get on the net, worried that something had gone wrong on the GRUMEC boat, when the crack of the round reverberated across the harbor.

I immediately stood up in the tire, reaching the top of the gunwale. I saw my target slack-jawed, holding a small Skorpion machine pistol, and looking at me like I was the devil.

His brain finally began to engage, and I saw the weapon begin to rise. I held on to the rope with my weak hand, raised my Glock in my right hand, settled the red dot of the holosight on his forehead, and broke the trigger.

Knuckles took another glance at his watch, leaned back into Brett, and said, "Pike is cutting it real close here. BMNT is about twenty minutes away, with the full sun in about thirty."

Brett said, "Must be the Ranger thing. Dawn's when the French and Indians attack, so he's going to do the same."

Both of them were whispering, pretending to be asleep, but even so, Willow Radcliffe rolled over, staring at them. Knuckles winked at her, and she snuggled into her son, eyes still on him.

Brett said, "We need to be prepared for disappointment here, and I can't go another day without sleep if we want to solve this problem on our own."

Knuckles kept his eyes on Willow and said, "He's coming

in the next thirty minutes. Trust me. When he does, we need to neutralize the unknown."

Brett glanced at the man they called the "unknown." He was fast asleep, his right hand still inside his jacket pocket. He said, "That shouldn't be too much of an issue."

As soon as the words were out of Brett's mouth, Knuckles caught movement on the starboard side. The resting terrorist sat up, rubbing his face. He picked up his weapon and walked sleepily to the toilet at the rear of the boat.

Knuckles whispered, "Shit. Now there's another problem. With the time they've had to analyze this crisis, I'm betting Pike is counting on at least one terrorist being asleep."

The man passed by them, reached the possible threat, and glanced at the mass of hostages all curled on the floor or benches, asleep. He surreptitiously patted the man on the shoulder, waking him. He whispered something before moving on.

Brett said, "Guess that answers the 'unknown' question."

Knuckles said, "And now that asshole is awake, too. You have him. I'll take the sleeper guard."

"How?"

"I'll just keep him close enough to strike."

Before Brett could say anything else, Knuckles slid off the bench and rolled next to Willow. She opened her eyes at the movement, saw him, and said, "Is this it? You're going to attack?"

Knuckles saw no fear and wondered what her brother had told her about situations like this. She seemed to have absolute faith that he held some magic ability to save her and her son, not realizing the vagaries that the god of war took, no matter the planning. One such vagary just went to the toilet, and he planned on using her to short-circuit it.

He said, "No, we're not attacking just yet, but I want to keep a handle on that guard who just went to the bathroom. I need to leave Brett here, so I was wondering if you'd go to the bathroom with me. Since we have to go in pairs."

She said, "Why does he need to stay here?"

Knuckles thought, *She doesn't miss a thing.*

He said, "He just does. Can you help me?"

"Will it put my son in danger?"

"No. The opposite."

She nodded. Knuckles looked at his watch and said, "You get in the toilet and stay for at least ten minutes."

"Why?"

"Because we're on the clock. After ten minutes you can come out, but not before."

She started to ask something else, and the man came out of the toilet, walking back to his pallet. Knuckles stood, holding his hand in the air. The terrorist approached, and Knuckles said that they both needed to use the bathroom. He grimaced, looked at his pallet, then nodded. They walked to the rear of the boat, and the man raised his pistol, waving it. Knuckles let Willow go first.

She entered the bathroom, and Knuckles edged closer until he could get to the man in one leap. He felt the adrenaline rise for no reason whatsoever, wondering where the hell Pike was. The phone alert had to have been sent from him. He checked his watch and saw they were nearing what the military called Before Morning Nautical Twilight—the time when the earth began to glow with the light of the sun before the sun actually rose in the sky.

The guard grew antsy and banged on the door. Knuckles was sure it scared the hell out of Willow. She shouted something and refused to come out. The guard looked at Knuckles with suspicion, then turned to bang on the door again.

Knuckles heard a split in the air, a distinct crack that he recognized immediately. The guard looked confused, turning around trying to identify where the noise had come from. The terrorist at the stern of the boat, the one on duty, stood up, and Knuckles saw his head explode. The guard to Knuckles's front shouted and raised his weapon, aiming it at the toilet as if the woman inside had caused the attack.

Knuckles slammed the barrel high, and he squeezed the trigger, sending bullets through the roof of the ferry, firing spasmodically until the machine pistol locked open on an empty magazine. Knuckles ripped the weapon out of his hand and lashed out with a foot, hammering the man in his gut. He sprang against the gunwale, reached into his jacket, and jerked something out.

Knuckles flicked open the blade from the child and slashed forward, slicing for the tendons in the man's wrist. The blade connected, biting deep. The man screamed again, dropping the detonator. Knuckles spun the blade in his hand, getting a reverse grip, grabbed the man by the head, and punched him in the throat with a glancing blow, letting the blade do the work.

A fountain of blood blurted out of the wound, and the man sank to his knees. Knuckles put his foot in his chest and pushed him over, then grabbed the detonator off the floor, making sure it was secure.

He turned to the rear, seeing Brett had subdued the "unknown." He held up another wireless detonator with a grin on his face.

Knuckles shouted, "Watch the rest of them. There might be another sleeper."

He caught movement next to the toilet and whirled, seeing a BOPE policeman dressed like a ninja searching another dead terrorist on the other side of the latrine. Knuckles raised his hands, showing he wasn't a threat, and the policeman pulled up his balaclava for a second. Knuckles had a hard time believing what he was seeing. It was the Israeli, Aaron Bergman.

Aaron removed the detonator from his target and stood up, saying, "You look like you've seen a ghost. Is that the thanks I get?"

Knuckles laughed and said, "No, no, you get the thanks. I was just surprised to see a policeman, but you're the last thing I expected. I thought this would be a Taskforce show."

Aaron moved into the interior with his weapon out, looking for threats and saying over his shoulder, "It's a Pike show. There is no Taskforce."

And then Knuckles heard, "Seems like I'm always bailing you out of trouble."

Knuckles turned and saw another policeman, his face also covered, holding only a Glock and standing above the hostages lying facedown on the deck. Next to him was Brett, a huge grin plastered across his face. He knew who was under the balaclava.

And so did Knuckles.

He smiled with genuine emotion for the first time in his ordeal. Pike's words were the exact quote Knuckles had said to him when he'd saved his life in Bosnia so long ago. He said, "I guess we're even."

Pike said, "Nope. I still owe you. Let's clean up this place. Clear the hostages of any threat and get out."

He remembered Willow in the bathroom and said, "Brett's got a sleeper. Pretty sure that's the last threat."

He knocked on the door of the bathroom and heard nothing. He said, "Willow, it's okay. Come out."

She opened the door, saw him, and sank to her knees, saying, "Is it over?"

He nodded, and her son ran over to her, wrapping his arms around her neck. Knuckles squatted down and held out the Zero Tolerance knife. He folded the blade, saying, "Thanks for the loan."

The boy took it, nodding solemnly.

Willow pulled her son close, hugging him fiercely. She took in the activity on the boat, watching the men separating hostages and searching for threats, her gaze finally reaching the man at Knuckles's feet.

Initially shocked at the slaughter, Knuckles saw her expression change when she realized who the dead man was. A raw smile crawled across her face and she said, "You weren't lying. You *are* worse than my brother."

52

Ignoring the gentle rise and fall of the boat, Knuckles kept his eyes glued to a set of binoculars, watching the ferry slowly advance to the dock on Itaparica Island. He said, "You should have brought off Willow and her kid. They're American citizens, too."

Pike said, "Couldn't happen. Sorry. You disappearing as a nobody is one thing, but making her disappear would have been impossible. It would have busted our little play."

Eyes still jammed to the binos, Knuckles said, "I'm pretty sure your play is already busted. You really think the hostages believe you're BOPE? You were speaking English."

Pike said, "Best I could do. They might talk about English speakers, but with Felipe controlling the debriefs it won't go any further than conspiracy theories told around a dinner table. Willow is the only one I'm worried about talking."

Knuckles dropped the binos and said, "She's good. I spoke to her. Her brother is a SEAL, and she gets it. She won't say anything."

Pike smiled and said, "I thought you were fighting so hard to bring her with us because she's a little bit of a hammer. Should have known it was some SEAL crap."

Knuckles returned to looking at the ferry and said, "It was neither. She thinks the entire thing was a setup to kill her, and with what you said about the Russians, I think she's right. She's still vulnerable."

After the assault, after Pike and Aaron had declared the crisis site secure, Pike had called in Jennifer, then had taken Brett and Knuckles to the second deck, out of the eyes of the other hostages. The sun had begun to rise and Knuckles had seen a boat in the distance coming closer. It was military gray, sleek and fast. He saw four BOPE officers on the deck, and then recognized Jennifer and Shoshana.

He said, "Those real BOPE or more Taskforce?"

Pike said, "Real BOPE. We're turning the crisis site over to them; we're getting on that boat and disappearing."

"What about the backpacks with the explosives?"

"That's a BOPE problem now. We're not touching them. Felipe's got EOD on the island, but he said he wanted to get the hostages off first before he screwed with them."

Knuckles said, "That female below is an American citizen. She and her son need to come with us."

Pike said, "I can't do that. The only reason I'm taking you off is because there's going to be an in-depth debrief of all the hostages, media attention, a veritable circus on the island. You probably don't realize it, but this thing made international news. Everyone in Brazil wants to know what's happening."

Knuckles started to shake his head and Pike said, "She's a Petrobras executive. She's been on the news. They've blabbed about her and the State Department's engaged because of her—sorry, they didn't really give a shit about you. Everyone knows she's on the boat. She can't simply disappear."

He said, "Okay, I get it, but I need to talk to her before that boat gets here."

"Not going to happen. We're walking right across this deck,

over the top of the hostages, and dropping into that boat to be replaced by real BOPE. You're gone. You're a ghost now."

Knuckles said, "I talked to her during this crisis, extensively. Christ, her son gave me the knife I used on the fourth terrorist. *She* was the diversion that allowed me to take him out, and she did it knowing the risks. You want this to work, I need to tell her to keep quiet."

He saw Pike considering the request and ended with, "I'm going to talk to her before I leave. I'm not asking."

Pike slowly nodded and said, "Okay, okay. Stay here." He put on the balaclava and went downstairs. When he returned, Knuckles saw Willow in tow. Pike pointed at Knuckles in the captain's chair and waited outside.

Confused, Willow entered and said, "What's going on?"

"You remember what you said your brother did? How it was all secret?"

She nodded, and he said, "That's basically what we have here. I'm going to disappear, and the BOPE are going to take over this boat. You're safe now, but you can't mention anything I did. As far as this goes, it was a BOPE rescue. Can you do that?"

Alarmed, she said, "Take us with you. Take Beau and me. Don't leave us here."

It tore at Knuckles, but he knew what Pike said was correct. "Willow, I can't. You're a bigwig with Petrobras. You got on the boat with a security man, which is enough for you to be remembered. His body is still on the boat, and the news has been reporting on you as the lone celebrity of the crisis. The U.S. State Department got involved because you were on the ferry. If you don't show up, there are going to be questions. Questions that could lead to me, and the men who saved your life."

She said, "I told you this wasn't random. They may have looked like criminals, but *I'm* the reason this happened. They were trying to eliminate me and make it look like criminals."

Knuckles said, "You don't know that. And anyway, they failed now. You're safe. You ride the ferry in with the BOPE men, and you'll be home in a few hours, back at your Petrobras desk."

She scoffed and said, "I'm through with Petrobras. This isn't worth my son's life. I'm done. These savages can have this place."

"Well, there you go. Get out of here and announce your departure. That'll stop anyone from trying to kill you. Why kill someone who's leaving?"

She considered his words, then nodded, saying, "Thank you. Thank you for what you did. Beau thinks you're like Captain America or something."

Knuckles laughed and said, "Tell him Captain America's got nothing on this crew."

She finally gave a tentative smile, then turned to go. She reached the door and Knuckles said, "Hey, I didn't get any way to contact you, after this is over."

She turned, fished through her clothing, then handed him a card. She said, "That's my private card, with my real address and direct number. Give me a call and I'll take you and your men out to dinner."

He nodded, and Pike led her down below. When he returned, Aaron was behind him. Without fanfare, Pike said, "Boat's here."

They walked across the top deck, climbed down the ladder outside of the latrine, and dropped into the well of the fast boat, crouching low.

53

Knuckles saw Pike scuttle behind the transom, out of view of anyone on the ferry, and he, Brett, and Aaron followed. Knuckles looked toward the bow and saw Jennifer and Shoshana slithering forward, almost on their bellies, keeping out of sight.

Shoshana went to Aaron, checking him for wounds like she was inspecting a household pet for ticks. He endured it with a grin. Jennifer came to Pike and Knuckles, and Knuckles could tell she'd been under significant stress through the night. She was glowing with relief at the sight of them.

He said, "You the one who made that shot on the guy from the upper deck?"

She nodded, and he said, "What idiot told you to take a precision rifle shot from a moving boat deck?"

Pike chuckled, and she looked confused. She said, "Pike did. He said it was no different from the range."

Now Knuckles laughed and said, "And was it?"

Vehemently, letting off the last four hours of doubt, she said, "Hell no! I couldn't keep the reticle from bobbing. I was petrified I'd miss."

She turned to Pike and said, "Is he right? Did you lie to me?"

Pike leaned in and pecked her cheek, saying, "No, I didn't lie. I said you had the skill, and you did. If I'd have said that this shot was hard, you would have started second-guessing. And by the way, that was a damn good shot."

Incredulous, Jennifer looked at Shoshana, and she grinned, saying, "Told you. He believes in you like I do. You made the bullet go where you wanted."

Jennifer's eyes flared, but before she could say anything, Felipe came forward, fully kitted out like the BOPE commander he was.

His face aglow, he said, "This has been a miracle. All of the hostages saved, all of the terrorists dead. I can't thank you enough."

Pike said, "Our pleasure. Just remember our deal. You get to be the hero. We get to disappear. You control the debriefs and tell anyone that mentions English speakers that they're confused and traumatized by the crisis."

He nodded his head, saying, "That will be *my* pleasure. I've already alerted the government. It is going out all over the news. The president is claiming it as a great win. It's the least I can do. Nobody will know you have ever been here."

"And you need to keep that entire episode with your wife under wraps. I know you want to punish the men who did it, but that's my lane. I want to talk to that final man. Make sure he doesn't 'escape.'"

"Of course. I understand. And my men understand. Look, I have to get you out of here if you want to stay hidden, and I have to remain on the ferry."

Pike stuck his hand out and said, "I'll contact you in a few days. Good luck with the press on this mess."

Felipe shook his hand forcefully and said, "This will be the first time in a week when I'm glad they're here. They're going to film our entry into the harbor. This is going to be a great day."

Pike said, "Felipe, you deserve it. I appreciate the help."

Solemnly, Felipe said, "No, no. It is I who appreciates what you've done."

Someone shouted at him from the ferry, Pike slapped him on the shoulder, and he left.

The fast boat detached from the ferry, and in minutes they were back in deep water, away from the harbor and able to stand up. Knuckles had immediately taken to looking through binoculars at the ferry, watching for Willow's exit and fighting Pike over his decision to leave her.

Pike said, "She'll be okay now."

"I'll believe that when I see her leave the ferry. She really seems to think the entire crisis was about her."

"Maybe, but it wasn't engineered. The hostage takers were truly a bunch of terrorists, but the Russians were trying to cause the assault to go bad, in effect, killing all the hostages. I thought it was because they'd found you here in Brazil, but maybe it was her. I don't know. What I do know is that we're going to make the rest of them pay for what they've done."

Knuckles lowered the binoculars and said, "You sure about that? We're successful here. From what you've said, we were successful in Charleston as well. You want to press this? I mean, what if it leads back to Moscow? You planning to go on a killing spree there?"

Pike exhaled and said, "I honestly don't know right now. I'm not sure about this whole ferry thing, but what I do know is that a bunch of Russian mercenaries recognized you here in Brazil, and because of that, they tried to kill me in Charleston. I don't know why, and I don't know how. What I do know is that it happened. I didn't start this war, but I'm going to finish it."

Knuckles listened to him, and something finally clicked

in his memory. "Wait a minute . . . Pike, these fuckers were in Switzerland. That's how they know us. It wasn't *me* they recognized. It was Brett. This was from rescuing Amena. Remember, he left his target alive? You and I were forced to kill ours, but he was able to subdue his. I'll bet that guy is here, in Brazil."

Pike said, "No way. Those assholes were Ukrainian and Chechen. Not Russian. There was no Russian government involvement there. It was some private mafia thing."

"Ukrainian and Chechen *is* Russian. Well, at least some of Ukraine, and definitely the Chechen part. That's it. They aren't private. They're like us. A slim veneer of private over a government-sanctioned entity."

Knuckles saw his words held weight with Pike. He brought up the binos again and said, "You messed up their plans in Switzerland, and then we were spotted down here. They thought you were going to screw up whatever they have in play down here just like you did in Switzerland, and they went after you."

Knuckles heard nothing from Pike, and turned, finding him deep in thought. Pike said, "You really believe that?"

"Yes, I do. It's the only thing that makes sense. Nung told you that they'd recognized members of GRS down here, and Brett and I are the only ones that could possibly be. Nothing else explains how they started tracking us—much less *why* they would."

Pike nodded, and Knuckles could see the anger bubbling just underneath the surface. Pike said, "If that's the case, they're professional killers. The man I took down in Switzerland was as good as you and me. He was a killing machine, and the others here are probably selected and trained the same way."

Knuckles smiled and said, "Well, I guess we should count

our blessings for getting away." He saw Pike's face and said, "Right?"

Pike glared at him, the lava of rage spilling out. He said, "I'm going to burn it down. Whatever those fucks have planned, I'm going to stop it."

Wanting away from the conversation, Knuckles raised the binoculars, seeing the ferry arrive at the terminal. A mass of cameras and newspeople streamed forward, a phalanx of BOPE police trying to stop the onslaught.

He said, "We have no sanction for that, Pike. I understand the problem, but we can't run amok whacking Russians here in Brazil."

Pike said, "We can, if you'll come with me. Wolffe is on my side. And Amanda Croft is as well."

Knuckles glanced at him and said, "Amanda? How?"

"She's the one who got me the access to Felipe, because she cares about you. Not everyone in D.C. is a sniveling coward."

Knuckles laughed and returned to the binoculars, saying, "Amanda won't support what you have in mind. I know her pretty well, Pike. Biblically, if you get my meaning. She won't sanction us ripping through Brazil on a suicide run."

He saw the BOPE men surround the exit of the ferry, then saw Felipe giving orders to the press. The first one off was Willow, and he waited to see if she would turn and wave, knowing that was stupid because he was four hundred meters offshore.

Her son held her hand, Felipe helped her to the stairs, and then the side of the ferry exploded, shredding the police captain and launching Willow's body into the air.

He blinked in disbelief. A second later, the echo of the explosion reached the boat. Pike stood up, saying, "What the fuck was that?"

Knuckles dropped the binoculars and said, "One of the IEDs just went off."

He sat down heavily and put his head in his hands. Pike snatched up the binoculars and trained them on the ferry port.

Jennifer ran up, saying, "What happened?"

Pike surveyed the chaos and said, "One of the bombs went off. As the hostages were exiting."

Jennifer took the binoculars, saw the carnage, and whispered, "That's not fair. That is *not* fair."

Pike turned to Knuckles, his voice grim, saying, "Willow was right. This wasn't about you. It was about her. You still want to go home?"

Knuckles felt a fury unlike anything he'd ever experienced. He'd often thought about the rage Pike kept bottled up inside of him, wondering why he couldn't keep it at bay.

And now he knew.

He thought about Willow's love of her son. Thought about her courage even with the risk of death. And then thought about the men who had done this.

He balled his hands into fists, trying to squeeze the pain away, then slammed them into the side of the boat hard enough to cause the BOPE policeman behind the wheel to jump. He locked eyes with Pike and said, "No. I don't want to go home."

He looked at the mushroom cloud forming over the ferry terminal and said, "I want to burn it all to the ground."

54

Nikita could tell Kolva was worried. Afraid that Nikita would somehow blame him for the debacle that had befallen his team. And ordinarily, Nikita probably would, but this time Kolva had an out: his sniper shot had eliminated the ombudsman target, the American woman. And Alek had a lead on the next one, conducting reconnaissance today with an execution tomorrow. That left the final one. The big one.

They were still on track, and, while the loss of the team was a serious problem, what really aggravated Nikita was that he had been forced to leave his high-rise life of luxury and relocate to a crappy dive hotel near the airport. One without even the basic necessity of a minibar.

Nikita said, "So two of the team are unaccounted for—including the leader, Maksim—and three are confirmed dead?"

As far as he was concerned, the team had gotten what they deserved. They had become lax, and because of it, the BOPE had made them pay. There was no reason to bemoan the deaths, but the ones that had disappeared were a different story.

"Yes, sir. I didn't get a chance to sterilize their bodies before the church custodians found them. They'll be reported with the Saint Kitts passports. It might raise our level of heat state when we use ours."

"That's the least of my worries. My concern is Maksim. Artem was just a guard and knows nothing. They can torture him until he dies, but Maksim knows everything."

Kolva simply nodded, and Nikita could tell he wanted to be anywhere but here. Nikita said, "You're sure that nobody realized your sniper shot set off the explosives? They believe it was a police mistake?"

"Yes. I was able to break down the sniper's hide and escape just by walking out of the bell tower on the island. I loaded up the vehicle with the kit and returned to the scene. Nobody paid the slightest bit of attention to the church. The weapon was suppressed, so there was no gunshot for them to pinpoint. Just the bullet breaking the sound barrier, and that was overshadowed by the explosion."

"Good. Good. Killing Felipe is icing on the cake. How that bastard managed to free his wife and then assault the ferry is beyond me. He didn't appear that formidable of an opponent. It would have been perfect if you'd have killed the two Americans, but you can't have everything."

Kolva's face soured, like he'd eaten something rotten.

"What?"

"Sir, I hung around as long as I could, and saw all of the hostages left alive exit the boat. I didn't see the Americans."

"Maybe you missed them. It was chaotic, yes? Maybe they exited while you were making your escape from the church."

"Yes, sir, that's possible, but I overheard a snippet of conversation from a BBC news reporter. She said that some of the passengers claimed that their rescuers were wearing BOPE uniforms, but speaking English."

Nikita leaned forward, saying, "Speaking English? On the ferry?"

"Yes, sir. That's all I heard. I tried to get closer, and they shut down the conversation, moving past the ropes segregating the press pool."

And it became clear to Nikita what had happened. He snapped, "Leave me. I have to make a call."

Kolva snapped upright, springing out of the chair at Nikita's tone. He said, "Yes, sir. What are my next orders?"

His false eyeball bulging out, Nikita screamed, "To get the fuck out of this room. Go!"

Kolva scrambled out the door, slamming it behind him, and Nikita picked up his cell phone, going through the dance with the Wagner control and gaining a conference room number. He dialed up the VPN on his laptop, and waited.

Thirty seconds later the screen cleared, and he saw Dmitri Pavlov scowling at him. Dmitri said, "I'm assuming this is good news, since it's an unscheduled contact."

Nikita had little time for his aggrieved attitude. "Sir, how is Charleston proceeding? What's the status of Grolier Recovery Services?"

Dmitri's scowl deepened, and Nikita knew it wasn't going to be good news. "Charleston was a debacle. The men I sent— the ones you vouched for—are gone. Three of them are dead, and one is missing."

Nikita ignored the implied placing of blame. He said, "How? They were going up against a nanny and a child."

"They went up against a buzz saw, and now I have to clean up the mess, just like I did before, when your men screwed up the initial attack against GRS. The only good news is the police have no idea what's going on. It's a quiet beach community and three murders are unheard-of. After the other two deaths in Charleston, they're going crazy over a Caribbean drug connection. That's the only good news."

The ramifications flashed through Nikita's head like an electric current. He said, "You followed protocol, correct? You didn't tell the men *why* they were hitting the targets, right?"

Dmitri exploded, "Are you actually questioning me?"

Nikita backpedaled and said, "No, sir, I'm just trying to understand the threat to Operation Harvest. If the missing man knows about our mission, we might be compromised."

Slightly mollified, Dmitri said, "They only knew about Grolier Recovery Services. They didn't know *why* they were interdicting, just that they had to."

Nikita said, "Good, very good, but we still need to deal with the man from Grolier Recovery Services. He's as bad as you said he was. He's mucking up my mission down here."

"What's that mean?"

Nikita told him about the loss of the team and his suspicions about the ferry rescue, ending with "We need to send in another team. One that's prepared to fight this time."

"What about Harvest? Did you at least get the target?"

"Sir? Did you hear what I just said? These men might prevent successful execution of Operation Harvest."

Dmitri spoke in a slow, measured cadence, repeating his question. "Yes. I heard you. Did—you—get—the—target?"

Riled at the lack of concern, Nikita stifled what he was about to blurt out. He said, "Yes, sir. We did. I placed a sniper in a bell tower of a church overlooking the harbor as a contingency. I thought it would be because those idiots on the ferry might give up, but it turned out the Americans managed to kill them all. One of the IEDs was positioned right at the exit ramp of the ferry. When the target left the ferry, stepping on the ramp, he initiated the explosives. We killed the BOPE police chief."

Dmitri nodded and said, "And the target? What about her?"

"She was standing directly behind the police chief. He absorbed the blast and shrapnel, but she was blown off the ramp and slammed into the pylons of the dock, along with her son. They're both in the hospital and probably won't survive. She's eliminated."

Dmitri leaned back, thinking. He said, "She's not eliminated. In fact, having her in the hospital is the worst case. You need to pull her plug. Make sure she's dead."

"Sir, she's no longer working for the foreseeable future. If ever. She's done. We have two more targets. One—the mining minister—has been reacquired. I expect him to be eliminated tomorrow. We have his pattern of life, and we have a plan to make it happen without exposure. The other is the political target, which will require extensive planning. Harvest is on schedule, but we need to press ahead."

Dmitri said, "You need to understand what we're doing here. It's not about killing. It's about replacing. The deaths mean nothing unless the man who assumes the position is in our pocket. She's still alive, which means she still holds the job title. Which also means we cannot replace her with our chosen successor. Best case, her office just quits operating while she's in the hospital. Worst case, someone takes her job on an interim basis. Someone we don't control, and when she dies, we now need to kill him. That won't do. Make sure she's dead. Force the succession process to work. Make our man get the job."

Nikita recognized the truth in what Dmitri said, even as he didn't want to believe it, because he had only so many men. He finally said, "Okay, sir. I have Luca and Simon from the Amazon mission. They were going to target the politician, but

I can use them for this. I'd recommend hitting the other two targets and then circling back. Let me do Harvest as planned, and then take her out."

"Taking her out now is the easiest thing. She's on her deathbed. Do it now."

Nikita wondered if the man had actually ever been in Spetsnaz. Ever worked a sensitive mission on the ground. He carefully laid out what he saw.

"Sir, she's going to be in the hospital for the duration of Harvest, making killing her problematic. Let me execute the missions we have planned, and then take her out. She might be dead by then anyway. Why raise a signature now? When we kill her, it will be the first that won't look like an accident. Think."

He saw Dmitri bristle yet again, and was growing weary of the show. *He* was the one on the tip of the spear, not that fat, pompous ass in Russia, earning money off the blood his team had spilled. He'd feared Dmitri when he'd been given the mission, but gradually, with the debacle in Charleston and other mistakes, his fear was melting away.

Dmitri said, "Don't question me. Unless you want to spend some time on the sharp end of a government inquiry on how you've been operating."

Nikita couldn't believe what the man had said. Technically, private military companies were illegal by the Russian constitution, but Putin had used Wagner for every one of his escapades. Dmitri was telling him to tow the line, or get jailed for doing the very thing he was hired to execute. Telling him he was expendable. Which was the last thing on earth Nikita would tolerate. *He* was the apex predator. Dimitri was just another man paying the bills. The threat opened a fissure in Nikita's commitment. Not to the mission, but to the man.

He simply said, "Understood, sir. But think about what I said. The best path is to continue forward. The political target is the endgame. We don't get him, then the rest is irrelevant."

Dmitri tapped a pen on his desk for a moment, and Nikita saw he was confounded that his threat had been dismissed. He said, "Okay, okay. I see the logic. But she's in a hospital now, and, if she lives, will be moved to her home. A hardened target. I want someone tracking her status."

Nikita said, "I'll have Luca and Simon on it, but that's it. I'm stretched too thin."

"Do it."

Nikita nodded to the camera, paused a beat, then said, "What about the man from Charleston? We have to hit him again. I need him off of my back."

Dmitri leaned back and said, "That's not going to happen."

"Sir, he's here and he's skilled. We need to get him out of Brazil."

"Do you not understand what happened in Charleston? What the damage is? Everyone there had a Saint Kitts passport. All of the men entered the United States under that flag, and with five dead, it's going to raise the level of inquiry. *You* are operating on a Saint Kitts passport."

"Sir, I really think that the risk is worth the reward. I have no handle on the men down here, and they've proven deadly. They're still on the loose. I have no idea what information they've gained from Maksim's capture."

"It's not going to happen. I've already prepared our Saint Kitts foreign ministry contact for the questions out of Charleston. I told him if he wants our investment fund to continue, he needs to play ball. He's agreed, and can deflect on the dead, but I'm certainly not sending another team with

Saint Kitts passports back into South Carolina, and Russian passports are out of the question."

"Sir, that man is still here. Still hunting."

"All that means is that you have your work cut out for you. You need to look both ways now. Unlike you did in the Donbass."

Nikita heard the words and wanted to jump through the screen, strangling the fat toad where he sat. Instead he said, "Understood, sir. I'll get it done."

55

Nikita stabbed the keyboard with his finger, disconnecting the VPN. He considered throwing the damn thing against the wall, shattering the laptop in a satisfying explosion of plastic, if for no other reason than Dmitri's face had been on the screen.

He did not.

Nikita stood up, pacing the room, Dmitri's last insult biting deep. Much deeper than Dmitri knew. It was why he was relegated to working for that bloated maggot in the first place.

In his own way, Nikita was a patriot, and always had been. He had little time for men who served in the military and then transferred to Wagner, ostensibly for the motherland but in reality for the money. Dmitri was one such man, growing rich off the blood of others. Nikita was not. He was forced into the arrangement because of the wounds he'd sustained in Ukraine.

A Spetsnaz special forces expert in the Russian GRU, in February 2014 he'd deployed to Crimea as one of the fabled "little green men" who had engineered a "spontaneous" uprising, seizing the parliament building as "Crimean" citizens. The action was relatively bloodless and incredibly successful. After that, he was detailed to train pro-Russian separatists in the Donbass region of Ukraine, building a fighting force that might topple the pro-Western government of Ukraine.

He'd taken to the mission with a starry-eyed naivete, proud to be serving Mother Russia training rabid, wild-eyed Russian patriots in the Donbass. Eventually his little band of mercenaries became a powerhouse, and men flocked to his banner. One of them, a man he'd personally recruited, showed more skill than the others. They'd become close friends, right up until the man had put a barrel to Nikita's head in the dead of night, trying to assassinate him.

With reflexes honed by a decade of training, Nikita had reacted instantly, managing to save his life, but the man had squeezed the trigger, blasting a bullet through his head that took his left eye and part of his orbit.

His next memory had been waking up in a hospital, having no recollection of winning the fight against the assassin. He expected a hero's welcome. After all, he'd defeated a trained killer after being shot in the head. Instead of sympathy, he'd been greeted with ridicule for recruiting an insider threat. The force he led was disbanded as untrustworthy, and he was cast aside as a failure. A cautionary tale of hubris for the other Spetsnaz men. This, after all he had done for his country.

Discharged from the army on medical grounds, he'd returned home a pariah. Nobody gave him his due as a combat veteran, spilling his blood for the Russian state. He was shunned by even his military comrades—his stench of failure treated like a communicable disease that they could contract.

Never a loving husband, his wife left him after he began taking out his frustration on her. She would have stayed even with the beatings, if he hadn't been viewed as a loser in the

GRU hierarchy. He began drinking vodka like it was a health elixir, downing a bottle a night to chase the demons away, until one night he found himself toying with an old Makarov pistol, placing it against his head over and over, but failing to have the courage to pull the trigger. And then Wagner had called, wanting his skill.

The initial contact had been dismissive, saying they weren't really interested, but his name had come up on a security screen. They'd toyed with him until he was frothing at the mouth to serve again. Deep inside, he wanted validation. Wanted to prove he wasn't what everyone said. He'd begged to join, and for his eagerness, they'd let him.

He'd returned to the Donbass, but not the same man who'd left. He developed a reputation for ruthlessness, taking out his shame on the enemy, his actions becoming legendary in the Wagner fold. He had a skill few men possessed, and he used it to great effect in the name of the nation he served, but his previous trials had severed something. His rage became legendary, and his actions on the battlefield earned a mythical status of brutality. He no longer had any trust in the Ukrainian men he served alongside, and thus no longer discriminated between combatant and noncombatant. *Everyone* was a potential combatant; some just hid it better than others.

He had no use for the stories and wasn't trying to create a legend. All he wanted was to prove his worth. To outrun the rumors and innuendo that had dogged his life.

Dmitri bringing up the loss of his eye on the VPN, accusing him of being weak or a failure, broke something inside of Nikita. He was sick of kowtowing to them for the acknowledgment of his value. Had he been more self-aware, he would have said he'd finally realized his own worth was held inside of him, and not gleaned from what others thought.

He would accomplish this mission not for Wagner, but for himself. And the mission was more than Operation Harvest. The man from Charleston had just put him back in that hospital bed, waking up and finding everyone thought he was to blame. That could not stand. Regardless of what Dmitri wanted, that man and his entire team would pay.

Nikita heard a bottle drop outside, breaking him out of his revenge fantasy. He put his good eye to the peephole of his door and saw a drunk staggering down the sidewalk, the parking lot littered with trash.

He went to the bathroom, turned on the sink, and splashed water on his face, looking in the cracked mirror and thinking. With his current manpower, he couldn't dedicate anyone to find the men from Grolier Recovery Services at the moment. That would have to wait. But he did need to get them to return to Charleston, somehow. Dmitri was no help, which left his other contact.

He left the bathroom and sat on the bed, flicking a bit of dirt off the ratty cover. He booted up his laptop and clicked on the WhatsApp icon. He dialed a number, wondering if he could convince the contact to get involved.

Clyde Marion's icon appeared, and he saw,

-Hey. How's it going down there?

He typed,

-Not good. I need more pressure.

He waited, then saw,

-Pressure how? I'm doing everything I can to manipulate the vote. I can't affect the election directly. That's not what you pay me to do.
-*Pressure from Kurt Hale. What's the status with his investigation?*

Nikita waited on the answer. After a minute, he typed,

-*What's the status?*
-Look, there is no status. My friend did his investigation, and it went nowhere. There was nothing to find. He's quit looking, and he's a little pissed that I put him on it. He burned some blue chips trying to find a guy in the CIA and now looks like a fool. Sorry.

The answer amazed Nikita. There was enough smoke around Kurt Hale's death to glean an investigative journalist award if someone were willing to look. Of that he was sure, because he lived in the same world. He typed,

-*You need to get him interested again. Feed him something else.*
-What? I have nothing else.
-*I have information that will interest him.*
-I can't do that. How can I? I'll look like a Russian spy, giving him niblets that nobody else has. Eventually, he's going to ask how I know this supposedly classified information as a computer geek. You're putting me in an awkward position.

Nikita thought for a moment, then typed,

-*Is there another way? Can you get this out without him?*
-What do you mean?
-*If I feed you information, can you get it out into the mainstream?*
-Like to the press?
-*Yes.*
-No. I don't have any press contacts. I don't want any contact with the press. My whole operating mechanism is precisely staying away from the press.

Nikita thought about his own past psychological operations with the GRU, when he'd generated a rumor that had eventually made the news as fact. The Russians were experts at seeding stories for propaganda purposes, and he could use those skills here. In the old days, it took weeks, but with the internet, it could take only hours.

He typed,

-*Can you access conspiracy blogs in the United States? Is that possible?*
-Yes. There are plenty. Why?

Nikita knew that an organization like Grolier Recovery Services would have Google alerts for any mention of them. If he could feed a blog with specifics of the actions in Charleston, they'd panic, collapsing back to the United States and hunkering down to weather the storm, spending their free time manufacturing cover stories to protect themselves instead of interfering with Operation Harvest.

He began typing, giving him everything he knew about the deaths in Charleston, and tying it all to Grolier Recovery Services. When he was done, he typed,

-Will that work?

Clyde Marion typed back,

-Is this shit for real?
-Maybe. Maybe not. Just get it into the system.
-Okay. But it can't be tied back to me. I never had this conversation. All I do is social media.

Nikita scoffed at the answer and typed,

-Along with our investment fund to get Saint Kitts passports. Dmitri told me about your involvement in that. Don't play innocent. Just do it.

He waited on a response and didn't receive one. He typed,

-Did you get that last message?
-Yes. I got it. And I got it. I'll seed the crazies, but I can't promise success. This isn't what I do.

Nikita grinned and typed,

-It's close enough. You manipulate elections for a living. Now you're manipulating an organization. It's the same damn thing.

He shut off the VPN and his mind, like it always did, returned to the mission, thinking about the hit tomorrow against the Mines and Energy minister.

56

Alek watched another small tour group enter the cathedral, blocking his view of the front door to the Petrobras headquarters building. He waited for them to enter, feeling anxious that he was going to miss the target leaving the office while they screened his view. And would thus lose his chance at one Galbino Alves, Mines and Energy minister for the country of Brazil.

He smiled at the tour guide as he approached, wanting to tell him to get his small band of tourists out of the fucking way, and waited. They passed by him, and he returned to his smartphone, slaved by Bluetooth to a miniature digital spotting scope just outside the door.

He had a clear view of the door across the street, watching people coming and going from the Petrobras building, but the chosen observation post was strange to say the least. The Petrobras headquarters was located in a high-rise on Republica do Chile Avenue, in the heart of downtown Rio and just across the street from the church Alek had chosen as his observation post.

Called the Metropolitan Cathedral of Rio de Janeiro, it was unlike any church he'd ever seen. Built as a giant pyramid, full of stained glass, the outside looked more like an Aztec temple than the Gothic designs of every other Catholic church in the city. The inside was just as strange, with an enormous seating area that could house upward of twenty thousand people, all circling around a central stage with the roof rising hundreds of feet into the air, the sides of the pyramid allowing a gloomy light to enter through massive stained-glass panels.

The tour guide stopped just behind, telling the history of the chapel, and he held his phone low, not wanting anyone to see why he was using it. He rotated his body away from them, and saw a group exit the office building. Four short men and a single tall one. He leaned closer, the spotting scope not having the best resolution. He saw that the four men were Asian, and the taller one was of Hispanic descent.

The target.

He glanced at the tour group, saw them move deeper into the chapel, and pulled out a handheld radio. He keyed the mic and said, "Target's on the move. Are you set?"

"Yes. I have control of the fruit juice stand, but I'm not sure this is going to work. What if he doesn't come to me?"

"He'll come. He'll give them the total experience. Just stand by. I'm moving to the train station."

Alek had taken command of the mission the minute he'd arrived in Rio and had spent the previous day conducting reconnaissance along the route from the Petrobras headquarters to the top of Mount Corcovado, the sight of the gigantic Christ the Redeemer statue known the world over. He'd searched for an interdiction or ambush location that would allow him to terminate the target in a way that looked natural—or at least would not point to the Russians—and had failed.

He'd considered ramming the vehicle en route, pushing the man to his death from the cliffs on Mount Corcovado—even derailing the train that took tourists up to the top—but none of the courses of action were viable. The minister was traveling with four potential Chinese investors, which complicated the mission exponentially. Ramming the car would not guarantee a death, and there was no way he could follow up without killing all four of the Chinese as well. Pushing him to his death was the cleanest, as Mount Corcovado had sheer cliffs that could be utilized, but when he'd conducted the recce, he'd found the monument packed to the gills with people, a multitude of tourists crawling all over the place, each snapping away with cell phones and cameras. There was no way he could shove the man to his death in front of them.

He'd circled the monument twice, then taken the granite stairs back down to the elevator that led to the train, and had stopped at a juice stand. He'd ordered a mango smoothie and had sat at a chipped plastic table overlooking the view to the coast, thinking through the problem. He noticed that just about everyone who came down from the top, after taking their selfies and YouTube videos, had stopped to admire the view from the small piazza, with most buying a juice drink. And he'd had an idea.

He'd gone back to the counter, waited until it was clear of customers, and had bribed the worker there, telling him he wanted to play a prank on a friend of his. He'd flashed a wad of American dollars and the man had readily agreed.

He'd returned to the hotel and asked if Pushka had been given poison in his bag of tricks. Pushka had stated he had nothing that could be wiped on a person, but he had a fast-acting neurotoxin based on the venom of a cone snail. The plus was the poison was very hard to detect and made the death look like a natural heart attack. The downside was it had to be ingested—which wasn't really a downside given Alek's plan.

Alek told him his course of action, and Pushka said, "But

you don't know he's going to get a juice drink. He could just take them back down the mountain."

"True, but if we're going to get him today, that's the only feasible plan. If we miss here, we know he's taking them to the Petrobras refinery in Manaus. We'll just have to follow."

"We have one other problem: he's with the Chinese investors. How will I know which one to put the poison in?"

"He'll order for them. They'll all be served first. The last will be his."

Pushka didn't seem happy with the looseness of the plan, but he'd agreed. First thing in the morning, he'd traveled to the Christ Redeemer monument, and Alek had begun his surveillance of the Petrobras headquarters.

He watched the men waiting on the sidewalk, then saw a black SUV pull to the curb. He left the church, recovered his digital scope in front, and jogged to his car, wanting to beat them to the train that led to the monument.

He raced through the Rio traffic, passed the train station, and turned down a narrow alley. He crossed a bridge over a thin creek and entered a square tucked off the main avenue, seeing a fountain and a small courtyard surrounded by abandoned mansions from the golden age of the rubber barons. He parked, locked the car, and jogged out of the courtyard.

He reached the avenue and began speed-walking back the way he'd come, seeing the train station a block away. As old as the abandoned mansions he'd just left, the train line had been built before the statue itself. Originally designed to service the coffee plantations that encased Mount Corcovado a century ago, it now was used solely to transport tourists up the steep incline to see the monument.

He waded through tour groups and individuals, purchased

a ticket, and took a seat, watching the line begin to grow for the next train. He glanced toward the avenue for his target, but didn't see anything resembling a black SUV. Not that it mattered. He had no intention of waiting for the target here, as there were two ways to get to the top—the train and a van service—and he wasn't sure which one the black SUV would seek out.

All he wanted to do was get to the top before they did.

57

George Wolffe heard a knock, spun around in his chair, and saw Creed in the doorway fidgeting like a child. Wolffe held up a finger, and into his phone he said, "So you're good? Safe?"

"Yeah. We went to Savannah. Back in the day, when I was a somebody in Air Force special operations, I made some friends in First Batt. A guy who's now deployed is a platoon sergeant in 1/75. We're in his house. We're safe."

"Good to hear. Kylie and Amena okay?"

"Kylie's a little freaked out. Amena thinks it's a blast."

Wolffe chuckled and said, "Get any more from the police response?"

"Yeah, it's the biggest news story in the Southeast. A bunch of Saint Kitts passport holders killed in an apparent drug smuggling operation gone bad. They're chasing their tails trying to find the connection to the port of Charleston. I think we'll be okay."

"No mention of the missing man? No indications of 'looking for one more person of interest'?"

"Nope. These guys were good at sterilization. Whatever they turned up didn't lead to the man you took with you."

"Good, good. Look, I've got Creed here about to wet his pants. I gotta go."

Veep said, "Is it bad news?"

"I have no idea. I'll call you if I need you."

"Don't you leave me. You'd better call."

"I won't. Take care of the precious cargo right now. The threat is still out there, and that's your mission now."

He hung up the phone, turned to Creed, and said, "Okay, what?"

When Creed was done, he picked up the phone and said, "Get me the president. Prometheus override. And I need the principals there."

Wolffe entered the West Wing and was immediately confronted by National Security Advisor Alexander Palmer. He said, "What's going on? Why the alert? Is it Pike?"

Wolffe looked at him in disdain and kept walking, saying, "You can hear it with the rest of the council."

Hurrying to match Wolffe's pace, he said, "I want to know what the fuck has happened before we enter. I want to know right *now*."

Wolffe kept walking, saying, "Must be nice to want something."

Palmer snatched his elbow and said, "You don't run the Taskforce. *We* do. Get that through your head. I want to know what you're going to say in there."

Tired of the political games, knowing Palmer was just looking for an edge, and, truthfully, because it was a little enjoyable, Wolffe grabbed his hand, pulled it away, and twisted until Palmer yelped.

The security men and passing aides looked on in shock. Wolffe locked eyes with Palmer and said, "Don't ever grab me again."

Without another word, he continued walking, straight to

the Oval Office. When the onlookers saw his destination, they relaxed. Palmer stumbled, and rushed to catch up.

Wolffe entered the Oval Office and saw President Hannister behind the Resolute Desk, the rest of the principals on the couch. He started to close the door, and Palmer pushed it open, coming in behind him holding his wrist.

Hannister took one look at Palmer's blanched face and said, "What the hell happened to you?"

Wolffe said, "He slammed his hand in a door."

Palmer said nothing, taking a seat on the couch. Hannister went from him to Wolffe and said, "Okay, you got us here, what's this about? Are we at risk for Pike's actions in Brazil?"

And that answer was why George Wolffe, like Kurt Hale before him, trusted the president of the United States. Hannister had already been told about the rescue of the ferry, which meant he already knew that Pike had gone off the reservation to save Knuckles and Brett, but he didn't care about that. There were no recriminations in the question. No "I knew this would go bad. I told you so." No searching for someone to blame. He was all business.

"No, sir. That was clean. A good hit. They're secure, and we're under no scrutiny. It was a BOPE action all the way."

Palmer said, "I still want to know how Pike got involved in that. He had no sanction to do anything, and then he's conducting a rescue?" He looked at Amanda Croft and said, "And apparently there was some State Department help."

Only two people in the room knew of the connection between the man on the boat and the secretary of state, and one of them, George Wolffe, wasn't going to utter a word.

He saw Amanda start to say something, and Hannister spoke first: "That's water under the proverbial bridge. If we're clean, we're clean. Can we get to why you're here? I don't have a lot of time."

And Wolffe saw Amanda sink back, a small smile on her face. He went from face to face, and when he reached hers, she winked.

He said, "Sir, you told me to hide in Charleston from the inquiries into Kurt Hale."

"Yes, and that worked. The Senate staffer fished around for a little bit, and then gave up. Why is that a big deal?"

Wolffe took a deep breath, then let the bomb free. He said, "Pike was right. He was targeted for elimination because of his company. While I was in Charleston, they attacked again. We killed three men and captured another. Someone in Russia is hunting Grolier Services."

The room was silent, with most sitting on the couch showing an open mouth. Hannister was the first to break the silence. "Did you just tell me you killed three men in Charleston?"

"Yes, sir. From a Russian private military company called Wagner. They've figured out a GRS connection to the Taskforce. We don't know how, and we don't know why they care, but they're trying to kill us."

He went through a detailed report of what had happened, ending with, "They're still out in the wild, and Pike is on the trail in Brazil. It all leads to that country."

When he finished, there was absolute silence. Amanda Croft broke it first, saying, "Where is the man you captured?"

"He's in the cloud. A terrorist holding cell in Utah. I didn't have another alternative."

"The cloud" was a nickname for the incarceration of terrorists captured by the Taskforce. Exploiting small town jails throughout the United States, it was the most sensitive aspect of Taskforce operations. Due to the publicity and ongoing fiasco with military tribunals in Cuba, the prison at the Guantanamo Bay naval base was out of the question, and so the Taskforce had built an alternative. They'd reviewed police human resources databases throughout the United States, zeroing in on the ones run by ex–special forces, finding more than a handful. They'd individually interviewed each law enforcement person that they'd found, and had come up with four sites, all in the Southwest, with each law enforcement officer signing nondisclosure statements. It had been a win-win for the police. The Taskforce paid to refurbish and expand their regional jails, and they kept a prisoner for as long as the Taskforce wanted. A terrorist who'd disappeared into the "cloud," as it were.

Palmer exploded: "You have a Russian national in our classified terrorist rendition architecture? Have you lost your mind?"

Calmly, Wolffe said, "Well, after he tried to kill me, I suppose I could have taken him to a cornfield in Iowa and put a bullet in his head, then buried him in a shallow grave. But that's not my style. I don't kill prisoners I catch."

"What the fuck are we supposed to do with him now? Have you thought about that?"

Wolffe glared at him and said, "Yes. I have. Option one is for you to come with me and I take him to that cornfield. You can pull the trigger. You got the stones for that?"

President Hannister regained control of the room, saying, "Okay, so you have him. What's your recommendation?"

"Let him go."

Palmer said, "What?"

"Let him go. We've interrogated him, and all he knows is he was targeted against a company. He has no idea why. I say we keep him until we've bled him dry on Wagner, giving us individuals and scope of operations, but when we're done with that, we just put him on a plane."

Palmer said, "How? How can we do that? He'll scream to high heaven about being kidnapped."

"He won't scream to anyone. He says anything here and he gets arrested for Charleston. No, he'll go home and shut the fuck up. There is no upside to him saying he'd been captured. They'll wonder what he said, and put a bullet in his head just for insurance. I want to reiterate, he knows nothing. He has no reason to rock the boat. It'll get him killed by his own people. He goes home, spins some tale about escaping the carnage in Charleston, and he'll shut up after that."

Palmer started shouting again, and Hannister raised a hand, saying, "Okay, okay. It's something to think about. He's secure now?"

"Yes, sir. He's secure."

"So why the emergency meeting? It's obviously not because you just found out about this. Since you engineered the whole thing."

58

Alek stood up when the train arrived, a two-car carrier powered by electricity that, while no longer an ancient nineteenth-century vehicle, still looked like it hadn't been updated since the seventies. He boarded with everyone else, sitting next to a young couple who couldn't keep their hands off of each other.

Within minutes, they'd left the concrete of Rio behind and entered a forest, the vegetation close and huge, reaching out to the open windows of the cars as the train cut its way through, as if the jungle resented the intrusion.

Once barren earth from rapacious clear-cut logging in the nineteenth century, Mount Corcovado had been deliberately replanted in the twentieth to heal the years of abuse, and was now a national forest, with the jungle greedily reclaiming the land from the coffee plantations that existed a century ago.

Twenty minutes later they arrived at the top, Alek having spent most of his time dodging out of the frame from tourists snapping pictures. He exited first, wound through the line of people waiting on the return trip, and rapidly walked to the first chokepoint leading to the monument: two long escalators traveling to the crest of the mountain, the back of the Christ Redeemer towering over them. From his earlier reconnaissance, Alek knew that it didn't matter if the target arrived via train or van, the group would end up here. There were stairs that could be used, but Alek refused to believe that the minister would make his potential Chinese investors walk up two hundred and fifty steps when an escalator was available.

He took a seat on a concrete bench and watched the flow of tourists heading upward. He didn't have to wait long. Within eight minutes he saw the small entourage walking to the escalators, bobbing along with the rest of the tourists like empty beer cans in a river, the target talking animatedly with his guests and gesturing to the statue.

Alek let them get to the top of the escalator, then followed. Ignoring the statue rising above him and the spectacular view spilling out below, he circled around the stone plaza, reaching the staircase leading down to the piazza with the juice stand. He glanced back at the target, saw him taking pictures of the Chinese, and pulled out his radio. He started to press the push-to-talk when two uniformed policemen began climbing the stairs.

He hid the radio and walked halfway down, letting them pass as he pretended to gaze at the view to his left. When they reached the top and disappeared into the crowd, he put the radio to his mouth and said, "Pushka, Pushka, you there?"

"Roger."

"Get ready. They're here. It'll be about ten minutes."

"And if they just keep going?"

Letting some exasperation leak out, he said, "Then they just keep going. Are you set?"

"Yeah. I'm acting as a bar-back for free. I've got a handle on it, and the locals appreciate the help. One of them has been outside smoking cigarettes since I arrived. I should confiscate his salary."

"Just stay on your toes. Out."

Alek remained in position for twenty more minutes, then began to think Pushka had been right and they'd simply taken the escalator back to the exit. There just wasn't that much to do up top. Take a selfie in front of the statue, take a panorama of Rio below you, maybe visit the chapel at the base of the monument, but that was about it. There were no interactive displays or other things to see, and was precisely why he was sure the target would bring them to the piazza for a fruit smoothie. The minister wouldn't want the trip *to* the monument to take longer than the tour of the monument itself.

Alek began walking back up the stairs when he saw them at the top. Unable to pull out his radio in front of them, he kept his gaze forward and passed them by. He reached the top and found himself face-to-face with the police now returning down from their patrol.

Shit.

He walked into the mass of people around the Christ statue, milled for a second, then returned to the stairs, pulling out his radio and hissing, "They're coming, they're coming."

He got nothing back, and hoped it was because Pushka was engaged. He bounded down the granite stairs, reached the bottom and scanned the area, seeing the police milling about on the flagstone, tourists sitting in the cracked plastic chairs he had used yesterday to come up with his plan, and then the group of Chinese at the fruit stand, the target explaining the menu.

He glanced around for a place to loiter as a singleton without drawing attention, and spied a cluster of tourists snapping photos of a marmoset monkey cleaning itself in a tree branch, begging for food.

He went to the back of the group and brought out his

phone, pretending to snap photos. He reversed the camera to selfie mode and held it up, now looking at the stand.

He watched the target play local host, recommending various flavors, then the Chinese make their choices. One by one the target passed out the selected juice drinks, until only one was left. The target had chosen a mango smoothie, showing bright yellow through the clear plastic cup. He turned to the group in time to see one of the men from the delegation grimace with a sour face, having taken a sip of his pink-colored guava drink.

The target said something to him, and Alek put his phone down, turning around to face them. He saw the target hold out his own mango drink, trading his smoothie for the guava-flavored one he'd recommended.

No, no, no!

The Chinese took a sip of the mango smoothie, smiled, and nodded his head. The target sipped the pink guava juice he'd traded and smiled as well, saying something. They all touched their cups together before taking deep gulps. Alek sagged against the concrete railing, causing the lone marmoset to scamper upward in the trees and the tourists to complain at his actions. He ignored them, glancing at the fruit stand.

Pushka locked eyes with him and nodded his head, telling Alek that he'd accomplished his mission. Alek flicked his head high, ordering him to vacate by way of the escalator and not the stairs. He watched Pushka leave, then saw the target point toward the stairs headed down to the landing area for both the vans and the train.

The men began walking, laughing and finishing their smoothies. They reached the top of the stairs when one of the Chinese clutched his chest, his face contorted in pain. He fell to his knees, dropping his smoothie as his other hand grasped the railing, his mouth bubbling a froth, the yellow mango juice spilling into his lap. The target began shouting and waving his arms while the other Chinese stood by in bewilderment.

Alek had seen enough. Cursing his luck, he took the steps back to the top two at a time, getting on his radio and saying, "Pushka, Pushka, contact your Petrobras security source. We're going to need his itinerary in Manaus."

59

Wolffe remained quiet, considering what he should say. President Hannister repeated, "What's the emergency? It has to be bad if killing three people in Charleston didn't even rate an update."

"Sir, I just came home last night. I haven't even had time to create a situation report when this new information surfaced. This is all rolled in together. It's all the emergency."

Hannister said, "Continue." Wolffe caught the president's tone of voice, realizing that the president wasn't pleased with his actions, but once again, wanted to solve the problem. It gave him courage.

"Sir, you know that the Taskforce keeps track of all web activity related to any of our cover organizations?"

"Yes."

"Well, there is a story on both the website 4chan and another site that was just created, detailing the attacks in Charleston, both of them. It has information about Kurt Hale, Grolier Services, and his manner of death, and the recent attacks at Sullivan's Island. It's not random. The Russians are trying to split us. They haven't been able to stop Pike by force, and now they're using an information campaign to get us to quit."

"How bad is it?"

"It's bad. There is stuff on the blogs about what Veep and I did in Charleston, with real information only the Russians would know, along with a huge conspiracy theory of how Grolier Recovery Services is a front organization for a pedophile sex ring."

Wolffe saw the brows furrow and Hannister said, "What?"

"It's just a tactic. For some reason, pedophilia causes certain websites and twitter handles to go crazy. The Russians did the same thing with PizzaGate. They're trying to generate interest in Grolier Recovery Services with this wild conspiracy idea in the hopes that mainstream press will pick it up and investigate. Whether they're investigating to debunk the story or investigating for real, it'll lead to the Taskforce."

The secretary of defense finally spoke, saying, "I thought we were shielded from all of that? I thought we were completely black?"

Wolffe said, "There is no such thing as completely black when operating in the world. We've covered our tracks well from a cursory exploration, but if they start digging into GRS, they're going to find some connections. Just like that staffer did with me. It's a digital world now."

The room took that in, and Palmer said, "We need to call off Pike. Get him home, and then shut down the entire experiment."

Wolffe said, "I think that's the wrong approach. Pike is hunting the men right now, and terminating his efforts will still leave a threat, one whose breadth will be unknown. It's exactly what they want."

Hannister said, "I'm inclined to agree with Palmer. We have no imminent threat to national security in Brazil. Let the Russians do what they're going to do, and call it a day."

"Sir, you do that, and you're calling it, period. We can't operate around the world knowing that there is a Russian agency that might have enough information about how we operate to thwart our efforts. Best case, the terrorists we hunt are tipped off. Worst case, they actively set traps to kill us. We can't function that way."

"So what's your solution?"

"Find the guy releasing the information. He's involved with the Russians, but from what we can glean, he's an American citizen—or at least he's operating from the United States. He's covered his digital tracks well, but whoever he is, he's in contact with the Russians. We need to stop him before some mainstream press element starts to look."

Hannister said, "An American citizen. One expressing his First Amendment rights. That's where you want to go?"

"Yes. Whoever it is is hell-bent on destroying us, and he's doing that with information fed to him by the Russians. He's a traitor."

Hannister took that in, then said, "I'm not sure I want to step across that Rubicon. We did what we did, and because this guy is spouting on conspiracy websites, we should silence him? Isn't that proving his point? I mean, he's actually telling the truth."

Wolffe sensed the room and relented. At least out loud. He said, "Okay, so we let him go. If that's what we want to do, we need to be prepared for the fallout, because if he persists, and a real news organization picks up the scent, it's going to be ferocious. We need to begin rolling up all of our cover organizations and start building some firewalls."

Palmer said, "First thing is to get Pike back home. Get GRS out of Brazil before he makes more noise for the press to dig up."

Wolffe unconsciously grimaced at his words. President Hannister saw the reaction and said, "Is that going to be a problem, George?"

Wolffe took a deep breath, let it out, then said, "Yes, sir."

Miffed, Hannister said, "Why? Just call him back home."

"Sir, we told Pike that the Taskforce was done, while leaving Knuckles in the wind to die. We told him to stand down when he knew that Kurt's death wasn't an accident. We told him his family was safe even as the Russians were hunting them. We've told him nothing but lies."

Palmer said, "I don't get it. This isn't a debate. Who cares what we said before? Give him an order. Get his ass home."

Wolffe remained focused on the president. He said, "There's a difference between following an order and doing what's right. He won't listen to an order from an organization we've told him no longer exists. He's going to do what he believes is right."

Palmer said, "What does that even mean? 'What he believes is right'?"

Wolffe said, "He's going to destroy whoever killed Kurt and tried to kill his family."

President Hannister said, "He's already done that. Hell, *you've* already done that."

Wolffe reflected on the president's words for a moment, then said, "After all of this time, I don't think you understand Pike. Because of what happened to his family, he takes protecting those he loves to a level you and I can't comprehend. When I say destroy, make no mistake, it will be total. He's not concerned about low-level soldiers. He's hunting the control, and when he finds it, he will rip it apart like a grizzly protecting her cubs."

Palmer said, "Then we get everyone else back. He can't operate by himself. Order Knuckles and Brett home."

Wolffe chuckled and said, "Did you not hear what I said about family? You people in this room come together out of a shared sense of duty. The people with Pike follow him because of *him*."

Palmer said, "It sounds like you *want* him to continue. Like you believe in what he's doing."

"Sir, I'd be lying if I said I didn't appreciate avenging Kurt's death, but how I feel is irrelevant. Pike is with his family. They won't listen to us, either."

Wolffe turned to the president and waved his hand toward the couch, saying, "The people in this room have an inflated sense of their own power. Pike does not care what you think. He does not care what you order. Trust me, nothing we say will stop what's coming."

60

Sitting on a park bench in the shadow of the famed Manaus Opera House, I began to regret taking the outdoor position instead of the bumper locations inside in the air-conditioning. It wasn't overbearingly hot—yet—but I could feel the sweat building on my neck.

I'd been outside for more than four hours, and my hand was itching to click on to the net for a situation report. My subconscious mind—like every commander I'd ever known—believed that a radio call would magically cause something to occur. My conscious mind knew better. All that would do was clog up the radio net and annoy the team. There was nothing worse than getting bugged by a team leader for a status update when none was required, as the implicit thought would be, "You don't trust me?"

With Brazil rolling into springtime, the weather had been pleasant in Salvador, but Manaus was a different story. A large city at the head of the Amazon basin, it was much warmer here, and not in a soothing, wrap a blanket around you in front of a winter fire sort of way. It felt more like a sauna. Lacking the sea breeze of Salvador, the air held a cloistering humidity that caused your clothes to cling to you like wet toilet paper.

I thought about calling Jennifer off the net just to break the boredom, when, like magic, my radio came alive. "All elements, all elements, this is Carrie. Both targets are on the move. Leaving the hotel with a purpose."

About time.

I came back, "This is Pike. Roger all. Blood, you ready?"

"Roger."

"Good copy. All elements, feed the beast. Give Brett a vector. When the target breaks the box, he needs to already have a lock-on. If we lose them here we're aborting."

In the movies, surveillance is either depicted as a clownfest of cars chasing each other through red lights and racing the wrong way down one-way streets, or a secret arcane art that the average human can't understand, full of tradecraft that only the men on the screen know. In truth, surveillance is nothing more than any other skill, and, like an NBA basketball team, there are certain principles that are always in play.

The primary one is identifying the target at an endpoint to initiate the operation. While it seems like common sense, more surveillance efforts fail at the start because the target escapes undetected, making the trigger the linchpin. Because the trigger is usually exposed to the target, he or she never, ever begins the follow. As the name suggests, the trigger does one thing: trigger the surveillance effort.

Once the target is acquired, the next step is simple: cover all possible avenues of escape in what is called the "box." Not knowing the intent of the target, he could go in any direction, but eventually, he'd break the box, and when that happened, the true surveillance could begin. Done correctly, there is no way the target will know that he's being followed.

In this case, the targets could go in one of three directions: Right, down the street and deeper into the concrete mess that was Manaus. Left, toward the opera house and the square it sat on. Or around to the back of the hotel and down an alley. I had the left bumper position because that's where I thought the target would come. We knew they had a car, and the only parking near the hotel was at the square where I was located.

I'd put Knuckles on the right position, down the road toward the city center, and Jennifer at the rear of the hotel, where the alley spilled out. If they chose either of those directions, we'd pick them up. But I didn't think that would happen.

The triggers were Aaron and Shoshana. They were in the lobby sitting around a table and drinking coffee. It cost me an extra man—or woman in this case—but two people were less memorable than one.

One person on a lobby couch makes everyone passing by wonder why he's there. Waiting on a friend? Burning off time for a cab? Room not ready yet? Or, worst case, waiting on me to leave the hotel? No matter what the target thought, a singleton would potentially be remembered, but a couple was much less likely to register.

I stood up from my park bench and walked to a trailer serving gelato on the edge of the square, the line of people waiting helping me to blend in. I couldn't be involved in a surveillance effort if I was wasting time on a frozen treat, right? I mean, who gets gelato prior to tracking a guy for a hit?

I glanced back at the hotel and saw the targets exit, then take a left toward me. On the net, I said, "All elements, all elements, this is Pike. I have the eye. Targets are moving east, toward the square. I'll let you know if it's a restaurant or a vehicle."

The opera house was surrounded by bars and restaurants ranging from a hole-in-the-wall pizzeria to an upscale

Brazilian steak house, so while I believed they were moving to a vehicle, they could just as easily be going to lunch.

Jennifer came on, saying, "What do we do if they don't get in a car and leave? We're going to need at least an hour to access both rooms."

"I'll send Brett in to whatever restaurant they enter. We're still good."

I heard nothing back, and knew she wasn't convinced. I said, "Relax. I'll bring you a gelato when we break into the rooms. You've earned it for that beacon placement."

It had taken some time to extricate ourselves from the Salvador crisis site, not least because the police chief who'd sanctioned our actions was now dead, but eventually we'd managed to get a clean break through the confusion and fog, leaving the fallout to the police on the ground.

We'd reconsolidated, and I'd taken a little straw poll about our next actions. I most definitely wanted to continue hunting the men who had made the mistake of killing those I held dear, but I couldn't order everyone else to do that. I knew Jennifer was on my side, and suspected Shoshana and Aaron would do whatever I asked, but I wasn't sure. I couldn't demand they help me, and I most certainly couldn't order Brett or Knuckles to follow me, because we were way outside of the Taskforce charter. It had to be their choice. I wasn't going to force it.

I'd sent Brett and Knuckles on a reconnaissance to see if there had been any change to the story of a unilateral BOPE raid, and after they'd left the hotel, I'd asked the Israelis. I'd expected some hesitation. Some waffling or questions about the mission, but I got none of that. Aaron had looked me in the eye and said it didn't even need to be asked, and Shoshana had actually been insulted.

She said, "I want to talk to you alone."

I felt her reading me and said, "I don't have time for this."

She said, "Make the time."

I looked at Aaron, then Jennifer. Jennifer touched my arm, whispering, "Let her talk. Go with her."

I realized that Jennifer had sensed something I had not. I'd followed Shoshana into the bathroom of our hotel, and she closed the door.

She'd turned her weird glow on me and said, "Aaron and I are here for you. You and Jennifer. Like you were for us. That bond is sacrosanct, but you need to understand why."

Exasperated, I'd said, "Look, I don't need a lecture. You're either in or you're out."

Her face as cold as a granite wall, she said, "I will not let you destroy yourself. I will kill who you ask, but only if it is necessary. I will not take a life for vengeance alone. I am done with such things. Is that understood?"

Her words hung in the air, and I felt the anger grow inside of me. I said, "Don't give me a sanctimonious speech. Don't *you* do that. You and I know what this is about. You alone understand. You *are* me. Don't make me the bad guy."

She said, "You don't even know what you're asking of me. I see it in you. You want to kill to quench a fire, but the men you are slaughtering are not the reason for the fire."

I said, "What the fuck kind of babble is that? They murdered my friend and commander and tried to kill me. They attacked Kylie and Amena. Are you telling me to quit? Let them go? Turn the other cheek or some other bullshit?"

She'd become supernaturally calm, saying "No. But you're on the edge, and you're taking Knuckles with you. I saw Knuckles when the woman was killed. He wants to slaughter anyone, guilty or not, just to release the pain, and he will do so, but the damage to him will come later. He hasn't seen what the abyss can do. Very few can look into it and return. I have. And so have you. Don't make him do the same, because he might not come back."

I said, "Look, I don't even know if Brett and Knuckles are on board to continue. They may just go home."

She said, "You know that's not true."

I clenched my fists and said, "They *killed* our men. They murdered the woman on the boat. Don't ask me to stop, because I'm not going to do that."

She slid close to me and cupped my chin, the gesture surprising me. She said, "I'm not asking you to stop. I'm asking you to have some control. Watch out for Knuckles. Just keep him in check."

I said, "He can take care of himself."

She ignored me, saying, "When I was a child, I lost my parents in a suicide attack on a bus. One minute I had a family, the next I did not, and because of it, all I wanted to do was kill. I learned I had a talent for it, and I ended up in a unit that exploited my skill, ordering me to kill whoever they targeted."

I saw her face grow stern. "And I did so, but all the people I killed didn't bring my family back. All it did was twist me, and I won't let that happen here. You are *me*, but Knuckles and Brett are not. I've already seen you lose control on this mission. Don't let them do the same. Do *not* let them become me."

Aggravated, I said, "What do you want from me?"

"I want Pike. Nothing more. I want the man I respect. Not the one I want to kill."

I held up my hands in surrender, saying, "Okay, okay, calm down. I get it. What I did in the alley was bad, and it won't happen again. I won't murder someone, but I *am* going to take these guys down. Whatever the Russians are doing, it's not good, and I'm going to stop it."

She studied me for a moment, then said, "Okay. We're in."

61

Relieved to be away from the conversation, I smiled, saying, "Let's not get ahead of ourselves. I still have to ask the others, and then there's that little problem of talking to the Taskforce."

I opened the bathroom door and saw that Brett and Knuckles had returned from the reconnaissance mission I'd given them. I was pleased to learn that there were no conspiracy theories swirling around about English-speaking hostage rescuers. Brett was as easygoing as ever, but he flicked his eyes to Knuckles when he saw me, letting me know that something was amiss.

Shoshana had been right. Knuckles wasn't himself. The death of the woman had hit him hard, as if he believed it was his fault she'd perished, and because of it I could sense a simmering rage.

He said, "We *are* getting payback, right?"

Which answered my question of whether he was in, but not in the way I'd hoped. I wanted vengeance for Kurt and what they'd tried to do to Kylie and Amena, but I needed Knuckles on an even keel to do so. Both of us having a bloodlust might be asking for trouble.

Calmly, I said, "Yes, but before we go off half-cocked, we need to develop a plan."

He said, "The beacon Jenn placed is in Rio. What more do

we need? We wait, and it'll run out of juice. It's the one lead we have."

Before I could answer, my Taskforce phone went off, with a ringtone that told me it was an encrypted call.

I looked at my screen and saw it was from George Wolffe. *Speak of the devil.*

I answered, "Hey, boss. I was just about to call you."

He went straight to business, "What's your status?"

"Still in Salvador. It looks like we're clean from the hostage rescue. BOPE are taking credit."

"So you're coming home?"

"Soon, yeah."

"What's that mean?"

"You know what it means. I'm not going to spell it out because then you'll just order me home. Leave it at 'soon.' Go report that back."

"Pike, I have to give you a direct order to come home, right now. No further actions. The Russians have started an information operation up here that can potentially expose us. It involves you and GRS. Every time you do something against the Russians, it gets reported up here on a conspiracy site. Nobody's picked it up mainstream yet, but if it goes viral, we're done."

He then told me about the discussions with the Oversight Council and the information that had been leaked. I said, "Seems like the solution is to stop the leak, not run from it."

"I tried that. I was told to stand down."

"Okay. You've done your duty."

"No, I haven't. I need to talk personally to Brett, Knuckles, and Jennifer. I need to give them the order."

I said, "Good luck with that," and passed the phone to Jennifer.

She took it with a question on her face, listened, then said, "I understand."

She looked at me and said, "No, sir. I'm not coming home."

She passed the phone to Knuckles, and then he passed it to Brett, all with the same results. Eventually it came back to me. I said, "You want to talk to the Israelis? Or are we done?"

He ignored that, saying, "What are you doing next? At least tell me what's coming."

I said, "A few days ago, Jennifer tagged one of the Russians. We have the beacon track in Rio. That's where we're going. We'll develop the next steps from there. I'll send in reports to Creed back-channel to keep you in the loop. Put it all on me, sir."

He said, "Veep has Amena and Kylie in Savannah, with some Ranger Battalion friend of his. They're good to go. I'm not ordering him to return until this is over."

And in that moment, I knew he supported my actions. He couldn't come right out and say he was with me, but he *could* turn off the beacon track. That he completely shifted gears at the mention of the beacon told me he just didn't want to know.

He'd also demanded to speak to everyone on my team, ordering each of them individually to come home—all the while knowing they wouldn't. On the other hand, he *didn't* ask to speak to the one team who could really gum up my ability to operate: the pilots of the Rock Star bird. Those guys had no allegiance to me or the team, and would absolutely listen to him about coming home, which would render me toothless. Losing the aircraft would be more than just travel. I'd lose the ability for tagging, tracking, and locating the Russians, along with my entire arsenal of weapons to deal with the problem.

He held the ability to prevent me from operating, and

because he'd failed to cut me off at the knees, I knew he wanted me to continue.

I said, "Thanks for keeping track of them. I appreciate it, sir."

He said, "I'll give the Oversight Council your decision. Expect some retribution when you get home."

Which was the same as saying, "I'll put you in time-out, young man!"

We packed up and went ripping from Salvador to Rio, only to find out by the time we'd arrived, the beacon was gone. At first, I'd thought it had finally expired, the liquid battery eating the brains of the beacon to prevent follow-on forensics, and had wasted time setting up surveillance at its last known location, a fancy hotel on Copacabana Beach. We'd established a box and waited to spot the guy Jennifer had beaconed, burning an entire day, and then the damn thing had surfaced again, in Manaus.

We had no idea why, but our target had fled Rio. We'd boarded the Rock Star bird and gave chase, landing in Manaus early in the morning only to find the beacon had quit transmitting again, and this time I feared it was gone for good because its battery had already exceeded the service life.

It had remained stationary for our entire flight up, which meant it was no longer on the target, but that might not be a catastrophe. Jennifer had put it on a jacket, and Manaus was definitely too hot to wear one, so maybe it had simply died in his suitcase in a hotel room.

We'd repeated the maneuver from Copacabana, boxing in the Hotel Villa Amazonia, now a day behind whatever the Russian had planned. By noon, I had started to believe that we were wasting our time yet again, and then Shoshana had triggered.

Now I was one person back in the gelato line, with a clear view of the targets. I called Shoshana and said, "Did you get a photo of the other Russian?"

"No. I didn't get the opportunity. They walked right by us."

I said, "Roger," and pulled out my phone. They walked behind me passing the line and entering the square, heading to the front of the opera house.

I surreptitiously snapped a couple of bad photos, saying on the net, "I don't think they're moving to a car. They're cutting through the square, probably to a restaurant."

The opera house was a gigantic, ornate building sporting a gilded domed roof that towered over the square, looking like something from the Middle East that was in sharp contrast to the colonial style of construction it rested on. Flowing down from the front terrace were two sweeping granite staircases that circled toward themselves until they reached the pavestones of the square I was on.

I bought my gelato just as they passed by the first set of stairs. I remembered one for Jennifer and stepped out of line in time to see them turn into what looked like a small alcove in the wall between the staircases. They disappeared from view.

What the hell?

Intrigued, I took a seat on a park bench and waited, calling on the net, "Target temporarily unsighted."

Brett said, "This is Blood, what's my vector? Do you want me to exit my vehicle?"

"No. Stand by. Something strange going on."

Five minutes later, the wall at the back of the alcove swung open and the men exited, now carrying, of all things, two guitar cases.

I said, "I have them again. They're crossing the square."

They stopped at a minivan, unlocked it, loaded the guitar cases, and prepared to drive away. I gave a description of the vehicle and the direction of travel, hearing Brett say, "Got them. I'm on them."

I said, "Roger all. Give us a status every ten minutes. Carrie, you provide close-in early warning. Koko, meet me at the front. Time to crack the room."

62

Alek ordered Pushka to drive even though he was the one who'd conducted the reconnaissance of the park. He wanted to think through the plan one more time, knowing it was borderline insane. Something more out of a James Bond movie than a well-planned assassination.

After the failure in Rio at the Christ Redeemer, Alek couldn't afford another mistake. He'd had to tell Nikita of the fiasco, and it hadn't been pleasant. Nikita had ordered Alek off the mission and Alek wondered if he should fear for his life. The only saving grace was that Pushka's security contact at the Petrobras building had managed to obtain the Mines and Energy minister's schedule in Manaus, a mixture of both work and pleasure.

Alek had begged Nikita to let him continue—to make it right, in his words—and Nikita had allowed it, even as he said he doubted the man would travel up to Manaus after the death of the Chinese investor. Alek prayed that wasn't true, because it would set back their entire mission. And would set off Nikita.

Luckily, they'd found the minister and his Chinese guests— now down to three—exactly where they said they'd be, staying at the Hotel Villa Amazonia near the historical city center. Alek and Pushka had reserved a room and set about designing a plan of attack. They had two days to find a "firing solution," as Nikita called it. Two days while the entourage was out discussing the refining of oil and the potentially lucrative returns for China should they invest.

He'd given Pushka the close-in reconnaissance of the tour locations in town, to include the mansion of an old German rubber baron who helped found Manaus, the Adolpho Lisboa open air market, and the Manaus Opera House.

That left the CIG nature park for Alek, located about an hour outside the city, a zoo full of Amazon flora and fauna staffed by the Jungle Training School of the Brazilian army. He'd hired a local guide to show him around, ostensibly to learn about the creatures of the Amazon, but in reality to see if the park would facilitate an "accident."

He'd learned that there were plenty of things in the Amazon that could kill a man, and most of them were located in the park, but he could see no way to cause the minister to fall into a pit of anacondas or slip off the bridge spanning the jaguar enclosure.

There were plenty of hidden spots and solitary jungle paths, all of which would make a perfect ambush location if he were allowed to employ lethal means such as a rifle or his bare hands, but nothing that he could leverage as an accident—especially since the minister would be surrounded by the three Chinese. Alek would have to kill all four to make it work, and he just couldn't see a way to do that inside the park.

After an hour of wandering around, listening to the guide, Alek had begun to think the trip had been a waste of time. They reached the very edge of the park, running into a tall chain-link fence surrounding a lake, a sign in Portuguese out front that he couldn't read except for one word. *Perigo!* So something dangerous was beyond the fence.

The guide saw him looking into the lake and said, "We can't go out there today. It's closed."

"What is it?"

"The piranha pit. It's pretty cool if you're the bloodthirsty sort, but also a little cruel."

"How so?"

"Piranhas aren't really the deadly killers the movies make them out to be. They're dangerous, no doubt, but don't really attack large animals unless they're threatened or extremely hungry. Or trained."

"Trained?"

"Yeah. They feed the piranhas live animals here. Rabbits, other things. Basically, they've trained them to ignore their instincts so they can put on a show."

He pointed to a small dock with a medium-sized rubber Zodiac boat and said, "They take VIPs out to the middle, smack the water a few times, then throw in the live bait. To make sure they're really in a frenzy, they don't feed them for days beforehand, which is why we can't go out today. Apparently some important government official is coming here tomorrow, and they want a show."

Alek knew who that government official was, and his plan began to form. Batshit crazy, but a plan nonetheless. He'd returned to the hotel and learned that Pushka's reconnaissance had turned up no viable alternatives, and so he'd decided to go with the crazy idea instead of telling Nikita they'd failed. He'd called Nikita and asked him to leverage his contacts in Manaus for the equipment he'd need, and, after more threats from Nikita, he'd been given the drop location: the Manaus Opera House.

He'd thought Nikita was screwing with him at first, his boss describing a secret tunnel the city founders had used to smuggle in mistresses to the theater, allowing them to bypass the front door for an orgy in the box seats. If that weren't weird enough, he'd been ordered to leave a stack of cash in Pushka's room to pay for the cache. He'd done so, of course, but wondered how the contact placing the cache would even know what room Pushka was in, much less have a key to retrieve the money.

Alek hadn't told Pushka his reservations about the cache, but he had been pleasantly surprised to find the tunnel existed, and then was surprised again when they'd located the equipment deep in the tunnel, next to some artifacts that had been lost to time. That meant Nikita had a much greater grip on what the two of them were doing than he'd given him credit for.

Now, driving out to the park, he began to doubt the plan he'd created. There were so many different variables, any one of which was a single point of failure. He felt an enormous pressure, so much so that he hadn't even told Pushka what the plan was, afraid he'd balk before they'd even begun. He'd decided to wait to tell him only after it was too late to back out.

The GPS showed they were within five minutes of the park and Pushka said, "You want to tell me what you have in mind? Why the sniper systems? We can't shoot him, especially not in front of the Chinese."

Alek took a deep breath, paused a minute, then told him. When he was done, Pushka smiled and said, "That is diabolical."

Relieved not to be told he was insane, and appreciating the confidence, Alek said, "If it fails, and it looks like they're going to escape, put a bullet in the target's head. The others can live."

Pushka said, "You sure about that?"

"Yeah. It's not like there will be much to autopsy."

Pushka passed a single-track road snaking off the hardtop into the jungle and Alek shouted, "That's it, that's it!"

Pushka turned the minivan around, and they bounced through the woods for a few minutes until the road grew so rugged that Alek was afraid they'd get stuck. He said, "Stop the vehicle. We walk in from here."

Pushka turned off the engine and exited, meeting Alek at the rear of the van. Alek opened the first guitar case, seeing a Heckler & Koch MSG90 sniper system. Next to it was a camouflaged smock that looked like a mechanic's jumpsuit. He pulled it out and began snaking his legs into it, Pushka following suit.

Five minutes later they were following the GPS into the jungle on foot, Alek surprised at how open the forest floor was. After seeing the dense foliage on the way to Christ Redeemer, he'd expected to be beating the bush, thrashing through vines and ferns, but the natural jungle here was more like a hardwood stand, with little in the way of ground foliage. The trees blocked out the light from above, but it wasn't hard movement.

They walked for close to a half an hour, both stalking like they were hunting deer, taking a few steps and then halting, listening for the signs of compromise. Alek had stressed that they were literally infiltrating the Brazilian army's jungle training center, and neither wanted to be found in the bush wearing camouflage and carrying sniper rifles.

Eventually, Alek saw sunlight spilling out through the trees at the edge of the jungle and called a halt. He left his weapon with Pushka and low crawled toward the light on his belly, breaking through a stand of sawgrass. He saw the lake to his front, the shore he was on elevated above it, the grass sloping to the water from the tree line. He called Pushka forward and they started preparing firing positions, one right next to the other, using the grass as cover.

When they were done, satisfied they could range the lake, they took their positions behind the rifles, beginning the patient wait of the sniper. An hour and eighteen minutes in, Pushka saw movement at the dock. Alek settled his scope and recognized the target, along with the three Chinese and a man in an army uniform. It was a shame he would have to die, but that was just the way of it.

The Chinese and the minister boarded the boat, sitting in the front, and then the army guide loaded a cage holding three rabbits, the beasts sniffing the air nervously. The guide picked up a pole and began pushing them out into the lake, the guests sitting in the front and the guide standing in the back, giving the impression he was a native of the Amazon providing a realistic experience. It might have worked if he was poling a wooden raft down the Negro River, but pushing an army Zodiac boat seemed a little ridiculous.

They reached the center of the pond and the guide set the pole in the boat. He grabbed a small paddle and slapped the water once, twice, three times. Alek saw a flicking on the surface and said, "Remember, you have the port chamber. I'll take the starboard side. Put in at least three rounds."

Pushka nodded and settled behind his scope. Alek did the same, seeing the man pull out a rabbit, hold it over the water by its back legs, then drop it. The rabbit began to swim for a split second, and then the water started boiling next to the boat, the guests in the front with looks of shock at the savagery.

Alek said, "Fire at will," and squeezed the trigger. He saw

his placement was good, heard Pushka firing, and shot three more times, with each bullet puncturing the inflated boat twice—an entrance and an exit wound. He quit firing and focused on the action in the boat, seeing the men panic as it deflated, the army guide grabbing the pole and attempting to push them to shore, the boiling water following them.

Eventually, the boat began to sink in on itself like a withering balloon, the men clinging to themselves and desperately trying to find a solution. One of the Chinese decided to make a break for it and jumped into the water, swimming furiously. His thrashing was overcome by a shredding of the water from below. He screamed, the sound carrying across the lake, and Alek watched him fight a monster he couldn't find, the hundreds of fish killing him one bite at a time.

The others in the boat looked on in horror, and then the rubber collapsed completely, the metal ribs in the hull dragging the boat down until the remaining men were bobbing on the surface. The guide began swimming to shore, the minister and final two Chinese attempting to follow. All the motion caused was a redirection of the piranha shoal as the swarm came looking for fresh meat. Alek watched the water boil, wincing at the screams, but wanting to make sure none escaped. The guide came the closest, but he eventually succumbed like the others, sinking beneath the surface.

Alek breathed a sigh of relief and picked up his rifle. Pushka said, "What happens if they pull that boat out and find bullet holes?"

Alek stood, folded the bipod to his rifle, and said, "You think anyone is going to go diving in that lake for a boat on the bottom?"

63

I met Jennifer on an outdoor patio at the front of the hotel. I handed her a gelato and said, "You ready to get to work, spider monkey?"

I saw the excitement in her eyes and wanted to rib her, but I didn't have the heart. It was gratifying enough to know she really enjoyed the mission, even as she spent an inordinate amount of time claiming I was a Neanderthal. She was just as big a meat-eater as I was, but she didn't want anyone to know. Like admitting it was uncouth or dirty, and I found that adorable. Yeah, I guess that does, in fact, make me a chauvinistic Neanderthal, but if I was, so be it. I still got to go to bed with an operator at the end of the day, which made it all worthwhile.

She shoved a spoonful of chocolate gelato into her mouth and said, "I'm thinking about wearing body armor on this one. We get caught in the room, there's no escape, and these guys shoot first, ask questions later."

I said, "If you think you need it, put it on, but we aren't getting caught."

She took another spoonful and said, "So you don't need it?"

I started walking up the outside stairs to avoid the front desk and said, "Not today. We'll know in plenty of time to leave."

The Hotel Villa Amazonia was a pretty high-class establishment, maybe the best in Manaus, but it was small, with only three floors, each with twelve rooms, and you still had to put your toilet paper in the trash instead of flushing it, something that annoyed me no end. The last time I'd had to do that, I'd been shitting in a palace Saddam Hussein used to own, not paying for a five-star hotel.

It had a small pool out back and a bar inside, with the second floor above the lobby housing a restaurant with about ten tables. Each room faced out to the pool, a sliding glass door leading to a tiny balcony that ran the length of the hotel with only potted plants separating one room's balcony from the next.

The hotel had a modern key-card system, which, given my limited Taskforce reach-back capability, was something I wouldn't be able to crack, but the sliding glass doors were typical—meaning it had a cheap tubular hook-lock. Which made sense, because who would climb up the outside wall to the balcony, in full view of the pool, to break into a room?

Me. That's who.

We entered the restaurant above the hotel lobby and walked to the elevators, taking it up one floor. I passed by a maid and unlocked the door to our room, waiting until Jennifer was inside before I began my pre-mission questions. I closed the door and said, "You're good with the door lock, right?"

She said, "Yes. I can get in."

"And the hotel safe? You can bypass that?"

"Yes. Pike, you watched me practice."

"Okay, okay, but if something goes bad, you climb up, not down. Get back to our room."

Exasperated, she said, "Pike, I'm more worried

about *your* climbing skills to get down than you should be about my lock picking. Let's go."

The target rooms were located right next to each other on the second floor. She had one room, and I had the other. To get there we had to climb down, and she was giving me a not-so-subtle jab that there were some things she was better at than me. Not many, but climbing was one of them.

I smiled at her and said, "Touché, little spider monkey. Touché." I keyed my radio, saying, "Carrie, we're about to enter. You and Aaron got the front?"

"Roger all."

Aaron came on, saying, "But someone's going to pay for the appetizers. Not sure how much longer we can stay. We've eaten the entire menu."

Knowing he was telling me they had been there long enough to cause someone to question, I said, "Thirty minutes, max, and we're out. Just give us early warning of the target returning. Break, break, Blood, what's your status?"

"You're good. I'm out here in the boondocks about a half hour from the city center. They went down a dirt road into the jungle. I didn't follow."

"Dirt road? Does it lead somewhere else? Can they get back here without you seeing them?"

I heard a touch of disgust. "Pike, I've been doing this more than a day. Unless that minivan can turn into a fan boat, they're coming back out the same way they went in."

"What are they doing?"

"I have no idea. The mission was early warning, not identification of actions. You want me to interdict now?"

"No, no. You're good. It's just strange is all. We're about to enter the rooms. Break, break, Knuckles, are you at the pool?"

"Roger all. And you're cleared to execute. Pool area is empty."

"Make sure you interdict anyone trying to enter the back courtyard."

"Got it."

I looked at Jennifer and she let a grin slink out, saying, "It's showtime."

I smiled and moved to the sliding glass door, pulling it open and looking down. I saw Knuckles on a chair drinking something frothy, but nobody else. He casually raised a thumb. I exited, followed by Jennifer. We both took a look over the balcony, judging how to get down.

It was only a four-foot drop from the hang, but those four feet were huge, because a miss would turn into thirty. She came up next to me, bumped my hip, and said, "I'll catch you if you fall," and then launched over the railing like a spider monkey crawling down a vine.

I leaned over and watched her drop onto the balcony below us. I crawled over the railing, shimmied down, and hung, my feet swinging in the air. Which was the moment of truth. I had to hit the balcony below, but in order to do so, I had to fall at an angle.

I hated this type of shit.

I heard, "On the balcony. Pike? Status?"

And I started a slight swing. I went back, then forth, then back, then let go, trusting I was in the sweet spot.

I cleared the railing, but not far enough for my upper body. I slammed into the iron, grunted, then heard Knuckles say, "Pike, you okay?"

Knuckles had seen the fall, but I'd be damned if I would give Jennifer ammunition. Holding my side, I squeezed out, "I'm set. Keep eyes on."

I heard, "Yeah, sure. That looked textbook. Except I saw Koko."

I knew I'd never hear the end of it and set about working my lock. Within seconds, I called, "I'm in. Koko, status?"

"Still working."

And I took a satisfactory victory lap, but said nothing on the net. No reason to rub it in.

I entered, seeing the room layout was just like ours. There was a small suitcase on the floor and I went through it, finding nothing but clothes, then turned to the hotel safe, seeing the same brand that was in my room.

Everyone is encouraged to put their valuables in the room safe, but no hotel will tell you that the safe itself is a joke. You believe it's secure because you give it a secret passcode that only you know, but the hotel has to have an ability to access the safe if you forget the code or if you just leave after setting it. The concept was sort of ridiculous, really. People put their most valuable belongings in a safe that had no protection whatsoever at the end of the day.

I pried off the brand plate, seeing a normal lockset, and went to work. I didn't have the master key the hotel did, but I had a skill that would defeat it.

Within seconds, I had it open, seeing a laptop computer. I pulled it out, hooked up a DragonBall extraction tool to the computer's USB port—a special Taskforce device designed to drain the entire hard drive—and let it work. While it did so, I placed three recording devices in the room: one under the bedside table, one behind the television, and one in the bathroom.

I waited on the DragonBall to do its thing, thinking about drinking the bottle of free water on the counter, then heard,

"Pike, Koko. I've got nothing over here. No computer, no tablet, no phone."

I said, "Not a problem. I've got a laptop. Place the listening devices. We'll get something from them."

"There *is* a pile of cash on the table, with a note in Portuguese. American dollars. And it's a lot."

I thought through what that could mean, then said, "Let it go. Don't touch it. Place the bugs and take a picture of the note."

She said, "Roger."

I watched the DragonBall drain the computer, seeing it go from 20 percent to 50. Like every human on the planet who's ever conducted a download, I wondered how accurate the readout was. If it was like my computer at home, one second it would say "20 minutes remaining" and the next second it would jump to "12 minutes remaining," before jumping back to "1 hour remaining."

I took a seat in the only chair in the room, watching the readout, and then heard, "Pike, this is Koko. Someone's at my door."

64

I jerked upright, saying, "A maid?"

I heard her running, her breath exhaling, and then, "No. He had a key. I'm in the bathroom."

Shit.

I stood up, looking at the balcony door that separated us. I said, "Do I need to interdict?"

I heard a whisper. "No, no. I'm okay. He's in the bedroom. He won't come here."

I didn't believe her. I went out on the balcony, walked over the plants that separated the rooms, and sidled right next to her door, saying, "Carrie, Aaron, who the fuck is this?"

Shoshana came back, "There was only one guy who entered the hotel since you dropped. A local. Not the target."

I saw movement inside, but couldn't determine what was happening. I said, "Roger. Koko, Koko, you still okay?"

She whispered, "Yes. I'm good. I'm in the tub, behind the shower curtain. Whatever he's doing, he won't find me unless he wants to take a bath."

I saw the shadow leave the doorway and breathed a sigh of relief. Then I heard a crashing, followed by a single shout, "Pike!"

I jerked open the sliding door and saw Jennifer half out of the bathroom, held in a headlock by some Brazilian guy that looked like he'd taken steroids his entire life, a single teardrop tattoo on his face right below his left eye. He caught my movement, whirled in my direction, and torqued Jennifer's neck, causing her to scream.

I held up my hands and said, "Hey, hey, let's not get crazy here. Let her go."

He didn't understand my words. He stretched Jennifer's neck again, and I heard her grunt. I knew he was close to killing her. Seeing her in his embrace caused my body to begin to vibrate, looking for release, but I knew he could end her life before I could reach him.

It was like watching Kurt's death all over again. I was impotent.

Panting, squeezing my fists, wanting nothing more than to replace myself with her, I said, "Let her *go*."

He backed into the wall, his eyes wild, looking for an escape. I held up my hands again, trying to calm him, and Jennifer felt the wall behind her. She pushed off, gained space, and then walked up it with her feet, using his own grip to allow it. He started to turn at her motion and her body reached parallel to the floor.

In the flash of an eye, she rose above him, her head popping out of his hold. She pushed off the wall with her feet, flipped in the air, and landed on his shoulders like a Chinese circus act, cinching his head between her legs. Her momentum carried both of them down, him slamming his chin on the marble floor in an explosion of blood and her landing on his back. The weight of her body snapped his neck like a piece of rotten wood. His eyes went slack. She rolled away.

I was honestly stunned. I had never seen Jennifer go beast mode in person. It was on tape, one fabled in the Taskforce, when she'd killed a man who had assassinated a teammate, but I'd never seen it in person. In that moment I realized something profound. Jennifer *wasn't* my better half. No matter what she said on the surface, she was a killer.

She sat upright, saw the damage, and went white in the face. She said, "He was . . ."

I cut her off, saying, "No time for that bullshit. We need to get him out of here."

I started thinking about what we could do and heard, "This is Blood, we're ten minutes out. I hope you're complete."

Well, that's just fucking perfect.

I said, "We have a problem. We need a delay."

Shoshana came on, saying, "What delay? Get out."

I hissed, "We need a delay because *you* missed a threat. Stop them from entering."

Shoshana said nothing back. I turned to Jennifer, seeing she was still a little out of it. I said, "Jenn, check the door. See what's out there."

I started cleaning up the blood on the floor and she turned from the peephole, saying, "There's a maid in the hallway."

Shit. Shit, shit, shit.

On the net, I said, "Knuckles, what's poolside?"

He said, "Nothing. Just me. And it's getting dark."

I said, "Okay, we're exfilling out of here. Body will be in the foliage at the end of the pool."

Shoshana said, "Seriously? Body? That's not going to work."

I said, "We have nothing else. If the targets enter, stop those fucks at the door. I don't care how. Stop them."

I hoisted the carcass into a fireman's carry and said, "Jenn. The door."

She stared at the body on my shoulder, and I said, "Jennifer. Open the door."

She did so, and I walked down the balcony, going two

rooms over until I was at the last room on the floor. I looked below me, seeing nothing but shrubbery. I dropped the body into the foliage, the fall loud as hell in my mind.

I crouched for a second, waiting, then Knuckles said, "No reaction. Get back to the room."

I scuttled back to Jennifer, saying, "Close the sliding door."

She did so, now focused, and I said, "Let's get back to our room."

She nodded, and I laced my hands together, giving her a foothold. She repeated my maneuver, holding her own hands at my knee. She said, "I'm pretty sure I'm not the one that needs the help."

And she was right. I winked at her and said, "Good job in there." Before she could react, I put my right foot into her hands and hoisted up, grabbing the railing of the balcony above us.

I raced upward, cleared the balcony, and saw her right behind me, somehow climbing faster than I had without any help.

65

Alek entered his room, opened the minibar, pulled out a beer, and sagged into a chair. For once, things were working out. He took a long pull, then heard a knock on his door. Aggravated, he stood up and opened it, seeing Pushka.

He said, "What now?"

"The money is still there. They didn't take it."

Confused, Alek said, "What do you mean?"

"I mean the money is still on my table."

Alek thought a moment, then said, "Well, they've lost their right to it. I'm leaving tonight. You stay until it's full dark, then replace the weapons. If they didn't want the money, that's on them."

And then he heard the police sirens. Alek looked at Pushka, but neither one could explain the noise, and it grew closer and closer. Eventually, it was right outside the hotel.

Alek walked onto the balcony and saw a flurry of people by the pool, along with someone on a stretcher, his face covered.

He ducked back into the room and said, "I think I know why the money wasn't taken."

"Why?"

Alek ignored him, dialing a cell phone. When it answered, he said, "Sir, we have an issue here."

He heard, "Tell me the target is gone."

"Yes, sir, the target is gone. Dead, and there's no connection to us. But there's a police presence at our hotel. The man you sent to collect the money is dead."

"How do you know?"

"Because I'm looking at the police getting ready to wrap his ass up in a body bag!"

Alek heard nothing for a moment, then an ice-cold voice. "How do you know the man you're looking at is the contact?"

Alek took a breath, relaxing. What Nikita said was true. "I don't know. You're right. It could be anyone. But the money is still in Pushka's room."

"Can you see him?"

Alek walked to the balcony, saying, "Yeah, I can now. He's surrounded by the police, but he's splayed out on the ground."

"Does he have a tattoo on his face? A teardrop under his eye?"

Alek stared hard, saying, "I can't tell. His face is hidden. Why? Is that the man?"

Alek saw the dead body hoisted onto a stretcher, and then hauled down the walkway. He heard, "You need to make sure," and the stretcher reached the light. He saw the teardrop on the face.

He said, "It's him. I see the tattoo. Who is he?"

For the first time, Alek heard fear from Nikita. He said, "That's irrelevant now. The Americans are there. They've found you. Get back to Rio, right now. Get out of there."

Alek said, "Americans? Here? I thought you took care of them."

"So did I, but clearly that's not the case. Get out of there and come here, tonight."

A man who'd seen his fair share of disasters, most staring down the barrel of a gun, Alek let the problem set swirl in his brain for a moment, like a blender mixing things until it created something new.

He said, "Sir, you're wrong. We're okay here. Why would an American team kill the contact and not interdict me or Pushka? Why leave the body outside the pool instead of in our room? And why let me eliminate the minister if they knew I was here? That makes no sense. We've had no contact at all here, and we've been looking. There was one woman who I thought was tracking us, but she ended up being with some guy who was clearly a tourist. He's from Israel, and more out of place here than we are."

Alek heard nothing from the phone, and plowed ahead, saying, "Sir, this death is from something that jackass did. It's not an indicator for us. How well did you know him, if I may ask?"

He walked back into the room from the balcony, waiting on the answer. After a moment, Nikita said, "You may be right. He was recommended because of his ability to get weapons, but I don't know his history. He wanted to transfer the weapons at the hotel, and I told him that was not happening. But I let stand the transfer of money in the room, which I'm now regretting. Whatever happened, you're compromised just by the police presence."

Alek knew he was right. He put the phone on speaker and said, "Okay, sir. I have Pushka here. Where are we going?"

"Come here to Rio de Janeiro. We have a new safe house. Luca and Simon figured out where the ombudsman is living. She was discharged from the hospital and went home. I'm now sitting in it."

"So she's dead as well? We only have one more target?"

"No. Not yet. When we leave here, it will be a murder, and I'm hoping she succumbs to her wounds first. In the meantime, we need to kill the next target just like you killed the last, as an accident."

Alek nodded his head, saying, "Okay, sir. Okay. Since the contact is dead, do I need to replace the weapons?"

"Yes. We fulfill our obligations. If no one retrieves them, it's not on us."

"Got it. No issues. Do we know the final target's pattern of life?"

"Yes. He's going to an event on Sugarloaf Mountain. We have a plan, and it's a little bit like yours. A little crazy, but once we get rid of him, our chosen candidate will win. There will be nobody else."

"Okay, sir. I'm on the way. I'll have Pushka replace the weapons and follow."

Nikita said, "Good. Get here without any more theatrics."

Alek glanced out the sliding door, seeing the police wrap up the body, and said, "I'm not the one creating drama."

66

We gathered in my room, taking stock. Brett said, "They know we're here. They *have* to know. There's a dead guy on the hotel grounds. A guy who had a key to their room. We need to vacate this hotel before they start to look."

Aaron said, "They know he was killed, but they don't know why. You left the money. It has to make them guess. We have time to figure it out."

I let them talk, then called downstairs, "Knuckles, what do you have?"

"A lot of police, and nothing else. Targets are still in the room."

I looked at my assembled team and said, "I agree with Brett. We need to get out of here. We've got the bugs in place, and they're feeding to the Taskforce, but I don't even know if anyone is listening. This ended up a mess, but staying here is asking to make it worse."

Jennifer whipped her head to me, and I spoke directly to her, "You didn't cause this. You did what was right, but we need to go."

Knuckles kicked in on the net, saying, "I've got beacon boy. He's leaving the hotel."

I snapped upright at the call, saying, "To a vehicle?"

"I don't know. I'm on him."

Then, "Yes, he's in the minivan. He's gone."

"By himself?"

"Yep."

Shit. This was falling apart faster than I even expected. I dialed up Creed on my phone. He answered and I said, "What do you have? What did they say?"

"Pike, I don't have a Russian linguist here. I've got about six minutes of audio, and all I heard was Rio de Janeiro. And I'm not even sure that's right."

I said, "I need that audio. Right fucking now."

He came back, and I could feel the embarrassment through his voice, not liking letting me down. "Pike, I just can't. I don't speak Russian, and I'm not even supposed to be doing this. I can't help."

I retreated. It wasn't his fault things were going south. I said, "Hey, sorry. That was uncalled for. Get it to me when you can. I have to go."

I looked at the people in the room and said, "This just got real. We have one guy left, and no intel from the Taskforce. Creed thinks they're headed to Rio, but that's even shaky. We need to roll up the guy who's still here before we lose him as well. Kit up. We're going to his room."

For a split second there was stillness in the room, everyone realizing I'd just ordered a hit. There was no self-defense rationale. No one to rescue, no one being threatened. We were going on the offense, and we had no sanction.

I said, "Anyone got a problem with that?"

And the room turned into a beehive of activity, everyone kitting up for the inevitable, jamming bullets into magazines and slapping gear into pockets. In the middle of it, Knuckles called, saying, "The other guy just exited."

The room stopped movement, and I said, "Where?"

"I have no idea, but he's leaving the hotel. He's carrying the two guitar cases."

I thought, *He's putting them back. And then he's gone.*

On the net, I said, "Get on him. We're taking him down."

I heard, "Taking him down?"

I said, "You heard me."

While I'm sure he was wondering if I'd lost my mind, all he said back was, "Roger all. On him."

I sprinted to the door, saying, "Jennifer, on me. Everyone else, when we exit the hotel, fan out. Give me a mobile box. Don't let this fuck get away."

I exited without even seeing if they agreed, running down the hallway to the stairs. I reached the restaurant and sprinted through it, bouncing down to the exit on the front patio. I slammed onto the ground floor, seeing two couples drinking cocktails and looking at me like I was insane. I ignored them, sprinting past the wall of the hotel entrance and calling Knuckles.

"Give me a lock on."

"He's walking to the front of the opera house. Still has both guitar cases."

Panting as I ran, I said, "He's going back to the place where he picked up those cases."

Knuckles said, "The opera house is active for a show, and I'm about to lose him. This place is crawling with people."

And I saw he was right. I entered the square, Jennifer right behind me, and we were immediately stonewalled by a throng of people. There was an outdoor stage with a band, vendors selling popcorn and glow sticks, and a mass of humanity.

I said, "Knuckles, you have the eye?"

He said, "No. I lost him. He's in here somewhere."

Aaron came on, saying, "We have the top. If he comes to the front of the opera house, we have him."

I began moving to the stairs, believing I knew where he was headed. I said, "Good to go. You find him, take him out, but not permanently. We need answers."

Shoshana said, "So I can't kill him?"

I grinned, knowing she was tweaking me. I said, "We'll kill him later."

Moving through the crowd, parting the people left and right, Jennifer heard what I said and looked at me. I caught the stare and said, "I'm just kidding. You and Shoshana take everything too seriously."

Doing a double step to keep up with my pace, she said, "I never know with you."

I said, "Well, now you know. I promised Shoshana."

She heard the words and jerked her head to me, saying, "What? Wait a minute, what did she say to you in the room?"

I kept walking, saying, "You made me go talk to her. Don't tell me you aren't in cahoots with her. I promised I wouldn't murder anyone, and I'll keep that promise."

We reached the stairs for the opera house and I keyed the radio, saying, "Knuckles, Knuckles, what's the status?"

"He's unsighted. I lost him in the crowd."

I stared hard at the alcove between the stairs and saw a shadow threading through the crowd, the two guitar cases standing out. I said, "I have the eye. We're moving in."

I turned to Jennifer and said, "You ready?"

She nodded her head, her eyes wide, the adrenaline flowing. I grinned and said, "Looks like you're ready. Let's go get some."

I keyed my radio and said, "We're taking him down. Knuckles, I need you to close the back door. Don't let anyone access the tunnel. Blood, get our vehicle and stage it on the square. Carrie, Aaron, stay up top and give me early warning of any police response. All elements, acknowledge."

I saw the target enter the alcove and heard my team repeat my commands, one after another. I threaded through the crowd, getting up to the wall, right next to the tunnel. Jennifer slammed into the brick next to me like she was in a television cop show, much harsher than was necessary. I looked at her and said, "You good?"

She nodded, and I saw her breath coming in and out, like a dog panting. I said, "Easy, easy. He can't shoot back. I'll take him down. You cover him. Okay?"

She nodded her head fiercely and said, "Let's go."

I entered the tunnel, seeing blackness in front of me but a dim glow at the very back from the lighting of the stage above. I saw a shadow break across the illumination and knew our target was still inside. I began moving, Jennifer to my right, both of us trying to remain quiet, and then my world was split apart.

67

Gunfire blasted to my front, splashing the darkness like a mistimed flash from a smartphone. I slammed my body against the wall, screamed at Jennifer to take cover, and it boomed again, the explosion of the rounds elevated by the tunnel, slapping my ears. I drew my weapon and fired back spastically, trying to get him to quit.

I had no idea how he knew we were behind him, but now we were in a killing field. A tunnel. The worst place on earth to be in a gunfight. If aimed rounds missed you, the ricochets would finish the job. This one was so narrow that two men could stretch out their hands and touch the walls, with a ceiling that was only inches above my head. Made of rough brick, it created a funnel of death. I dropped to the ground and whipped my head to Jennifer. She was on a knee, pressed against the wall, fear on her face, her weapon out and extended. I saw a bullet strike her in the chest. It lifted her up for a moment, and then she collapsed into herself and folded onto the floor.

In a firefight, there was one rule: eliminate the threat before treating the ones hit. I had adhered to that maxim my entire military career, but when Jennifer went down, I broke it. I launched myself across the tunnel, landed next to her, and saw her eyes open and slack, fluttering up and down. The bullets kept coming, and I lost my mind.

I leapt up and began shooting, putting down suppressive fire just to keep the enemy at bay. It worked. The return fire slacked off and I started running. I keyed the radio, and in a disembodied voice said, "Koko is down. I say again, Koko is down. I'm in pursuit."

The radio came alive, the chatter erupting, but I ignored it all, the beast inside me exploding. A rage filling the narrow space. The bullets kept ripping by my head but I knew they wouldn't find me. I had a mission now.

I saw a light at the end of the tunnel, then the man who'd killed my partner, a look of absolute shock on his face that I was still coming. He lined up his rifle and shot twice more, the bullets spanking the wall next to me. His weapon locked open on an empty magazine, and I kept running. Incredulous, he dropped the rifle, turned, and sprinted to a ladder, scrambling up in a panic.

I heard the theater above me, someone singing onstage, the audience clapping, and felt a coldness settle on me. The target was about to enter a public arena in an attempt to stop me from killing him, but it would do no good. Nothing would prevent me from ripping the life out of the thing that had taken Jennifer.

I followed up the ladder, exiting behind the stage, startling a multitude of people working the set pieces for the show. They looked at me in fear, and they had a reason to be afraid. I was willing to kill anyone who crossed me.

I snarled, "Where did he go?"

Three stagehands pointed to the left, and I took off running. I entered a darkened hallway and saw my target searching for a way out. I advanced on him and he held up his hands, saying, "No, no, no. I didn't want this. I didn't ask for this."

I centered the dot of my holosight and said, "Yes, you did."

He stood, waiting on the bullet, but that would be too easy.

I tossed my weapon to the floor, my rage coming forth, a bubbling mass of puss. I wanted to kill him with my bare hands, and in so doing, I sealed my fate.

I raised my fists, closed the distance, and he whipped his arm to his back, then leveled a small derringer.

In that moment, I knew I was dead, my hubris of beating the life out of him exposed as the failure it was, and the thought was debilitating. This sack of shit had managed to kill everything I held dear, and now he was going to kill me. It was unfair. A cosmic injustice.

He snarled, "Good-bye, Rambo."

And he was engulfed in a cyclone of violence, a wraith enveloping his body. He was hammered into the wall, then slammed onto the ground hard enough to bounce his head against the stone. He desperately tried to fight back, but it was like a child trying to defeat a lion. Shoshana ended his efforts, controlling his body with a joint lock and turning his face into a mask of pain.

Kneeling on his back, she flashed her eyes at me and I saw the dark angel in all of its fury. She said, "I heard the radio call. You want this one? Or do you want me to do it?"

I felt the beast inside of me, writhing and slithering. I realized we were both in the abyss. Her eyes were locked on to mine, and I knew she wanted to kill the man below her for taking the life of someone she held dear. But she was giving deference to me.

Giving me the satisfaction.

I said, "Hold his neck up."

She pulled his head off the ground and he said, "No! Please! I didn't mean to kill anyone!"

I said, "Me either."

And I kicked his throat like I was punting a football. I felt his cartilage crush and his vertebrae fracture, the crunch eminently satisfying. Shoshana dropped his head. He writhed on the ground like a worm trying to escape hot pavement. I watched it without empathy, wanting him to suffer, now swimming deeper into the blackness.

Knuckles came on the net, saying, "Blood, Blood, get the vehicle up here. I'm coming out with Koko."

Shoshana heard the call, and I saw the same pain I felt. She said, "It wasn't your fault."

I said, "Yes, it was. She followed me into the tunnel. She was following *me*."

She started searching the body, saying, "She was following family. You would do the same."

Her words should have been some solace, but they weren't. I'd managed to kill everything I'd ever touched. My wife, my daughter, Kurt Hale, and now Jennifer.

Knuckles came on the net, saying, "Pike, Carrie, we're exfilling. What's your status?"

I looked at Shoshana, saw the sadness, and said, "We're inside. Target is down. We'll meet you at the hotel. Leave the body in the vehicle. I'll call the Taskforce about disposition."

His next words didn't register for a moment. "Why do you want to extract the body? Search it and be done."

Shoshana heard me and I saw her eyes open wide, making a connection from his confusion. Not daring to believe, I said, "Koko. I'm talking about Koko."

"What about Koko? She's fine."

And then I heard, "This is Koko. I cannot believe you ran off and left me."

I sagged to my knees, unable to speak. Knuckles came

back, saying, "She was wearing body armor. She's bruised, but okay. We're exfilling now. Do you need help?"

Grinning, her face lit up like a Christmas tree, Shoshana keyed the radio, "No. We won't be needing any help."

She pulled me to my feet, pointed at the dead man on the floor, and said, "We won't talk about this little incident, okay? Don't tell Jennifer what happened. I slipped a little bit when I heard your call."

She smiled, looking just like a schoolgirl out on a date, the dark angel long gone, disappearing into the ether. I grinned back, the whipsaw of emotions overrunning me. I swam out of the abyss.

I said, "I won't if you won't."

68

Willow Radcliffe opened her eyes, seeing the same man sitting in a chair next to her bed, a pistol in his lap. Next to him, lying prostrate on the floor with a blanket over his face, was the head of security for her house, the blanket soaked through with blood.

So it wasn't a dream. The last twenty-four hours had been all too real.

She'd awakened in a hospital with second-degree burns, a broken clavicle, and a punctured lung from some piece of debris that had acted like a bullet from the explosion on the ferry. None of the injuries mattered to her. All she'd cared about was her son.

She'd learned he'd suffered a concussion from being thrown off the dock, and luckily that was it. She was worried about traumatic brain injury, but there was no way to tell at this early stage. Only time would determine that.

After she'd recuperated enough, she'd demanded to leave the hospital, against the wishes of her doctors. They were concerned about her medical status, but she was more anxious about her health for a different reason. It wasn't until she was home, surrounded with security, that she realized she'd made an enormous mistake.

She'd felt vulnerable in the hospital, knowing she'd been targeted for death on the ferry. She'd watched every orderly that entered, sleeping barely minutes at a time, only relaxing once she was pushed into her house in a wheelchair, an IV bag above her head and her own trusted nurse draining the fluid from her punctured lung.

Then the Russians had come, walking right up to the front door in broad daylight, evading all of the security the house had in place simply by being brazen. They'd killed her two guards at the door, rushing in like they were storming the bastion of Hitler. She'd jerked upright in her bed at the gunshots, causing her wound to split, and she'd seen them kill her head of security right in front of her.

They hadn't even bothered to remove the body. After he fell, a man had entered with a weird false eyeball, the pupil aimed up at the ceiling. He'd said, "I'm sorry for the intrusion, but we're going to need your house for a couple of days."

She'd curled up against the headboard and said, "Where is my son?"

He flicked his head at a man behind him, and Beau was brought into the room, running to her bed. Before he reached it, a man with a tribal art tattoo crawling up his neck snatched him in the air, holding his squealing body.

The leader remained focused on her, his weird eye staring into space, saying, "My name is Nikita, and if you behave, everything will end okay. Do you understand?"

Petrified, she'd nodded.

They'd allowed the nurse to clean her wounds, which was a small victory. She'd spent the day trembling, the man with the neck tattoo next to her bed, and eventually her body drifted off to sleep, no longer able to stave off the weariness.

When she woke up, the first thing she saw was the man with the pistol. She sat up in bed and he said, "Good morning," as if there weren't a dead body next to him.

She remained quiet. He said, "Don't worry. It'll be over soon."

As always, her first thought was Beau. She said, "Where is my son? He has a concussion."

"He's fine. We understand the medical condition and want no harm to come to him."

"I want to see him."

Neck tattoo clicked on the radio, said something in Russian, and the weird eyeball entered, scaring her by his very presence.

"Glad to see you awake. You had the nurse worried."

They were empty words. She sensed no empathy from him, and understood he would have been happier if she had died in the night.

He said, "I promise, this will be over today. I'm sorry we had to inconvenience you, but it will be over soon."

"I want to see my son."

He said something in Russian on the radio, and a man-mountain entered, bristling with muscle, a ponytail down his back and veins bulging out of his forearms. He was the one who'd killed her head of security, right in front of her. She recoiled in the bed, and Nikita said, "Don't worry. The violence before was necessary for our goals."

He flicked his good eye at the rotting body on the floor and said, "If he hadn't resisted, he'd still be alive. We don't execute violence just to do so. Bring in her child."

The mountain of muscle left, then returned, leading Beau. He broke free of the man and sprang onto her bed, hugging her fiercely. The muscle advanced and Nikita held out his hand, stopping him.

She wrapped her arms around Beau, kissing him on the head.

Nikita said, "Okay, you know he's alive."

She put her hands on her son's head and looked into his eyes. She said, "Are you okay?"

He nodded, glanced back theatrically to Nikita, then returned to her. She said, "What?"

He said nothing, sliding his hand under her leg. She felt metal. Nikita said, "Okay, enough. Get him out of here."

She said, "Wait, wait. Please."

They ignored her, jerking him off the bed. Nikita said, "We have a busy day today. Sorry."

She said, "Don't hurt him. Take me, but don't hurt him."

Nikita said, "Don't worry. We're not going to harm either of you, if you behave."

He left the room, leaving the tattooed man in his chair. She leaned back, then felt the bulge under her leg.

She slid her hand down and felt the metal of the folded knife her son had left for her. She curled it in her hand, feeling the tears well in her eyes.

Her son thought she could use it like the man on the boat. She could not. They were going to be killed because she didn't have the skill to fight back.

She thought about the man from the ferry. The predator.

And wondered if he would come calling, like he said he would.

69

George Wolffe looked at the transcript from the hotel and said, "Are you sure about this? No fuckups? No bad translation?"

"No. That's real."

He opened a folder and said, "And this is from the computer?"

"Yes, sir. Not much there besides a repeated reference to something called Operation Harvest. They have something big going down in Brazil, but their operational security is pretty good. We couldn't decipher what it is, and they never spell it out. Something to do with oil, but that's about as far as we could get."

Wolffe looked at the transcript, seeing a break in the words. He said, "Why'd we lose the comms here?"

"We think he left the room. Went out on the balcony or something. The listening devices weren't powerful enough to pick up what he said. We just heard unintelligible garbage. When he comes back in, he puts the phone on speaker."

Wolffe read,

UNSUB ONE—Okay, sir. I have Pushka here. Where are we going?

UNSUB TWO—Come here to Rio de Janeiro. We have a new safe house. Luca and Simon figured out where the ombudsman is living. She was discharged out of the hospital and went home. I'm now sitting in it.

UNSUB ONE—So she's dead as well? We only have one more target?

UNSUB TWO—No. Not yet. When we leave here, it will be a murder, and I'm hoping she succumbs to her wounds first. In the meantime, we need to kill the next target just like you killed the last, as an accident.

UNSUB ONE—Okay, sir. Okay. Since the contact is dead, do I need to replace the weapons?

UNSUB TWO—Yes. We fulfill our obligations. If no one retrieves them, it's not on us.

UNSUB ONE—Got it. No issues. Do we know the final target's pattern of life?

UNSUB TWO—Yes. He's going to an event on Sugarloaf Mountain. We have a plan, and it's a little bit like yours. A little crazy, but once we get rid of him, our chosen candidate will win. There's nobody else even close in the polls.

Wolffe set the transcript down and said, "I suppose we have no idea what this is about, either. A candidate for what?"

Creed fidgeted and said, "We don't know. Clearly they're targeting somebody, and they know he's going to be at some place called Sugarloaf Mountain, but that's it. What they mean by crazy is anyone's guess."

"Who's this ombudsman? The one with the house? That's the key."

Creed said, "Once again, we don't know. Could be anybody. All we know is that it's in Rio. I know that's not a lot of help."

Wolffe nodded, knowing Creed was doing his best. With the Taskforce on stand-down, he couldn't even leverage the intel analysts who covered South America. All he had was a skill with computers and an undying loyalty to Pike.

He said, "Where's Pike now?"

"He flew to Rio."

"Okay, thanks." With that, he dismissed Creed from his office, lost in thought, not even noticing when the door closed.

Wolffe couldn't leverage Taskforce assets, but he was still a member of the CIA, with deep contacts from a lifetime of covert activity. He picked up his gray line, a secure link allowing him to talk encrypted, and dialed up a buddy of his in the Western Hemisphere mission center.

The phone connected, and he heard, "Brubaker."

He said, "Hey, Phil. It's George Wolffe here."

"Wolffe? I heard you'd retired."

"I sort of did, but they still give me a gray line. Hey, listen, do you have a handle on the elections going on in Brazil right now?"

"Yeah, we're tracking that fiasco. Half the people running are in prison, and the other half are nuts. Why?"

"You hear anything about the Russian Federation doing something down there?"

"No, not really. They're tied up in the Venezuelan shit show. What do you mean?"

"Keep your eyes out for something called Operation Harvest. I have no idea what it is, but it's crossed my path over here."

There was a pause, then Phil said, "And where, exactly, is 'over here'?"

Wolffe said, "Just a different cell, but still in the game." He shifted gears, saying, "Do you have a granular view of the current campaign down there?"

"What do you mean by granular?"

"Do you track campaign events? Know where the candidates are going to be on a given day?"

"Yeah, a little bit, but it's not like we have their schedules stapled to our wall. We just track the big movements."

"You know of anything happening on Sugarloaf Mountain in Rio in the next couple of days?"

"I'd have to check. What's this about?"

"I honestly don't know. That's why I'm asking."

He felt Brubaker wrestling with a decision, then heard, "You got a high-side address I can send it to?"

Wolffe said, "JWICS or SIPRnet? What's the classification?"

"Either one. It's only classified secret."

Wolffe gave him a SIPRnet address and then called Creed, telling him to be on the lookout.

Thirty minutes later Creed came running into his office holding a printout. He said, "You're going to want to see this."

Wolffe took one look and said, "Holy shit. Get me Alexander Palmer. We need to brief President Hannister."

70

Jennifer saw me standing in front of the sink, water running, and came into the bathroom. She said, "You okay?"

I said, "Yeah. Just tired."

"Team will be up here in a few minutes. Have you made a decision on what we're going to do?"

After consolidating at our hotel, we'd packed up and flown straight from Manaus to Rio, landing at a domestic airport right next to downtown, away from the giant monstrosity of the Rio de Janeiro international airport up the coast. The reunion with Jennifer had been anticlimactic because of the need to vacate the area due to our actions. There was still a police presence at the hotel, with a crime scene next to the pool, and now a police presence at the opera house down the street because of the body we'd left.

We'd found nothing of interest on the man I'd killed, and had no other lead besides Creed saying he thought the Russians were in Rio, so I'd ordered everyone to pack up, and we'd fled, leaving a mess behind.

The only anchor we had was the Bellmond Copacabana Hotel, which we'd boxed before, where the beacon had been, but the odds were slim that the man from Manaus—beacon boy, as Knuckles called him—had returned there. Even so, it was the one lead we had, so we'd checked in, getting a confused "welcome back" from the staff.

Now we were running on fumes and coffee. Jennifer sensed that something wasn't right with me, and it was more than just being tired. She said, "What is it?"

I turned to her and said, "I'm not sure I can do this anymore."

Taken aback, she said, "This being what?"

"Hunting these Russians. Getting vengeance for Kurt. It's debilitating. Feels like I'm living in darkness."

She took my hands and said, "Whew. I thought you were talking about us."

I knew she was just kidding, but also that she didn't understand what had happened in Manaus. She continued, "You've done all right. You haven't lost it like I thought you would."

The Russian writhing on the floor flashed in my head. I said, "Jennifer, last night I thought you'd been killed. I thought you were dead, and I went from zero to a hundred in a nanosecond. I went full black. I caught that guy with Shoshana's help, and I killed him with my bare hands, after he was under our control. I actually dropped my pistol to do it."

Her mouth fell open and I said, "He deserved it. I don't feel bad about that, but I was completely out of control. I would have killed anyone who tried to stop me. I mean *anyone*, good or bad."

I turned to her and said, "I don't want to go through that again. Doing missions for the Taskforce is one thing—we all signed up for it—but this mission is all because of me. I can't put anyone in jeopardy for that. The team will follow me, just like you did last night, but the deaths will be my fault."

She let go of my hands and raised my chin. I saw a little fire come out of her. "That's not fair. You can't blame yourself for me getting shot, any more than you can take credit for me deciding to wear armor. In fact, it's a little insulting, like you think the damn universe revolves around you."

I said, "Jennifer—"

And she cut me off, saying, "Don't 'Jennifer' me. Don't play the martyr here. And you don't get to search for excuses because you committed a war crime. That's not on me. That's on *you*."

She quit talking, her eyes locked on to mine. I said, "I know. It's why I think we should go home."

"Would you be beating yourself up if it were a Taskforce mission you were ordered to do?"

"Of course not, but that's sort of the point. Those are just missions. This is personal."

She said, "Then make it a mission. Take the personal out of it."

We both paused, not speaking. I leaned against the sink and said, "I can't make it a mission. Only the Taskforce can do that."

I heard a knock on the door to our room. I said, "Here we go," and left the bathroom to let in the team. She came out to find them circled around me, all looking at me expectantly. I said, "We got nothing from the Taskforce. We can stay here and see if they turn up something from our listening devices in Manaus, or we can go home."

I went from face to face and said, "I'm leaning toward going home."

Knuckles said, "What about Willow?"

"Who?"

"The woman on the ferry and her son. What about them?"

"What *about* them?"

"I'm not letting those fucks get away with what they did."

"That wasn't your fault, and you don't want to go hunter-killer here, because if someone else gets hurt by your need for vengeance, it'll rip you apart. Trust me."

He said nothing for a moment, then, "I followed you when you asked. Will you do the same?"

I looked at Jennifer, wanting some support, but her face remained stoic. I reflected on what he was asking, and knew I couldn't say no to my family. I said, "Yes, I will. If it's what you want, but think hard about it. We have no sanction here. No backup, and you're asking to do nothing more than kill someone for revenge. You're not solving a problem."

"Did we solve anything last night?"

I glanced at Shoshana, catching her eye. I said, "Yes, we did. We solved that I don't want to go back into the abyss. But if you want to try it out, I'll lead the way. Just be prepared for what you find."

Shoshana said, "No. That's not what we're going to do."

Knuckles turned to her, his fists balled, saying, "I didn't ask for your help. I don't need your help. You want to leave, then leave."

I got between them and my phone started ringing on the TV stand. I said, "Jennifer, get that."

I turned to Knuckles and said, "I know what you're feeling. Trust me, I know, but taking it out on Shoshana is not going to get the mission done. You want to wait here for the Taskforce, then we wait. But the odds of them finding anything are pretty low."

Jennifer held up my phone and said, "It's George Wolffe. He has a mission for us. A sanctioned mission."

71

Alek felt the sweat break out on his spine beneath his backpack, his pace on the hiking trail faster than anyone who was out to enjoy the view. He turned back to Kolva, saw he was twenty feet behind, and said, "Pick it up. We're running out of time."

He'd arrived in Rio at dawn, taking a cab straight to a ritzy island called Clube Dos Caiçaras on the Rodrigo de Freitas Lagoon, a small body of water in the neighborhood of Lagoa. As instructed, he'd given his name to the local guard out front and had been allowed through the gate. Following the directions Nikita had given him, he'd walked to the end of the island, passing by tennis courts, swimming pools, spas, and other workout areas, finally reaching a short drive and another iron gate with a guard shack. Behind it he could see a low-slung mansion sprawling out across the grounds, a large yard in front and the lagoon falling away behind it, the Christ Redeemer monument in the distance looking down on the water.

Alek was surprised to find Kolva inside the shack. He said, "Nikita's been waiting. He keeps asking what's taking you so long."

Alek looked at the mansion behind the iron fencing and said, "How did you guys manage to take this down?"

Kolva opened the gate and said, "Bribed the guards out

front to let us in. After that, it was easy. We walked straight up to the front door, hitting them before they had a chance to react. And this place has some serious security. Luckily, that's Wagner now."

He stepped off the pavement and said, "Watch this."

He walked three feet in the grass and Alek heard a buzzing. Overhead, a small quadcopter drone came circling down, hovering above his head. As he walked, the drone followed. Alek said, "What is that?"

"It's called a sunflower. This entire area is seeded with heat and motion detectors. When they trigger, it launches that thing in the air, which then reports back to a central control room in the house. Pretty neat, huh?"

Alek said, "Yeah, I guess if you have someone watching. Didn't do these people any good."

Kolva laughed and said, "Oh, they were watching. They just didn't see the wolf coming."

They reached the door and it opened without them even knocking. Alek saw Luca and his rippling muscles, then Simon behind him, the tribal tattoo crawling up his neck looking as ridiculous as ever. Alek shook their hands and was led into a small room full of CCTV cameras, Nikita sitting behind a desk.

He said, "It's about time. You need to hurry. Pedro Cardosa is headed up the mountain in a few hours."

Alek waved his hand at Luca and Simon and said, "What's up with these clods? I thought they were the super team. I just got here."

Simon scowled and Luca made a show of flexing his biceps. Nikita barked a laugh and said, "They haven't been sitting still. They're the ones that set the trap. All you have to do is initiate. Look, I like what you did in Salvador. I want that same thinking here. You'll take Kolva and head to the mountain. You two are the team. I need Simon and Luca here."

"Why? Looks like you have pretty tight control with that drone thing on the lawn and the guards at the front gate of the club."

"Because of the Americans. They're still hunting, and they're good. If *we* can take this place over, so can they. Did you see them? Any indication when you left?"

"No, but I've lost contact with Pushka. He won't answer his phone."

Nikita banged a fist on the table. He said, "Did he know anything?"

"No. Other than you ordering us to Rio, he knew nothing. And that's pretty much where I am. Can you tell me what the plan is?"

Nikita did. Thirty minutes later, Alek and Kolva had been dropped off at the trailhead for the walk up the Morro da Urca, the smaller hill below the one known as Pão de Açúcar—Sugarloaf Mountain.

It was an easy hike, without any technical skills needed, and they reached the top within an hour, finding the first cable car landing among a smattering of souvenir shops and snack stands. The area was oddly empty, and then Alek saw why: a hefty police presence around the entrance, preventing anyone from getting close to the cars.

That was fine by him. He had no need to get to the gondola. That work had already been accomplished. He only needed to achieve line-of-sight radio contact to the upper mountain.

They slunk around the hill, staying in the foliage and away from the concrete at the base of the cable car system, gingerly walking through the woods, hearing the marmoset monkeys chattering at them. Through the trees he could see Sugarloaf Mountain towering above him about eight hundred meters away, the cable systems for the cars rising steeply into the air to another landing at the top.

He gestured to Kolva, then walked down the slope, leaving the hiking trail for the woods. He circled around the concrete and steel of the cable car stop, walking until he was right up against a sheer cliff face of rock, the valley spilling out two hundred meters below him. He looked behind him, wanting to ensure there was no way a stray tourist would find them, then scraped out a shallow cut, satisfied.

He unspooled a kernmantle rope from his pack and anchored it to the trunk of a tree, saying, "Break out the security weapon."

Kolva did so, setting another H&K system like he'd used in Salvador on its bipod, this one colored coyote brown instead of black. He said, "Now what?"

Alek threw the rope over the side and tested the anchor, making sure their escape route was good. Satisfied, he said, "Now, we wait. And pray that whoever placed the explosives on the car knew what he was doing."

72

Everyone in the room looked at Jennifer like she was carrying the Holy Grail. She held the phone out to me expectantly. I took it, still looking at her, and said, "Hey, sir, we're talking about coming home."

He said, "Home? Forget about that. I have a mission for you. The Russians are about to kill the lead presidential candidate in Brazil."

Clearly agitated, his words came out so fast I had trouble assimilating them. I said, "Sir? Say again?"

He said, "Pike, we don't have a lot of time. Pedro Cardosa, the guy leading in the polls, is going up to Sugarloaf for a campaign stop. He's going to be there in the next five hours. The Russians are going to kill him. You're going to stop it."

"How do you know this?"

"From your implants in Manaus. They're holed up at some house with a hostage. We don't know where that is, but they're going to kill her, too. We can't stop both, but we can stop the assassination of the candidate."

"What are they attempting to do? What's their end state?"

"They're conducting something called Operation Harvest. We don't know the scope, but the analysis is they're trying to get a foothold in South America. Venezuela is falling apart, and they want to spread from there. The CIA says they're messing with Brazil's election just like they did with ours, only using WhatsApp instead of Facebook and Twitter. They have a preferred candidate, but he's miles behind."

"Why Brazil?"

"It's a tit for tat. They want to get into our near abroad because of what we're doing in *their* near abroad. They don't like all the new NATO countries. Shit, they just tried to conduct a coup in Montenegro for this same reason. And they're going to succeed if they eliminate that candidate."

I looked at the team, all of them hearing one-half of the conversation, and said, "So my little vengeance mission just became a national security threat?"

I heard him sigh, and then, "Yeah. You want an apology, or do you want to start operating?"

"What do you want us to do?"

"Get up to Sugarloaf. You know the Russians on sight, right?"

"Well, yeah, we know *some* of them. But we don't know how many are down here."

"Pike, I can't tell you what to do. I can only tell you that you're sanctioned. I've been authorized to pull in anyone you need for reachback. Anything that I can give, you have."

"The Oversight Council agreed to that? Based on a single intercept? What happened to the news stories on conspiracy sites? If we miss, this is going to be a big posting. The Russians will eat us alive."

"The Oversight Council doesn't know. They *will* soon, but right now this is between us and POTUS."

"Hannister agreed to this?"

"Yes. It's growing legs. The CIA is on it now, and they're finding threads tied to that Carwash scandal and the Lulu oil fields. Petrobras has had some strange deaths lately. You were right all along. It's not vengeance. It's real. And you found it."

As comforting as those words were, they still didn't help me to solve the mission. I said, "Do you have anything at all about what they have planned? Anything I can use as an anchor? I mean, I can't just wander around at a campaign rally like Clint Eastwood from *In the Line of Fire*. I need something. Is it a sniper? An IED? What?"

"All we know is that they have a safe house with someone called the 'ombudsman.' They're going to murder that person when it's through, but we don't know where that is. We only have the anchor of Sugarloaf."

"Ombudsman? From Petrobras? She's dead. They already killed her on the ferry."

I saw Knuckles perk up and raised a hand. I heard, "The person on the ferry with Knuckles was the Petrobras ombudsman?"

"Yes."

"Well, that makes one more strange death. Look, we don't know who the ombudsman is that they have, but the candidate is the target. That's your focus."

Knuckles was practically jumping up and down. I waved my hand at him and said, "Okay, sir. We're on it. But I expect the support you promised. With this little information, it's going to be messy, and I'm not hanging my ass out here just because some Russians want to kill a Brazilian."

"You have it. Give me some Pike magic. Like you did with Kurt."

"Will do, sir, but you need to prepare for the magic. Because it's probably going to be black."

I hung up the phone and Knuckles said, "What was that about Willow?"

"We have nothing on Willow. There's a target being held

labeled as the 'ombudsman.' It's a safe house for the Russian control. That's all we know."

He locked eyes with me and said, "She's not dead."

I ignored him, saying to the room, "We have an anchor of Sugarloaf Mountain. The Russians are going to kill the next president of Brazil. We're going to prevent it."

Knuckles pulled a card from his pocket and said, "I have the bed down. This is her house."

I said, "Knuckles, we have a mission. We're going to Sugarloaf."

He held the card out, the silence growing. When I didn't take it, he put it in his shirt pocket and said, "You're going without me. She's an American citizen. I give a fuck about some politician. I'm going to the house."

"You don't even know if it's the right target. We have a *mission*. The Taskforce is back."

He said, "*I* have a mission. It's not like you said before. This is no longer vengeance. It's not revenge. It's a rescue."

Shoshana stepped forward, saying, "He's correct. We have a choice. One is a politician we don't even know. Another is a person who risked her life to save Knuckles. I do not care about the politician, or the political implications. I do care about family. She has earned the right to be saved."

Exasperated, I said, "I don't have sanction for the woman. I have sanction for the politician. How do you think this is going to play out if I got ordered to save the next president of Brazil, and I chose to save an unknown American citizen? I hear you. I really do, but we have a single team."

Completely out of character, Brett said, "I'm with Shoshana and Knuckles. Those fucks on the Oversight Council did nothing to help us. They would have left me on the ferry to die because of politics, and now we're supposed to save a guy because of politics? We have a woman who saved our lives. Saved *my* life. I'm going with Knuckles."

And I remembered he had been on the ferry. That left Aaron. I said, "And your vote?"

He held his hands up and said, "Don't enter me into this. I will do what I'm asked, but if you ask now, Shoshana is right. In Israel, the soldier is the one you save. The ombudsman is a soldier. And she deserves to be saved."

I felt like I was losing control. I turned from him to Jennifer. "What's your vote?"

She paced around in a tight circle, and everyone in the room knew I was asking her to side with me when she clearly didn't want to.

She stopped pacing and said, "My vote is for both. Do them both."

Wanting a way out, I said, "How?"

She said, "We don't even know what's going on at Sugarloaf. We do know the address of the ombudsman. Let Shoshana and me go explore Sugarloaf on a recce. You guys take down the house."

Her words sank in, and, unbidden, I felt a revulsion about letting her go alone. I realized I didn't want to put her in danger again. In that moment, I learned that I was afraid of losing her. Again. I said, "No. That's not going to happen."

Shoshana floated her eyes over me, reading my intent, and, alone in the room, understood why I'd said that. She came to me and said, "Don't make a decision based on emotion. Make it based on the mission."

She held my eyes, then said, "I won't let her die."

She meant it, like she had some preternatural control over life and death. And I believed her. It was enough. I said,

"Okay, Knuckles. You have a four-man team. Let's figure out how we're going to crack this nut."

Surprised at how quickly I'd changed my mind, he said, "You going to call Wolffe about that decision?"

I said, "What the fuck for? No matter what he says, it won't alter my decision."

My words told him I was all in. He was my second in command. My family, and I was going to protect the family.

He pulled the card out of his pocket and held it up. Brett snatched it out of his hand, booting up a computer, and like an anthill had been kicked over, everyone began working, with Shoshana, Jennifer, and the rest of the team researching their prospective missions.

A wolf grin slipped out and Knuckles said, "Looks like we're back."

73

Jennifer arrived at the cable car entrance that took tourists to the top of Sugarloaf and saw they had a problem. They weren't letting any cars go up. She asked a man at the gate what was happening, and he said, "It's full up top. We can't let any more people in. You should have arrived earlier."

A backpacker behind her, a blond guy with a two-day growth of beard, muttered, "That's bullshit."

She ignored him, asking the man behind the window, "What time is the rally?"

He looked at his watch and said, "Three hours."

"And it's already full?"

He smiled, saying, "Yes. People came very early."

She left the window, saying to Shoshana, "What are we going to do now?"

Shoshana pointed at a policeman on the street and said, "I know what Pike told you, but maybe we should rethink not telling the police."

"No. I agree with Pike after the BOPE thing in Salvador. The Russians have a long reach, and we don't know who to trust."

The backpacker came up to them, saw the rucksacks the two women carried, and assumed they were fellow global travelers. He said, "That's a crock. I don't care about the rally, I just wanted to go to the top. If they'd have said something on the website about the cars being stopped, I would have prepped to climb it."

Shoshana said, "Climb it? There's a trail up to the top?"

"Yes, but it's a little hairy. You need ropes or risk a pretty big fall."

Jennifer said, "Where is it?"

He pointed to a road that ran parallel to the beach, then disappeared into the forest at the base of the mountain, saying, "It starts over there, but I'm telling you getting to the top of Sugarloaf isn't a beginner trail. You'd be better off walking up to the top of Morro da Urca. That's more of a day hike."

Jennifer's eyes followed where he pointed, thinking about what he'd said. He continued, saying, "Or we can just call it a day and go get a beer?"

Shoshana saw the look on her face and knew what was going through Jennifer's head. She watched Jennifer pull out her phone, searching the internet. She told the backpacker, "Thanks for the invitation, but we've already got plans."

He started to say something else, and she settled her gaze on him, a disquieting stare that caused him to rethink wanting to have anything to do with her.

She took Jennifer by the elbow and walked out of earshot, saying, "You're thinking of climbing that damn thing, aren't you?"

"Well, yeah. I just found a bunch of tour guides on the web that'll take amateurs up to the top. They say no climbing experience necessary. It can't be that big of a deal."

"Jennifer, take a look at what you're talking about."

Before them were two peaks, both looking like a giant had made a sand castle from a bucket on the beach, the mountains rising straight up out of the ground. The first, Morro da Urca, was about seven hundred feet tall; the second, Pão de Açúcar, rose thirteen hundred feet above the ocean, looking almost vertical the entire way. Connecting them and landing back to earth behind Jennifer were the cables for the gondola.

Jennifer held up her phone, saying, "Here's a picture of a twelve-year-old going up. Come on."

Shoshana said, "She's wearing a climbing harness and a helmet."

"She's twelve."

"We have backpacks full of equipment."

"She's twelve. I'm going up."

Jennifer started walking toward the edge of the forest. Shoshana shook her head, but followed. The road ended at a concrete pillar, a sign in Portuguese and English proclaiming danger beyond. Jennifer could see a worn path snaking upward.

She took it, and for the first thirty minutes, the route was fairly easy. It was steep, and there were a couple of rock faces they had to traverse on their hands and knees, but it wasn't like they were going up Everest.

Standing back upright after scuttling across a face of bare stone, she said, "I told you this wouldn't be that hard."

The trail rounded a bend and dead-ended into a rock wall, the stone rising almost vertical for twenty meters. Shoshana took one look at it and said, "Yeah, not hard at all."

In the center of the rock was a cut about two feet wide that ran the length of the face, like someone had taken a rake to the stone when it was still molten, leaving a jumble of handgrips and footholds. Jennifer spied anchor bolts alongside of it and said, "That's the way up."

Shoshana said, "Are you serious?" She looked behind her, seeing the rocks of the beach far below. She said, "We slip on that, and it's a long, long way to the bottom."

Jennifer put her hands in the cut, tested the stone, and rose up four feet, saying, "Then don't slip."

She began climbing and reached a shelf halfway up. She sat down and looked below her, seeing Shoshana standing where she'd left her. She said, "What are you doing?"

Shoshana said, "I'm afraid of very little, but this is apparently one of those things."

Jennifer laughed and said, "It just looks bad. It's really not that hard."

Shoshana muttered something and began climbing. In ten minutes, she reached the shelf, sweat running down her face. Jennifer pointed up to the last bit of cliff face, saying, "This one's a little steeper."

She stood and began scrambling up the cut again. Shoshana muttered, "Great. Just what I wanted to hear," and followed. She had one harrowing moment when her foot slipped, leaving her dangling by her hands, gripping the rock face like a vise.

She found her footing, and after twelve more minutes rolled over the top, her breath coming in gasps. Jennifer held out her hand and she took it, saying, "There will be payback for this."

Jennifer grinned and pointed behind her, saying, "We're back on the trail, and I can see the top through the trees. We're almost there."

They scrambled upward, using tree branches and bushes to pull themselves along the path. After a few more minutes of climbing, the trail ended at a bricked overlook, the back lined with benches. Behind the overlook was a concrete path zigzagging up the side of the mountain to the top.

Jennifer stood on it and gazed outward, saying, "Look at that view."

Shoshana looked at her watch instead, saying, "I don't give a shit about the view. We're running out of time."

Jennifer turned to the path, saying, "You're just aggravated that you'll have your callsign changed from Carrie to some sort of gorilla, like me."

Shoshana said, "I told Pike I wouldn't let you die, but that meant from someone else's hand, not your own."

They walked up the concrete sidewalk, going left, then right, roping back and forth on the mountain crest, and eventually heard the buzz of a crowd. They reached the top, the path ending at a restaurant, the outdoor balcony jammed with people. Jennifer threaded through them, reaching a small amphitheater next to the cable car station, seeing hundreds milling about, all waiting on the arrival of the presidential candidate.

The sheer scope of the problem overwhelmed her. She said, "We're never going to find a Russian in this crowd. He could be anywhere."

Shoshana surveyed the mob, then turned back, her face granite, the dark angel seeking a release. She said, "He's here. I can feel it."

74

We boarded the small Yamaha jet boat before the rental process was even complete, throwing our kit onto the floor. The rental agent looked at us with concern, and I waited on Knuckles to finish proving he was able to operate it. I said, "Last time I was in a boat with Knuckles, he couldn't drive it."

Brett started sorting out his bag, saying, "Well, the guy's not giving us a driving test. All he wants is a captain's license. And Knuckles is the only one with that."

I said, "I'm pretty sure he Photoshopped that thing."

Aaron laughed and said, "Whatever it takes."

Knuckles boarded and said, "We need to go, before he runs my license through some system."

Brett took off the aft moorings and I did the same to the stern, and Knuckles fired up the impeller, a jet of water goosing us forward. He put some distance between them and the dock, then slowed down, pointing at the island a thousand meters away, a speck of green on the water.

He said, "That's it. You boys ready?"

Everyone in the boat knew what he was asking. We'd done as much of a data dump as we could on the island and found that there was no way to attack from the land side. There was only one entrance for vehicles—trucks bringing in supplies for the various club amenities—and a single pedestrian gate manned by a local national guard.

We had no idea if he was part of the plot, but it didn't matter. Even if we got past him, we were looking at a fight. The island was only two-hundred meters deep, but in a gunfight it might as well be a million. And once the alarm was raised—*if* we made it to the house—we'd have to fight our way back out, shooting at a police response that had no idea what we were doing. It was a nonstarter.

We'd decided to attack from the water side, where the house butted right up against the lagoon. If we were successful, we could control the outcome, but worst case, if things went bad, we could flee on the boat, dumping it at another dock on the lagoon.

And make no mistake, we were all thinking about the worst case.

Thumping a target in daylight was always a risk. Hitting one that held Russian Spetsnaz mercenaries who were spoiling for a fight was something else. It was insane.

There was only one way to succeed, and that was through violence of action. Luckily, if I were asking God for the best at that skill, he would have put the same three men in my boat.

I pulled out a plate hanger holding level III body armor and seated it over my torso, then withdrew an integrally suppressed AR-15 chambered in 300 Blackout. The rest of the boat did the same. I seated a magazine and said, "We're wasting time."

Willow Radcliffe saw the tattooed man grow antsy, fidgeting in his chair and staring at his watch. Whatever they were going to do, it was going to happen soon. And she felt the press of death hovering over her.

She said, "May I see my son?"

He said, "No. Not now."

"Please. Let me see him one last time."

"Look, this will be over soon. In a few more minutes. Just wait."

She felt the blade underneath her sheet and decided. She would not be the only one to die today. She said, "Can you help me with my drainage tube? Please? Or get the nurse?"

Distracted, he said, "The nurse is gone. Just wait a minute, I'm listening." And she realized he was glued to his radio.

She said, "It's starting to overflow."

He said nothing, and she heard a shouting from the other room in Russian. The tattooed man jumped up and clapped his hands together like he was enjoying a show. She showed confusion and fear, and he said, "He's on the way. He actually got into the car."

She had no idea what he was talking about, only wanted to find a way to get him to move closer to her. She said, "My drainage tube. Please."

He began to walk toward her and she curled her hand on the handle of the folding knife, silently releasing the steel from its hold in the handle, the flick making a small noise.

He reached the edge of her bed, hovering over her, and she tensed, preparing for an act of violence she'd never contemplated. Someone shouted in Russian outside of the room, and she heard a flurry of footsteps. He leapt back and slammed against the wall, drawing his pistol.

Jennifer surveyed the mass of people, all waiting to hear the next president of Brazil, and said, "We have to get out of the crowd. Get the drone up."

Shoshana said, "This way," and led her through the throngs until they were on the far side of the pavilion, the smaller peak to her front, the cables for the car dropping steeply away.

She glanced left and right, then scooted over the wall, landing softly in the dirt next to the cable car station. Jennifer followed, and they scuttled into the woods, leaving the noise of the crowd behind them. Shoshana threaded through the trees until they reached the barren edge of the mountain, the stone falling away into the valley below. She found a rock shelf and said, "Here. Launch it from here."

Jennifer dropped her backpack to the ground, pulling out a two-foot tube with legs on the bottom. She extended them, then laid the tube on the stone over the edge of the valley, it now perched at a forty-five-degree angle. While she was setting up the launcher, Shoshana had extracted the control mechanism from her own pack, a small tablet with two rubber joysticks on either side.

She said, "Do we arm it?"

"No. Not yet. Just get a flyover. Maybe we'll get lucky."

The UAV was a Taskforce development based off the Switchblade loitering munition. In essence, it was a flying bomb, but it had some special modifications. One was an increased loitering time of thirty minutes instead of ten, which came at a cost of explosive power. While the Switchblade could take out a vehicle, the Taskforce version could only take out a human or two. But it had some special modifications to make that occur.

Called—tongue in cheek—the Nailclipper, it had one purpose: find and kill a human who had been loaded into its software. Using the latest facial recognition technology on the planet, Jennifer had loaded every single picture they'd ever taken of the Russians they'd tracked.

Shoshana worked the tablet, then said, "Ready for launch."

Jennifer hit a switch at the back of the tube, and a pneumatic pump threw a little bundle in the air. It spread its deadly wings and began to fly.

Jennifer heard a cheer go up from the crowd, incongruously thinking they'd seen her. Then she realized what it was. The candidate was on his way.

75

Knuckles hit the engine and we raced across the lagoon, streaking toward the island. A passing boat waved at us, and he returned it, looking like a surfer out having fun, bringing a grin from me.

If that family only knew what the hell we were about to do.

He came within one hundred meters of the dock jutting out of the back of the house and cut the engine, drifting in. All in the boat pulled out binoculars and began searching the shore, looking for a threat.

We'd studied the layout and found a small structure at the beginning of the dock for storing whatever maintenance stuff was needed, just inside the compound fence—an eight-foot-tall iron structure that looked like something a zoo would use to keep in the tigers. From the left side of the dock, the shack blocked the view from the house, and we intended to stop there, then get over the fence behind it, but before we did, we needed to make sure nobody was patrolling the back lawn.

After a few seconds, I said, "I got nothing. Anyone else?"

Knuckles said, "Nothing."

Brett and Aaron echoed the sentiment.

I glanced around the boat, looking each man in the eye. I said, "Okay. Let's take it in."

The comment was more final than it sounded. We were

now committing to an assault against a hardened target in broad daylight.

Knuckles guided the boat forward faster than necessary, sliding against the dock hard enough to gouge the fiberglass. Before it had even stopped moving, I leapt out on the wood, saying, "That's not going to look good on the rental voucher."

The rest of the team piled out behind me and we sprinted down the dock hunched over, using the building to hide from view. We reached the iron fence and I grabbed the bars in two hands, offering my back. I felt one set of boots, then two, then three, and sprang up, climbing the fence like Koko and dropping to the far side, my adrenaline starting to pump.

I saw Aaron on the left side of the building and Brett on the right, both pulling security and waiting on the call to launch. Knuckles was against the wood, furiously building a breaching charge from his rucksack. I slid in behind him, took a breath, and said, "Bottom of the ninth. Time for a home run."

He grinned, working the Nonel tubing into the initiator, and said, "Good thing Babe Ruth is at the plate."

I heard a whirring in the air and looked above me. There was a quadcopter drone fifteen feet over my head, the lens of the camera staring at me.

Oh, shit.

I raised my rifle, lined up the sights, and blasted the thing out of the sky.

I jumped up and said, "Game on."

Alek saw the cable car leave the station far below and said, "Here he comes. Radio Nikita."

Kolva did so, then smiled, saying, "He says don't fuck this up."

Alek said, "All we have to do is push a button. If it doesn't go off, it's his fault."

He watched the cable car rise, slowly coming to meet the death he offered. It reached the station, and then docked. He waited for the transfer to the second car, the one that would take the future president of Brazil to the top of Sugarloaf.

The one with the explosives.

After an interminable time, he saw the second car lift off, rising rapidly in the air. Right above the wheels rolling on the cable he saw a small bundle, and knew what it was. Once initiated, it would sever the cable holding the car in the air, and plummet all to their death in the valley below.

He turned on the transmitter and checked to make sure he had a green light, meaning the device had connected to the detonator on the cable car. It was still red. The car rose higher and higher. He waited.

Finally, the car reached the midpoint of the trip to the top of Sugarloaf, and he could wait no longer. He jammed his finger into the detonating button.

Nothing happened.

I rounded the edge of the building, took three steps to the large double doors at the back of the mansion, and a window shattered. I saw a barrel come out and engaged it, suppressing the incoming fire.

Another window exploded, and a second gun began raking rounds across the lawn. Sprinting forward, I heard Aaron scream next to me, and saw him go down. We were now in a buzz saw of death, with only one way out: we needed to get inside the structure and off the killing field.

I dove into the prone, trying to dig a fighting position with my buttons alone, hearing the rounds rip next to my head. I aimed into the window, squeezing off round after round and shouting, "Knuckles! We need inside!"

Brett was at the corner of the maintenance shack, on a knee and shooting into anything he could see, but he was driven back by the volume of fire. Knuckles sprinted through the volcano, carrying his breaching charge, and I knew it was our final chance.

Out on the lawn, we were exposed. Get us inside, and there was no way they could survive our ability to destroy them. But we needed off the lawn.

I saw Aaron roll over and shouted, "Stay down!" Brett rounded the corner of the shack following Knuckles, and I saw a bullet crease his thigh, knocking him to the ground. Knuckles made it two more steps before he was hit, a round striking the faceplate of his armor and another hitting his bicep, and I knew we were in deep shit.

I leapt up, sprinting to him, firing all the way but honestly doing nothing more than wasting bullets. I saw him holding his arm, snatched the breaching charge out of his hand, and was through the cone of fire, inside their ability to target me. I slapped the charge against the door, rolled backward, and capped off the Nonel. I heard an enormously satisfying blast split the air, pieces of wood and metal flying everywhere.

I turned into the shattered breach point and began looking for death, knowing we were on the cusp of victory. Like the breakout on Omaha Beach, the end state was now preordained. But only if I could clear the gap.

I entered a foyer, moving through the smoke, and saw a

man right in front of me, stunned by the explosion. I put two rounds in his chest, saw him twitch, and he went down.

Brett ran up behind me, limping on his wounded leg. He shouted, "Door!" and a man exited. A towering mass of muscle with a ponytail, the Russian collided with Brett, throwing him against the wall.

Brett bounced upright and I heard him say, "You've got to be shitting me." The man drew down on him with a rifle and Brett knocked the barrel aside. I raised my own and put two bullets into his skull, killing him outright.

Knuckles came sprinting inside, blood running down his arm, but he could operate. At that point, I knew we'd won. I asked, "Aaron?"

He said, "He's okay. Got an in-and-out of his thigh. He's coming."

Two men charged from a room on the left, and we cut them down with surgical precision, still racing forward. Aaron joined the stack and we started clearing, looking for threats. None appeared, and we slowed down, adjusting our pace, now knowing it was a cat-and-mouse game. Somewhere, someone was waiting for us.

I reached a door and held up. I tested the knob, finding it unlocked. I nodded my head, felt a squeeze on my shoulder, and burst in, seeing another empty room. We regrouped on the entrance leading back to the hallway and I whispered to Brett, "What was that comment about the ponytail guy?"

"He's the guy whose ass I kicked in Switzerland. The one who tried to kill Amena."

Which explained a lot. Knuckles hissed, "Willow. We need to find Willow," and I exited the doorway, moving down a hall, my barrel leading the way.

76

The one-eyed man entered Willow's bedroom dragging Beau by the neck. She shouted, "What are you doing?"

He hissed, "Shut the fuck up."

She struggled to get her wounded body out of the bed, and he raised his pistol, pointing at her head. She ceased movement. She'd heard the gunfire and the explosions, knowing something bad was happening. Someone else was in the house, and they probably wanted to kill her, too. For thirty seconds it had sounded like a war movie, but now it was quiet.

Nikita hissed at the tattooed man in Russian, and he began to back up, hiding behind her bed, squeezing himself between the headboard and the wall. She realized what they were doing. They were setting up an ambush.

She said, "Stop. Stop right now."

Nikita put the barrel of his pistol against Beau's head and said, "If you utter another sound, he's dead."

She sagged into her pillow, the terror ripping through her. Whoever the one-eyed man was afraid of, it had to be worse than him, which made it bad indeed.

She heard soft footsteps outside her door, then the doorknob turned slightly. It grew still, just like in a horror movie, and she knew the beast was outside. She saw Nikita lock eyes with the tattooed man and nod. Then he stood, holding her son as a shield.

She screamed, "Don't shoot! Don't shoot! There's a child in here!"

Nikita turned his pistol on her, the barrel a gaping maw, and she waited on the bullet. The door burst open like a dam splitting from a swollen river, men piling inside the room. Nikita turned from her, aiming toward the entrance.

She saw the predator from the ferry, his eyes feral and dangerous, looking to kill. She shouted, "No!" and he recognized the child. He held up, the men behind him halting their movement, taking in this hostage situation. The tattooed man rose from behind her bed, standing between her and the Americans, now aiming his weapon at them.

She raised her son's blade and jammed it between his shoulders to the right of his spine, burying it as deep as she could, bringing out a scream. The last man in the room, the black man from the ferry, whirled and fired, splitting his head open.

Her tormentor dropped to the floor and a man she didn't know, another apex predator, said, "Put the pistol down and let the boy go."

Nikita said, "No. You leave, or I kill him."

The predator's face turned grim, and Willow felt the death he held, knowing her child was in the balance.

Aiming his pistol at Nikita's head, he said, "You killed a friend of mine in Charleston, didn't you?"

He said, "I'll kill you, too. I promise."

Knuckles took two steps forward, jammed the barrel of his pistol into Nikita's head, and pulled the trigger, spraying the wall with brain matter, the action so fast that it stunned everyone in the room.

Everything went still for a moment, and then the boy began rolling on the floor. Knuckles helped him to his feet. He jerked his hand away and leapt across the bed, cowering in his mother's lap.

She was nearly catatonic, clearly stunned by all that had just happened. She hugged her son and waited on the men to say something, unsure if she'd left the frying pan and had entered the fire.

The apex predator said, "Start searching this place. Find an attack point for Sugarloaf." The men spread out, leaving the room to her and Knuckles.

She kept her arms wrapped around her son, her eyes wide, wanting to believe, but not wanting the pain if she was wrong. She said, "What do you want? Are you going to harm us?"

Knuckles came forward and peered at the injuries to her face. He brushed her cheek, taking in the IV bag and the damage to her chest. He said, "Harm you? We're the rescue."

She wasn't convinced, wondering how he had known to come here. Wondering if he wasn't just one more enemy hunting her. He pulled her card out of his shirt pocket, laying it on the bed. He said, "You helped me once. And now I'm helping you."

She recognized the card, and then remembered giving it to him. The relief washed over her like a wave, leaving her at a loss for words. He said, "Can you move? Get out of here?"

She squeezed her son fiercely and said, "Yes, I can move. I can go wherever you want. I just can't walk."

Knuckles said, "That's not an issue." He unhooked her IV bag and handed it to her, then slid his arms under her body. She let him, giving in to his protection, succumbing to the stress of the last week. He lifted her off the bed and stepped over the man on the floor. He saw the knife sticking out next to the spine.

He looked at her and said, "That blade is turning out to be pretty handy."

And she smiled for the first time.

Jennifer did one more lap around the crowd with the drone and didn't earn a positive response. She said, "I've got nothing. The drone doesn't recognize anyone, and I can't see anything suspicious."

Shoshana said, "The candidate is on the second cable car. He's on the way up. Maybe we'll see a signature when he arrives. Focus on changes in the crowd."

Jennifer banked the drone over the throng one more time, the computer furiously trying to identify the images they'd given it.

She said, "I'm afraid that will be too late."

She desperately wanted to call Pike for advice, but knew he was fully committed. She'd been the one to suggest this course of action and asking him for help would potentially screw up both missions. She felt impotent and hoped at least he was having some success.

Then she felt her Taskforce phone vibrate in her back pocket.

She stuck out her butt, still flying the drone, and said, "Shoshana, my phone is ringing!"

Shoshana pulled it out, and Jennifer kept one eye on the tablet, one ear on the conversation. She heard Shoshana say, "You're complete?"

Jennifer heard Pike shouting. Shoshana said, "Wait, slow down. The attack isn't at the rally?"

A pause, then, "The cable car? It's almost here."

Shoshana leapt up, slapped Jennifer's arm, saying, "Where? Where is he?"

Frustrated, Shoshana said, "I don't have the diagram you're looking at. Just tell me where to go."

Shoshana looked at Jennifer and said, "The other mountain. He's on the other mountain. Arm the drone."

Jennifer did so, then flew it across the valley, saying, "We have less than five minutes of flying time."

The UAV reached the far side and Jennifer started scanning the small crowd next to the cable car stop on Morro da Urca. She got nothing. Shoshana saw a flash of light on a shelf at the edge of the cliff, like a signal mirror beckoning her. A piece of glass attached to a rifle.

She said, "On the edge, on the edge. Come toward the edge."

Alek couldn't believe the explosive charges had failed to detonate. He pushed the button again and achieved the same lack of results. Kolva said, "What's happening?"

"This fucking thing isn't working."

Alek looked at the cable car and saw it had passed the halfway mark. It began to climb higher, the small blob of explosives growing smaller and farther out of reach.

And then he remembered the ferry.

He kept jamming the button, holding the transmitter in the air like it would help, and shouted, "Shoot the explosives! Just like you did in Salvador."

Kolva said, "What?"

"Shoot the damn explosives. Quickly!"

Kolva got down behind his rifle, seated a cheek weld, and

began scanning. Alek hissed, "Hurry! Before it gets to the top. We need to drop it before it goes into the dock."

Kolva released a breath and said, "Stand by."

He squeezed the trigger, and the rifle spit fire. He said, "Shit. Missed."

Alek cursed and Kolva took in another breath, lining up the crosshairs. Alek focused on him, willing the bullet to reach, and then he heard a buzzing in the air. A vibrating noise.

Alek made the mistake of looking up, into the lens of the suicide drone, the machine making a thousand calculations a second, then settling on one. Making a match.

Alek saw the thing streaking toward him, said, "What the fuck?"

And was obliterated.

77

The sky was cold and gray, the leaden clouds threatening to open up, which was about perfect for a funeral at Arlington. A bright and shining day would have been unfitting.

The crowd included most of the available Taskforce personnel, along with a smattering of Kurt Hale's former unit members. I saw Kurt's sister on the edge, Kylie holding her hand, but didn't go over. I was unsure how she'd receive me after losing her uncle, and didn't want to cause a scene on this hallowed turf. She had Veep next to her, which was good enough.

I just stood in the back with Jennifer, feeling her hand in mine on the left, and Amena's on the right, wanting to be invisible. Both of them jumped when the rifle salute began, each round puncturing the air on command. The mournful notes of Taps floated out, and I heard Jennifer sniffle. The flag was folded, then taken to Hale's sister, and Jennifer began to cry, the tears flowing freely.

The chaplain said a few more words, and the service ended. We stood still for a second, and then the group of mourners began to break up. I turned and started walking through the expanse of grass to our car, the solemnness of the grounds overwhelming me. Amena said, "Does everyone in America get to be buried here?"

I chuckled and said, "No. Only the special ones."

She looked up at me and said, "Are you special?"

And it almost made me weep. Jennifer saw the flood of emotions, squeezed my hand, and, while looking at me, said, "Yes, he's special. One of the few."

Amena sensed the shift in my emotions and said, "What did I do?"

I said, "Nothing. Nothing at all."

I faded back from the crowd, pulling Jennifer and Amena with me, not wanting to talk to anyone. In truth, I hated these things, but went out of duty. I had almost made it to the car before George Wolffe found me.

Shit. Here we go.

He shook my hand and said, "Hey, I didn't get a chance to talk to you after the Oversight Council meeting."

I said, "Sorry about that, sir. But at least the meeting paid for the per diem here today, so I guess that worked out in the greater game of bullshit in D.C."

He grimaced and said, "It's not like that, Pike."

I said, "Oh, yeah it is. Last night was proof."

We'd wrapped up the operation in Brazil in about thirty seconds, which is to say, I'd made the call to do absolutely nothing to cover our tracks. In the past, I would have stayed, doing some sort of cover development, getting Willow into a hospital with a story of a mugging and making up other tales to allow us plausible deniability for the mess we'd left behind, seeding my wake with receipts and digital bread crumbs.

But I had grown weary of the dance. I'd received no help from the Oversight Council at the outset, then had been called on to save the day. If it hadn't been for Wolffe a great many people would have died, but even he had warned me about a flaying upon my return, even though I had, in fact, saved the day. So they could deal with the mess I'd left behind.

We'd evacuated the house, leaving all the bodies and taking Willow and her boy on the boat with us. We'd raced across the lagoon and tied up the boat at a dock that wasn't where we rented it, then fled to the airport like a group of high school kids who'd taken a joyride in a car then left it in a ditch.

Of course, we weren't a bunch of high school students, and we hadn't just taken a joyride. We'd killed a bunch of people, and we had the living proof of Willow and her son as evidence.

While we waited for Jennifer and Shoshana at the Rock Star bird, I'd had Brett, our designated medic, replace the hasty combat trauma patches of the wounded with more precise medical care. Aaron had been hit the worst, but even he was healthy enough to fly once Brett was through with him. Nobody needed to see a doctor here, which was good, because I really didn't want to explain a gunshot wound to a Brazilian emergency room.

The wait took a little longer than I expected, but luckily nobody at the executive airport dared to bother the "important people" with the expensive jet. Growing anxious, I'd called Jennifer, and it turned out those two had gone out of their way to accomplish the mission by scaling Sugarloaf like it was Everest. Shoshana had answered Jennifer's phone, and she was panting coming back down the mountain. She told me what they were doing, and if I didn't know better, I'd have said she was scared.

I'd said, "Where's Jennifer?"

"She's at the bottom of a cliff. She seems to think this is fun. I'm only halfway down, and I'm really pissed she made me do this. If I make it to her, you might not see her again."

I'd laughed, then asked, "How is she?"

I knew Jennifer was the one who'd targeted the Russians with the suicide drone. It was a tough, unforgiving call because nothing about that piece of equipment is 100 percent. The potential to turn it loose on the wrong target was there. You ceded control to a damn computer algorithm instead of human intuition, and I didn't want that eating at Jennifer. The presidential candidate was alive and well, so I was positive they'd hit the right men, but I wasn't sure she felt the same way.

Shoshana said, "She's fine, Pike. Give her a little more credit."

"Okay, okay. I just don't want her second-guessing the decision."

"Before we exfilled from the top, we took a look at the strike zone with binos. There was a rope dangling down the cliff for their escape and a sniper rifle next to the bodies we shredded. She's not second-guessing *anything*. We killed the right men."

Which was a relief. I said, "Good. Really good. Get your ass down the mountain. I'm ready to go home."

She said, "What *I'm* second-guessing is this damn cliff and her talking me in to this."

I started to respond, but she'd hung up. Letting me know she wasn't pleased. Two hours later, they both showed up, sweaty and disheveled, but pretty proud of what they'd accomplished. But not as proud as I was.

On the aircraft, leaving Brazil's airspace, I shacked up a message to George Wolffe, sending it through Creed, and I hadn't held back on the cowardice I'd felt from the Oversight Council. By the time I'd landed, it had caused quite a stir, not the least because my top secret aircraft held an American citizen and her child, who had been marked for death. I should have just turned her loose at a Brazilian hospital, but I didn't think that was right, or safe.

The Council had lost its mind, but Willow was my hole card. I knew they would want to bury her somehow, and that would take any heat greater than an ass chewing off of me, which was good, because I still had one more mission to execute.

We'd landed and immediately been met with a phalanx of officers from the Department of Homeland Security. They camouflaged their actions as a customs review, but I knew why they were there: to get my planeload of people through immigration control without a record.

I'd been separated from the rest of the team, a man saying, "Which one of you is Pike?"

I'd raised my hand and he started to lead me away. I pecked Jennifer on the lips, said, "See you soon," and let him take me. Knuckles stepped forward and gave me a fist bump.

Willow said, "Wait."

The agent stopped and let me walk to her. I leaned over, getting a kiss on the cheek.

She'd said, "I still don't even know your real name, but I greatly appreciate it. If I can help with any trouble for what you did, I will."

I said, "Just remember what we talked about on the plane. You stick to that story, and that's thanks enough."

She nodded, then looked at Knuckles, saying, "I was really, really lucky being on that ferry. Anywhere else, and I'd be dead."

I said, "No, you were just unlucky in your job. But you *were* lucky to run into that asshole."

Knuckles grinned at me and the Homeland Security guys began to lead me away. Shoshana broke from the pack and

left the ring of officers, coming toward me. They stiffened,
like they were going to put her in cuffs. Which would have
ended badly, given who was walking.

I said, "Hold your roll there, commandos. She just wants
to say good-bye."

And they did. She came up to me, her eyes bubbly, and
said, "Looks like Jennifer was right about that message
you sent."

Jennifer, of course, had told me to tone down my report.
And, of course, I'd refused.

I said, "It wouldn't have mattered what I sent. This was
going to happen."

She smiled, then said, "We're working on that computer.
You get done over there, and we'll clean up the rest."

I nodded, and she said, "It's close. I can feel it."

I said, "What's close?"

"You and Jennifer. It's close. Something's going to force it."

I looked at her like she was crazy, which, of course, she
was, and was led away. We left Dulles airport in a caravan
of black SUVs, and I wondered how much money the U.S.
government was paying for vehicles.

The meeting was much ado about nothing, with Secretary
of State Amanda Croft standing up for me, National Security
Advisor Alexander Palmer and the rest wanting to roast
me, and the president of the United States ending the whole
damn thing by asking about the breach of the Taskforce and
GRS. It was surreal. I'd been running for about forty-eight
hours without sleep, and would have said I was hallucinating
like I was a candidate at Ranger School, but it was just the
government at its finest.

In the end, the Taskforce had foiled a Russian operation to
take over control of the new Lulu oil fields in Brazil—which

potentially would have given them sway over the government itself, putting a near-peer enemy in our backyard—and I was being grilled about the manner with which I'd accomplished the mission. It aggravated the hell out of me, and after Kurt Hale's death, coupled with the subsequent waffling of the men at the table, I had little patience for the circus.

The only plus from the event was President Hannister himself saying that my actions proved the worth of the Taskforce. He mentioned the GRS stories being published, saying they were something to watch and a reason to keep the Taskforce on stand-down, but I knew *that* threat would end tonight.

I'd answered all of their questions, then left, meeting Amanda at the door as I exited. She'd said, "No matter what anyone thinks, I understand what you did, and I appreciate it."

I came close to saying, "You'd better up your game, because there's a Petrobras chick that'll close the deal with Knuckles as soon as she can breathe without a tube."

But I didn't.

Now walking across the grounds of Arlington, Jennifer to my right and Amena to my left, I wondered if Wolffe really wanted to talk about the meeting, or something else.

78

Without preamble, Wolffe said, "There's a tech guy with a Department of Defense contract who was found dead this morning in Crystal City."

So it was something else. I said, "Do tell."

He said, "The police did a dive on his computer. They entered it into a database to help solve the murder, and it pinged with us. We, of course, aren't going to help solve the crime, but it turned out that his IP address was connected to the stories posted about the Taskforce. About GRS. You get in any extracurricular activities last night?"

Truthfully, I said, "No. I had nothing to do with that."

Untruthfully, I failed to mention that I'd turned Shoshana and Aaron on to him from Nikita's computer. On the flight home we'd found WhatsApp messages from Nikita to one Clyde Marion, a man who'd made a living altering election results around the world, manipulating voters by inserting messages into social media.

His name had been archived in the traffic, and the messages had been damning. He'd conspired with the team that had killed Kurt, attacked Amena and Kylie, and almost killed me. When I'd read the messages, I'd felt the rage grow.

Jennifer had seen the pain on my face and said, "Let it go. It's over."

I'd agreed, and let the team go to sleep on the ten-hour

flight. When I was sure Jennifer was zonked out, I'd awakened Shoshana.

I knew I was going to be carted off as soon as the plane landed—not officially arrested, but separated for sure. I also knew they'd leave my team alone. There would be too many questions if they raised a stink. I knew they'd be set free.

I'd slunk down to Shoshana's seat and gently rubbed her arm until she opened her eyes. And then I'd asked her for one last favor. One last step into the abyss.

She'd heard the request, turned to Aaron's slumbering form, then back at me. She said, "This is a big ask."

I said, "I know. I know."

She said, "Do I have to crawl up a rock wall?"

Confused, I said, "No. Not at all."

She smiled, then turned serious, saying, "The abyss waits for us both. You need to understand that. You need to avoid it."

I nodded and said, "You know I wouldn't—"

She cut me off, saying, "I'll do it for you. Only for you."

I'd kissed her on the forehead and returned to my seat, finding Jennifer awake. She said, "What was that about?"

I said, "Nothing. Just thanking her."

Now, hearing Wolffe's words about the death of the computer contractor, Jennifer put two and two together, and looked at me sharply.

Wolffe said, "Yeah, I know it wasn't you, because you were getting grilled by us all night. Right?"

I said, "Right, sir. Right."

We kept walking, the expanse of the hallowed ground of Arlington spilling out behind us, the crowd breaking apart, and out of nowhere, Kylie caught up to us, saying, "Hey, Amena."

Amena hugged her, and then Kylie looked at me. I said, "I'm sorry, Kylie. More than you know."

She released Amena and wrapped her arms around my chest, leaning into me and saying, "I know you are. I know."

I awkwardly hugged her back, then said, "Amena, you want to ride with Kylie to the restaurant for lunch?"

She sensed that something was about to happen and said, "Why?"

I said, "Because I need to talk to Uncle George here."

She slitted her eyes, but let Kylie drag her away.

Wolffe said, "Thanks for that. I have to ask about the original problem. Given what's gone on, the Council is more worried than ever about someone tracking down Amena's admittance. She has no sponsor and has no reason to be here."

Jennifer and I had talked about this on the flight home, and she had a pretty good solution. She said, "We've figured this out. There's an all-girls school called Ashley Hall in Charleston that has an international boarding program. They have students from all over the world, and we're sure they'll take a Syrian refugee. It'll play well politically for the school."

He walked a few feet and then said, "That's not the answer they want."

I saw Amena glance back at me, walking slowly with Kylie, looking like she wanted to return.

I said, "I don't give a shit what they want. I just spilled blood for them to scream at me right up until they cheered me on. Get it done. It's the perfect solution. She boards with them while we're gone doing Taskforce missions, then she can see us when we're home."

He said, "Can you get her into the school?"

"Yeah. We can do that with a little help from your end."

"I'm not sure I'll get that help."

I stopped walking and said, "Bullshit. Amanda Croft can make one phone call to get her in. I'd prefer it to be discreet, but if you want to make a stink about it, I'll do it loudly. She's *not* going back to Syria."

He said, "Hey, hey, don't get upset. I don't make the rules. I just follow them."

Which set me off. I snarled, "Sorry, sir, but this was actually the last conversation I had with Kurt Hale. You might want to have someone start your car for you after today."

Jennifer latched on to my arm, squeezing, and I calmed down.

She said, "I'm the one who did the research. This will work. It's the best solution."

I saw Amena coming back to us, running through the grass, having changed her mind about leaving with Kylie. As if she knew her fate hung in the balance of our conversation.

George sighed and said, "You know someone will have to officially sponsor her. Do you have anyone for that?"

"Yeah, me."

He laughed and said, "Pike, a lone bachelor with a shady past can't be a sponsor. We're going to need something more than that for the State Department records."

"Well, Jennifer, then."

"Same thing. Look, I'm not shooting down your plan, but we need to think it through."

"So you need a stable married couple? Someone who is vetted, guaranteed not to talk, that sort of thing?"

Amena reached us, and he whispered, "Yeah, something like that. Now you see the problem."

I said, "You got it. Right here."

Jennifer snapped her head to me, wondering where I was going.

Her expression trying for carefree, but the angst leaking out, Amena said, "What are you guys talking about?"

I looked at her and said, "We're talking about you."

George's face showed consternation. Amena went from me to Jennifer, then back to me. She said, "What did you decide?"

I said, "Looks like you're going to be a part of our family."

George said, "That's not how it works. You need to be married. You can't just legally call yourself a family."

I said, "I understand that, sir. That's what I'm saying."

Amena caught on before Jennifer did, jumping up into my arms. Jennifer said, "I don't get it. What married couple are you talking about?"

Her head on my shoulder, Amena said, "You. He's talking about you."

Jennifer's mouth fell open, and I said, "If you'll have me."

Acknowledgments

I had no intention of writing about Brazil and South America for this book, but as usual, something piqued my interest and caused me to focus there. In this case, after *Daughter of War*, I still had alerts up for stories about Wagner and/or Russian mercenaries causing havoc in the world. I read a story about Wagner men surreptitiously entering Venezuela, and zoomed in for a closer look, trying to ascertain the significance of it all—not for a novel, but because it interested me. I started studying the geopolitics of the region and came across the presidential elections in Brazil. Unbelievably, an ex-president was running for re-election from prison because of the Carwash scandal, the largest corruption case in history—and was winning. He was so popular that the largest off-shore oil find in the last thirty years, something Russia would love to control, was named after him. That was just crazy enough for a story.

As usual, I had my deputy commander of everything plan the trip, and as expected, she slipped in some spots that had nothing to do with the book because *she* wanted to go there. First up was a four-day stay in the Amazon jungle, which included everything from Cayman hunts in the dead of night to walks through the jungle eating everything the guide plucked from the ground and shoved in our face. While the stay was absolutely fascinating, I had no intention of using this setting in the book. I just couldn't see how it would fit. The hotel drove us to the Amazon lodge in a bouncing van over pocked pavement for a nearly three-hour hell trip, with me complaining about wasting research time and Elaine about to vomit. When we arrived, I saw a seaplane land on the river. I asked how we could take the seaplane back to Manaus instead of riding in the van, and was told primary election voting was scheduled for our departure day, and the plane was dedicated to a candidate. So right then and there, I decided to blow it up in the book. Make me take another three-hour hell trip? Suffer the consequences.

Brazil is an enormous, beautiful country, and I really wish I could have captured everything I saw on my trip, but it became impossible—like trying to capture the entire United States. Salvador was my favorite spot, with its blending of the old and new, and I decided to laser in on discrete aspects of the country versus trying to capture an overall feel. The town was fascinating, but like Rio de Janeiro, it held its own dangers. For the most part, Brazil is safe—in the tourist districts—but I needed to go a little farther. To that end, I'm indebted to several locals for showing me just how far I could go before I reached a bad place. (One guide said he had been afraid to return to his car the night before. I felt like a heel for keeping him out until the sun set.)

A special thanks to the man who showed me around the Brazilian Jungle Training Center zoo on the outskirts of Manaus. It's a place that's very similar to our own Birds of Prey encampment here in South Carolina, in that they take wounded animals from the Amazon and rehabilitate them, only putting the ones that can't be returned to the wild in the zoo for patrons to see. Unfortunately, there is no piranha lake for real, but come on, that death was pretty cool, wasn't it? And I got in free because I'm a veteran!

After seeing a bunch of tourist destinations in Manaus, I finally heard about something that truly interested me—the secret tunnel underneath the Manaus Opera House. I begged the guy showing us around to take me there, because it was most decidedly not on the menu, and he agreed. We snuck over the ropes and he led me to it. Sometimes not being the ugly American pays off.

Everyone in this novel is a fabrication with the exception of one: I donated a name for an auction at the American Heart Association's Charleston Heart Ball, and Clyde Marion won. I told him he'd be a Russian traitor, and he was unfazed. If you're wondering why the owner of Monte Cristo Analytics changed his name—there it is.

As usual, the tech and weapons in this novel are real, but I sometimes use artistic license to make it something else. Not that it couldn't be done, but simply because nobody has done it yet. The Switchblade loitering munition is real and is being used in Afghanistan as we speak. The Nailclipper is my own invention, but it most certainly could exist. The leaps and bounds in artificial intelligence and facial recognition are real, and it is a threat that we haven't given near enough consideration (say . . . that sounds like an idea for my next book). Alexa is, in fact, listening to you, and it can, in fact, be hacked. The Sunflower drone perimeter protection is real, as are all the other tagging, tracking, and locating technologies. The world is moving to a scary place, but as with everything in evolution, it creates both a pro and a con. I always research the con, because it scares the hell out of me.

Finally, this is my first book with William Morrow, and I'm

indebted to my editor, David Highfill, for making the move as seamless as possible. Any change in life involves angst, and I've had very little. I'm looking forward to working with this team for a long, long time. If my DCOE doesn't kill me in the Amazon first. . . .